About the Author

Terry O'Shea grew up in Dublin's North Inner City Sherriff Street during the 1960s and 1970s. He was schooled at St Laurence O'Tooles and then O'Connells North Circular road. After leaving the Army in 1980 he was employed by Dublin Bus as a driver. He then started a small business in the late 80s, which he continued until 2007. In 2008 he went to Spain to live and worked as a singer and entertainer. Whilst in Spain he wrote and self published 'Sandals or Slippers'. He returned to Ireland in 2013 and currently lives in Cavan where he splits his time between writing and working in the entertainment business.

Dedication

To my wife Linda, my daughters Emma and Sara, and my seven grandchildren. Thank you for the support and encouragement. To the old friends and neighbours past and present in Sherriff Street, where I was privileged to be part of this close inner city community.

Terry O'Shea

AN INNER CITY

AUSTIN MACAULEY
PUBLISHERS LTD.

A CIP catalogue record for this title is available from the British Library.

ISBN 978 184963 946 0

www.austinmacauley.com

First Published (2015)
Austin Macauley Publishers Ltd.
25 Canada Square
Canary Wharf
London
E14 5LB

Printed and bound in Great Britain

Acknowledgments

To John Roberts (IRRV) hons, for all the help in compiling this work. To Dougie (Lord Baldry) for his help with the London references to this work. To Austin Macauley publishers and the team. Thank you for all the help involved in bringing this work to fruition.

Introduction

In 1967, Ireland was rife with unemployment. The boat to England was the vehicle in which we haemorrhaged our unemployed masses. Families found themselves being separated, and the social fabric was being decimated in this time of a government's inability to cope with recession. Money and work were very scarce. Ireland was stuck in a time warp, whereby the powers that be were still stuck in civil war politics. In a republic that was hard fought for by the blood sacrifices of our forefathers to enable each citizen to partake in the building of a state where opportunities should be open to all citizens, the truth was after forty-five years from the formation of our first republican government there was still a social divide.

The working class lived mainly in inner city flat complexes or very run down tenements. The new housing schemes were being built in the fields surrounding the city of Dublin. The outside world – America, England and the rest of Europe – were light years ahead of Ireland. People's attitude to the church, to the state, and to authority, was starting to change. The younger generation saw another life outside Ireland, as they watched the world through television and listened through the radio. The old order was changing. They no longer accepted the status quo that their parents had accepted as the norm. They had the privilege of free information that streamed through the television every evening. This is the first of three books following the lives of the main characters throughout their lives. Beginning in 1967 "An Inner City" gives the reader an insight into the lives and the hopes and aspirations of the main characters. Books two and three follow them into the seventies, eighties, and nineties.

The story is set in Chapelgate Gardens, an inner city flats complex in Dublin, an area near the docklands. It was typical of most small communities in Ireland. The main characters are Mick, Gerard and Rory Foley, Larry Burke and Imelda Bradshaw, Angela Hopkins, Pancho, Jem, and Joxer. Two detectives Dermot and Patrick.

Mick is a quiet and a somewhat innocent twenty year old. He is always concerned about his appearance and is quite shy. He is unemployed and trying to get work, but no matter how well he does on interviews for jobs, his address, is always the final hurdle to jump.

Gerard is nineteen and more cynical in his attitude to life. He goes to the local boxing club three times a week and loves the strict training regime. He has given up on trying to find a job, so he spends his time stealing, gambling, and hustling his way through life. He knows he is capable of better and is always looking for an opportunity to get out of Chapelgate Gardens.

Rory the younger brother at fourteen is a lovable rogue. His mop of curly black hair, his bright blue eyes and wide smile makes everybody warm to him. He has no fears for authority or the law. He skips school, and his scrapes with the law are an everyday part of his life.

Larry Burke is nineteen and works with his father cleaning windows around the Clontarf area along the coast. He is tall and handsome and very clever, always looking for new ways of making money.

Imelda Bradshaw is eighteen and works in a sewing factory in Talbot Street, a few minutes' walk from Chapelgate Gardens. She is very attractive with her long black hair and her Sophia Loren looks. Her friends, Angela, and Linda Hopkins look up to her and admire her gutsy no nonsense approach to life. Her direct approach to life and her attitude to authority, boys, and sex means she is older than her years.

Jem O'Donnell, Joxer, Pancho McDermot, Angela and Linda Hopkins who are all friends and live in the flats complex make up the main characters in the story.

Dermot Kelly and Patrick O'Reilly are two detectives from the local police station who keep an eye on the day to day events that transpire in Chapelgate Gardens.

There are other characters introduced from time to time.

The story starts in March 1967, and it follows events during that year that will impact on their future. It is the most important year of their lives to make decisions about their futures, if any. The story starts off with Mick Foley in his bedroom looking at himself in the mirror.

Chapter One

"Is that really me?" said Mick to himself, as he looked in the mirror. At twenty years of age, he thought to himself that he was a "good looking fella". He stood sideways and tucked in his stomach and thought "Jeeez … not bad!" Then he turned to see his back in the mirror, and the row of white pearl buttons up his back looked comical and out of place. He had his mother's new black lamb's wool cardigan on back to front, and he thought if he put his jacket on it would hide the buttons, and from the front it would look like a stylish crew neck sweater.

"Ahh bollox to this, I'll never pull it off. It means I can't take this jacket off all night, and if I get off with a girl … well that won't happen … ah fuck it, I'll take a chance and wear it," he thought.

He looked in the mirror again. "Is that really me? Mick Foley, ya handsome bastard." He stood with his jacket on and tried to see if the small pearl buttons could be visible through the fabric of his black leather jacket. He brushed his black hair back and picked up the tin marked Brylcream. After a few more minutes he took one last look in the mirror and thought to himself, "Well here goes nothing".

About a half an hour later he was walking through Chapelgate Gardens on his way to meet one of his best friends, Larry Burke.

Larry worked with his father in Clontarf and the surrounding areas as a window cleaner. Larry was very cunning and had a good business acumen. . He had started work with his father after he had lost his job as a delivery boy in Boyle's fruit and veg store in Fairview strand beside the affluent area of Clontarf. A job he had had since he left school at fifteen. He was always on the make, and he had a nice little earner going by skimming from the orders. A little here, a little there before he dropped them off at the addresses on the daily delivery book. He would have enough fruit and veg left over to make up another order and sell on to someone in Chapelgate Gardens, to bring his wages up a little bit extra. He never looked at this as stealing. His take on it was that the people he delivered to in most cases had money and jobs and lived in nice houses, and most of them never gave him a tip, so he took it upon himself to remedy this. It all went well for a few years, but one day he was brought into the office and got the sack, because one of his deliveries had been taken back to the shop by the woman who knew it was short in weight, and also some fruit was missing. He took being sacked badly, so he tampered with the messenger bike before he left, so it would have been out of action within a couple of days from when he left.

"Fuck you, I suppose a reference is out of the question," he said to the owner of the shop as he picked up an apple and walked out with his head held high from the shop. So he had started work as a window cleaner with his father, and from day one he turned his father's little window cleaning business into a nice little earner. His father was very old fashioned, and if he cleaned windows for someone and they didn't have the money to pay him at that time he would say, "Ahh, no problem, sure – fix me up next time." But as he never wrote anything down, because he couldn't read or write, and the customer would either genuinely forget, or just would not bring it up the next time they had their windows cleaned, that they owed money. More often than not, he would only have about half the money he should have had at the end of the day if he'd been keeping a proper set of books. Larry saw this flaw from day one, and he wouldn't let anyone off from paying. He would write down everything and record who owed what, and where he could put up the price. Larry found that if he recorded things on paper it was easier to remember and also it gave him a true record of earnings, a thing his father had never done because of his inability to be able to read or write. Larry had a code that he lived by

His uncle had given him some words of advice, and Larry never forgot them. His mother's brother, Jimmy, had come back from England to spend a few days with Larry's mother. He brought Larry for his first pint, to The Bell, with Larry's father. He was telling Larry's father about how he was doing so well in England. He didn't tell them what he did for a living, but the way he was spending money, he seemed to be very prosperous.

During the course of the conversation his uncle said to Larry, "Lar, there are three things I've learned since I left Dublin. First, the myth that cheaters never win. Well, that's a load of bollox. Second, the myth that hard work never killed anyone. That's another load of bollox – and third, the biggest fucking myth of them all. That crime doesn't pay. That's the biggest load of bollox of them all! So listen to me Larry, use your head and keep ahead of the posse. Stick it to them before they stick it to you." So Larry kept these little sayings in the back of his mind, and would draw on their meanings over the course of his life.

Larry had also started a little scam within weeks of working with his father where he would put a piece of slate in the end of the roof gutter, and when it rained the gutter would overflow. He would then offer to clean out gutters. This brought in a bit more money. His dad didn't approve of this, as he was a very honest man. He said to Larry that it was a form of stealing, but of course Larry would outline his take on it, and would be able to justify it to himself, even though his father didn't approve, and so this little earner continued. Larry's ability to record everything would be his strength in business in the years that followed.

That evening, Mick met Larry, who was standing outside The Bell public house with another friend of theirs, Joxer. Joxer was twenty years old and together with another friend, Jem O'Donnell, they collected turf in a box car they had made together, and delivered it to people around the Chapelgate Gardens area.

Mick walked towards the two lads.

"How are things Mick, jeez that's a lovely sweater pal, the girls will have to watch themselves tonight, am I right Joxer?" said Larry.

"Fuck off, don't take the piss out of me Lar. Hello Joxer come on are you coming in for a pint?" said Mick.

Joxer was standing with his hands buried deep in his worn jacket shuffling on his feet. Joxer was nineteen and had learning difficulties. He wasn't stupid or backward, quite the opposite in fact. He was just different from other lads of his age. . Joxer was delighted to tag along with the lads and never proffered an opinion on anything.

"That bollix O'Brien is very odd if he's in a mood. He won't serve us drink, but he knows you well, Mick." Larry replied.

They were standing outside The Bell public house, where Mr O'Brien the owner ran a strict shop, and if he didn't like the look of you, or he didn't know your parents, he would not serve you a drink. Mick's parents drank in The Bell, and Mick was well known there. His father and mother were well respected.

"Did any of you see Gerard? He was supposed to see me at the flat, but he never came," said Mick.

Joxer looked at Larry in a peculiar way and Mick picked up on this.

"What? What's wrong, lads? Did Ger do something?" said Mick.

Joxer looked down at his shoes and then at Larry. Larry looked at Mick. Mick turned to Larry and said, "Come on mate what's the story?"

"Well do you know that gear you had to sell, the scrap metal you hid, and it was stolen on ye, well I think I know who took it," said Larry.

Mick had found a bag containing lead, and copper near the canal a few days earlier. He had told Gerard about it and hid it till he was ready to sell it on.

"You do. Who?" asked Mick.

"Well the other day me and me da were walking back from Clontarf, and we went by Ballybough to get chips, and guess who we saw coming out of the scrap metal dealers with a bundle of ten shilling notes?" said Larry.

"Gerard," said Mick. Mick knew it was Gerard as soon as he heard about the ten shilling notes, as Gerard always changed his money into ten shilling notes. Gerard said he would always change his pound notes into ten shilling notes because it made him feel that he had more money in his pocket than he actually had. Mick was annoyed when he heard this.

"Fucking bastard! Jesus, I never thought Ger would rip me off like that. Are you sure it was him?" replied Mick.

Larry looked at Mick. Mick knew he was telling the truth.

"I like Gerard, but he fucked up there, mate," said Larry.

Joxer felt uncomfortable, and shuffled on his feet. Joxer hated rows or any sort of confrontation.

"Fuck him," said Mick. "Come on in. We will have a pint, and fuck that fucker – I'll get him later," said Mick.

They went into the pub, and Mick went over to the bar and ordered three pints.

"How'ya son, is your da coming in tonight?" said a red faced Mr O'Brien.

Mr O'Brien called everybody son. He couldn't remember names, so this got him out of remembering each person's name.

"Yes, me ma and da are coming in later. Was Gerard in this evening?" asked Mick.

Mr O'Brien squinted his eyes and looked into space. This looked very comical, as one of his eyes was turned in towards his nose permanently.

"No I don't think so son," he replied, and proceeded to pull the three pints.

Mick turned and looked around the lounge bar to see who was there. The lads, Joxer and Larry, had sat over in Crab's Corner, beside a few of the local girls, Angela Hopkins, her sister Linda and Imelda Bradshaw. They called it Crab's Corner because Mr O'Brien who owned the bar was a keen fisherman and he wanted to give the lounge a theme, so he strung some old nets into the ceiling and put dried out crab shells and lobster shells into the nets. It just so happened that the girls would always sit in that particular corner. One night when Larry was drunk he tried to get off with Imelda, but she knocked him back. So when he returned to where the lads were sitting at the bar he turned to the lads and said. "Look at them, shower of crabs the lot of them". So from then on it was known as crabs corner.

Mick nodded to Angela and she went red and turned to her best friend Imelda.

"God! There's Mick Foley, he's feckin' gorgeous, Imelda, and that black sweater he has on. God, I'm scarlet," whispered Angela.

Angela was a shy girl, and her best friend Imelda was the complete opposite. Imelda called it as it was, and a lot of the local lads only went with her because she was easy where sex was concerned. She had no problem having sex with any of the lads. She had no steady boyfriend as a result of this.

"He's a fucking ride, Angela. Would you do it with him?" she asked Angela.

Angela nearly choked on her glass of Harp lager.

"Imelda, God, do you ever think of anything else?" laughed Angela.

"What did she say?" asked Angela's sister, Linda. Angela looked at Imelda and laughed.

"Nothing, Linda – just Imelda being Imelda," she said. "There's that Joxer fella Linda, I think he has the hot's for you" laughed Imelda as she pushed Linda on the shoulder. Linda picked up her drink and threw her head up in the air.

"He's a gobshite," she said

Mick picked up the pints, and went over to the corner of the bar where the girls were sitting. Larry winked at Imelda, who stuck her tongue out at him. Larry had gone off with Imelda a few weeks before and had sex. The next day, when he saw her he just blanked her, and she was a little upset over it. But she was used to this treatment by lads – it had happened to her a few times. This made her very cynical and sharp in her dealings with people. Larry smiled, shrugged his shoulders and sat down. Mick looked around at who was sitting beside them, and he saw it was Mr and Mrs Dillon, a married couple from Chapelgate Gardens who had nine children, but were always in The Bell public house. The Dillons acknowledged the three lads as they sat down beside them. Nobody liked to sit near the Dillons, because if they weren't singing into each other's face, they would be arguing. And as they spent all of their money on drink, they would often try to bum drink from whoever would sit beside them. Mr O'Brien had warned them before over this, but wouldn't bar them, as they both sang, and sometimes they would keep people in the pub with their lovely singing. Mr O'Brien would often give them drink on the house.

"How's things Mick? Love the sweater. Angela thinks you're a ride," quipped Imelda to Mick as he sat into his seat. Angela nearly choked on her drink when she heard Imelda. Mick cheeks flushed up and he laughed it off.

"Yeh bitch," said Angela but she was delighted to see Mick taking notice of her.

Just then the door opened, and Gerard and his friend Pancho walked into the bar. Larry saw Mick getting upset over this.

"Hold on Mick, relax, come on out to the toilet. Don't go starting a fight with Ger now, or we will get barred," said Larry. Mick knew he was right, and they both got up and went to the toilet.

The smell of urine in the toilet was horrible. Mrs Pluck who cleaned the pub every day put a dollop of bleach into the urinals every morning, and that was to do all day, so by the evening the smell was terrible. They both stood at the urinals, and then Larry, not thinking, turned to talk to Mick. As he turned, he pissed on Mick's trousers.

Mick jumped back and shouted, "Larry, for Jaysus' sake, watch where you're fucking pissing, mate!"

"Sorry Mick, but look Mick, don't go accusing Gerard of taking your stuff, you have to have proof," said Larry.

Mick knew he was right.

"OK, but Jaysus, I have to let him know that I know it was him who took my gear," said Mick.

"I know, I know, but just leave it to me. I will sort it. Just keep easy, right?" said Larry, as he patted Mick on the back.

"Jesus, you're a boney fucker. You have a back like a mackerel!" laughed Larry. Mick had forgotten about his mother's cardigan that he was wearing.

As they came back into the bar, Gerard had sat down beside Joxer, and he nodded to Mick and Larry as they walked towards the table. Mick and Larry nodded back.

"It's fucking warm in here," said Pancho, as he stood up and took off his coat. Gerard stood up also.

"Yer, right," replied Gerard, and he did the same.

Mick was warm now, but he couldn't take off his coat because of the buttons running down his back. The Dillon's had started to sing, and Mr Dillon, who was a lovely singer, was standing up with his hand to his heart, and was singing to Mrs Dillon.

"*Mona Lisa, Mona Lisa, men have named you,*" sang Mr Dillon.

Gerard turned to Mick.

"How'ya, brud?" he said.

Mick looked at him and grunted, "How'ya?"

Mick was older than Gerard by a year, but he was a little bit afraid of Gerard, as any time they had had fights when they were younger, Gerard was stronger and always won.

"Did I tell you about the oul wan I rode the other day?" said Larry.

They all looked at Larry.

"More bleedin' spoofs. You're always making up stories." laughed Gerard.

Larry ignored Gerard's taunts.

Larry had a vivid imagination and always made up stories for the lads that either had him being ravished by lonely widows or him finding a piece of jewellery that he would sell for a few quid.

"No seriously, I was cleaning windows in Clontarf the other day, and this fucking oul wan, well she's about forty or so, but she asked me not to forget the back windows. Anyway she closed the door and I went around the back to clean the windows. I was on the ladder cleaning the bathroom windows, and in she came to have a bath. I couldn't see properly, that bleedin' bubble glass, you know. Anyway, she stood there in her nude, and I nearly fell off the fucking ladder," said Larry.

"What happened next, what happened, next?" said Joxer, who was getting excited. He always liked Larry's stories.

"Wait, for fuck's sake, I'm getting there," said Larry. Mick couldn't help but laugh, because Joxer always fell for Larry's stories. Larry would always make up these stories, and Joxer just swallowed every line.

"If you were to believe Larry, he must have rode nearly every customer that he cleaned windows for in Clontarf. Where the fuck does he get time to clean the windows?" laughed Gerard. Larry put his two fingers up towards Gerard and continued. In fact Larry and Gerard had great respect for each other and truth be known they were both sides of the same coin.

"Anyway, she called out to me – 'Laurence, can you put the kettle on for me?'" said Larry.

Joxer rubbed his hands together, and looked at Larry waiting for the next line.

"You're a fucking spoofer, Larry Burke. Your mickey is the size of a small sausage. It's like one of them, what do you call it, pigs in a blanket," laughed Imelda Bradshaw, who was going to the bar, and had overheard Larry telling his story.

The lads never noticed Imelda standing listening to the story, and were taken aback at the outburst. The lads all laughed, and Larry at first was hurt, and then laughed himself. Imelda flashed a quick smile to Gerard, and went on her way to the bar.

"Bitch," said Larry, as he picked up his pint and took a long mouthful.

"Do you smile to tempt a lover, Mona Lisa
Or is this your way to hide a broken heart?" sang Mr Dillon breaking the mood of the story.

The people in the pub all clapped for Mr Dillon as he sat back into his seat. Gerard let out a little laugh.

"Do you find something funny, Gerard?" said Larry to Gerard.

"You and your fucking stories, and you have poor Joxer believing you. You're a fucking spoofer," said Gerard.

"I'll give you a laugh if you want then," said Larry.

"I saw you coming out of the scrap yard the other day with an arm full of ten bob notes. Now that's fucking funny, do you not think so?" said Larry to Gerard in a sarcastic tone.

Gerard was taken aback.

"So what the fuck's that got to do with you," snapped Gerard.

"You robbed me bleedin' gear, ye bollix," said Mick.

The lads all looked at Gerard. Gerard laughed a nervous laugh.

"I was going to tell you but, I ..." His voice tapered off.

Mick stood up and pointed at Gerard.

"Right, outside now," he said. Angela and Linda looked on as Mick raised his voice. Angela had never seen Mick being so aggressive. She felt a strange feeling of admiration for him.

Gerard put his hand on Mick and tried to reason with him.

"Look, I was going to tell you brud – I got a tip for a horse and I needed ...," he pleaded with Mick. He didn't get a chance to finish the sentence, as Mick was already walking towards the door.

Gerard picked up his pint and turned to Pancho.

"Come on let's get this over with, I was going to tell him anyway," said Gerard to Pancho, who just looked blankly at him. Larry and Joxer followed.

Angela turned to Imelda and said, "Jesus, Imelda, I think Gerard and Mick Foley are going to have a fight. They are all gone outside." Imelda put the drink on the table and headed towards the door. Angela and Linda followed her. When the girls got outside they saw Gerard and Mick standing face to face.

"Mick, I was going to give you your money, brud. I got a tip for a horse and I needed the cash, so I sold that gear and borrowed the money brud, believe me." Gerard remonstrated with Mick.

"I don't believe you, Ger, you fucking robbed me, and that's not on, brothers don't rob fucking brothers," replied Mick, and he pushed Gerard in the chest. Gerard knew he would have had the measure on Mick. His boxing experience told him that Mick was agitated and not in control. He didn't want to hit his brother and he thought if he would only hear me out things would be sorted.

Larry got behind Mick, and said, "Here, Mick, take your coat off," Larry pulled Mick's jacket off his shoulders.

Mick pushed Gerard in the chest, and they both put their fists up to start a fight. Then they heard a laugh come from the three girls. Then Pancho started laughing, and then Larry and Joxer. Mick looked at Gerard, and Gerard looked back at Mick, and they couldn't understand why everybody was laughing.

Mick turned to Larry, who was standing behind him, and said, "What the fuck are you laughing at?"

Then Mick heard Gerard laughing also. Mick turned around to see Gerard laughing. And just as he turned, he caught his reflection in the plate glass window of the pub, and he knew then why they were laughing. He could see the neat row of pearl buttons all the way up his back.

Then a voice came from the door of the pub.

"Michael, is that my best black cardigan with the pearl buttons? I was looking for it everywhere."

It was his mother, who had just arrived with his father to the pub. Mick couldn't help but laugh himself, because he looked so comical in the mirror.

"Yes, Ma … I … I …was going to ask you, but I …I …just …," replied Mick.

His mother just smiled and went into the bar with his father. Gerard took out a bundle of ten shilling notes and thrust them into Mick's hands.

"Here this is yours. It's half the money I won from that tip for that horse. It romped home ten to one, brud. I was just winding you up," said Gerard in a very sincere voice.

Mick looked at the fistful of notes in his hand and then at his brother and laughed.

Joxer was delighted that they had made up. He didn't like confrontation, and more so not between his best friends.

"OK pal, sorry, but you know me, jumping the gun," replied Mick.

"Mick your me brother, I wouldn't fuck you over," replied Gerard in a sincere voice.

"A pint?" said Gerard, as he pointed towards the door.

"Yeh, why not," replied Mick.

Larry helped Mick with his coat and had a little giggle whilst doing it.

"Fuck off, Larry!" laughed Mick.

They all went back into the pub, where Mrs Dillon was singing a song... Mick went to the bar with Gerard, where his father was waiting on Mr O'Brien to serve up his drink.

"Are you lads alright?" said his father, as he looked at Gerard and Mick.

"Yes, Da, we are, were ok. Go on down to Ma, we will pay for that drink," replied Gerard. "I'll pay for that, Mr O'Brien, and can you put a round of drinks for the table there also," said Gerard to Mr O'Brien.

The lads sat at the table, and Mr O'Brien brought the drinks over.

Mick paid Mr O'Brien, and said, "Can you get the girls over there a round of drinks also?" and he handed him the money.

"Thanks Mick, Jaysus, you're a generous bloke, the backbone of the community," laughed Larry.

The lads all laughed at this quip.

"Fuck you very much." laughed Mick, as he lifted his pint up to all the lads at the table.

Mr O'Brien came back with his change. Imelda called over.

"Thanks, Mick."

Mick looked over at the girls, and Angela looked straight at him.

"She's lovely," he thought. Angela picked up her drink, and holding the glass, lifted it to him and smiled in a thank you gesture.

"Jesus, I think you are in there, Angela. He can't take his eyes off you," said Imelda to Angela.

"Ahh feck off Imelda, he's just being nice," joked Angela.

Angela blushed, and with that Imelda went over to Mick and sat down beside him. Angela was embarrassed, and didn't know what Imelda would say to Mick. Imelda talked to Mick and Angela noticed that he was taken aback at the things she was saying to him.

"Oh, Jesus what's she saying to him," thought Angela.

Imelda came back to the table.

"What did you say to him?" asked Angela.

"You're meeting him Tuesday night and going to the pictures," replied Imelda.

Angela nearly choked on her drink.

"Imelda, Jeeez, I'm …I'm …God I'm scarlet …" she replied.

"If I was to leave it to him or you to get yourselves together, we would be drawing our old age bleedin' pension, so just meet him, for fuck's sake, and do it with him," replied Imelda.

Angela sat back in her seat.

"Imelda Bradshaw – you're a mad bitch," she exclaimed.

Mrs Dillon was in full flight now with her song.

"No-one knows what I go through, and the tears I cried for you, you go to parties, dances and shows - , my heart is breaking but no one knows!"

Chapter Two

Mick waited on Angela the following Tuesday outside the church at Chapelgate Gardens. He was a little nervous meeting her on his own, as he hadn't been out with many girls. Angela walked towards the church with her friend Imelda.

Angela was wearing a black pencil skirt and white top and black high heels she borrowed from Imelda. When it came to clothes Imelda had great style. Angela was very straight laced and when she turned up at Imelda's flat wearing a flower pattern dress and flat shoes Imelda pulled her into her bedroom and gave her a makeover. She fixed her hair and gave her the skirt and top to wear. As Angela looked in the mirror she was surprised at how Imelda had transformed her into a sexy looking woman.

"Imelda if me Ma sees me wearing this skirt she'll kill me. It's so tight," said Angela. Imelda walked around her fixing her hair and smoothing out the top. She took pride in making her friend look her best for her date.

"Don't mind your aulwan, sure she won't see you. Just put on that old coat your wearing when you go home tonight and you'll be grand," said Imelda.

Angela put her hands on her hips and smoothed out the tight fitting skirt. She felt like a woman now.

Mick was a little nervous as he pulled on a cigarette as he stood waiting for Angela. He had known her for years but never had the courage to ask her on a date. When Imelda talked to him the other night she had told him that Angela had asked her to ask Mick would he go to the pictures with her. He was glad now that he agreed as he did like Angela. He heard the clicking of high heels behind him and he turned to see Imelda and Angela coming towards him, their arms linked together.

"Jesus Angela looks bleedin great," he thought to himself as he watched them both walk towards him.

"There he is, Imelda. I'm in bits – me legs are going to give in," said Angela, as she linked her friend's arm.

"You'll be grand love. He's the nicest out of the whole lot of that bunch of wasters from round here. Look! He is as nervous as you," replied Imelda.

They walked towards Mick, and he smiled when he saw them.

"Don't worry, Mick, I'm not going with you. She's just a bundle of nerves." laughed Imelda.

Angela pushed Imelda in the arm.

"Feck off, I'm not," she replied.

The three of them stood there for a couple of seconds, and then Imelda just said, "Well, I've done my bit now – you two can take it from here, and don't forget to be careful when you do it with him!" laughed Imelda, as she walked off.

Angela blushed.

"Imelda," she squealed.

Mick went red.

"Don't mind her, Angela. She loves winding people up," Mick replied, as he took Angela's hand, and they walked towards the cinema.

Mick had applied for a job in CIE as a porter on the train station. It was a very low paid job, but in his heart he knew if he got the job and stuck at it, one day he would get a better job within the company, with more pay. His father's friend who worked for the company had put Mick's name forward for the job that had become available.

He mentioned this to Angela.

"I'll go half on the picture money Mick," said Angela as they walked towards Talbot Street.

Mick stopped in his tracks and looked at her.

"If I bring you out Angela I pay. You're my girlfriend, it's only right," said Mick and he kissed her. As shy as he was he just felt at ease with Angela.

She kissed him back and her thoughts went racing through her mind. 'Girlfriend'" was all that she heard him saying as his lips touched hers. Angela hadn't gone out with many lads before and she hated when they tried to kiss her, especially when they had a smell of stale Guinness on their breath. As they walked she thrust her hand into his jacket pocket.

Mick had enough money from his windfall from Saturday to pay for them to go to the pictures, and maybe go for a pint on the way home.

"You looked great the other night, Angela," he said as they walked.

Angela blushed.

"Thanks, Mick, and you were looking well too."

"Even in me mother's cardigan?" laughed Mick.

They both laughed. They walked together, and before they got to the pictures they were holding hands tightly. Angela felt comfortable with Mick, and he with her. They both wondered why they had never got together before, as they'd both known each other since childhood.

*****

Larry loved his job with his father. He helped his father cleaning windows in Clontarf and Dollymount – very affluent areas of Dublin in the sixties. They cleaned chimneys in the winter time, and Larry also had started to clean gutters in the houses.

It was the Monday morning after the Saturday night out with the lads in The Bell. His hangover wasn't as bad as the hangover he had had the day before. Mick and Gerard had been buying him pints all night that night, and when he woke up on the Sunday morning he had a lot more money in his pocket than normal.

His father looked at him and said, "Well son, you look a lot better today than yesterday. You go and clean number forty-eight and I will do a few houses on the other road."

"No probs, Da, I think she owes from last week. You never got the money from her," said Larry.

"Are you sure, Larry? OK, but only take it if she offers it son," replied his father.

Larry hated it when his father wouldn't ask for the money he was owed. His father was a socialist, and believed in sharing the wealth. This was fine if you had "wealth to share in the first place", thought Larry.

Larry's father was easy going about collecting money that was owed to him by his customers. The arguments in the Burke household over money always upset Larry's mother. Larry's father was very old fashioned in his thinking, and he saw the people he cleaned the windows for as his employers, whereas Larry saw them as customers. After the first month of working for his father, Larry realised that his father was not the best businessman in the world, as he had nothing written down. Of course, this was because his father couldn't read or write, so Larry decided to take control of that part of the business.

In fact his father didn't see it as a business at all. The first thing Larry did was to put the price up. Some of the customers refused to pay this increase, so Larry refused to clean their windows. When his father found out he had lost these people he argued with Larry. But Larry talked him around, and said to his father, "Fuck them, Da. They are mean fuckers anyway, and how many times have they left you short with money? The fuckers!"

A few weeks later, Larry bought a set of chimney rods and offered to clean their chimneys also. This was a great little earner during the winter months, when they would be rained off from cleaning windows. Larry was a good worker, and very smart. He wrote everything into a small book and loved seeing the columns of figures indicating the amount of money earned. He saw opportunities and exploited them. One day while cleaning windows, a lady asked him to check the gutters, as when it rained there was water overflowing from the gutter. When he looked into the gutter he saw that it was free from dirt, but the outlet was blocked by a piece of loose slate, so he just picked it out and stayed up on the ladder for over half an hour pretending to clean them, whilst he had a cigarette. It was then he came up with the idea of placing a blockage into some of his customers' "guttering", and when they saw the rain overflowing, they would get him to clear it out. This brought in a bit more money. Between the windows, the chimneys and the

28

gutters, Larry was building up a nice little business. His father was glad to take a back seat where the money was concerned, but when Larry told him about his methods, his father wasn't very happy with the situation, but he said nothing. But the result was that Larry's mother had a little bit more money at the end of the week.

Another little scam Larry came up with, was cleaning the football gear for his team that himself and Mick Foley played for on Sundays. He didn't get money for cleaning the jerseys, but his mother would wash them on the Sunday evening and then pawn them on Monday morning. She would then redeem them on Saturday afternoon, in time for the match on the Sunday. Of course, the manager of the team thought Larry was doing this out of loyalty to his team, but Larry only did things to suit himself, or if there was an earner in it.

The manager's wife used to carry out this task, and she was glad that Larry had taken it on. Once she asked her husband, "Did any of the lads who wore the shorts ever wear any underpants? With the amount of skid marks on the shorts, no amount of money would pay you to clean them!"

Larry parked his bike outside number forty-eight, and took his ladder from the bike and set it against the upstairs window. He liked cleaning the windows for Mrs White, the woman who lived in forty eight. She was about thirty five, and was a very attractive woman. She always talked to Larry as an equal, as opposed to being just the 'window cleaner'. He rang the bell and went around the back of the house to get water from the outside tap. Usually she would come to the back of the house and acknowledge Larry, and see if he wanted a cup of tea, or just wish him a good day.

As he filled the bucket, he waited for her to come to the back door but he heard no noise from inside, so he assumed she had gone out. He was a bit disappointed that she was out. He went back to the front of the house and proceeded to prepare to get the job done. He thought he heard a low whistle and he looked around to see where it had come from. As he started to climb the ladder he heard the low whistle again, and also he heard his name being called out in a loud whisper. He looked up to see a black curly head of hair looking down from the upstairs window. It was Rory Foley, Gerard and Mick's younger brother leaning out the bedroom window above him, with his big broad smile across his face. Larry nearly fell off the ladder with the sudden appearance of Rory Foley.

"Fuck! Jesus, Rory, what the fuck are you doing up there?" said Larry.

Rory laughed his infectious laugh, and said to Larry, "Come on in Lar, I'll open the back door for ye."

Larry looked up and down the road to see if anyone had seen Rory Foley looking out the window. The road as usual, was deserted.

"Jesus, that Rory Foley is something else," he thought to himself.

Rory was fourteen years of age and he was the youngest of the Foley clan. He seldom went to school, but he loved trying scams and stealing. He was well known to the local police. He was always being caught stealing. When he was six years old, he stole some sweets from the counter of the local shop and ran towards the door, but hit his head on the corner of the counter and fell in a heap on the ground. It took him ten minutes to come around. This was a bad start in a career of crime, but he continued undeterred, and before reaching his twelfth birthday, he had a string of charges for petty crime. His mother always worried about him, and she was afraid he would be sent to an industrial school. Once, he stole a box containing new shoes from the back of a delivery truck, as it drove through Chapelgate Gardens. The name "Clarkes shoes" was emblazoned on the side of the truck.

As he was running away from the truck, trying hard to carry the large box of shoes, the parish priest saw him and called out, "Rory Foley come back here with those shoes".

Rory looked back at the priest and called back, "Sorry, father, we haven't got your size."

This was Rory. He had no fear of police or church, and had no conception of right or wrong.

The back door opened, and Larry could see the lock on the door was broken.

"Rory, if the police see you around this area, they will know you are up to no good. What the fuck are you playing at, Rory?" said Larry.

Rory ignored what Larry had said and walked back into the house and up the stairs.

"Larry, come on up and look at the gear this oul wan has. It could be worth a few bob," he called out to Larry.

Larry followed him but was very nervous being in the house, as he liked Mrs White, and he thought she might return any minute.

He followed Rory upstairs to the bedroom. As he walked into the room, Rory was stood smiling at the dresser, and there was an array of jewellery strewn about the bed. Larry looked around the room, and the smell of perfume reminded him of Mrs White.

"Look, Rory, you'd better get the fuck out of here – she could come back at any minute," said Larry.

Rory laughed and picked up the jewellery from the bed and started to put it into his pockets. He let some beads fall to the ground, and as he bent down to pick them up he saw a lady's sexy basque lying on the floor. He picked it up and pulled it around his front, and jumped around the room.

"Hi, Larry, do you want to do the business with me?" he said in a high pitched voice, mimicking a woman.

Larry laughed at Rory's jumping around with the basque around him. Just then, they heard the front gate opening. Larry ran to the window and saw Mrs White walking up the path.

"Bollox, she's back, Rory – we're fucked," said Larry. Rory thought for a moment whilst Larry paced up and down thinking to himself, "If he was caught stealing from this house the word would get around and his father's cleaning business would be fucked".

"Right, chase me out the door, Lar, and shout out for me to stop, but give me a head start," laughed Rory, as he ran from the room.

Larry stood there for a couple of seconds and couldn't take it all in. Then he heard the front door open, and with that Rory, ran from the room shouting and screaming. Larry took his cue!

"Stop, come back, stop," he shouted as he ran after Rory.

As Mrs White opened the door, she jumped back as Rory pushed by her and she heard the shouting from Larry. Rory ran out the gate, turned right, and ran as fast as he could. He looked behind him to see Larry saying something to the woman at the door.

"He was stealing from the house Mrs White," Larry said as he passed her in the hallway. Mrs White couldn't take it all in what was happening, and she froze as Larry brushed by her in pursuit of the robber.

A few minutes later Larry caught up with Rory.

Rory Foley was sitting on a wall laughing his head off.

"You'd never make a robber, Lar, you're in bits. Take it easy. When you go back to that oul wan, she will think you're a fucking hero," said Rory.

Larry slowed as he approached Rory.

"You're fucking mad, you! Listen, you'd better get the fuck out of here, she might call the police," he said.

Rory took a small pair of pliers from his back pocket.

"No, she won't. I cut the wires!" laughed Rory.

Larry looked at him and smiled.

"Go on, get the fuck out of here, ye mad bastard, before you're caught," he laughed.

"I'll split the money with ye, Lar if I get anything for this lot," said Rory as he held up a handful of trinkets and gold chains.

"You fucking better ye little bollix," laughed Larry as he tussled Rory's hair and turned to walk back to the house. Rory ran off and Larry could hear him laughing his infectious laugh.

"The little rascal," giggled Larry to himself.

Larry walked back towards the house, and as he approached the house he could see Mrs White standing there with her hand to her mouth, and an elderly woman standing beside her, trying to console her. He increased his pace when he saw Mrs White.

"Are you alright, Lawrence?" said a very upset Mrs White.

Larry put on a great act pretending to be out of breath.

"Are you!" alright, Mrs White?" he exclaimed, as he stopped beside her.

"I'm a bit shook, but never mind me, Lawrence. You are very brave – he could've had a knife!" exclaimed Mrs White. Larry was amused at this because he knew Rory Foley wouldn't hurt fly.

The elderly lady who was consoling Mrs White was an old customer of Larrys'. She had stopped getting the windows cleaned when Larry had put the price up. Larry thought she was a mean fucker, and was glad to have lost her as a customer. She looked at Larry and saw him in a different light. She had never really liked him since he started helping his father.

"You're a very brave boy," she said to him.

"Well, I just heard someone in the house, and I thought it was Mrs White, but when I called out I knew something was wrong. That's when I came in to investigate," said Larry to the two women.

"I will go and phone the police from my house," said the elderly woman, as she went to go into her house. Larry was a bit uneasy, and to stall her and give Rory a few more minutes to get away, he held on to the railings at the side of the path and pretended to faint.

"Merciful God, he's fainting," said Mrs White, as she took Larry's arm.

"I'm OK – don't worry about me. I think you should sit down and take it easy, you've had a nasty fright, Mrs White," said Larry, as they both held each other and walked towards the front room. The elderly lady followed them into the front room.

"Will I put the kettle on?" she asked Mrs White.

"Thanks Mrs Quinn, but don't put yourself to any bother. I'll phone my husband and get him to get on to the guard's in Clontarf. You go home and look after Mr Quinn, he'll be worrying about you," replied Mrs White.

The elderly lady thought for a second and remembered she had left her husband in his wheelchair in the kitchen.

"Oh God I forgot about him in all the commotion," she replied and she walked towards the door. "I'll call in later to see how you are, and Larry, well done you're a very brave boy," she said as shuffled out of the room.

Larry sat down in the front room, and Mrs White went to the kitchen to get a glass of water for him.

When he was left in the room on his own, he looked around to gather his surroundings. He had only seen this room from the outside through the net curtains. It was full of golfing trophies and crystal. He walked over to the dresser and picked up a silver framed photograph. It was a picture of Mrs White from a few years before.

"Jesus, she was a bit of a ride when she was younger," thought Larry. He put the frame down, but noticed a leather wallet just to the right of a crystal glass decanter. He swiftly picked it up and put it inside his underpants. He returned to the chair where he was sitting. Mrs White returned to the room. He was really nervous now, and started to sweat.

"Here, Lawrence, drink this," said Mrs White, as she sat beside him and handed him a glass of water. She held his hand as he cupped the glass. He found this strange but she looked concerned. He felt a little bit guilty about the situation, because she was being so nice to him.

"Thanks, Mrs White. I'm sorry I couldn't catch him," replied Larry and he took a sip from the cup.

"Marie – call me Marie. And don't worry about not catching him. Just as long as no-one was hurt. He could have stabbed you, or me. He looked nasty from what I could see of him," said Mrs White.

Larry knew Rory Foley and thought to himself how wrong she was about him. Mrs White got up and went over to the dresser and poured out two large glasses of brandy for herself and Larry.

"Here Lawrence' drink this," she said as she handed him the glass. He put the water down on the mahogany table and thanked her.

He drank the liquid in one gulp and it hit the back of his throat. He spluttered and coughed, and Marie patted him on the back. They both laughed. Larry looked at Marie and she looked back and for a split second there was a moment between them. Larry looked at her and for the first time he could see that they had something between them. There was a couple of seconds of awkward silence. Larry broke the moment and he jumped to his feet.

"I better get going. Me Da will be wondering where I am," said Larry, as he put the glass down on the dresser.

"Hold on there for a minute, Lawrence," said Mrs White, as she got up and left the room.

Larry watched her leave the room, and noticed she was a very sexy woman. His mind raced back to the bedroom and the basque that Rory had been prancing around in. He could just imagine Marie in the basque. He looked around the room again and it was then that he noticed the picture of a man in a police uniform holding a silver trophy in his hands smiling at the camera. He didn't hear her as she came back into the room.

"That's my husband," she said as she noticed Larry looking at the picture.

"Sorry Mrs White I wasn't being nosey I ...I ... just," he didn't finish his sentence.

"Marie, call me Marie, Mrs White is my husband's mother's name" joked Marie.

"Here, take this Lawrence, and thanks again. Go and have a drink on me," she said as she handed Larry two pound notes.

"Ahh, no. It's ... it's ... OK, no ..." Larry protested, but she just pushed the money into his pocket.

Larry hoped that she hadn't felt the bulge where the wallet was hidden. They both stood there looking at each other for what seemed to be a long time, when the elderly woman broke the silence as she entered the room.

"The police are on the way," she said.

Larry thanked Marie and as he walked towards his bike he looked behind to see Marie staring at him. He strapped the ladder to his bike and wheeled it out towards the road. He looked back again and she lifted her hand with a slight wave. He waved back and for no apparent reason winked at her and smiled.

He went onto the next road and saw his father on the top of the ladder stretching to clean the windows. He stood looking at his father for a while and thought to himself, "Poor bastard – he's breaking his bollocks day in day out, and fuck all to show for it. I'll be fucked if I'm going to clean widows for the rest of my life". He entered the garden and told his father what had happened. Of course he didn't tell him it was Rory Foley.

When he had a chance to inspect the wallet later on, he opened it up to find twenty seven pounds, ten shillings.

"A good day's work," he thought to himself, as he popped the money into his pocket. He checked the contents of his father's money bag that they used to keep the earnings for the day and counted just under one pound five shillings.

"Fuck, my uncle Jimmy was right. The biggest load of bollocks of them all. Crime doesn't pay. Fucking sure it does."

Chapter Three

Paul Mc Dermot or Pancho as he was known was eighteen and lived in a corner flat in Chapelgate Gardens with his mother and three of his six sisters. His father had died years before in an accident on the docks. He had been working unloading coal from a ship. In the hold of the ship he was crushed as the load shifted and tons of coal engulfed him and two other men. As a casual worker his widow received no compensation. Pancho's mother had brought up the seven children on her own. He played football every day of his life – he loved football more than anything else in the world. He was eighteen years old, and the only job he had ever had was a job in "Varien's" brush factory as a messenger boy delivering parcels and letters on the big black messenger bike. He loved his job, because the big old iron bike he peddled around Dublin, was great at building up the strength in his legs. Even when they asked him to go to work inside on the shop floor for more money, he refused.

He loved being out and about, and every afternoon on his lunch break, he would play football with the other messenger boys in Stephen's Green. Even after work, his mother and older sisters made him run errands for them, so he was constantly running to and from the shops. He was once picked for a trial for an English football team, but he never left Ireland to pursue this chance in a lifetime. His mother cried and cried the day he was leaving for the boat. He really wanted to play football in England, because the wages were very good, and he would have been paid for something he had a passion for, but he could not break the hold his mother had over him. In reality, he passed up on a good career in football for the whims of an over-possessive mother. When he returned to the brush factory to look for his job back, they had already given it to another lad, so he hadn't worked in a proper job for nearly three years.

Pancho was playing ball with some kids in the Chapelgate area when an unmarked police car pulled up beside them. Two detectives who were sitting in the car beckoned Pancho to come over. Pancho approached the car, bouncing the ball as he went. He recognised the two detectives as he approached the car. Dermot Kelly and Patrick O'Reilly, the two detectives who had beckoned him were well known in Chapelgate Gardens, and were not liked in the area.

"McDermot, you are mates with that Rory Foley lad, aren't you?" said Dermot Kelly, as he pulled on a cigarette.

Pancho put the ball down and sat on it and looked right into the car.

"Yeh, so what?" replied Pancho.

"Did you see him today?" asked Dermot Kelly.

Pancho didn't know whether to answer yes or no to the question. He didn't know if Rory had been up to something illegal and he might need Pancho to verify his whereabouts at a certain time

"What do you want him for?" said Pancho to the detective.

Dermot Kelly looked at his partner.

"Now where does it say in the police handbook that we have to answer their questions first?" he replied in a sarcastic tone.

Patrick Reilly got out of the car and came around to stand beside Pancho.

"Just answer the fucking question, Mc Dermot, or your arse will be in a cold pissey cell in the next five minutes, ye little bollix," replied Patrick O'Reilly, as he glared at Pancho.

"Now, I'll ask the question again. Did you see that robbing little toe rag Foley or not?"

Pancho turned to the young lads behind him, and winked at them.

"He was with us all morning here, kicking ball, isn't that right lads?" said Pancho.

Dermot Kelly nodded at Patrick to get back into the car. They were getting nowhere with Pancho.

"Lying bastards the lot of them," said Dermot.

"We better get the "Rory" fella before they put him wise to us," replied Patrick.

"It has to be him that broke into the Whites' house – fits the description. Of all the fucking houses to break into he would have had to pick a house belonging to our feckin' boss. The hassle we will get if we don't catch the fucker. It doesn't bear thinking about," said Dermot Kelly, as he pulled two cigarettes from a box and handed one to his partner.

"Where to now?" asked Patrick.

They both looked at each other and in unison replied, "The White House". As they drove away they laughed at the obvious joke they had just cracked.

Pancho and the lads ran in all directions to look for Rory Foley, to warn him that the police were looking for him.

*****

Rory Foley stood outside the pawn shop in Marlborough Street thinking of a story to tell the pawnshop owner, for the jewellery and baubles he was going to pawn.

"Where did you say you got this jewellery, boy?" asked the man behind the counter in the pawn shop.

The man held the eye glass to his good eye and inspected the pieces of jewellery. His other eye was actually a glass eye. He looked at the little boy with his head of black curly hair.

Rory shuffled from foot to foot, and looked as if butter wouldn't melt in his mouth.

"Er, me auntie, she is home from England for me granny's funeral, and she needs the money to go towards burying her," replied Rory.

The man picked up another piece of jewellery, and through the eye glass inspected it with his good eye.

"Hmmm, she needs the money for a funeral … er, your granny's funeral, you say?" replied the pawnbroker.

"Yep, Me auntie is loaded! Lives in England!" replied Rory. "But she's waiting for her husband, me uncle, to come over from England with money," lied Rory

The man put his eye glass in his waistcoat pocket. Then what he did next took Rory completely by surprise. The man put the jewellery on the counter and placed his hands flat on the counter and leaned across to stare at Rory.

Rory looked into his face and gave him his innocent smile.

"This stuff is just a load of glass, just like the glass that's in me eye here," replied the man, as he took out his glass eye and held it in the open palm of his hand.

Rory Foley jumped back, and nearly shit himself. He didn't know the man had a false eye, and just seeing it looking back at him in the palm of the man's hand freaked him out.

"Now, son, do me a favour. Go home to your dead granny, and tell your wealthy aunt to go and buy a shovel and dig the bloody grave herself, because she will be getting no money from me for this heap of crap," said the man, as he broke his heart laughing at the look of fright on Rory's face.

Rory was in shock, but he walked towards the counter and started to pick up the baubles and put them back into the box they had been in, to the chuckles of laughter from the man behind the counter. As Rory turned and walked towards the door the man called him back.

"Here, boy, here, take this. I've heard some whoppers in my time, but that sure tops the lot," he said, as he took sixpence from the waistcoat pocket with one hand and put his glass eye back into its socket with the other hand.

Rory took the sixpence and put it in his pocket, and then he put the box under his arm and smiled his big smile at the man.

"Thanks, mister," he replied.

As Rory left the pawnshop to the sound of the man's laughter he thought to himself, "Bollocks to that, a load of fucking cheap tat for all that effort. Pity there was no cash in the house – ah well, there's always the next time."

As he walked away from the shop, he heard his name being called from a young lad in the street.

"Rory, Rory, come here. The police are looking for ye," said the lad as he ran up to Rory.

"Me and the lads were kicking ball in the area and them two fuckers, Kelly and O'Reilly, came sniffing around looking for ye. We told them that you were with us all day, so make sure you keep to the same story. What did you do – rob a bank or something. They're pissed at ye?" said the lad.

"No, just turned a house over, but got fuck all out of it. Fuck me, I hope it wasn't a judge's house," said Rory.

"Well, they are pissed at you Rory for some reason, so be careful," said the lad.

Rory thanked the lad for the information, and decided to head to Chapelgate.

"What the fuck am I going to do with this load of shite," he thought to himself. He walked back towards Chapelgate, and as he walked towards the train station, he saw his brother Mick coming from the train station after his interview.

"Mick! Mick! Hang on – I'll walk with ye," said Rory, as he ran up beside his big brother.

Mick stopped to wait for Rory, and as they walked towards Chapelgate Gardens, Rory told Mick about the police and about meeting Larry Burke that morning when he was robbing the house.

"Rory, for fuck's sake, you'll be the death of me Ma. You know she worries about you. She's afraid you'll be sent to the industrial school. Try and keep out of trouble Rory, for Jaysus' sake," said Mick, as he tousled Rory's hair. "You're a scoundrel" laughed Mick.

They walked towards Chapelgate Gardens and Mick told Rory about his interview.

"I'll say a prayer that you get the job Mick," said Rory. Mick looked at his younger brother and smiled.

"Thanks Rory. Thanks," he said as they both walked together towards home.

Rory took the small box from under his arm, and opened it up as he walked along under the railway bridge, out of sight of passing cars.

"Here, Mick. Give this to Angela – it will look lovely on her," said Rory, as he handed Mick a small bracelet.

Mick looked at the little bauble in Rory's hand, and hesitated for a second before taking it from him.

"Thanks, Rory, she will love it," replied Mick.

"What are you going to do with the rest of that stuff, Rory? It looks expensive," said Mick.

"It's just cheap tat Mick. Probably had the real gear in a safe or something. Not even a fucking pound note in the place. I'll give this stuff to Ma – she loves a bit of shiny stuff," replied Rory.

They walked along the street, and Mick couldn't help smiling at his brother. He had tried to keep Rory from stealing, and always gave him lectures about it, but to no avail. Mick knew that Rory was always up to something or other, but he knew his brother had a big heart.

"Rory, why do you keep stealing stuff? You know it's wrong," said Mick, as he put his arm around Rory's shoulder.

Rory looked up at Mick.

"Don't know Mick. Them coppers call me a kleptomaniac. What's that mean?" he said.

"It means someone who steals things or takes things not belonging to them," replied Mick.

Rory thought for a couple of seconds about this.

"So if a person puts things back, would they call him a 'manokleptic'?" laughed Rory.

Mick looked at his brother and smiled.

"Ye mad bastard – what goes on in that little head of yours?" he replied.

They walked towards Chapelgate, Mick's arm around his brother's shoulder.

Chapter Four

Pancho walked into his flat and the smell of fat from the chips cooking in the pan filled his nostrils.

"Ma, is me dinner ready?" shouted Pancho over the noise of his three of sisters, as they argued over clothes in the small bedroom they shared. Pancho threw his coat on the chair, and went into the small scullery that served as the kitchen, utility room, and sometimes confession box, where his mother would sort out all the problems of the world. Her favourite saying to Pancho and the girls would be, "When you're all working we will be on the pig's back!"

But in reality, as the girls got older, they met boys, got married, and moved out. There were just the three girls and Pancho left in the flat, and the only ones working were two of his sisters.

"Madeline, Emily, Annette, stop that fighting and come out here for your dinner!" shouted his mother.

The three girls came out of the bedroom still arguing, and Pancho found it hard to understand who was saying what and who was listening to whom. It was just noise to him, but this was a regular occurrence. They always talked over each other this way. As they sat at the table, the mother came in with the plates of fish and chips. As usual, the fish was just a scrambled mess on the plate, with a few greasy soggy chips beside it. Pancho's mother was not a good cook, and the sisters all looked at each other and giggled when the mother put the plates in front of them.

She came back with a plate of buttered batch loaf, and plonked it into the middle of the table. The girls and Pancho dived into the plate to take a piece.

"You're like fucking animals the lot of yis, no fucking manners!" shouted his mother.

"Ma, she got more bleedin' chips than me!" shouted Madeline, pointing her fork at the youngest, Annette.

Her mother slapped Madeline on the hand.

"Don't point your fork, and don't be fucking cursing. I told you's about that bad language, there's no fucking need for it, I don't know where you get it from," replied her mother. The girls looked at each other and burst into fits of laughter.

The picture on the black and white television in the corner of the room jumped periodically.

"Pancho, give that a kick, son," said his mother as she slapped Annette on the hand for taking another slice of bread.

Pancho reached out and patted the top of the television, and within a couple of seconds the picture rolled twice then settled. The Irish language programme, *Buntas Cainte*, was shown at the same time every evening. Even though they didn't take much notice of it. The next programme was *Lolac and Bolac*, a cheap animated cartoon imported from Poland. Radió Teilifís Éireann was still in its infancy, and the programme selection was very poor.

"Turn that shite off," shouted his mother from the kitchen.

"You wouldn't be saying that if it was "Charles Mitchell" on the news," quipped Annette. The girls laughed out loud as they knew their mother loved the popular newsreader.

"Ahh, very fuckin' funny, very funny" shouted their mother sarcastically from the kitchen.

"Did you get any work today son?" asked his mother.

Pancho picked up a chip with his thumb and finger, tossed around the vinegar on the plate, and threw it into his mouth.

"No, Ma, I went down the docks to see if I could breast on a truck, but there wasn't many trucks about," replied Pancho.

"You won't see too many trucks driving through the fucking playground where you were playing football with them wasters all day!" remarked Madeline sarcastically.

"You fuck off and mind your own fucking business," snapped Pancho, as bits of chip flew from his mouth.

He felt a stinging pain in his right ear, from his mother's open palm.

"Give up fucking cursing at the table I told you before. I don't know where you pick it up," replied his mother ironically.

"Tell her to mind her own business, Ma," said Pancho, as he rubbed his sore ear.

His mother turned to Madeline, and said, "It would be better if you made sure that waster Hickey you're going out with, was looking for work, instead of making smart remarks to your brother." Madeline was vexed at the way her mother turned on her.

"He is, Ma," she protested.

"Well, he won't find much work lying in fucking bed day after day," her mother snapped back.

John Hickey was Madeline's boyfriend and he had never had a job in his life. He leeched off Madeline. She would pay for his cigarettes and his beer when they went out, and as she worked in Guiney's clothes shop, she also dressed him. She couldn't see this, though, as she was besotted with him.

"He's waitin on the right job to come along," she replied defending her boyfriend.

"Ooooh, waiting for the right job is he? Well it's good to know he has such high opinions of himself ... the little bollix," replied her mother sarcastically.

"Do you know who the police were looking for today?" said Pancho, changing the subject.

"Rory Foley!" they all chorused in unison.

The girls laughed at the way they had all said it together.

"No, no, which police were looking for him? Two detectives – Kelly and O'Reilly – that's who," replied Pancho.

"The police are always looking for that fella. God help his poor mother, hardworking family, the Foleys, and that little bugger is always getting into trouble," said his mother.

"Rory Foley is gorgeous," said Emily out loud, not realising she had said it so loud.

She went red, and the other two sisters prodded her and were cooing and aaahing to annoy her.

"What did he do now?" said his mother.

"Fuck all, they just like picking him up to hassle him," replied Pancho, as he tossed another chip into his mouth.

He felt another stinging pain to his ear.

"Pancho, I told you about using that language at the table. Now give it fuckin' up," replied his mother as she drew out again and slapped Pancho across his already sore ear.

"Ma, will you stop slapping me, Jesus!" cried Pancho.

His mother finished the plate of chips she was eating, got up from the table, and headed for the scullery. As she stood in the scullery she let out a loud fart. The girls giggled when they heard it. Pancho walked into the scullery to put his plate in the sink.

"Ma, Jesus, the fucking smell," he said.

His mother turned to him and slapped him across the head again.

"Have respect for your mother," she snapped.

Emily turned to the girls and said, "I think he's a ride."

The girls giggled.

"Ride or no fucking ride, you keep away from that fellah. He will come to a bad end, mark my words!" roared Mrs McDermot, from the small scullery. "Mark my words!"

*****

A few days later Rory was sitting on a wall facing the seafront in Clontarf when he heard the police car pull in behind him. . It was too late to run.

"Fuck," he thought to himself, "that's O'Reilly, driving. I'm fucked!"

The police car drew up beside Rory. He sat smiling at them, as they pulled into the kerb.

"Well, well, look who we have here, the bold Rory Foley. Thief, stroke puller, and a general fucking nuisance," said detective O'Reilly.

Rory jumped off the wall and walked over to the car and kneeled down to come face to face with the driver, detective O'Reilly. The other detective got out of the car and walked to where Rory was kneeling at the car. Detective Kelly took hold of Rory's ear and pulled him to his feet.

"Now me bucko, do you know anything about a little burglary in this area the other day?" asked the detective

Rory pulled away from the detective, and rubbed his ear.

"For fuck's sake, me bleedin' ear's in bits. I know about the burglary," replied Rory.

The two detectives looked at each other, puzzled. No-one in Chapelgate Gardens ever gave information voluntarily.

"Yep, and I know who was involved as well," replied Rory.

Detective O'Reilly got out of the car and stood beside Rory. The detectives looked at each other, and were puzzled at Rory's laid back attitude.

Kelly whispered into the other's ear, "Well it can't have been this Rory fellah who has done the job. He's too confident, and he seems to want to give us information."

O'Reilly nodded and agreed with his partner. They stood in front of Rory and detective Kelly said to him, "Right, ye little fecker – who was it?"

Rory looked at the two detectives and replied, "Well, I know Larry Burke was involved. I think he was trying to catch the robber," said Rory innocently.

The two detectives knew they were being had by Rory, and that he was just playing a game with them. Patrick O'Reilly slapped Rory across the head. Rory stumbled back and came over all dizzy.

"Jesus!" shouted Rory as he rubbed the side of his head.

He nearly blanked out for a split second, and the pain stung his head. The detective went to hit Rory again, but his partner held him back.

"For God's sake, Patrick, take it easy, the young fellah is nearly after fainting. Leave it now," said Kelly, as he pulled his partner back to the car.

Patrick O'Reilly was a very hot headed man, and he lost his temper quite quickly, but Detective Kelly, was, more easy going. The hit to Rory's head was quite a heavy one, and Kelly, thought it was a bit too heavy handed.

Patrick O'Reilly went back to Rory.

"Right, now empty your pockets out. Let's see what you bought with all that money you stole," said detective O'Reilly.

Rory started emptying his pockets and was saying to himself, "What fucking money? There was no money. Them people in the big houses are no better than me. They must have told the insurance that there was money stolen, the robbin' bastards."

Rory put a lone cigarette and a match on the ledge of the wall, together with a small gobstopper sweet he was keeping for later. Detective O'Reilly was surprised that there was no money in Rory's pockets. "Not even a penny. If this fellah had robbed that much money, he would have had at least a few shillings. And one cigarette ... mmm ... and the look on his face when I asked him about the money. Something's not right here – I'm in this game a long time and I don't think we have the right person here. Maybe he didn't rob the house after all". He decided to leave it until later, and he would talk it over with his partner.

O'Reilly turned to Rory and looked into his face.

"Now son, I'm going to give you some sound advice, so you better take it on board. You have been causing an awful lot of trouble around the area here, what with robbing and stuff, but you have just gone and broke into a policeman's house; not an ordinary policeman but a very high up policeman. Detective Superintendent in headquarters, of all people. He is going to break our bollox over this and in turn we have to break your bollox. Now that is crossing the line. This is going to come back on us, so I will advise you to get back to the Gardens where you belong, and keep away from this place. If we see you around here again I won't stop that man there, from giving you a good feckin' hiding. Now get out of here!"

Rory looked at the detective and he nodded as he rubbed his head.

"Ok, Mr O'Reilly, I'll go home," replied Rory, who was feeling very strange after the hit to the head.

The two detectives got back into the car and Dermot turned to his partner.

"That little fucker did it. The description that White's missus gave us fits, and Burke's description was not the same as hers, so he was covering for him," said Patrick.

The other detective nodded in agreement and sat back into the seat.

"I know Patrick, I know, but take it easy with the fists. That was some bang you gave that young fellah," replied Dermot Kelly...

"Feckin' deserves it the little fecker," replied O'Reilly as he pulled away from the kerb and passed Rory who was still rubbing his head.

Detective Kelly had been worried about his partner for the last few weeks. He was noticing changes in his moods, and he was losing his temper at the least little thing. As they passed Rory, they didn't see him sticking his two fingers in the air after them.

"Bastards, me fucking head is spinning." He walked on for a while until he came to the train tracks. He walked towards Killester and from the tracks he could see into the back gardens that bordered the train line. He looked into one particular garden and saw lovely apples hanging from a tree.

"I think I'll bring a few apples home for me ma, she makes a lovely apple tart," he thought to himself.

Chapter Five

Larry was standing beside Mick Foley at the corner of the church beside the convent. There was a little chapel off the convent which was open to the public and it was where the older people would go and pray from time to time. The nuns would look after this chapel with flowers, and candles. It was surprising, but this little chapel was never vandalised, or interfered with, as in the Ireland of the time people had a huge amount of respect for the Church.

The nuns also looked after the poor of Chapelgate Gardens, of which there were many. Larry handed Mick a cigarette.

"Mick, that Rory fellah is as mad as a brush," said Larry.

Mick took a long pull on the cigarette.

"Tell me about it! He has me ma's heart broke with his antics. If he doesn't watch himself, he'll go to Letterfrack Industrial School" replied Mick.

Why, what's he done now, Larry?" replied Mick.

"He was robbing a house where I was cleaning windows the other day. Well, I was climbing me ladder, and I hear a voice coming from upstairs, and of course it was Rory. Frightened the bejaysus out of me he did. But anyway the woman that lives there, a nice woman, Mrs White, Marie – she's a bit of a looker Mick – but anyway, she came home early, and I let on that I came across him and chased him out of the house," said Larry.

Mick shook his head and said, "I'll talk to him Larry. He's a little bollix. Ger and me are always at him to go to school and settle, but he's a mad bastard."

"He can rob any house he wants to Mick, but tell him to be careful around Clontarf. I don't want to lose me window round. If he gets caught and they know he knows me, well things could get tricky for me," said Larry.

"OK, Larry, I'll talk to him," replied Mick.

"Just tell him to be careful, Mick, that's all. But listen, when I got back to the house she brought me in and gave me a brandy. She thought I was a fucking hero. But the gas thing was, when she was out of the room, I found a wallet behind a picture frame and swiped it. After all, if the place was burgled, she will assume that the burglar has taken the wallet. There was a good few fucking quid in it, Mick. Poor Rory missed out on it. Anyway, when you get home, give him this," said Larry, handing Mick five single pound notes.

Mick laughed and took the money.

"He will be made up. I saw him the other day with some jewellery, well just cheap ould tat! That must have been the proceeds." laughed Mick.

Larry told him about how he found Rory in the house, and the way he had to chase him off when the woman returned. They both had a good laugh at the antics of Rory Foley.

"Do you know what, Mick? I think the woman has a thing for me. She was acting strange, like different, you know," said Larry.

Mick knew Larry was always making up stories about his customers on his window cleaning rounds, and he knew he just made them up to keep the lads amused. Mick knew that most of the stories had no real truth in them. But it was the way Larry was telling him that told him this wasn't just another yarn from Larry.

"How'd you mean, Lar?" said Mick.

Larry took a long drag from his cigarette, and blew the smoke into the air.

"Well, I do the windows for this woman twice a month. Everybody else only have them cleaned once a month, but Marie always asks me to clean them every two weeks. She said me dad is ok, but she prefers me to clean them. But anyway, the other day after I had chased Rory, I came back to her. She was looking at me in a kind of strange way, like she was waiting for me to make a move on her," replied Larry.

Mick knew Larry was being serious by his demeanour.

"Marie, well at least you're on first name terms with her!" laughed Mick.

"Fuck off, Mick! But seriously, what do you think?" asked Larry.

"Did you do anything with her?" asked Mick.

"No, Mick. God's honest. I just stood there with the drink in me hand. She gave me a large glass of brandy as well, Mick. I forgot to tell you that, but no, I just stood there, and I mean it Mick, she was waiting for me to make a move. What would you have done, Mick?" asked Larry.

Mick let out a little laugh.

"Jesus, you asking me about women? I know fuck all about women, as you know Larry. The large brandy might have gone to your head mate. But she is a customer, so be careful. If you pick up the wrong signals and make a move, you'll be in the shit!" replied Mick.

Larry thought about what Mick had said.

"Yeh, you're right, Mick. I must have drank the brandy too quickly. Anyway, she is old, about forty, with loads of money. What the fuck would she want with me?" replied Larry.

"It must be your Rock Hudson looks!" laughed Mick. Larry did have a slight resemblance to Rock Hudson. This was why he never had any trouble getting girls to go off with.

Larry thumped Mick on the arm.

"Piss off, I look nothing like Rock fucking Hudson," he laughed.

They were both laughing when Jem O'Donnell joined them.

"How's the lads?" asked Jem, as he took out a cigarette and lit a match and puffed on the cigarette.

Larry looked at Mick and nodded towards Jem. Mick knew what he was drawing attention to. It was the way Jem held his cigarette. He held his cigarette like a girl. Jem copped this nod from Larry to Mick.

"Fuck off you pair of cunts! I know you're slagging me. I can't help the way I fucking smoke." laughed Jem, and he pushed Larry on the shoulder.

"How's the Joxer fella? Have you's made your first million yet?" laughed Larry.

They had a good laugh, and Larry didn't talk about the incident with Marie in front of Jem. Mick picked up on this, but said nothing.

Joxer and Jem had a large box car and they collected turf from Portland Street and would deliver it around the flats complex for a small fee. It was hard work for small gain but in the winter months they earned quite a bit of money. They also helped people moving items from place to place. A sofa for Mrs Pluck to go to her daughter's flat, or a bed and mattress to Mrs Kealy. They had made the box car with large wheels and it could take six large bags of turf.

"A million? That will be the day. No, but we are getting a few bob every week. We had Pancho giving us a hand last week, moving some stuff for a woman moving from a three bedroom to the two bedroom flats in Seville Place. Joxer and him are like an old married couple, telling each other what to do, but fuck me, Pancho is strong," said Jem.

Jem had asked Pancho for help the previous week, and Joxer wasn't happy but Joxer noticed that Pancho worked a lot harder than Jem that day. Jem would always try to get out of working hard, and this was the only thing that Joxer didn't like about him.

*****

Jem helped Joxer collecting turf from the local turf depot, and they distributed it around Chapelgate Gardens. People who were on welfare were given a fuel docket in the winter period, and it entitled them to two bags of turf every week, free of charge. But they had to collect it themselves. So Joxer built a large box type trolley, and went around the flats asking people if they needed their turf collecting. For this he would charge a shilling. But when the turf was piled high on the trolley, it would be heavy to push, so he roped in Jem to help him. Joxer couldn't read or write, and he was described as 'being backward' – the term used by the locals in Chapelgate to describe someone who was mentally challenged. Jem and

Joxer got on well, considering Joxer didn't take to many people.

Once, when they were taking the turf back to the Chapelgate Gardens, they nearly run over by a truck. The box trolley was quite big, with two large pram wheels at the back, and two smaller wheels at the front which had two pieces of rope attached to enable Jem to steer with. They normally collected six bags of turf at a time, and this filled the trolley.

The depot was in the Portland Street, and they had to push the trolley down a hill towards a junction called the five lamps. The way they worked it was like this. As Joxer was quite strong, he did most of the pushing, and Jem would sit astride the bags of turf and steer the trolley. They had no braking system as such, but Jem would just put his foot to the large back wheel, and the friction would slow it down slightly. But this day, as they were coming back with a full load, six bags of turf, they came across a young lad at the top of the hill which took them down to the five lamps. He had two bags of turf on a small child's pram. Unfortunately the wheel had fallen off this lad's pram and he was just standing by the side of the road with it, when Joxer and Jem came upon him. He asked them if they could take the two bags of turf back to Chapelgate for him, and he would give them the shilling. Joxer said no, as he was the one doing all the pushing, and an extra two bags of turf would overload the cart. But Jem said to Joxer that they only had to push the trolley to the edge of hill, and if they timed the traffic lights properly at the bottom of the hill, they would sail right through the set of traffic lights at the five lamps junction, all the way down Seville Place, and right into Chapelgate.

Joxer was a bit sceptical about the load, but he agreed to take it if the lad would help them push the trolley down the hill. With enough momentum and the timing of the traffic lights, Joxer would be able to climb on to the back of the trolley, and the weight and the speed would mean an easy ride. So they agreed to take the extra bags. They put a small plank at the back of the trolley, to load the two new sacks against it. Then Jem sat astride the new bags. He found that he was higher up than normal, but he felt ok, and he imagined himself as a stagecoach driver in the old west. He imagined himself as John Wayne in a cowboy film.

Then Joxer and the lad started to push the trolley – slowly at first, due to the extra weight. As they started rolling down the hill the trolley started to sway from side to side. Joxer was getting a bit worried.

"I think it's too heavy Jem," said Joxer.

But Jem was delighted to be up on the cart, and he was steering it towards the crossroads at the end of the hill.

"Me bollox, it's grand! We'll get the load through," shouted back Jem, who was now in a film in his mind.

He imagined himself as a stage coach driver in the old cowboy films they used to watch when they were younger.

"We just have to time the traffic lights properly and we will be OK," said Joxer to the young lad helping him push the trolley.

As they gained momentum on the hill Jem saw the traffic lights just change to green. From going up and down the hill so often, he knew that if they started to get a bit more speed up, they would just make it through the traffic lights before they changed back to red. But because of the weight, it was taking longer to get up to the correct speed. Halfway down the hill, the trolley was now going much faster than normal, and Joxer and the lad were finding it hard now to keep up with it.

Jem was calling out, "Faster, faster, giddy up!" The trolley was now speeding towards the crossroads, and Jem was still calling out "Faster!" Jem was astride the turf and the ropes he held, to control the steering were pulling at his arms. He was finding it very hard to keep it in a straight line. The cart had picked up quite a fast pace now and the young boy and Joxer were finding it hard to keep up with it.

As they picked up speed Joxer went to jump onto the back of the cart but miscalculated it and tripped. He fell, and the young lad tripped over Joxer, and he fell too. The trolley was now speeding and swaying dangerously, with Jem steering. He looked around to see Joxer and the lad in a heap in the middle of the road behind him. When he looked back to the traffic lights they had changed from green to orange. He was going too fast now to try and stop the cart. He tried to reach the wheel with his foot but the extra bags he was sitting on meant he couldn't reach it.

"Jesus, I'll be killed," he thought to himself. Then the lights went red for the traffic going forward, and a car had just stopped in front of him.

He pulled the rope to the right, and the trolley started to steer around the car in front. The trolley then started to tip over to the left, so he pulled his rope to the left. It straightened up. He missed the car by inches. The trolley continued and he managed to get some sort of control. He proceeded towards the junction, and the cart was going very fast now.

From the corner of his eye, Jem could see a truck pulling away from the traffic lights to his right and if it continued it would cross his path within seconds.

The truck was loaded with bags of cabbage, which were piled high and tied loosely. The cart continued to trundle along at a very fast pace.

Jem closed his eyes.

"Holy Mother of God, I'm going to die," he thought to himself.

The trolley was swaying dangerously as it sped through the junction at breakneck speed. The truck driver saw the trolley to his left coming in front of his truck, so he jammed his foot to the brake. The load of cabbages were pushed forward, and the rope holding them broke. The cabbages fell onto the road. The bags containing the cabbages burst open as they hit the road, and they spilled everywhere. Jem had closed his eyes as he sailed through the junction, and only opened them when he reached the other side. He looked back to see cabbages rolling around the street, as men, women, and children came from every corner to pick them up. He looked back at the driver of the truck waving his fist in the air, and heard him calling out, "Ye feckin bastard!"

There was mayhem on the road as people came from everywhere and picked the cabbages up and walked off with them. The driver could do nothing as he saw his load disappear before his eyes.

"What will we do about the cabbages?" said his helper, a young lad of about sixteen, as he climbed down from the truck.

The driver pulled a cigarette butt from behind his ear and put it in his mouth. He struck a match off the arse of his corduroy trousers, and as he lit the butt, he watched the rest of the load being cleared from the road.

"They are like fucking locusts," he thought to himself. He looked at the young lad, who was standing outside the truck waiting for an answer to his question.

The driver took a long pull on the cigarette and said to the lad, "Fuck the cabbages. At least they are going to deserving causes. Let's get back to the depot."

Jem continued on down Seville Place, and as the trolley slowed up, he thought to himself, "Well, that was fucking close – the things we do for money!"

Chapter Six

Rory was walking along the railway tracks towards Chapelgate. He was near the signal box a mile from the main train station. He had his sweater tucked into his trousers, and had apples stuffed into his sweater. He looked like a pregnant woman, with his belly full of the stolen apples sticking out. He had jumped over a wall and had taken the apples from the trees in the back garden of a house. He thought to himself that he would give his mother the apples, and she would make her lovely apple cakes for tea, which he loved. His head still hurt from the clatter he had received from O'Reilly

The signalman in the signal box up ahead sat reading, and then he looked up from his book and when he saw a movement in the tracks. A few minutes before, he had just pulled the switch to reroute the incoming express train from Belfast. He saw a small figure with a head of black hair moving along the line.

"Jesus, Mary and Joseph, what the bloody hell is that?" he said to himself. He watched the boy scramble after an apple as it rolled around the tracks.

Rory was stepping from sleeper to sleeper along the tracks, oblivious to what was going on around him. Trying to keep from stepping on the gravel between the sleepers required a degree of concentration.

"I'm going to give up robbing and go back to school," he thought to himself. An apple dropped from his sweater and rolled along the tracks. He bent down to pick up the apple, and again he thought to himself, "Yeh, I'll give up robbing and go back to school just for me ma's sake. This is the last time I take anything that doesn't belong to me. No more seeing me ma crying over me."

The signalman saw the train speeding up behind Rory.

The Belfast express was making great progress towards Dublin, and the driver sat in the cab watching the green scenery pass by in a blur. He reached for his pipe, and pressed the tobacco into the hole... In a few minutes he would be having his break and a few games of cards with the lads in Dublin, he thought to himself. He struck a match and started to light the pipe. . Through the smoke that came from the lighted pipe, he saw a small figure move on the tracks about two or three hundred yards in front of him. He froze as he saw the figure bend down and pick up things from the track.

He reached for the emergency stop lever as the pipe fell from his mouth.

Rory picked up the apple that had fallen, and put it down the front of his jumper.

"Me ma loved that jewellery I gave her. She looked great with the ear rings on and the ... what's that noise?" he thought to himself, as he turned around and on bended knee saw the train come hurtling towards him. He saw the man in the cab pulling on a lever.

"Oh my God," he said to himself as the train came closer and closer. On his bended knee he closed his eyes, and his mother's smiling face was the last thing he saw.

The signalman in the box saw the whole thing in slow motion. As the young boy turned to face the train, he was mown down in a split second. The sparks from the wheels only started to show when the train was near the signal box. That's how fast the train was travelling. He saw the look of fear in the face of the train driver. He couldn't look at the spot where the train had passed over the boy. All he could see was a few apples rolling around the area where the boy had been. He cupped his head in his hands, and tried to blot out what he had seen.

As the train was slowing down, the people in the carriages were wondering why they were coming to a sudden stop. The driver had just seen for a split second the young boy's face, as he looked up into his eyes. One second he was there, and in a flash he was gone. The train eventually came to a shudder and then stopped. The driver put his hands on the dashboard of the cab, and bent his head. The pipe, had dropped to the floor of the cab and was still smouldering.

"God have mercy on the poor little fellah," he said, as he blessed himself. He sat staring straight in front of him.

The signalman came down from his box and ran towards the spot where Rory had been hit. As he approached the front of the train, the driver was climbing down from the cab. The signalman had seen this driver bring this train into the station over many years now, and they always waved to each other, but they had never talked or met before. They nodded to each other and their faces were white with shock.

They walked back the length of the train.

"I didn't see him till the last minute, the poor wee mite," said the driver, in his distinct Belfast accent, the tears welling up in his eyes.

"I know, I saw the whole thing. I don't know where he came from. One second he wasn't there, the next he was," said the signalman, as he put his hand on the shoulder of the driver to console him.

As they approached the spot, they saw the apples strewn around the tracks. The body of Rory Foley lay like a rag doll behind the train, his black curly hair matted with blood. The driver and the signalman stood there, and as other workers approached from behind, the signalman just kept saying, "May God help the poor wee lad."

*****

Dermot Kelly sat in the patrol car waiting for his partner to join him. They had just had a pint whilst on a fifteen minute break. The radio crackled and Dermot picked up the handset.

"Two ten, where are you?" crackled the radio.

Dermot pressed the button.

"Amiens Street, near the train station," replied Dermot.

"An incident in the station on the incoming track. Can you go and check it out?" replied the controller.

Patrick jumped into the front seat.

"Well, where to?" he asked.

Dermot pulled away and indicated they were going up the ramp to Amiens Street train station.

"Something happened on the incoming track. We've to check it out," he replied to Patrick.

A couple of minutes later as they walked down the track out towards Fairview, the signalman, who had witnessed the accident, approached them with tears in his eyes. He explained to them about the incident and how it happened.

"The driver hadn't a chance. I only saw the boy myself at the last minute. He came out of nowhere." the man explained drying his eyes with a handkerchief. .

As they came upon the track where Rory had been hit, they saw that there were two men folding a blanket over the mangled remains of Rory Foley as he lay on the tracks. One of the men knew Patrick.

"He's only about thirteen or fourteen years of age sir, God bless him," said the man to Patrick.

The man lifted the blanket and Patrick winced at the image he saw. Rory's face peered back at him, eyes open. His curly hair covered on one side with blood. There were some splats of blood on his forehead.

"Do you know him?" asked the man.

Patrick O'Reilly said nothing. He hadn't expected to see someone he knew, but nodded his head.

His partner Dermot noticed Patrick's changed demeanour. He walked up to where Rory lay and was surprised to see Rory's face looking back.

"Poor little Rory Foley. We were only talking to him a couple of hours ago," said Dermot to the signalman. "What happened?" Dermot asked the signalman.

Patrick walked over towards a wall and leaned into it and his stomach heaved. It was just black liquid, the pint of Guinness, he had earlier that came up. He held one hand on the wall and wiped his mouth with a handkerchief with the other. His thoughts went to his brother Jack who would have been about Rory's age if had still been alive. He died ten years before in an accident, when the wheels of the tractor that Patrick was driving caught Jack and crushed him. The incident came flooding back to him in an instant. He remembered the day as if it was yesterday. His father had given him the keys to the tractor, to fill it up with diesel at the local garage. He jumped into the driving seat and started it up. His younger brother Jack, who had been playing behind the house, heard the noise from the tractor and came around to where Patrick was just about to reverse it out of the barn. Jack called to his older brother to take him with him, but he could not be heard over the noise of the engine. As he reversed the tractor, he felt the bump but he just kept going.

Seeing young Rory brought all the memories flooding back.

Dermot Kelly had taken out his notebook and was writing a statement from the train driver. He looked across to see where his partner was.

"I could have done with his help," he thought to himself. He looked across and saw his partner standing hunched over at the wall, his shoulders heaving up and down as he sobbed his heart out. "What the feck! Jesus, I bet he is regretting the thump he gave the young fellah earlier," thought Dermot. He decided to continue taking statements, and to leave his partner with his thoughts for the time being.

As they walked back towards the car in silence, Dermot offered his partner a cigarette. Patrick stopped, took it, and struck a match. He offered a light to his partner.

"Where you thinking about the thump ye gave the young fellah earlier?" asked Dermot.

Patrick sucked the smoke into his lungs. "Yes, I was a bit too hard on him. God, he was only a kid. About the same age as the brother Jack, the little fella I told you about. – yeh, Jack would have been his age now," replied Patrick to his partner as he exhaled his smoke.

"Ah, I remember, that's the little fellah ye told me about. God bless his little soul," replied Dermot.

"He would be about sixteen, same age as young Foley there," replied Patrick.

They walked on towards the car, and Dermot offered to drive to Chapelgate to inform Rory's mother.

"I will give her the sad news, Patrick. You stay in the car, me oul pal," said Dermot.

Patrick said nothing but looked straight ahead and took another pull from the cigarette. As they drove towards Chapelgate, Dermot looked at his partner. The tears were rolling down Patrick's face. They drove on in silence.

Chapter Seven

"Here comes fucking trouble," said Gerard, as he walked towards the three lads, Mick, Larry, and Jem. They looked at where Gerard was nodding his head. The car with the detectives was driving slowly into the flats complex. Gerard looked at Patrick O'Reilly as the car passed them. He couldn't help noticing his sad looking face. The detective never glanced at them once, which the lads thought unusual. They drove over towards where the Foleys lived.

Mick looked at Gerard.

"I think they are going towards our place, Ger," he said.

Mick stubbed his cigarette out and walked towards the car, with Gerard walking behind him.

As they got out of the car, Dermot turned to Patrick.

"I'll inform the mother, you stay here," he said.

Patrick got out of the car and walked around to his partner and put his hand on his shoulder.

"Dermot, I would like to do this. I need to do this. I know what this woman is going to go through. My own mother went through it, and I think I should inform her," replied Patrick.

Dermot looked at his partner and saw the sincerity in his face.

"OK, Pat, if you think you can handle this, you should do it. Do you need me to go in with you?" replied Dermot.

Patrick shook his head. He knocked on the front door and waited. The grey hair of Mrs Foley appeared at the bubble glass panel on the front door. Mrs Foley stood in the hallway wiping her hands on her apron.

"Oh, hello, sir. Are you looking for Rory? He should be in for his tea soon. What did he get up to now, sir? He's not a bad lad really – just a bit mischievous." Mrs Foley rambled on.

Patrick just stood there in the doorway, and he let Mrs Foley finish what she was saying. She looked into his eyes and she saw that he had been crying. There was nothing said, and the silence hung in the air.

Patrick stepped into the hall and held her two hands.

"Mrs Foley, it's Rory. He ... a train ... It..." he didn't finish his sentence.

Mrs Foley stepped back into the hallway, and her hands went to her mouth.

"Oh God, no. Oh, Jesus, my Rory," she cried out.

Patrick walked towards her and put his arms around her shoulders. She buried her head in his chest and she sobbed. They stood together in the hall for what seemed like ages.

Outside, Gerard and Mick talked to Dermot Kelly, and he told them what had happened to Rory. Dermot put his hand on Mick's shoulder, and told him how sorry he was about Rory. Gerard ran towards the door, and as he entered the hallway, he saw his mother sobbing into the detective's shoulder.

Gerard held his mother by the shoulder and acknowledged to the detective that he would take over. They went into the kitchen, and Gerard sat his mother down.

"Can I get you a cup of tea, guard?" asked Gerard.

Patrick nodded, and then sat beside Mrs Foley. She wiped her eyes in her apron and turned to the detective.

"What happened guard. Where?" she pleaded.

Patrick explained to them both the way Rory had been hit by a train. Gerard gave his mother and the detective a cup of tea.

"Thanks," the detective said.

Mrs Foley started to cry again, and Gerard and Patrick O'Reilly could only look on. Gerard didn't cry, he just sat in silence. A few minutes passed in silence, then Mr's Foley got up from the chair and went into the bedroom, and returned with a little jewellery box in her hands.

"Look, he gave me these the other day. He was a good boy, guard. I know he was a bit mischievous, but he really was a good boy who loved his mother," she pleaded with the guard, as she took out the little baubles from the box.

"He gave me these the other day, God bless him," she said, as she held the little pieces in her hand.

Patrick looked at the baubles, and knew from the description they were the pieces of jewellery that Mrs White had described to him a couple of days before.

Gerard looked over at the detective, knowing he was thinking the same thing about the baubles. As they looked at each other Patrick took out a pack of cigarettes and offered one to Gerard. Patrick saw the look on Gerard's face and he found himself in an awkward situation. He made a gesture to Gerard that all he was there for was to give some comfort to Mrs Foley, and he lit a match and offered a light to Gerard.

"Thanks," said Gerard as he took the light, but Patrick knew the real reason he was thanking him.

Patrick looked into Mrs Foley's eyes.

"Yes I know – he really did love his mother," replied the detective.

Gerard put his arm around his mother's shoulders. She bent her head forward and started to sob again. The detective got up from the table and put his hand on Gerard's shoulder. He nodded to Gerard and then left.

Mick was talking to Dermot Kelly as he approached them.

"Sorry, Mick," said Patrick to Mick.

"Thanks, guard. How is she?" asked Mick.

"She needs her sons now," said the detective.

Mick thanked the guards and went into the flat.

"Well, God bless her. How is she?" asked Dermot.

Patrick leaned against the car. They both smoked in silence for a few minutes.

"Come on, let's get back to make our report. Then we can have a few pints. God knows, I could do with a pint," said Dermot Kelly, as they drove out of the flats complex.

They drove by Angela and Imelda who were walking towards the Foley's flat. They had just heard the news about Rory. News travelled fast in Chapelgate Gardens.

"Poor Rory, he was such happy fellah, always smiling with that lovely big smile of his," said Angela.

"A little angel," said Imelda.

They walked into the Foley's flat and saw Mrs Foley being comforted by Mick. Gerard was standing at the window looking out towards the green area where Rory would often play football with his friends. Angela walked over to Mick and put her arms around his shoulder and pressed her face against his arm. Mick put his arm around her. Mrs Foley looked at Angela through eyes full of tears; she smiled at Angela.

"Sorry Mrs Foley," said Angela.

Imelda stood behind Gerard and put her hand on his shoulder.

"Are you ok Ger," she asked. Gerard looked over his shoulder to see Imelda. He was glad she was beside him now.

"Yeh, I, I just hope he felt no pain. Poor Rory," he said. There was a noise at the front door and they all turned to see Mr Foley coming into the room.

"Nora why is the front door wide open, are we living in a barn?" he said as he walked into the room. When he saw his wife with tears rolling down her face and Mick and Gerard with two girls standing there he knew there was something wrong.

"Dick, it's little Rory," sobbed Mrs Foley. The blood drained from Mr Foley's face. He sat on the chair beside his wife. He took her hands in his and they both sobbed and sobbed. Mick took Angela by the hand and walked towards the kitchen. Imelda and Gerard followed. A parent's grief is very private.

*****

A few days later, after the funeral, the Foleys returned back to The Bell public house, where the owner laid on sandwiches and soup for the mourners. The funeral was a big one, and nearly everybody from Chapelgate Gardens was there. The parish priest, Father Ball, celebrated the Mass. Father Ball, was a small fat man and was feared by a lot of people, as he had a fire and brimstone manner.

Once while saying Mass he bent in front of the microphone and farted. The sound bellowed through the PA system. At first, a few children laughed, and then the whole congregation went into fits of laughter. He wasn't liked very much in Chapelgate Gardens, for his rough treatment of children. Years later, the diocese decided to make him a canon, and the kids got great kick out of calling him "Canon Ball!"

Angela and Imelda had taken the day off work to attend the funeral, and they sat together in the lounge bar. They were joined by Gerard, Michael, Jem and Larry.

"Will you have a pint, Mick, Ger?" said Larry, as he approached the company.

"We're OK, Lar, thanks," replied Gerard.

They sat around the table talking about the antics that young Rory had gotten up to. Each of them had a story to tell about Rory, and how he had affected their lives.

Larry tried to lighten the conversation and recounted a joke about Father Ball.

"Anyway, he went to the doctor, and said to him, 'Doctor, I keep farting, when I walk, but the funny thing is my farts "don't smell!".' So the doctor said, 'OK, walk over there.' So Father Ball walks, and of course he farts … Brrp, brrrp, brrp! 'Come back,' says the doctor, so he walks back. Brrrp … brrrp … brrrp, goes Father Ball. The doctor turns to him and says, 'I know the problem. You'll need an operation.' 'On me arse, doctor?' says Father Ball. 'No, on your fucking nose. You're fucking rotten!' says the doctor."

The lads cracked up with laughter at Larry's joke.

The pub was full with friends and neighbours of the Foley's. It was always full after a funeral but today it seemed as if everybody from Chapelgate Gardens was in attendance. The Dillons were in their usual place. Mr Dillon had tried in recent weeks to keep Mrs Dillon away from the pub by taking her only pair of shoes with him when he went to work. But this hadn't stopped her, as she found an old pair of wellington boots in the wardrobe, and she wore them to the pub when he was out. Most of their money went on drink, and they were in arrears with all of their bills. Once, the rent collector from the corporation came to the door looking for overdue rent. Mrs Dillon was very drunk when she answered the loud knock on the door. He stood there with a clipboard in his hand.

"Mrs Dillon, I've come to look for the rent," he said in a strong firm voice.

Mrs Dillon looked back at him through her bleary drunken eyes and replied, "OK, well, come on in and we will look for it together!" Then she fell in a heap at his feet. Mrs Dillon was an alcoholic.

In the corner near the toilets sat Mrs Pluck and Ossiler Larkin. Ossiler was Joxer's father. Mrs Pluck and Ossiler were both widowed and were often together. They were in their late fifties, and liked each other's company, though they were not intimately involved.

Mrs Pluck had been married to a very violent man, who had knocked her about for years, and she was glad when he had died. In fact he had a heart attack six months before he died, and when she went to the hospital to see him, the doctor told her he had a slim chance of pulling through. The doctor told her it might be just a matter of days. She had pretended to be upset in front of the doctor, but inside she was delighted. In fact, when she left the hospital she went to the trouble of organising his funeral and the afters in The Bell. As he was insured, she borrowed fifty pounds from the Jewish money lender who lent money at very high interest rates to people in Chapelgate. The people of Chapelgate would have no access to bank loans. She needed the money to keep the household going, and to buy some black clothes for herself, in preparation for his funeral. She had two daughters and they hated their father for the way he treated their mother.

"Our lives will be a lot better when he goes," she said to them on returning from the hospital.

After four days in hospital, the doctor called her into his office.

"This is it," she thought to herself.

She had called in to see her sister Patty before she left for the hospital.

"This is it, Patty. The doctor sent for me this morning," she said to her sister, as she left for the hospital.

The doctor greeted her as she entered his office.

"Sit down, I have some news on your husband, Mrs Pluck," said the doctor.

Later that day, Mrs Pluck called in to see her sister on the way back from the hospital.

"Come in, love," said Patty, looking at her sister's ashen face, as she stood at the front door.

"Patty, it's bad news," said Mrs Pluck to her sister.

"Is he … is he dead, love?" said Patty, holding her sister's hand and putting on a sad face.

"Patty, the fucker is coming home tomorrow. He's sitting up in bed like a fucking lord. The doctor can't believe he's pulled through. How am I going to pay back the loan from the Jewman? I was depending on his insurance money to pay it off. The bastard can't even die when he's supposed to. He'll break me heart till the fucking end," she cried.

"The bastard, we'll have to put a stake through his heart, like fucking Dracula," replied Patty, as she put her arms around her sister.

They both looked at each other and started laughing.

Six months later, Mrs Pluck was sitting at the fire looking into the flames. Her husband, who had been bedridden since his release from hospital, called out to her.

"Joanee, bring me in the paper and a cu …"

He never finished his sentence. He died mid-sentence. Joanee Pluck sat there in silence for over an hour. She started to cry tears of happiness. Her prison sentence was over.

"Thank you, Lord Jesus Christ, for releasing me from my torment," she prayed.

In Catholic Ireland in 1967, when you married you married till death divided you.

Mr Dillon was singing now. His velvet voice could be heard in the gents' toilet, where Mick and Gerard Foley were talking.

"Where do you think Rory is now?" asked Gerard.

"Trying to get the keys to the pearly gates from St Michael, if I know him!" laughed Mick.

They both laughed together and hugged each other. Mick then cried and sobbed into his brother's shoulder.

"I miss him, Ger," he cried.

"I know, I know, brud. Me too," replied Gerard.

The strains of Mr Dillon's song came wafting through to where they stood holding each other.

"When I fall in love, it will be forever." sang Mr Dillon, as he stood in the midst of the crowd in the packed lounge. He was a lovely singer, with a soft velvet voice like Nat King Cole. *"Or I'll never fall in love. In a restless world like this is, love is ended before it's begun, and too many moonlight kisses, seemed to cool in the warmth of the sun,"* he continued. The lounge was silent as Mr Dillon sang, and tears ran down Mrs Dillon's face as she listened to her husband sing.

"Good on yeh, Jimmy!" shouted a man from the bar.

"Ssshhh!" went the crowd in unison at this interruption. *"When I give my heart, it will be completely, or I'll never give my heart. And the moment I can feel that, you feel that way too. Is when I fall in love with you."* sang Mr Dillon.

When he finished the crowd stood and clapped. The two detectives were walking by The Bell as the velvet voice of Mr Dillon came wafting from the bar. They both stopped and stood listening to the song. At the sound of the clapping, Dermot raised his eyes to his partner.

"That Dillon chap, lovely singer. As good as the main man himself," said Dermot.

Patrick just nodded. As the two detectives walked towards their car, Patrick thought to himself that Chapelgate Gardens and the people that lived there, were not unlike his own community, in the village where he grew up. He thought to himself that apart from the level of crime in the area, the people faced the same challenges in life, trying to struggle and survive, and trying to provide for their families in very difficult circumstances. Since he had broken the news to Mrs Foley, he was seeing a different side óf Chapelgate Gardens that he had not seen before. He saw them come together in grief for one of their own.

He remembered that when his own brother died, the village came together in grief, the same way this community was consoling the Foleys. When he was in Templemore training school before he graduated as a policeman, he was led to believe that the city people would eat you alive. So he had come to Dublin as a young guard on the back foot, ready to 'put manners on the inner city'. But the more time he spent in Chapelgate in the last few days, his opinions were slowly changing. He could see that this was a small village in the midst of a City.

They got to the car, and Dermot again tried to engage his partner in conversation.

"That Imelda Bradshaw is growing into a nice little filly, eh Pat? I'd say she's a grand little ride, what?" he quipped.

Pat smiled back.

"Yeh, I'd say she will be a right little goer," said Pat, and they both laughed.

Mick and Gerard returned to the bar and joined Angela, Imelda, Jem and Larry at the table. The smoke was heavy in the air as the lads came in from the toilet.

"Good turnout Mick. Your ma will be pleased – he was liked a lot," said Larry.

Mick nodded in agreement and Angela held his hand and squeezed it.

Gerard turned to Imelda.

"It was nice of you to come, Imelda, I know it's hard to get time off from work. But thanks, Imelda," he said.

Imelda had been with Gerard before, and they had sex on a number of occasions. But they were not boyfriend or girlfriend. In fact, Imelda did not want a boyfriend. She liked the fact that she was in control of her own body, and if she wanted to have sex with anyone, she let them know that she was the one in control. She had a reputation as being very strong willed. Once she had met a lad in a bar in town, and they had sex in a lane at the back of the bar. The lad thought that he was now her boyfriend. The next time he met her it was at a dance. He started to act as if she was his property, and was getting jealous when she danced with other boys. When he tried to pull her away from a lad on the dance floor, she turned and kneed him between his legs.

As he fell to the ground clutching himself, she stood over him and said, "I don't belong to you, or fucking anyone, so put your hand on me again, and I will fucking stab ye, do you hear me?" she shouted.

From that day, the lads in Chapelgate knew where they stood with Imelda.

Gerard and Imelda chatted about Rory and the scrapes he got in to. The conversation came around to what Gerard had in mind for the future.

"England? Jesus, Ger, we'll never see you if you head over there," said Imelda.

"Larry's Uncle "Jimmy" was back from England a couple of weeks ago, and we had a pint with him, Me and Lar, and he was saying there are great opportunities over there for anybody willing to take chances," replied Gerard.

"How'd ye mean … take chances?" said Imelda, eyeing Gerard suspiciously.

Gerard just laughed.

"Life's too short, Imelda. "Do it to them before they do it to you, kid!"

Larry overheard Gerard, and knew it was one of their sayings they would come up with when they were ranting about the system that kept the working class down. Larry leaned in between Imelda and Gerard.

"Don't let the bastards grind you down," he quipped.

"You'll never take me alive, copper!" replied Gerard.

They both laughed at their stupid sayings.

Imelda looked at the two lads, puzzled.

"You're a pair of fucking eejits," she replied as she took a sip from her glass.

"Every time you say goodbye I die a little, Every time you say goodbye I cry a little." sang Mrs Dillon. She wasn't too drunk to keep her singing in tune. The fact that herself and her husband were very good singers meant that at parties and weddings they were always the centre of attention.

The afternoon drifted into the evening, and more sandwiches were put on the table. Gerard and Larry were deep in conversation. Gerard was telling Larry that he was thinking about going to England to look for work, and he was asking Larry where could he meet his Uncle Jimmy.

"He's doing great over there, Ger. He's in to dodgy stuff, but he has plenty of money. He's always asking me over, but I have things going good with the da, so I don't see things changing for me. We're building up a nice little earner now with the chimney cleaning, and I can stroke a few bits and bobs here and there," replied Larry.

Gerard took a gulp from his pint, and took a drag from his cigarette. He blew out the smoke and looked around the smoky pub. The people who frequented The Bell were sat in the same seats as always. Mrs Pluck and Ossiler, sitting in the same seats. Mr O'Brien with his big red face, sweating profusely running from lounge to bar because he was too mean to employ another barman. The Dillons sitting in their usual seats singing their hearts out, hoping someone will throw the odd drink their way. His father and mother sat beside the door as they did every Saturday on their only night out together. His hard working father who, after working all week had just about enough money to bring his mother out on Saturday night, and maybe have a few shillings left over to have a Sunday morning drink with his workmates in The Bell.

"Is this it, Lar? Is this fucking it? Look around. Are we going to replace the Mr and Mrs Dillons and the Ossilers and the Mrs Plucks? Look at me da. He has a job. He works every day and still at the end of the week he has fuck all to show for it" pleaded Gerard with Larry.

Larry looked around, and he saw that Gerard was right. Larry thought to himself, "In a few years he would marry someone and have kids, and like his parents have more kids, and barely keep his bills paid." He would get a flat from the council and marry a local girl, settle down and have kids. It was the way it was.

Larry knew Gerard was right, but he refused to contemplate his future.

"Get off the cross – we need the fucking wood, Ger! Don't just talk about going to England. Do it!" replied Larry, who was getting a bit pissed now.

"I will Lar and soon, real soon, I'm fed up with this fucking life. No fucking work. No fucking money and no fucking life," said Gerard.

Larry was getting a bit drunk now and picked up his drink and raised it in a salute.

"To Gerard Foley!"

"Who wants a life," said Larry.

Gerard smiled at Larry.

"Cheers mate," he said as he clinked glasses with Lar. "You are right Larry. I do want a life. I want to make a life for myself," replied Gerard.

Imelda who had been talking to Angela and Mick earlier, came over and joined Gerard and Larry. She had been trying to get to talk to Gerard all day but with people paying their respects to the family there just wasn't an opportunity to get him on his own.

"How are you, Ger? Are you ok?" she asked.

She sat in beside Gerard. Larry was feeling a little bit sick and needed to go to the toilet.

"'Scuse me Imelda, I think I need a piss," said Larry as he got up from his seat and went to the toilets.

It was half nine, and they had been in the pub since the early afternoon. They both felt a bit drunk. The heat from the people and the smoke from the cigarettes made everything hazy for Gerard. Imelda moved closer in towards Gerard as they sat into the corner of the pub.

"Poor Larry, he looks as if he's going to throw up doesn't he?" giggled Imelda. Gerard laughed and agreed with her.

"Great fellah' but can't hold his booze," said Gerard.

"Ger, I'm really sorry about Rory, he was a lovely fellah," said Imelda, putting her hand on Gerard's shoulder and holding his hand with the other. Imelda liked Gerard. She knew he was special. He had taken her to the pictures a couple of times and there were moments between them. But Imelda wanted the same things in life that Gerard wanted, but they both knew they would have to pursue their own dreams and aspirations, in their own ways.

"Thanks, Imelda," replied Gerard, as he saw that the tears were swelling up in her eyes. "

She moved in towards him and put her hand on his leg. Gerard and Imelda had sex on a few occasions but Imelda had always made sure she wasn't going to get pregnant and would make him pull out of her before he climaxed. She wasn't going to be lumbered with kids before she had a life.

She put her hand on his leg and it started to arouse his feelings. They sat there in silence for a few minutes not saying a word.

He had used her, as much as she had used him. They both had a mutual feeling for each other, but Imelda was the strong one. She had decided years before that she would not end up bringing up a gang of screaming kids in Chapelgate. She wanted better for herself, and she was determined to have a better life. In her mind there was only one obstacle. Money! She didn't know what she wanted to do in life but she knew she didn't want to hang around Chapelgate Gardens for the rest of her life.

"Can I get you a drink, Ger?" asked Imelda.

She felt sorry for him, and she really wanted to mother him and look after him. That was another side to Imelda. She had a soft heart, and if she got close to anyone, and if she liked them, she smothered them with affection. She got up and went to the bar for a pint for Gerard.

Gerard looked around the room at the people. Mr Dillon was singing another song, and everybody was looking in his direction. He looked at the faces of the people. They were hanging on to every note that Mr Dillon sang. Gerard looked at his brother Mick.

"Angela and him will get married and settle down, and in a few years of struggling and surviving they will be Mr and Mrs Foley part two. They will have children and be a good family, but with fuck all else to show for it. All the years of working and keeping body and soul together. Is England the only answer? Why can't we have a decent way of life instead of fucking robbing and stroking? It's not my fault," he thought to himself. Is it too much to ask from life!".

When Imelda came back, she sat very close to Gerard, almost sitting on his lap.

Gerard slipped his arm around her waist and whispered into her ear, "Imelda, the last time we were together, I didn't mean to ignore you after we, well you know, but I ... " she put her finger to his lips.

"Ssshh ..." she said.

"Gerard I know the score. I'm a big girl you don't have to act the "big man" in front of me, for fuck's sake. How long do you know me. I loved the sex, but boyfriend and girlfriend we aren't," she said. Gerard liked Imelda a lot but he was afraid to get too close. Love wasn't in his nature. He didn't want stupid things and soppy things like feelings or love to get in the way of his life. That was Mick's life. His brother would be that type who fell in love and got married and have kids and settle down. "Nothing wrong with that" he thought but it wasn't for Gerard.

Mr Dillon was singing a lovely "Matt Monroe" song and the crowd in the bar were transfixed by his voice.

"*Walk away please go, before you give your life away*" sang Mr Dillon. It was a popular song sang by Matt Monroe.

Gerard put his arm around Imelda. His hand was at the small of her back, just between her top and her skirt. She put her hand around behind her and pulled the zip of her skirt down. She moved forward and allowed Gerard to slip his hand in between her skirt, and he could feel the soft fabric of her underwear. Gerard looked into her eyes. She smiled back.

"*We could have met some years ago, but for your sake I say walk away walk on*" sang Mr Dillon.

Imelda looked at Gerard and gave him a little smile. Her red lips and black hair gave her, a remarkable resemblance to Sophia Loren. He slipped his hand down inside her underwear and as he went lower, she lifted herself slightly off the seat to allow Gerard to put his fingers where she could get pleasure. The soft dulcet tones of Mr Dillon's voice wafted over the people. Imelda and Gerard, were sitting in the corner and everybody was facing towards where Mr Dillon was standing. She moved as Gerard explored deeper and deeper into her. She moaned in a low moan, and the excitement was heightened because of the danger of being seen. Gerard had never pleasured a girl like this before. It was new to him, but he just let his fingers explore. He felt her body shiver as his fingers worked back and forth. Imelda felt beads of sweat roll from her temple, and her face was flushed. It was usually her giving pleasure to a boy. This was different for her. She wanted to moan and bit her lip to stop her from moaning with the pleasure she was feeling. She felt Gerard's fingers touching intimate parts of her that only she touched. She turned her face towards him. He was facing towards the front and just glanced at her. He could see her red flushed cheeks.

She closed her eyes and bit her top lip. Gerard could see a bead of sweat roll down the side of her temple, and he could see that she was enjoying what he was doing to her. He looked around and nobody in the packed room was taking any notice of them.

"Do I love you but I told you walk away walk on..ooon" sang Mr Dillon bringing the song to a crescendo.

The song was coming to the end. As the people stood up to clap for Mr Dillon, Imelda felt a shudder of pleasure and ecstasy surge through her body. The noise in the room drowned out the moans that Imelda could not help exhale. Gerard felt the shudder in her body as it trembled, and she moaned in silent ecstasy.

Imelda climaxed and her head was a blur with emotions as beads of sweat rolled down the side of her red flushed face. She fell back into the seat, trapping Gerard's arm against the back of the seat. The people were clapping now, as the song came to an end. Imelda's face was flushed and her legs were like jelly. Gerard had never pleased a girl like this before, as he didn't really know how to please a girl. Nobody had noticed what had just happened in their midst, as they were all focused on the singer. Imelda reached behind her and pulled her zip up, and as Gerard tried to say something, she put her finger to his lips.

"Ssshhh," said Imelda.

She brushed the damp hair from her forehead. She picked up her drink and took a small sip. Gerard lit two cigarettes and handed one to Imelda. She took it and put it to her lips, and took a long drag from it.

She exhaled and turned to Gerard and said, "Thanks, Ger, thanks."

Chapter Eight

The two detectives parked the police car outside the police station. As Dermot handed over the keys to the desk sergeant, he nodded.

"Everything OK, lads?"

"Do you fancy a pint, Sarge?" asked Patrick O'Reilly.

Dermot noticed that Patrick had been acting very strange since the day they told Mrs Foley about Rory. He noticed the long silences between conversations, and he noticed that Patrick was actually drinking more heavily. They had a pint or two every day after their shift, but lately Patrick stayed on in the pub after Dermot had gone home.

The sergeant also noticed a change in the demeanour of Patrick. As a veteran in an inner city police station, he had seen a lot. He watched young recruits come into the station full of enthusiasm, and saw them face the reality of life in a major city.

Patrick was at the bar paying for the two pints of Guinness and the small whiskey chaser he would knock back while he waited for the pints to settle. Sean Burke, another policeman was sitting beside Dermot when Patrick came back with the pints.

"How'r ya boyo? How's she cutting like?" said Sean the Cork man, as he patted Patrick on the back.

"Great, Sean. Just going for a piss – back in a minute," said Patrick, as he supped on the pint and then put it beside Dermot.

"Sean, do you notice any changes with Pat lately?" asked Dermot.

Sean scratched his head as if puzzled.

"Not really. Why, is he OK?" asked Sean.

Dermot shook his head.

"I don't know. I can't put me finger on it, but the last few days, well since we took that young fellah off the tracks, he has not been the same," replied Dermot.

"Probably fightin' with the wife Dermot. He's only married a few years like. Ahh, I wouldn't worry too much – he'll be grand like," said Sean.

"I hope so Sean, I hope so," replied Dermot.

Patrick came back from the toilet and sat beside Sean.

"Good health, Sean, Dermot," said Patrick as he gulped the pint down to halfway.

There weren't many people in the bar. A couple of railway porters, one of whom Dermot recognised as the man who had been on the tracks after the accident, and a couple of men having a pint before the start of their nightshift in the bakery behind the police station.

"Tell me, Pat. I believe the pair of you took a lad of the tracks the other day like?" asked Sean in his strong Cork accent.

Patrick threw a look at Sean.

"Poor little bastard. Fifteen I think, right little character though wasn't he Dermot?" replied Patrick to his partner.

Dermot just nodded his head.

"Yeh, poor fecker, a regular little magpie. Anyway such is life. Did you play hurling on Sunday? Word has it you're up for a county place," replied Patrick, switching the conversation back to Sean.

"Is the Pope a catholic, like? Yes, I think I should get a call soon, and with a bit of luck a transfer back to me lovely County Cork," replied Sean. They passed the time talking about sports and work.

Dermot noticed that the sergeant had come into the bar. He stood up and said, "Three more pints lads?" and with that walked to the bar to have a word with his sergeant, leaving Sean and Patrick talking about the Gaelic football.

"What gives, Dermot?" asked the sergeant, getting straight to the point.

"Well, it's Patrick. For the past few days, he's been acting very strange. The day we took that young fellah off the tracks," replied Dermot.

The sergeant knocked back a straight whiskey in one gulp.

"I've seen it before, Dermot. Death of a child can have a strange effect on people. Did you know Patrick ran over his younger brother in a tractor years ago and killed him, so he could be getting flashbacks. I wouldn't take too much notice – he'll snap out of it when they start running rings around him down there in Chapelgate," replied the sergeant.

Dermot nodded and agreed with his sergeant.

"Yes, you're probably right. A child's death does have strange effects on people in different ways, alright," he said.

The sergeant nodded to the barman for another whiskey and drained the last little drop from the already empty glass.

"Sit down over there, and we'll have a few drinks and a bit of a session. Go on there now. I'll take a few small ones over," replied the sergeant.

Dermot sat back down and indicated that the sergeant was on the way over. He came over carrying five whiskeys, which were being held between his little fingers. His fingers looked like little sausages stuck into the glasses. He put the glasses down on the table and poured one glass into another for himself.

"Thanks, Sarge – cheers!" replied Dermot, Patrick and Sean as they picked up the drinks.

"Are you alright, son?" whispered the sergeant to Patrick as the other two guards started to talk about their home county football results.

Patrick gave a little laugh and sat back in his chair.

"Jesus yes, Sarge, why wouldn't I be?"

The sergeant drained the glass and looked at Patrick straight in the eye.

"I'm thirty two years in this job and I know the lads better than they know themselves. So don't fuck around with me, Patrick. I'm too long in the tooth for all that bravado shite. You can't go around carrying a cross for every little bollocks that gets scraped of the tracks, no more than feeling guilty because you might have given the little beggar a good fucking hiding the week before. That's an awful lot of baggage to carry around son, so put it behind you and move on. This job can break a man. It's not even a job it's a fucking vocation. The people in Chapelgate, or any other feckin' flats complex in Dublin. They're not bad people, well not all of them. They are a victim of their time and circumstance son. You, me, Dermot over there, none of us can change this. Only time can change it. So get your act together. You can move up the ranks and set yourself up with a nice pension when you retire. That's what I've been doing. "Me time"... That's the last time we will talk about it, now. Get up there and get a few more in before me throat dries up completely," replied the sergeant, and he gave Patrick a slight pat on the face with the palm of his hand in an affectionate gesture.

Patrick got up and went to the bar. He looked over at the sergeant and then to Dermot and Sean.

"Same again Paul," said Patrick to the barman. He dropped the drinks at the table and sat back in beside the sergeant.

"I know, Sarge. I know, we move on, yeh ..." replied Patrick. He excused himself and went to the toilet.

Dermot looked at his sergeant.

"Thanks Sarge, that might do the trick, and please God, he'll snap out of it," he said.

The sergeant nodded in agreement, saying, "Ahh, he'll be grand now. What's this I hear about you ye little Cork fecker making the county team? Are we to see the back of ye soon?"

As Patrick came back to the table, he heard them laughing.

"Come on Pat. For feck's sake lighten up and forget about that young fellah," the sergeant said as he patted Patrick on the back.

"The sarge is right. I have enough baggage to carry," he thought to himself. The sergeant picked up his drink and took a sip from it.

"Nectar from the Gods," he said.

He whispered into Patrick's ear, "I've recommended you for the sergeant's exams. Do you think you could cut the mustard?" he said.

Patrick was delighted at this bit of news.

"Thanks, sarge. Yes, I'm up to the challenge. I'll have to dust off the manuals, though," he replied.

"Well, the exams are in a couple of months' time, so get your finger out me boyo!" laughed the Sergeant.

*****

Back in The Bell, Mrs Pluck was handing around a plate with slices of cold white pudding, and as the plate was handed to Angela she pushed it away.

"God, how can you eat that stuff? The smell of it," she said to Mick as he chewed on two large pieces of white pudding.

Mick tried to talk, but his mouth was full, so he just rubbed his belly and went "Mmmmm" to Angela.

Larry sat in beside Angela, and he was very drunk now and his speech was slurred.

"Angela, I love ye. I mean I don't love ye like that, (hic!) But (hic!) I love ye 'cause you're with Mick, me best mate, (hic!)," he slurred.

Angela hadn't had much to drink – she was very cautious when it came to alcohol, and she also wanted to be there for Mick. Things were going good with them the last few weeks, and he had even come to her mother's flat for tea to meet her mother and her sisters. They still hadn't had sex yet, but they had been very close to it one night. She wanted to wait and see if Mick had any plans for them for the future. She loved Mick, and she knew he loved her, but she didn't want to take a chance and get pregnant. Condoms weren't something you could buy in the Ireland of the nineteen sixties. In fact, she had never seen a condom, and the only sex education she had known was from her mother, which consisted of, "Keep your finger on your button!" When she asked her mother what she meant, her mother replied, "Listen, boys just want to put their thing into you, and if they do, you'll get pregnant. So keep your legs crossed and save yourself for your wedding night."

"We have to take Larry home, Mick – he's very drunk," Angela said to Mick.

"Yep, I think you're right. I'll just see how me ma and dad are, and say goodnight to them," replied Mick, as he left the table and went over to where his mother and father were sitting.

Imelda was just coming out of the toilet, and she went over to her friend Angela to see if she was going home.

"We'll give you a hand with Larry," said Imelda, pointing towards Gerard.

Angela looked at Imelda. "Are you's like … are you two together?" she asked.

Imelda looked over at Gerard and saw him coming towards them. She liked Gerard, but wanted more out of life than he would ever be able give her. In fact Imelda wanted to be in charge of her own destiny, and not be tied to any one person.

"No, no, we're not together. I'd shag the arse off him, though, but you know me, Angela. They didn't make the one for me yet. I'm just too fucking fussy, Angie," she quipped.

When Mick came back to the table Gerard asked him about his mother and father.

"Are they ok Mick?" asked Gerard. Mick looked back at his parents and then back to Gerard.

"I think so Ger. It'll take a lot out of them; we need to be there for them," said Mick. Gerard nodded in agreement.

Gerard was trying to get Larry to his feet. Mick got to his other side, and they both carried him towards the door. Imelda and Angela picked up Larry's coat and followed the lads.

"Well Angie, you and Mick?" asked Imelda.

Angela put her arm into Imelda's arm and they both walked behind the lads who were struggling with Larry.

"We, well we are getting on grand. But Mick is waiting on news from that job he applied for. I think he feels it that because he has no job he's like, well, not a real man, do you know what I mean Imelda," said Angela.

"He's the nicest bloke in Chapelgate Gardens Angie. Don't worry he'll get that job. By the way did yis do the bold thing yet?" laughed Imelda. Angela pushed her friend in a friendly way.

"Go away you, is that all you think about ye hussy," laughed Angela. They walked for a few more minutes and Angela told her friend how they nearly came close to having sex, but she was nervous because she wanted to respect her mother's wishes and be a virgin on her wedding night. She told Imelda about her feelings for Mick and how she would love to settle down with him and have his children. Imelda listened to her friend and knew that Angela and Mick's life would be like so many in Chapelgate. But she also knew Mick was a good man and he would make a good father. All they needed was a break. A chance in life. Imelda told herself if she ever got the chance she would help her friend. She didn't know how she would help her or what she could do for her but she knew that all Angela and Mick needed was a chance.

"Don't worry Angie, as me ma always says, 'If it's meant for you it won't pass you by," said Imelda as they walked on towards Chapelgate.

*****

"Are you OK, Pat? Careful now, mind your head," said Dermot, as he helped Patrick into the front seat of Dermot's Ford Zephyr car. They had stayed on even after Sean and the sergeant had left. Dermot had had to tell him to keep his voice down in the bar, as with all the drink that Patrick had taken he was quite drunk and didn't realise that he was shouting. Dermot didn't take too much drink that night, as he thought he should be there for his partner, and just listen to what was going on in his life. Pat had been quite loud and the barman, Paul, was in an awkward situation as he knew all the policemen that came into the bar because the police station was situated right behind his bar, and he catered for retirement parties, promotion parties and all types of gatherings from the police fraternity.

Dermot saw Paul was uneasy and indicated that he would take Pat home.

As they drove through Chapelgate, Patrick was slurring his words and Dermot found it hard to understand what he was saying. He drove by The Bell and saw Mick and Gerard Foley help Larry Burke walk towards the flat complex. He saw Imelda walk with another girl he didn't know just behind them.

He knew Imelda, as he had seen her behind the local church with a lad about a year ago, and they were having sex against the railings. He and Patrick had been sitting in the car with the lights off that night, just having a cigarette break, when she had walked around the back of the church with this lad. They saw her pull her skirt up around her thighs and watched as the lad held her up against the railings.

Patrick wanted to go over and stop them, but Dermot told him to "Let the young fellah finish". So as he sat there smoking he looked at the way Imelda used her body. He couldn't help noticing that she was the one in control. At one stage he thought he saw Imelda looking at the car knowing the two policemen were watching her. He remembered thinking to himself, "What sort of a girl is this. She is taunting us, what sort of power has she got. Why am I not going over there and putting a stop to her antics". When they had finished and walked away, Dermot couldn't forget the image of Imelda with the suspenders from her stockings at the top of her legs, as she wrapped them around the boy. Patrick wanted to go over and have a word with them for as he said, "defiling church grounds", but Dermot stopped him.

"Leave it Pat, sure they're doing no harm," he said.

As he drove by Imelda and Angela he saw Imelda looking into the car. She knew the two detectives. She smiled at Dermot Kelly as he passed. He smiled back and thought to himself, "The cheeky little minx, but Jesus she looks very sexy." He drove on towards Pat's house.

Mick and Gerard didn't notice the car go by as they tried to carry Larry to his flat. When they got to his flat, Larry's mother came out to help take him in.

"Oh, God bless you's, Mick and Gerard, what with your poor mother and father having to deal with Rory's funereal. Lord have mercy on his soul. I'll say a decade of the rosary for the family. God knows your mother needs God's help now." pleaded Mrs Burke, who was a very religious woman.

"Thanks, Mrs Burke, but just look after Larry. I think he had a few too many," replied Mick.

Imelda came over and put his coat over Larry's shoulders.

"Thanks, Imelda love. Oh, by the way, your Uncle Paddy is home from London for a few days – he called in to see Mr Burke earlier. Your father and mother and himself are gone to the Sailor's Rest bar as far as I know. Your mother asked me to tell you if I saw you could you put a few sambos together for them for when they come home," said Mrs Foley.

Angela froze when she heard her Uncle Paddy was back. As they walked from the Burke flat, Angela paired off with Mick, and Gerard said goodnight to them and offered to walk Imelda home. As they walked towards her flat, Imelda went very quiet, which didn't go unnoticed by Gerard.

"Are you OK, Imelda?" asked Gerard.

She nodded, but said nothing. They walked on, and Gerard went to put his arm around her shoulder. He felt her freeze under his arm. He stopped and took out his cigarettes and offered her one. She took one and as they both smoked in silence, Gerard thought to himself, "Jeeez, I'll never understand women, and especially Imelda. One minute she's all over me – next she is cold as ice. Fucking women – I'll never understand them!" They smoked in silence as they stood just outside Imelda's block where she lived. Imelda broke the silence.

"Sorry Gerard, but me Uncle Paddy is a right fucking bollix. He always causes trouble when he comes home, the fucker," said Imelda. They sat there on a small wall for what seemed like ages.

"If you want me to go home with you just in case he kicks off, I will" Gerard offered. Imelda smiled at Gerard and put her hand against his face.

"Thanks Ger, but I can handle that fucker, but thanks anyway," she smiled.

Gerard told Imelda that as soon as he had the money he was out of Chapelgate and on the boat to England. He was telling her about Larry's uncle and how he might have some work for him in London.

"You should go Ger, there's nothing here for you. Take a chance on life," she replied.

"Come with me Imelda," he asked. She was just about to answer him when Imelda heard her mother singing from down the street as she made her way home.

"I better go, I can hear them coming," she replied. She said goodnight to Gerard, put her hand to his face and kissed him lightly on the cheek. She walked away but stopped and turned towards Gerard.

"Thanks Gerard. That was lovely in the pub. You're special," she said, as she slipped away towards her flat.

*****

As Dermot drove the car into the driveway of Patrick's house, he saw the light in the hall go on. He knew Helen, Patrick's wife, well. She had worked with Mary, his own wife, as a nurse in the same hospital before they were married. The four of them used to socialise together, but when Mary and Dermot had their first baby girl, their nights out were fewer, as Mary took on motherhood full time. Patrick and Helen had one little boy. Both couples would visit each other's houses and the four of them were very close. Dermot and Mary had just had their second child – a boy. Dermot had seen some changes in his wife since the birth of their second child. She had become withdrawn and depressed, and lately she had taken to sleeping in the spare room. She told Dermot it was because he would disturb her sleep when he came home after a night shift. When he started on day shift she still slept in the spare room. He thought in time she might snap out of her depression, but it was taking time. The one thing he missed was sex. They had had a good sex life, but lately Mary wouldn't let him touch her.

Dermot helped Patrick from the car. The front door opened and Helen smiled at Dermot as he helped Patrick into the house. Helen helped Dermot take her husband to bed. Patrick was babbling, and Helen just kept saying to him.

"Come on now love, take it easy, let's get you to bed." As they walked back down the stairs, Dermot couldn't help but notice that Helen had a lovely slim figure, when the light caught her silhouette through her nightdress. She was a very attractive woman. He followed her into the kitchen.

"He'll be fine, Helen. Just a few too many," said Dermot, as he sat at the breakfast bar.

She put the kettle on and leaned back against the worktop. Dermot noticed her breast was exposed as the nightdress wasn't closed properly. She hadn't realised that her breast was showing. It had been a long time since Dermot had made love to his wife, and looking at Helen now was starting to get him aroused. But he would never try it on with Helen, as he had too much respect for the friendship between them. And also he saw Helen as more of a sister figure. But he said nothing to bring her attention to her nightdress.

"I know, Dermot. He has been drinking a lot lately. Just in the past few days. I think he needs a break," she replied.

"Well, he has been put forward for the sergeant's exam, so he will have to get the books out and study," said Dermot.

"That's good news. He's been hoping for a promotion. By the way, the four of us have not been out together since before the baby was born. We should have a meal together. Let me sort something out in a couple of weeks, and you can come over for a meal," she said.

"That's great, I think Mary could do with a bit adult company. She's been out of sorts lately," replied Dermot.

"Is it the new baby?" she continued, as she poured out a cup of tea for Dermot.

He lit a cigarette and sipped the tea.

"Jesus, she's having a bad time of it, Helen. Her weight has ballooned and she's snapping like a Jack Russell dog when things are not going her way!" laughed Dermot.

But his laughter didn't fool Helen. She had worked with Mary in nursing for years, and knew she could be difficult. They talked for a couple of minutes about old times, and

Dermot divulged a couple of things to Helen regarding his home life since the birth of the new baby. He couldn't divulge everything that had been happening in his home. He would be too ashamed to tell her all the things that Mary had done on him. One night he slipped into bed beside her and tried to make love to her. She was asleep and as he ran his hands over her breasts she awoke and jumped from the bed. She started screaming and shouting at Dermot and suddenly she picked up the lamp beside the dresser and threw it at him. The wire stopped it from hitting him, and he knew that if it had hit him it would have done damage. That was some weeks ago and since then he tried to stay on in work so as he wouldn't get in her way.

"Listen, Dermot. She will come around. Just take your patience with her. That post-natal depression can feck the head up," she replied, as she rubbed his hand in an affectionate way.

Dermot smiled back at her.

"Thanks, Helen. Yes I know she will, but she can be … well, you know. But anyway, I'd better get going," he replied, and he rose to leave. She walked towards the front door in front of him, and again he saw the outline of her svelte body through her flimsy nightdress.

"Jesus snap out of it," he thought to himself.

"We will have you and Mary over in a couple of weeks and I'll have a good chat with her. We can catch up on old times. Seems like ages since we all had a meal and a few drinks together," replied Helen, and she gave Dermot a peck on the cheek.

He turned and stood looking at her.

"Thanks, Helen. I'll see you soon, and by the way, you should put that away, I haven't had it in months!" laughed Dermot and he nodded towards her exposed breast.

She looked down, and only then realised what he was indicating. She pulled her gown around her and laughed.

"Feck off, you men are all the same!" She pushed him in the arm with her free hand.

"Goodnight girl, now take care" laughed Dermot as he rubbed his shoulder and walked towards his car.

As he drove away he wondered what sort of reception he was going to get when he entered the house. Mary was being very difficult of late, and her depression was getting worse. She was a Jekyll and Hyde the last few months. On the streets, Dermot was the tough no nonsense detective, but when he entered his own home, it was like he left that cloak at the door and he would be at the beck and call of his wife, whom he loved very much. A couple of times she had thrown things at him, and also one night just after the new baby was born he was awakened by her slapping him on the face, screaming and shouting. He couldn't and wouldn't tell anybody about these incidents. He drove through the dimly lit streets towards his home, and hoped Mary was in good spirits, or even asleep.

Chapter Nine

Mick and Angela sat on the sofa kissing. Mick was stroking Angela's hair and she was getting very aroused.

"Will we get engaged, Mick? You know I love you more than anything," she whispered in his ear.

"If that's what you want, Angela. I love you, too, you know that," replied Mick.

He felt himself getting hard. Angela touched Mick where his bulge was clearly showing through his trousers.

"Do you want to?" asked Angela.

Mick was excited and he nodded his head. He rose and walked with Angela into the bedroom he shared with Gerard – and Rory, when he was alive. They stood and looked at Rory's bed.

"You must miss him." Angela said, as she stroked his arm and held his hand. Mick squeezed her hand.

"Miss him? I loved seeing his little head on the pillow when I would wake up in the morning. I loved seeing him joke with me ma and pull her apron strings, and watch her shout at him to stop it, even though she loved him playacting with her. Miss him? I will Angela … I will," replied Mick. Angela sat on the edge of Mick's bed and he joined her. They both lay back on the bed and Mick put his arm around her.

As they lay on the bed, Angela turned to Mick.

"Rory! Our first son will be called Rory. I love you, Mick Foley." Angela whispered to him.

*****

Imelda put the lights on in the flat. She put the kettle on the gas stove and looked in the cupboard for leftovers to make some sandwiches. She found some cheese and sliced some ham from the joint of ham they had for the dinner earlier. She heard her mother singing outside in the street. She heard her uncle Paddy, who was her mother's brother, also join in with the song. Then the door opened and her father came in shouting.

"Melda, Melda, put the kettle on, the "uncle Paddy's" here! Where's me only girl?" called her father as he entered the little scullery of the flat.

She loved her father even though she thought that her mother gave him a terrible life. Her mother was a very dominant woman, and she thought that was where she also got her strong will. Her father kissed her on her head. He still treated her as a little girl, even though she was nineteen years of age. He put a brown bag on the table and pulled out bottles of Guinness. As he poured out his beer and went into the main room, she heard the familiar voice of her uncle Paddy.

She was cutting the sandwiches with the large carving knife from the drawer. Her mind drifted back to the last time she had seen her uncle Paddy. It was nearly five years ago – the night before her uncle left for England. She was fourteen and she loved her uncle, as he always had a sixpence for her as his only niece. There had been a party that evening for her uncle, before he left for the boat. And during the night she sat on his lap sipping red lemonade. Her uncle slipped a small drop of whiskey into her lemonade.

"It'll put hairs on your chest," he said to her. "Don't tell your mother or she'll kill me," he laughed. That night there was a lot of people in the flat as Paddy was very popular with everybody. He wasn't married but always had a girl on his arm. Everybody used to say he would be a great catch for any girl as he had a good job and seemed to always have money. That is why her mother and father were surprised that he had packed his job in and had decided to go to England. The only reason people left for England was to get work but Paddy had a job already, and it was a bolt from the blue to Imelda's mother when he told her. That evening after a few sips from her glass she felt her head go dizzy and she felt sleepy. She hadn't remembered being put to bed because of the drowsiness brought on by the drink. All she remembered was being awakened from her sleep feeling someone touching her. The feeling was strange to her, and it felt nice, but she knew this was wrong somehow. She smelt the stale drink from the person beside her, who was touching her. His voice was familiar.

When she awoke the next day she looked down at her underwear, which was stained with blood. The night before came flooding back to her – she thought she had been dreaming, but she realised now that she wasn't. She knew the voice that had been whispering in her ear. She looked down into the sheets of the bed and saw the cufflink. It was the same cufflink her uncle Paddy had been wearing the night before. She never told anybody about that night. The night that she lost her virginity.

"Where is she? Where's me favourite niece?" came the familiar voice from the hallway.

Her uncle Paddy came into the scullery. He looked a bit older from when she remembered him, and his hair was a lot thinner.

"My God you have grown up. Come here and give your uncle a kiss," said Paddy as he approached Imelda.

"Hello, Uncle Paddy," said Imelda sheepishly, as she pressed her lips against his cheek. He grabbed her around the waist and pulled her roughly to him, rubbing her breasts on his chest.

"My God, you've gotten bigger," he laughed as he stared at her breasts.

Her mother and father were in the main room sharing the bottle of Guinness and weren't taking much notice of Imelda and her uncle, who were in the scullery.

Imelda pulled away from her uncle's clutches and turned to cut the sandwiches.

"You go on out, and I'll bring you something to eat, Uncle Paddy," she said as she cut into the sandwiches.

Her uncle looked behind and saw that Imelda's mother had left the room and gone to the toilet, and Jimmy, Imelda's father, was kneeling down in front of the radiogram, trying to put on a record. Paddy turned towards Imelda and cupped her breasts in his hands.

"Why don't you give your favourite uncle a big hello kiss," he whispered in her ear.

In a flash Imelda turned around and put the knife just under Paddy's throat. He drew back and his eyes opened wide. The blood drained from his face.

"You fucking messed with me before you left five years ago. If you fucking put your hands near me, I'll cut your fucking balls off. Do ya hear me?" she hissed.

"Jesus, please Imelda ... please don't. I was drunk. I had forgotten all about it, I swear, Imelda. God, I wouldn't do anything to hurt you sweetheart. You're me only niece. I ... I was very drunk that night, honest," pleaded Paddy.

Tears started to fall from his eyes.

"Imelda, really, I wouldn't hurt a hair on your head," he pleaded.

She backed down and dropped the knife from his throat. She felt sorry for him now.

"Why did she have this power over men?" she thought to herself. Paddy backed off, and tried to smile a sheepish smile.

"Where's the sandwiches, Melda?" asked her mother as she entered the scullery.

There was a silence.

"Is everything OK, Melda? Paddy?" said her mother as she noticed the situation.

Paddy looked at Imelda as if pleading for her not to say anything. Imelda looked at her mother and then a smile came across her face.

"Yes. It's Uncle Paddy. He told me he has fifty pounds for me as a present to spend it on anything I like. Isn't that right Uncle Paddy?" replied Imelda.

Paddy looked at his sister and a weak smile came across his face.

"Yes, that's what I was just saying to me favourite niece. I have fifty pounds for her to spend on herself," he replied.

Imelda's mother threw her arms around her brother.

"God, you've more money than sense! Is he the best uncle ever?" said her mother as she hugged her brother.

Imelda looked straight into Paddy's eyes.

"Yes, he is the best uncle ever," she whispered.

Her uncle Paddy smiled sheepishly and he pulled a bundle of notes from his pocket. Imelda put her hand out and stared at him.

"Here you are Imelda," said Paddy as he counted out the notes into her hand.

Imelda's mother called into where her husband was kneeling in front of the radiogram still trying to get a record to play. She turned and walked in to the main room and left Imelda alone with Paddy. He went to put the rest of the notes into his pocket and Imelda put the knife just under his crotch. He went white in the face. Imelda took the rest of the money from his fist and put it down her bra, still keeping the knife where it was. He just stood there not knowing what to do. Imelda took the knife away and turned to cut the rest of the sandwiches.

"Bitch," she heard her uncle whisper behind her. She turned and held the knife to his throat.

"Rapist," she replied. He jumped back and went into the main room. She heard him make some excuse to her mother and he was gone. When her uncle left for England suddenly two days later Imelda was pleased. After Paddy left for England Imelda was in her room and her mother was in the kitchen calling out to her.

Imelda's mother couldn't understand his sudden departure.

"Three weeks he said he was staying. I can't understand how he had to leave suddenly," she called out to Imelda, who was in her room counting out eighty five crisp English pound notes into her jewellery box.

"Do you hear me in there, Imelda?" she called out again.

"I hear you, Ma. I hear you." laughed Imelda as she put the box away. "Men are so fucking stupid," she thought.

*****

Gerard sat on the wall overlooking the canal that ran alongside the Chapelgate complex. He lit the cigarette and watched the match burn right down to the end, nearly burning his fingers. The last time he came here with Rory was to teach him how to swim. The canal wasn't the cleanest, but when you have no alternative, and in the hot summer days, you go to the nearest place. The day Rory came down he was about eleven or twelve, and just assumed he could swim. When he jumped into the canal the lads all laughed, but it was Mick who knew he couldn't swim. As he bobbed up and down swallowing water and spluttering, the lads thought he was joking. Mick jumped in and pulled him by the hair to the edge of the canal bank. But within a couple of days of perseverance, Rory was paddling about in the water without any fear.

He heard footsteps behind him, and turned to see Mick coming towards him. Mick had started work a few days earlier in CIE in the railway station as a porter. His father had put a word in for him through his union rep and it got him the job.

"You're thinking of the day he jumped in without knowing how to swim, aren't you," said Mick, as he squatted down beside Gerard.

They both laughed, remembering the way Rory had bobbed up and down.

"Yeh, Mick, the little fecker had no fear!" replied Gerard.

Mick sat down beside Gerard. They shared the cigarette and looked into the dark waters of the canal.

"I'm thinking of heading off to England, Mick. This place is doing me fucking head in. No fucking work. The money from the dole is shit, and I'm just fucking drowning, Mick," said Gerard.

"What would you do over there? Do you know anyone?" asked Mick.

Gerard took a long drag from his cigarette and looked into the dark waters.

"I was talking to Larry's uncle, Jimmy, a few weeks ago. He says there are jobs Mick, and plenty of opportunities if you have half a brain. He said if I go over he would put me in touch with right people. You met him before, Mick, he's no fucking fool. I know he's a bit dodgy, but let's face it, Mick, if you don't take chances you won't make advances," replied Gerard.

"That's a good saying Ger," replied Mick.

Mick took the cigarette from Gerard and pulled on it.

"Me ma would go mad, Ger. Jesus she's just lost one son. If you go, it will kill her," he said.

They sat there for few minutes in silence.

"You work, Mick, and you have a girl. Your life is sorted, and Mick, don't take this the wrong way – you're happy with that, and God knows there for the grace of God that would be me. But I want more. Is that too much to ask?" replied Gerard.

Mick looked around at the silhouette of the large flats complex. He turned back to Gerard.

"America! That's where I'd go. New fucking York," he replied.

Gerard let out a little laugh.

"Fuck's sake Mick, one step at a time. Getting the boat is one thing, but flying to America, Jeez, one step at a time," he laughed.

Mick handed the now depleted cigarette to Gerard.

"We're getting engaged," said Mick, and he looked at Gerard's face for a reaction.

Gerard stared straight ahead.

"I know Mick. I can see she's the one. A blind man on a horse can see you were made for each other. You're lucky to have found someone. Angela is a good girl, Mick, and I'm happy for both of you. Me ma will be made up," replied Gerard.

They sat there in silence for a few more minutes. Mick broke the silence.

"We done it!" he said to Gerard.

Gerard shouldered his brother in a playful way and laughed.

"Yeh dirty oul dog ye! Well, what's she like?" quipped Gerard.

Mick pushed his brother on the shoulder.

"Fuck off I'm not telling you, ye bollix," he laughed.

Gerard grabbed his brother around his neck and rubbed his head.

"I knew you had it in yeh, mate! Come on. Nora will be worried about us – let's get back to the nest," replied Gerard.

They stood up and walked towards their flat together.

Chapter Ten

A few weeks after the funeral, Larry was cleaning windows just a couple of doors up from Marie's house. It was a lovely day, and from the top of the ladder he could see Marie sitting in the back garden reading a book. The weather was very hot, and he could see that Marie was wearing a bikini top. She had sunglasses on, and was engrossed in the book she was reading. Larry leaned against the ladder as he watched her, and tried to figure out what had happened between them a couple of weeks before. He hadn't seen her since then. She had been away and the neighbour paid him for cleaning her windows, and told Larry that the Whites were gone to Kerry for one month to see her parents and her husband's family. The neighbour was the same lady who came to help Marie the day Rory had ran from the house. Since then she was very friendly with Larry, and in fact the word went around the area that he was the lad who chased the robber. Since then his cleaning round grew. A lot of people trusted him more since they learned what he had done.

Larry didn't notice Marie waving to him at first, as he daydreamed about her. Then he saw her take off the glasses and wave again. He snapped out of his daydream when he realised she was waving at him.

"Fuck, she's calling me. Did she notice I was watching her, I wonder?" he thought to himself. He waved back in acknowledgment. She indicated for him to come over to her. He put his thumb in the air to indicate he would.

As he descended the ladder, he wondered to himself why she was being so friendly with him. He gathered up his bucket and put the ladder on his bike.

"How will I handle this situation? Fuck, what if she comes on to me? Fuck, who do I think I am – she's just being friendly! Get a fucking grip ye thick fucker," he mused.

He leaned his bike against the back gate of her house. He knocked on the back gate and walked into the garden. Marie got up from the garden deck chair and came over to greet Larry like an old friend.

"Lawrence, how are you? It's been ages since I saw you – how are things?" she gushed as she came up to Larry and put her hand on his shoulder in an affectionate way.

Larry smiled a sheepish smile, and said, "I'm good, Mrs White, and how are you? How was the holiday?"

"Marie, Lawrence. I told you, Marie – you make me feel old. I'm only thirty-four, not sixty-four," she laughed.

"Marie, sorry, yeh, I forgot … and by the way, it's Larry. Me da is Lawrence and I'm twenty, seeing as we're saying how old we are," he laughed.

She gave his shoulder a slight rub, and Larry noticed this bit of affection.

"Come on, I'll get you a cold drink. I don't know how you work in this warm weather," she replied, as she turned and walked towards the back door of the house.

"For a thirty-four year old she was in fine shape'" thought Larry as he watched her walk towards the house.

Larry was a bit unsure of himself, but he decided to go with the flow and walked behind her towards the kitchen. He noticed that under her flimsy skirt she looked slim and fit. She turned and beckoned to him.

"Go sit beside me I'll bring your drink out," she said.

"Sit on that deck chair and I'll bring you out a drink," she repeated from the kitchen.

Larry turned and walked towards the deck chair, and sat down on it. He looked around the well kept garden, with its trimmed lawn and the clipped hedges. A far cry from the drab grey buildings of Chapelgate Gardens, with the clothes drying in the main square, rows and rows … each family's washing for all the world to see. The calm serene picture that he found himself in was relaxing and tranquil, and he started to settle and relax. He lay back against the easy chair and closed his eyes. He could hear birds chirping in the bushes behind him.

"Here Larry, take this," said Marie, as she gave Larry a glass with lemonade.

"Thanks, Marie," replied Larry, as he looked up from the chair at Marie, who was standing with the sun behind her. He could make out the silhouette of her legs right up to her waist. She stood in front of him and waited for him to take a drink from the glass. She turned and pulled another deck chair beside Larry.

"Well, is that nice?" she asked, and looked into his face for a reaction.

"Mmm ... that's fucki ... sorry, that's lovely," replied Larry, as he slipped up and nearly swore in front of her. From his point of view she was his customer, and not just any old woman he was talking to from Chapelgate Gardens.

"Ha, ha, Larry! Larry, you don't have to be so formal with me, for God's sake. Just because I live in this big house. I actually come from a council estate in a large town in Kerry. You don't have to have your guard up in front of me, Larry. Actually, my father is a window cleaner, so we have a lot more in common than you realise, Larry," she laughed.

They both laughed together, and Larry was able to finally relax in front of her.

"So your father is in the business well that's a coincidence. I thought you'd be a rich farmer's daughter or something," said Larry.

"Not all people who live outside of Dublin are farmers, Larry," she laughed. "Have you ever been outside of Dublin?" she asked.

Larry thought for a minute.

"I went to Enniskerry on the bus once," he replied.

"Well it's outside Dublin Larry but there is a whole bigger world out there," she said. Larry nodded in agreement. A few seconds went by without them talking. Larry broke the silence.

"So how long are you married?" asked Larry.

Marie brushed her dress down over her knees and held her arms around her knees as a teenager would.

"Well, believe it or not nearly ten years, and before you ask, no, we have no children, and yes I would love a child. But so far we have not been blessed," she replied.

Larry got a bit embarrassed with the way Marie was being so open with him about her life.

"Oh, I wasn't, I didn't mean … I … " Larry gushed with embarrassment.

Marie laughed again, and for a minute he thought she was laughing at his attempts to rectify his mumbling.

"Larry, relax! I'm just trying to get to know you a bit more. Now let's start again," she replied.

Larry laughed and then decided to drop his guard with her.

"OK, Marie. Right, let's start again. What does your husband work at, and how come you ended up here in, let's face it, fucking dreary Clontarf, full of old retired people. God's fucking waiting room?" asked Larry.

Marie leaned back in the chair laughing, and as she lifted her legs Larry could see right up under her skirt to her underwear. She was acting like a teenager, not a thirty-four year old married woman.

"Well, my husband is a detective inspector in the headquarters of the police, and we live here in "God's waiting room", as you call it, because he wants to impress his bosses. He needs to show them he has the perfect wife and lives in the perfect area, to enhance his prospects of climbing the promotion ladder in the police force," she replied.

"Well, at least you're honest and straight up. I wasn't being nosey, but, well a little bit, but I knew he was in the police because the two coppers investigating the burglary are going out of their way to find out who it was," replied Larry.

"Listen, Larry, whoever it was, well, he got nothing. A few bits of costume jewellery, and a bit of cash in a wallet. But my husband is making a big thing of it. He is paranoid – he thinks whoever it was knew that he lived here, and they were just letting him know, to keep his guard up. He thinks it was someone he put away in prison, and since the break in he has been giving me so much grief. Lock this, check that! Who's that window cleaner? I'll interview him – he must have seen his face. He just goes on and on," replied Marie, as she settled and her voice became a little more serious.

"Does he want to talk to me, Marie?" asked Larry.

"He won't be talking to you, Larry. I told him you saw nothing. That the thief had a scarf around his mouth. No, don't worry I don't want him annoying you. Anyway, he is a very jealous man, and he would try and insinuate that I was having an affair with you. You don't know him. He can be a very nasty man," replied Marie.

Larry leaned forward in his chair.

"Really? Why would he think you'd be having an affair with me? I wouldn't be in your league anyway, Marie, I'm sure – in fact I know you could do much better. I haven't got a pot to piss in anyway, so I couldn't give you the lifestyle you'd be accustomed to," laughed Larry.

Marie took a sip from her glass and looked at Larry.

"Why would you think that. That you are out of my league, Larry? You're a very nice looking lad, and I'm sure you already have a girlfriend?" replied Marie.

"No, I have no girlfriend … and me good looking? Well, my not having a girlfriend just reinforces that; good looking I am not," said Larry.

Marie smiled at Larry.

"Believe me, Larry, you are good looking, and not only that, you're a nice lad, don't be so hard on yourself," she replied.

Larry blushed. There was an awkward silence for a few seconds, and it was the next door neighbour who broke the silence.

"You hoo! Window man. You hoo!" the neighbour called over the hedge. Marie and Larry were startled, and looked to where the woman was calling.

"Oh, can you clean my windows today?" called the lady.

"Yes no problem," replied Larry.

"Hello Marie, how was your holiday?" asked the lady.

"Lovely. Nice weather, and saw the family," replied Marie as she turned towards Larry and made a face to him imitating the face of the woman. Larry couldn't keep the laughing in and bit his lip.

The woman looked at the pair of them and said, "OK, window man. Bye, Marie." and she disappeared behind the hedge.

"Window man," giggled Marie and laughed like a teenager.

Larry and Marie were giggling and Marie couldn't help it but she stood up, took Larry's hand and ran for the door, and as they entered the kitchen they both burst out laughing. Marie put her arm over Larry's shoulder.

"Mr Window man. Poor woman, God bless her!" laughed Marie.

Larry put his arm around Marie's waist, in a natural move to steady himself as he was bent over laughing. The laughing then subsided and Larry looked into Marie's face. She stopped laughing and then she looked back at Larry. There was a silence between them for a couple seconds. Marie moved her face towards Larry and kissed him full on the lips. Larry opened his mouth and searched for her tongue. She reached under his t-shirt and grabbed at his chest. She rubbed her hands to the front of his chest and then she slid her hands around to the small of his back. She dug her nails into his flesh. Larry arched his back as her nails dug into his flesh. He felt very strange, and he was feeling very aroused. His penis was starting to rise. Marie opened her mouth and sucked his tongue. She lifted her leg and wrapped it around the back of his leg. They embraced for what seemed like ages. Larry was touching her all over. Any time he had had sex before with a girl he was always drunk, or had some drink taken and it was always at night never during the day. This was the first time he was stone cold sober, that he had ever encountered this experience. Marie pulled away from Larry.

"Come, come upstairs, Larry, come," she pleaded with him.

She turned and walked towards the stairs grabbing Larry's hand. As they entered the room, Larry had a flashback to the day he saw Rory here. He didn't get time to remember as Marie pulled her bikini top off and her skirt down and stood in front of Larry in pink satin pants. Larry's head was bursting now – he had never had a moment like this before. He was sober, and it was the middle of the day.

They fell on the bed as one together and Marie clawed at his body, gripping into his flesh. Larry felt her nails cut into his back, and he loved it. Never before had he had a woman wanting him so much – her mouth open and her moans turning him on. She ripped at his shirt and then she got on top of him. She pulled his penis from his trousers and she forced it into her and as he entered her she closed her legs around it sucking him inside her, deeper and deeper. She was taking control. Her hair came within inches of his face as she leaned over him. She pulled his jeans down. She had kept her pants on and she pushed them to the side to allow him enter her. She arched her back to meet his thrusts. He turned her over and got on top. This play continued for ages with her taking control, then Larry.

Later, as they lay there on the bed wrapped around each other, with just the noise of their breathing, breaking the silence, Larry stroked her shoulder affectionately. He looked down at her face and saw the tears roll from her eyes.

"Are you OK?" he whispered in a soft voice into her ear.

She squeezed him to her.

"I am now Larry. I am now," she replied.

He lay there and looked around the large room. Marie was stroking his chest. The sheet was lying loosely over them, and the afternoon sun shone through the net curtains. Later, Marie rolled over on top of him and took control. Larry had never experienced anything like this in his life.

"The stories he used to make up for the lads would never live up to what had happened this afternoon," he thought to himself. He would never divulge to the lads what had happened today. This "real" fantasy was just for him.

Chapter Eleven

A couple of months after Rory's funeral, Gerard Foley was sitting in The Bell with his father and his brother Mick. Mick had told his mother and father about his engagement to Angela, and the wedding was to be in two years – June, nineteen sixty-nine. Gerard had decided to leave for England at the end of June. He had asked Larry to go, but Larry was acting very strange lately, and wasn't keen on it. Larry hadn't told Mick or Gerard about the afternoon with Marie, or about the other afternoons that they had together in her bedroom.

Mr Foley went to the toilet, and while he was away Gerard turned to Mick and said, "I'm glad you're here with me da and me, Mick. I'm heading to London at the end of the month, and I haven't got the heart to tell him – well, not so much the oul fellah as the ma. How will they take it, Mick?"

Mick didn't seem too surprised at the news, but Gerard noticed he was slightly distracted also.

"Are things OK, Mick? You don't sound too surprised." asked Gerard.

Mick took a sip from his pint and looked around to make sure his father wasn't on the way back from the toilet.

"I knew you were thinking of it, Ger, but to be honest, I have a little problem meself." He paused. "Angela is up the spout," replied Mick.

Gerard smiled and slapped his brother on the back.

"Well, that's good news, yeh? Well, a bit premature, but how do you feel? How does Angela feel about it?" replied Gerard.

"She's in bits, Ger. She said her mother will kill her. We'll have to bring the wedding forward, I mean really forward by two years," replied Mick.

"Me ma will be made up, Mick. She likes Angie, and don't worry, things will work out for yous," replied Gerard.

"Thanks, Ger. Yes, I know. Angela is telling her ma tonight, and I'm going to tell the da now, but we are looking at an October, maybe November, wedding. We are looking for a place to live at the moment, so it's going to be a busy few months," said Mick.

Mr Foley came back from the toilet and sat at the bar coughing. "The bloody smell out of that feckin' toilet! Brings water to yer eyes," he said as he picked his pint up.

"Da, I'm thinking of going to London for a bit of work," said Gerard to his father as he settled himself on his stool.

Mr Foley didn't act surprised.

"Yeh, I know. I was talking to Mr Burke, and he was telling me you were talking to "Jimmy" the brother in law that lives in London, and that you were thinking of going," he replied nonchalantly.

Gerard nodded at Mick, and whispered, "Well that went well – your turn, Bro!"

Mick called the barman over.

"Three pints there, Mr O'Brien please. Thanks," he said, and took a deep breath and turned to his father.

"Da, Angela is ..." He didn't finish his sentence as his father interrupted him.

"Pregnant. I know, your mother told me last week," said his father, as he put his pint down on the counter.

Mick looked at Gerard and then to his father.

"How! Who! ... Jesus, women," he retorted.

Mr Foley turned to the two lads and said to Gerard, "Listen, son, I can't blame you for leaving this Emerald Isle. Jesus, your grandfather would turn in his grave if he saw the way they're leaving in their droves to work for the enemy". Mr Foley's father was in the British army and fought in France in the First World War.

"Did you know when he came back from France after World War One, he joined Collins' crowd. He believed that Ireland would be united after fighting for king and country, and when he returned to Ireland they had brought in the Tans. His brother and uncle were killed in cold blood by the Tans as they were returning from a Gaelic match. That nearly killed him, so he joined a flying squad in the IRA, and with Collins set out to try and get an independent Ireland. You never knew that, did you?" replied Mr Foley.

"He must be pissed off with the way things have turned out here now, Da. The country is fucked," said Gerard.

Mr Foley wiped the rim of his pint. It was something he did. The lads used to take the piss out of him doing it . He would wipe his thumb across the rim of the glass, and then lick his thumb and wipe the rim again and stare at the creamy head of the pint of Guinness.

He took a long sip from the pint. Then he turned to the lads. Even though Collins is long dead, the war between him and "Dev" is still going on. As long as they put party before country Ireland will never be fixed.

"In time, things will change son, but in the meantime decent hard working people have to just make do. Go! Gerard – Go and seek a life. You have brains, and you're young enough to make something of yourself. Michael, you have a job and a lovely girl, and please God next year a new baby. Stick with it son – that job you have in the train station, you can be promoted., But it's a job for life. Anyway, setting up a home is hard work, so stick at it son," replied his father. Mr Foley was a man of few words but when he did speak he spoke words of wisdom and his words weren't wasted.

Mick whispered to Gerard.

"How did me ma know about Angela being pregnant?" said Mick.

Gerard laughed and said, "It's a woman thing."

Larry and Jem walked into the bar and came up behind the lads.

"Get up out of that," said Jem, as he slapped Gerard on the back. Gerard nearly broke his teeth on the glass.

"Jem, for Christ's sake, I'm nearly after fucking choking," spluttered Gerard.

The lads went and sat in the seats, and left Mr Foley at the bar talking to Ossiler Larkin. Larry sat in beside Mick, and Jem sat the other side of Gerard.

"How's the transport business going, Jem? I heard Joxer has big plans to expand. I saw him pushing you with a full load sitting on top of the pride of the fleet the other day!" laughed Gerard.

"The pride of the fleet, Oh the box car, ahh it's going great," replied Jem

The others laughed.

"Joxer, I swear he's as good as gold, but trying to get him to change things? I swear a snail would move quicker," replied Jem.

They sat and talked about Joxer, and Mick noticed Larry wasn't as talkative as he usually was. Gerard started telling the lads that he was going to "get the boat", as he put it.

"Don't forget the uncle's address. Ger. He's well got over there in London. He will put you right – the fucker is loaded. Don't know how or where he gets the money, but, well he gets it," said Larry to Gerard.

"He gave me an address the last time I was talking to him and he said he would sort out some work for me," replied Gerard.

Mick turned to Larry.

"Lar, why don't you go with Ger? Your oul fellah will still be able to carry on on his own, now that you've put manners on that fucking shower he cleans the windows for," said Mick.

"And don't forget the gutters and the chimneys." laughed Jem.

Larry picked up his pint and raised it to Gerard.

"No way lads, I'm very happy with me lot. We have a nice little earner going, and besides I know me oul fellah – he would go back to cleaning for free. He needs to be minded," remarked Larry as he sipped his pint.

"And all them oul wans you're ridin', what about them? Who'd fill your shoes there, Lar?" quipped Jem.

The lads laughed.

"They're all stories I made up." remarked Larry, quite seriously.

The lads looked at Larry in surprise. This wasn't the Larry they knew, as he was always ready to tell some sort of story about his day, and what happened during the day, even though he made most of it up to keep the lads interested.

Later on that evening, Mick and Larry were alone. Gerard and Jem left to meet Pancho, who was trying to organise a football match with a group of lads from the Sailors' Rest bar, the pub at the other end of Chapelgate Gardens.

"Right, come on Larry, spill the beans. You're not the same as normal, you've something on your mind." remarked Mick to Larry.

Larry pulled on his cigarette and dismissed Mick's concern, and in a minute turned the focus on Mick.

"Never mind me, what about you and Angela – engaged! Are you looking forward to the wedding? After all a couple of years will fly in," said Larry.

Mick went red and fumbled a little. This was enough to spark Larry off, and he knew Mick was holding back something.

"Come on, Mick, I fucking know you better than I know meself. What gives?" asked Larry.

"Well, to be honest, Lar, Angela is pregnant. We are going to bring the wedding forward to maybe October, or November," remarked Mick.

Larry nearly fell off the seat.

"Jeeez, you a dad! Fuck me, this calls for a celebration," he shouted.

"Ssshh, we are keeping it quiet till she tells her family. Sure I only told the da tonight, but me ma knew last week. Fucked if I know how she knew, but you know women. A different breed," said Mick.

Larry picked up his pint and they both clinked glasses, and Larry congratulated Mick.

"Jesus, Mick, fair fucks to ye. Anybody else would be pulling their hair out if they had gotten someone preggers, but fuck me, you're taking it well," said Larry.

Mick thought for a minute and replied, "Well, to be honest, Lar. I know Angela is the one. I am not ashamed to tell you, but I love her – really. I know we are meant to be together.

Don't ask me how I know, but I just … well I just know. Does that make sense?"

Larry nodded and reflected for a minute. He knew exactly what he meant. The afternoons with Marie were the only thing he looked forward to. Every waking minute he was thinking of her. He had never felt like this about any girl before. She had told him about her life and the control her husband had over her. The drive that was in him, to rise in the ranks of the police. Larry was falling in love with Marie. He couldn't fathom it but he had never been so serious about another person. He turned to Mick and decided to confide in his best friend.

"Mick, do you remember a few months ago I was telling you about, Marie, er Mrs White?" said Larry.

Mick looked at Larry curiously.

"Have you? Did you like have … I mean …?" stuttered Mick.

Larry nodded his head, and he was in a serious mood as he told Mick what had happened the day in the garden and then a few times since, when Larry would go into the house and they would spend hours in bed together. Larry also told Mick about her husband's high up job in the police. He also told Mick that her husband very seldom made love with her, and was always working or playing golf with senior policemen, to try and enhance his career. Mick was taken aback. Larry told him his feelings for Marie. He told him about the way she was the first thought that came into his head in the morning and the last thing he thought about before going to sleep. Mick knew what he was talking about because he was that soldier.

"What will I do Mick? We haven't talked about a future or anything like that. It's just sex … No, not sex, it's lovemaking Mick. We don't have sex we make love," said Larry.

Mick looked at his friend.

"I don't know the answer to that Larry," he replied honestly.

Since that first encounter with Marie Larry confided in Marie. Intimate things about himself. She in turn told him about her upbringing and how she wanted to pursue her dream of going to college as her father worked so hard all his life to get the money to send her to college. But when she met and fell in love with her husband all her future plans were discarded.

He told Mick that every time he tried to talk about where it was going she would change the subject. Mick tried to give Larry reassurance but he had his own dilemmas to consider.

*****

In the weeks following the first time they had made love that afternoon, Marie had confided in Larry that from the first day he came to clean the windows for her, she would try and talk to him at every opportunity. Larry recalled that on reflection he thought she was just being friendly, and he didn't know that she would be interested in him as a person. She told Larry that she was very lonely, and her husband's only interest in her was making sure she came across as the perfect wife. When they were at official functions for the police, or if he invited colleagues to the house for dinner. She also told Larry that her husband didn't like sex, but only had sex with her to try and make a baby. As they used no protection, they were puzzled that they had had no children after nearly ten years of marriage.

Larry told Marie about his life in Chapelgate Gardens. The friends he had. The scrapes he got into. He told her about Imelda. They laughed about the time Joxer and Jem caused mayhem when they crashed the box car through the lights at the five lamps. Larry had never been in a situation like this. It was surreal to him. Lying in bed whilst his father was cleaning windows a couple of doors away whilst he spent these summer afternoons with the sun streaming in the windows of Marie's bedroom, Larry couldn't believe where he was. He never told Marie about the day Rory robbed the house. He never told of the wallet he picked up from the front room. Even though he knew that if he had told her she would have accepted it. One day while she was sleeping after they had made love he looked at her with her long hair strewn across the pillow. He would have walked away from his life and gone with her wherever she would want to go once he was with her. But in his heart he knew that was never going to happen.

*****

"Is it going to last, or are you just using her?" asked Mick.

Larry shrugged his shoulders, and looked into space. "Mick, I'll be honest. I like her – I like, no I love her, but think about it. I'm twenty, she's thirty four, a good looking thirty-four, but nearly fourteen years difference in age, and she lives in that big house, with a husband on the way up the ladder, and me, living in me ma's flat, cleaning windows, and not a pot to piss in? It doesn't take a fucking genius to work out we won't be growing fucking old together, but Mick I really, really love her. Does that make sense?" replied Larry.

"Have you talked to her about it?" asked Mick.

"No that's just it. It is never brought up. I talk about my life, and she tells me about hers. Then I dress and I leave," replied Larry

They talked for another hour, and Larry realised that Mick would be a married man with a child in tow this time next year. The group was changing. Gerard was going to England, and God knows where things between Marie and him would go. They were being pulled apart as a group.

Chapter Twelve

Angela and Imelda would meet every day after work and go into the city looking for a wedding dress. It was common knowledge around Chapelgate that Angela was pregnant with Mick Foley's child, but as they were getting married, people weren't as judgmental as would happen if a girl was having a child outside marriage.

"Imelda, will you be my bridesmaid?" asked Angela one afternoon, as they walked home from work.

Imelda was delighted to be asked.

"What with Gerard best man and you bridesmaid, you never know what will happen!" teased Angela.

Imelda shrugged her shoulders.

"I wouldn't be bothered with Gerard . Anyway, he's off to England in a couple of days, so that's not going to happen," said Imelda, non-committal.

Since Gerard had decided to go away, things had changed with the lads. Jem had decided to go with Gerard, and Pancho was going to take over with Joxer on the turf runs. Jem had saved a lot of money, and they had given him the nickname 'the Squirrel'.

Gerard had also put some money away from a stroke he had pulled off. He had robbed a truck delivering boxes to a clothes shop. One day he had been walking by the back entrance to Guiney's clothes shop. He noticed the doors of a truck, which was parked outside, seemed to be open and not properly locked. At first he thought, "Fuck, they wouldn't leave a truck unlocked in Dublin City," and he moved on. But as he was walking by a sweet shop a couple of doors down from Guiney's, he noticed Jem. He was sitting on the box car outside the sweet shop waiting for Joxer, who was in the shop buying bars of chocolate.

"Jem, Jem. What are you doing up around here?" cried Gerard, as he approached Jem.

Jem turned around and greeted Gerard.

"We just dropped an old bed off at Cluxton's, the second-hand furniture shop. It was for Fatser Larkin," said Jem.

"Fatser Larkin! Make sure you get paid off him – he's a robbing bastard," said Gerard.

"Too fucking late, he's already fucking screwed us. We were supposed to collect the money off Mr Cluxton when the bed was delivered, but he had already paid Fatser. Wait till I get him. I'll knock the bollicks out of him," shouted Joxer, as he came out of the shop and heard Jem talking to Gerard.

Jem looked at Gerard and his eyes went up to the heavens, as they both knew poor Joxer 'Wouldn't beat snow off a rope'.

"Look, forget about that now. Do you see that truck there outside Guineys? Well, its back doors aren't locked, and there are boxes of stuff just crying out to be robbed. What do you think, lads?" said Gerard. The boys looked at each other and within minutes they had opened the truck, thrown two boxes onto the box car, covered them with the sacking cloth and they were away to Chapelgate as fast as they could run.

When they had opened the boxes, one was full of bright red ladies' sweaters, and the other had men's short jackets with a very large check pattern. After a few hours of wheeling and dealing, they had sold off the stuff to the people of Chapelgate, who were glad of a bargain, and didn't want to know where the clothes came from.

All Gerard said was. "They came off the back of a truck." This was true.

"Never look a gift horse in the mouth," said Angela's mother, when her youngest daughter asked where she thought the red sweaters came from.

The lads went to the Sailor's Rest, and split the money they had made, three ways.

Whilst they were there, Pancho saw the box car outside, and called in to see if Jem had Ok'd it with Joxer about taking over when Jem left for England. When Pancho came in, Jem jumped up and brought Pancho over to Joxer, and tried to convince him he would be better taking Pancho as a partner to help him do the turf, as Joxer couldn't do it all on his own.

Joxer was very set in his ways, and was taking some convincing. During the conversation, the door opened, and Fatser Larkin came in to have a drink. John Larkin had the nickname Fatser because he was very skinny, and it was a way of taking the piss out of him. Despite being skinny, he was very handy with his fists and hard as nails. He had a reputation of being a dirty fighter. As he stood at the bar he ordered a pint and went straight out to the toilet, not even glancing at the lads.

"I'm going to get me money off him," said Joxer, and he followed Fatser to the toilet.

When he went after Fatser, Jem explained to Pancho what had happened.

Gerard and Jem didn't fancy a bust up with Fatser, as he had a bad reputation, and he was liable to pull a knife. He had a bad reputation in Chapelgate as a nasty piece of work.

Joxer followed Fatser into the toilet. Gerard looked at Pancho and Jem.

"Right I suppose I have to do it myself," he said as he rose to go to the toilet knowing Fatser would have beaten up Joxer by now. "Fuck me, I have to look after these fuckers and when I go away who will do their fighting," thought Gerard.

Gerard didn't fear Fatser Larkin. Gerard had boxed him at the boxing club a few years before and had beat him to pulp. As he rose from his seat Pancho put his hand on his arm.

"Leave this to me Ger," he said and he walked towards the toilets.

"I w … w … waaant me m-m-money!" stuttered Joxer, who would stutter when he was nervous.

Fatser Larkin was standing against the urinal pissing. He ignored Joxer and continued pissing.

"Fats … s-s-sor-ry … John, c-c-can we have ouurr m-m-money?" repeated Joxer, who was really nervous now, but determined to get the money he was owed.

Fatser turned towards Joxer, still pissing, and looked straight at him as his piss hit Joxer on the shoes.

"Yeh, in a week or two, if I remember!" laughed Fatser.

Joxer jumped back as the water sprayed across his trousers and then the tiled floor. Pancho walked into the toilet and saw the scene before him. Without stopping to think he walked straight up to Fatser, grabbed him by the shoulders and head butted him right on the nose. Fatser fell back as the blood gushed from his nose like a burst pipe. Pancho flicked his foot under Fatser's feet, sending him reeling back into the urinal, and as Fatser hit his arse off the tiled floor, cracking something in his spine into the bargain, Pancho stood over him and pressed his foot against his neck.

"You! Money now, you cunt," he screamed.

Fatser's eyes rolled in his head. It had happened so fast. He was stunned. His hands came up in front of him, and he tried to put his penis back into his trousers.

"OK! OK! Don't hit me," he pleaded.

Pancho reached into his pocket and took the money. Without letting his foot off his neck, Pancho, who was very fit from playing football, reached down and grabbed Fatser by the hair.

"This boy here is my boss. He tells me what to do and he pays me. If you don't pay him, he can't pay me, geddit. How much does he owe us?" he called to Joxer.

Joxer couldn't believe what he had just witnessed.

"Er, t ...t ... ten shillins," he whispered.

Pancho pulled an orange ten shilling note from the notes he had in his hand. Then he took another ten shillings, and he threw the rest at Fatser. He took his foot off Fatser's neck, and kneeled in front of him, grabbing his balls through his trousers. Fatser felt the pain surge through him, and he opened his mouth to cry out.

"You fuck with me or my boss again, and these balls will be in your fucking mouth. Are we clear?" Pancho whispered into his ear.

Fatser couldn't speak, but nodded his head up and down. He stumbled from the toilet with blood still pumping from his nose, and headed towards the front door. As he passed by the bar, the barman held his pint up for him. He just stumbled towards the door and left. Gerard and Jem couldn't help but snigger as he went by.

"What the fuck happened there," said Jem to Gerard.

Then Pancho and Joxer came out together, with Joxer giving Jem the thumbs up.

"Well – is it sorted?" said Jem to Joxer.

Joxer looked at Pancho, who was as cool as a cucumber, and just about to sip into Fatser's pint.

"Er … yes. Yes – sorted – he's in," replied Joxer.

Pancho put his pint down and turned to the lads.

"Thanks boss. I never liked that fucking cunt anyway, the skinny bollix," said Pancho

Fatser could hear the laughter as he stumbled towards his flat.

"Bollix to that," he thought to himself.

"When are you guys off to the big smoke of London?" asked Pancho.

"A week on Friday. Are you coming to see us off on the boat? It leaves at ten Friday night, and we arrive in Liverpool seven thirty Saturday morning," said Gerard.

"Yeh, we'll all go down to the docks to wave you off. Will we need to bring hankies for the tears? Jesus, you'll be in England like the next day. That's quick, a few hours away, and years ahead of us "poor fuckers"," said Pancho.

"There are millions more people in England than in Ireland, Pancho, and even the small towns are nearly as big as Dublin. But London, that's where Larry's uncle is. That's where the money can be earned," replied Gerard.

"Earned, or robbed?" laughed Joxer, who was sipping a sparkling orange drink, as he couldn't drink alcohol because of his medication. They all laughed at Joxer's input, as he never really got involved in any meaningful conversations with the lads.

"Opportunities, Joxer! Opportunities," said Gerard, as he patted Joxer on the head.

"If you don't take chances …" said Joxer,

"…you won't make advances," replied Gerard.

They all laughed, and Pancho put his arm around Joxer.

"Don't mind them shower of cunts, boss. When they are locked up in Wormwood Scrubs, we will be running our very own transport company, so fuck them!" laughed Pancho.

A big cheer went up as all the lads stood and clinked their glasses together.

*****

Jem was excited about the trip to London. He had never been out of Dublin before. Pancho had been helping out with the turf deliveries. He was glad that Joxer had taken to working with Pancho. Even though they worked and hung around together, Joxer was difficult to get on with at times. From the day Pancho had hit Fatser Larkin, Joxer looked up to Pancho. Jem knew that he was not part of the team any more. He had had second thoughts for a couple of days, but it was too late to back out now, even if he wanted to. The lads were getting on well, and all of a sudden Jem was the outsider.

"So Jem, this Jimmy guy, Larry's uncle – is he getting you jobs and stuff?" asked Pancho, as he sat astride a sack of turf blowing smoke into the air.

Joxer was fixing the back wheel shaking his head.

"Pancho, we have to get another wheel. This one is fucked," said Joxer, ignoring Jem.

Jem was a little bit hurt knowing he was out of the team.

"I don't really know, but Gerard said he had something lined up for us," replied Jem.

"It's better having someone in the know over there. He'll look after you guys," said Pancho.

"I heard he killed a guy. Stabbed him to death," said Pancho.

"I heard that too but it was in self-defence," replied Jem.

"Well just don't get caught doing anything dodgy. They'll lock you up and throw away the key," said Pancho flicking his cigarette butt into the air.

Earlier in the week Larry had been telling Gerard about his uncle "Jimmy" and his life in London. He told him that when Jimmy had first gone to London in the late fifties, he had only been there two weeks when he had got himself into a fight in a bar, and had stabbed a man to death.

"When Jimmy first arrived in London, years before, he tried to integrate with some local heavies in a very rough part of London. Jimmy was smart, and took no prisoners. One night he was in the company of some Irish heavies, who had done a job with a London crew from the east end of London.

Jimmy had been introduced to the London gang, and one man in particular passed a couple of nasty remarks to Jimmy about him being Irish. His name was Oliver, and he kept calling Jimmy 'Mick' or '"Paddy'. Jimmy didn't want to upset things with the London gang, even though this "Oliver guy" was passing insults about Irish people at every opportunity he got. Jimmy was only young then and he wanted to just fit in with everybody so he laughed off the insults coming from this guy. He was at the bar and the main man of the Irish crew was sitting in deep conversation with local head man.

Later in the night as Jimmy was standing at the bar, and Oliver, who was quite drunk by now, shouted at him, "Hey you, Mick, bring over some drinks to the table here, and be quick about it, you spud picker."

The head man, Terry, known as Tell, of the London crew, was standing beside Jimmy at the bar, and he turned to Jimmy and said in his broad cockney accent, "Don't mind that facking twat mate, he's a facking moron." So Jimmy ignored Oliver and started up a conversation with Tell. Terry liked Jimmy, and as they chatted he could see that Jimmy Burke, was a straight talker. He wanted him in his crew.

Out of the blue, Oliver came up to Jimmy and pushed him on the shoulder. Tell stood back to see how Jimmy was going to handle this situation.

"Hey you Mick, where's my facking drink?" he said.

Jimmy turned to Oliver and said, "Listen Ollie, take it easy, and the name is Jimmy. Just fuck off and get a life." And he turned back to talk to Tell.

Oliver shoved him again on the shoulder.

"Here, you ye caun't, my facking name is facking Oliver, not facking Ollie ye Irish twat." And he pushed Jimmy in the shoulder again.

Jimmy turned around to face Oliver and grabbed him by the collar and said, "Listen here you fucker, the only other Oliver I know was called Cromwell, and he was English like you, and like you he was also a cunt. Now fuck off and annoy someone else!" and with that Jimmy pushed him away and turned his back on him. The pain of the knife plunging Jimmy's shoulder was excruciating. He turned back to see the blade coming through the air at his face. He caught Oliver's arm and pushed the knife towards his chest. It was over in seconds. The knife penetrated Oliver's heart and within minutes he was dying on the floor.

When the police arrested Jimmy, the head of the London crew told the police exactly what had happened, and the murder charge was dropped because it had been in self-defence. Jimmy was taken into the inner workings of the London and Irish gangs that operated in London, after that night. He had actually killed the man who had been informing the police about their activities. It was only after his death that Tell had found out who had been passing information to the police about the gang's activities. Over the years, Jimmy had built up a good reputation within the criminal fraternity in London. He ran his own crew, and he had built up a network of criminal activity between Ireland and England, importing small amounts of drugs to a small market, laundering sterling from bank robberies carried out in Ireland, and fencing stolen jewellery.

Jimmy had told Larry about this when he had been over for a couple of weeks' holiday. He had been trying to get Larry to come to London and work for his crew. But Larry had bigger fish to fry at that moment in time. Jimmy put it to Gerard about having to do some stuff and ask no questions. Gerard knew he wasn't going to London to work as a navvy. Jimmy needed a bigger network for his dodgy dealings and Larry was his first choice but when Larry told him about Gerard and how he needed to get away from Chapelgate. He told his uncle about

Gerard being loyal to his friends and that was why Jimmy decided to give him a chance.

Chapter Thirteen

Larry had fallen asleep in Marie's warm bed. The first time they had slept together, he noticed that the mattress was the most comfortable bed he had ever slept in, even though he hadn't slept in many beds. He hadn't cleaned many windows today, as it was a very overcast Friday afternoon.

The smell of perfume lingered on his nostrils. He had spent many days in Marie's bed since that first afternoon. He had grown more mature. He became more sensitive to her. He couldn't believe that he was with Marie. He had held this woman in very high esteem – almost afraid to talk to her at times, when he had started working with his father.

She had told him about her childhood, and she actually grown up in a very poor neighbourhood, but she had wanted to go to college. Her father had saved for her college fees. she applied for and got a good civil service job when she left school. But one night she went to a dance in Dublin, and that's where she met her husband. Within three years was married.

As with the law at the time she had to leave her job in the civil service if a woman married. Her husband, she came to realise, was only interested in one thing in life – his career!

Soon after they had married she would find herself alone for hours and hours on end in the big house they had bought. Her husband's family were all in the police force, and well connected to a large political party. Her husband Paidraigh, had an uncle who was a member of the parliament.

She never wanted for anything, as her husband organised everything from groceries being delivered to the gardens being maintained. He had actually got rid of the previous window cleaner of the house and got Larry's father to clean them instead.

One thing she had found out about her husband was that he was very jealous and paranoid. He would relate stories of what happened during his days at work, and the underhanded tactics he had used to inform on colleagues to his superiors, without their knowing about it. He was climbing the ladder to be a top policeman, and he didn't care who he would have to step over in pursuit of his goals.

When they went to functions, Marie could see the way his colleagues would be wary of him. Even their wives would be cautious around Marie, and she knew why. Most times she would end up talking to some old washed up chief super somebody or detective superintendent somebody, while he would be trying to further his career.

They had tried to have children but nothing was happening. Then over the years they just accepted it, and even though they slept in the same bed, sex was a quick poke when he wanted, and then he would just roll off her. He provided for her for all her needs … except love and affection.

The day Larry walked into her garden she couldn't believe how handsome he was. She also noticed he was polite, but with an edge to him. An independence – not cocky, but confident – a man on a boy's errand is how she thought of him. As she looked down at his black tousled hair and his strong chin, she kissed him on the forehead.

"Well, I can't hold it in any longer – he has to know. I hope he takes it well," she thought to herself.

*****

Larry's father looked up at the rainwater, spilling from the gutter.

"Where is Larry? He should have been here ages ago," he thought to himself as he took the big ladder from the bike.

"Da, we have the gutters in number twenty-three this afternoon, but it's not a real clean – just a bit of slate. But I'll do it, and you can hold the ladder. It's an awkward one, and higher than normal." Larry had said to his father earlier that day.

"Where the blazes is he?" he thought to himself.

His eyes opened and he looked back to see her staring down at him.

"What?" he smiled.

"Nothing, I was just looking at you," replied Marie.

She sat up and pulled her knees into her chest. Larry lay back and stroked her back with his index finger, sliding over the little bones protruding from her back. They stayed like that for a couple of minutes.

"I'm pregnant," she said, out of the blue.

*****

Larry's father walked to the gable end of the house and looked up.

"That's not right, what Larry is doing, blocking up the downpipes to get extra money. We'll have to stop doing that. Sure he has us earning enough with the windows," he thought to himself.

Larry shot up from the pillow.

"Pregnant, Marie, pregnant. Is … is …" he started to say.

"Yes, Larry, it's your baby, it's yours," replied Marie, half smiling, and not knowing how Larry would take the news.

*****

"It can't be that high. Sure I was up and down ladders before Larry's arse was the size of a shirt button," he giggled to himself as he moved the ladder against the gable. "Feck, I'll get it ready before he arrives, and sure we will fly through it and head to The Bell for a pint. Young Foley is going off tonight on the boat, so there should be a good crowd in The Bell. The Dillon's will be there anyway – they wouldn't miss a going away shindig," he hummed the little song to himself, a song he always hummed as he went about his work, and he started to pull the rope to extend the long wooden ladder.

*****

Marie looked at Larry's expression to see if she could gauge the way he was thinking. Larry reached out for Marie, and she leaned into him as he lay back into the bed.

"God, a ... a ... baby. It has to be mine, yes?" he said.

She stroked his face with her hand.

"Larry I've been married ten years and we couldn't conceive. I am with you a few months and ...well, what do you think?" she teased.

"Jeeez, that's ... er ... well good news, yes?" he replied. Larry sat up and reached for a cigarette.

"Larry, you know that this will change things between us," Marie teased out.

Larry couldn't help but smile. He hadn't even thought about a baby. Even though they had made love lots of times since that first day, it never dawned on him that she could get pregnant.

"Well, yes, I know, I know, but ehh, I'm going to be a Daddy! I'm going to be a Daddy, Dad Da Da Da! Dad Da Da Da!" sang Larry. Marie was pleased that Larry had taken it so well. She had already told her husband and all he could say was:

"Well there now that will keep me mother happy, she always thought there was something wrong with you that we couldn't have kids, great now," he had said and patted Marie on the head like child.

*****

Larry's father looked up and down the road for Larry.

"Ah, feck him, I'll get started. The wind has died down, so I should be OK up there. Just reach in and pick the bit of slate out," he thought.

He steadied the ladder against the gable. It was an old heavy wooden ladder with a rope that extended it to its full height. Larry had bought a few days earlier but this was the first time they had a need to use it. He shook it to make sure it was stable.

"I'll tie it off at the top when I get up there," he thought to himself.

He started to climb the ladder one step at a time. He passed the normal height of the window ledge, which he was used to, and looked up. He had still a good way to go to the gutter's edge. The wooden ladder started to bend in towards the house the higher he climbed. He reached the top and looked around. He had never climbed this high before, as Larry always cleaned the gutters. He could see the boats in the bay, and the two chimneys from the power plant miles away.

"God, what a lovely city we live in," he thought to himself, as he tried to reach the piece of slate which was stuck well into the downpipe.

*****

Larry was upset when Marie explained to him that even though she was going to have his baby, she was staying married to her husband.

"I know Marie, I know, this is great, you and me, but I know how you are married and … but Jeeez, a baby!" Larry blustered.

He kissed her on the lips and she opened her mouth to receive him. "I love you Marie White" he whispered in her ear. As he lay there, Marie put her leg across him. She opened her legs and he slipped inside her. She rolled over and he pushed hard into her. She felt the beads of sweat rolling down his back. He moved faster and faster, grinding against her pelvis. The sweat was dripping from his nose onto her cheek.

*****

"Just a little further, ahh yes, I have a hold of it now. Just a little more," Larry's father thought to himself.

He reached out and the ladder started to slide. He froze. He reached out and grabbed at the gutter. The ladder started to slide away from him. His hand slipped from the gutter and he started to fall. He grasped at the wall, but couldn't get a grip.

Then he started to fall towards the ground. As he hurtled towards the ground, his head hit the corner of the bay window that protruded from the front of the house. His small frame hurtled towards the ground, but the blow to his head from the window killed him before he hit the ground.

*****

"Arrrgh." groaned Larry, as he climaxed and slumped on top of Marie. She stroked his black hair and kissed him on his ear.

"How long will we be together?" he dared to dream.

Chapter Fourteen

Imelda and Angela were sitting in "The Bell" waiting on Mick and Gerard and the lads. Gerard and Jem were leaving for England that night on the boat. Imelda came down to the table with two drinks.

"God, do them pair ever go home?" said Imelda, nodding towards Mr and Mrs Dillon, who were sitting in the corner of the bar.

Pancho walked into The Bell looking for the lads. He had just talked to a woman who was a cleaner in one of the houses in Clontarf. She told Pancho that she heard there was an ambulance called to a house where the window cleaner had fallen off the ladder. She heard that the man who fell had died. Pancho thought straight away that it was Larry. He ran to Larry's flat, but there was no answer at the door.

"Have you seen Larry or his father?" he asked the girls.

The girls noticed that Pancho was very agitated, and they asked him what had happened.

"Mrs Loftus told me a window cleaner had fallen off a ladder and was taken to hospital, and she heard he was after dying on the way to the hospital," replied Pancho.

"Oh God, I hope it's not Larry." exclaimed Angela. "Should we go to the hospital and see if it's Larry?" asked Angela.

"Hold on, I'll phone the hospital from here," said Imelda. She went to the main bar where there was a payphone. A few minutes later she came back to the table where Angela and Pancho were sitting.

"Well?" said Pancho.

"They would only tell me that a Mr Burke was admitted this afternoon and as I wasn't family they couldn't give me any more information replied Imelda.

Pancho stood up.

"I think I'll head up to the hospital," he said.

"We'll all go. Come on Angela grab your coat," said Imelda.

*****

Larry pushed his bike to the road where he was to meet his father.

"A baby, fuck's sake a little baby, I hope it's a boy and ..." His thoughts were interrupted as he rounded the corner and he saw the ambulance and the people at number twenty-three.

As he came upon the scene, he saw his father's bike leaning against the wall, and there was a hive of activity around the ambulance.

"What the fuck's going on here," he thought to himself. As he approached, the woman who lived in number twenty-three came towards him.

"Lawrence, it's your father, he was cleaning the gutters and he fell," she said as Larry approached.

Larry just let his bike fall away from him, and ran towards the ambulance. The grey blanket was draped over the body on the stretcher, and Larry touched it, looking at the ambulance men to see if they could do anything.

"Da, Da speak to me, Da," pleaded Larry and he pulled the blanket from the still lifeless body. His father's face had large gash across his head with blood smearing his cheekbone. The woman from twenty-three held his arm and talked to him. Larry couldn't hear her words. All he wanted was to do was shake his father to wake him. The blanket fell away from his father's face completely, and Larry could see his eyes wide open and his lovely soft gentle face looking back.

"Da! Da," he called out.

Another woman held his other arm, and they were consoling him. He didn't hear their words, but all he could do was to hold on to his father's hand as they put him into the ambulance. He sat in the ambulance, and as the doors closed he could see his father's bike leaning against the wall of number twenty-three.

"I told him to wait for me," he repeated to himself over and over, as the ambulance sped towards the city.

*****

Marie was making the bed when she heard the ambulance siren.

"I wonder who that's for?" she thought. As she folded the sheets, she saw herself in the mirror, and she tried to imagine herself with a big belly. She looked at herself sideways, and then from the front. "I hope I can get through this OK," she thought to herself.

*****

Imelda and Angela were just about to leave for the hospital together, when Gerard Mick and Jem walked into the Bell.

Gerard was carrying a small duffle bag, and Jem had an old fashioned brown leather case. They were laughing and joking together as they entered The Bell.

"Where's Larry? He was supposed to be here." asked Gerard, as he approached the table. Imelda broke the news to the lads as they had heard it from Pancho.

"Should we go and see if he's at the hospital?" asked Jem.

"I phoned the hospital and they won't give any information over the phone, but they told me a Mr L. Burke was admitted today," said Imelda.

"I'll go. You stay here. No sense in all of us going," said Gerard. He got up and walked towards the door, followed by Imelda.

"Where are you going?" asked Gerard as she came up beside him.

"I'll go with you, I hope it's not Larry who had the accident," replied Imelda. "Well either way, if it's not him it's his da," replied Gerard.

They left The Bell and walked towards the hospital. They hadn't seen each other for weeks. They walked along in silence until they got to the five lamps cross roads, where Jem had caused havoc a few months before.

"Hope it's not Larry or his father," said Imelda.

"Well something's not right. Larry was looking forward to seeing us before we headed off to England. I was expecting to see him at the Bell," said Gerard.

They walked into the corridor of the hospital, and saw Larry's sisters and Larry with his arm around his mother. He looked up as they entered the corridor, and Imelda and Gerard knew that it was Larry's father who had died. Gerard put his arms around Larry.

"Sorry mate, God bless him, how did it happen?" asked Gerard.

Larry told Imelda and Gerard about the fall from the ladder. He looked at his mother as she sat there between his sisters, crying.

"She'll be lost without him. They were inseparable, Imelda. God help her," said Larry.

"Did you see it Larry, were you with him?" asked Gerard.

Larry felt a sudden pang of guilt.

"No, I ... I, was at another house," replied Larry.

Imelda was consoling Mrs Burke. Gerard and Larry stood in the long corridor, and looked out the window at the yellow hue from the street lights. They stood and smoked in silence.

After a few minutes Larry turned to Gerard.

"Listen mate, you'd better go. The boat sails at ten, so don't miss it," he said.

"No mate I'm here for you, I can leave in a few days," said Gerard.

Larry shook his head.

"No Ger, go on, you can't do anything here tonight. If you put it off you may never get the chance again, now go," replied Larry.

Gerard hugged Larry, and Imelda came over and hugged him too.

"You take care, mate, and write – do you hear me?" Larry said as the tears came to his eyes, and he wiped them with the back of his sleeve.

Gerard patted Larry on the shoulder.

"I'm sorry to have to leave you like this, mate," he added.

Larry looked at Gerard.

"No Ger – you go, we will catch up when you come back for the wedding. Now go and take chances, or you won't make advances," said Larry, and a weak smile crossed his lips.

Gerard hated leaving his pal like this but he knew there was nothing he could to help Larry. Gerard and Imelda left the hospital.

As they walked along the street Imelda turned to Gerard.

"Jesus, Gerard. Poor Larry," she said.

Gerard nodded.

"I hate leaving Larry in that state. God help him," said Gerard.

"There's nothing you can do, Ger. You'll be back for the wedding in a few months, so you can see Larry then," she said.

"Yes I will. I just hope he gets through this," said Gerard.

They walked back towards Chapelgate.

"Imelda, the night of Rory's funeral, I thought we were getting somewhere. The thing in the pub, and then later you just dropped me. I thought just maybe," said Gerard.

Imelda looked at Gerard as they walked along. She thought for a couple of minutes before answering.

"Gerard, we are too alike. I want more from life than a sewing factory job. I don't want a man thinking he owns me, just because I give him a ride! I have to do this myself, for myself. Ger, you're going to go places. Chapelgate is not for you, and the last thing you need is me, or another Imelda to hold you back from your future. If you stay here, you'll end up like the other men, struggling with a family you can't afford, and limping from day to day. You'll end up hating your life and then yourself. Go, Gerard, and grasp the world by the balls, and then if you come back, and if I am available, you can ride up on your big white horse and be my knight in shining armour," she replied.

Gerard knew she was right. He knew he didn't want a life in Chapelgate. He stopped and she walked on, and then she stopped to look back at Gerard.

"Imelda Bradshaw, I can't ride a horse but for you I will learn. We are a right fucking pair! Aren't we?" he laughed.

She walked up to him and kissed him on the forehead.

"Go and kill the dragon and return safe to me," she laughed.

*****

The doctor came out to Larry and his mother.

"I'm sorry, but we could do nothing for him. He had head injuries and we tried but …. I'm sorry," said the doctor.

Larry consoled his mother. She sobbed and sobbed. "Me poor Da" thought Larry. They sat in silence in the corridor for over an hour. When the nurse came to bring them in to see Mr Burke, Larry had to hold her up. Mr Burke lay there with a white sheet up to his chin. Larry saw the cracked broken leather shoes, protruding from the sheet. He saw his father's hands, with the broken nails, where he tried grip at the wall before he fell. There was a slight cut to his cheek and the corner of his eye was bruised. Larry's sisters cried as they saw their lovely father lying lifeless on the slab. They stood there for a long time. Mrs Burke's neighbour arrived, and she helped Larry take his mother back to Chapelgate Gardens.

*****

As Gerard and Imelda walked into The Bell the others looked expectantly at them awaiting the news.

"Is it Larry?" asked Angela.

Imelda shook her head.

"His father," she replied.

"Poor Mr Burke God bless him," said Angela and she made the sign of the cross. The pub was very quiet as the news travelled around. They sat in silence for a few minutes and it was Mr Dillon who broke the Silence. In his low dulcet tones he sang a lovely song by Ella Fitzgerald. "*Every time we say goodbye I die a little. Every time we say goodbye I want to cry a little,"* he just hummed the rest of the song as the tears fell from his eyes.

Imelda Bradshaw was standing looking up at the ship as it was departing from the dock. She had walked with Jem and Gerard to the ship, and together with Angela and Mick she waved to Gerard and Jem as the big vessel pulled away from the dock. She hadn't a chance to be alone with Gerard before he boarded but she knew that she had said all she needed to say to him earlier.

Mick and Angela stood arm in arm, and Mick was calling.

"Don't miss the wedding, Ger, you're me best man," he shouted.

They waited to see the big ship departing. As the three of them walked back towards Chapelgate, they heard a bus coming along the road heading for Chapelgate. It was only a five minute bus journey, but Angela asked Mick to get the bus as she was feeling tired. The bus pulled in, but Imelda decided to walk.

"Are you sure?" asked Angela, as she was a bit worried about Imelda walking on her own.

"Piss off, you pair! I'll be OK – see you tomorrow," said Imelda as she waved them off on the bus.

"We might go for a quick drink if you want to join us," said Mick.

"Maybe, maybe, go on now," replied Imelda.

She wanted to walk and clear her head. She was thinking of leaving the factory job, to try for a better job in a clothes shop. She loved clothes, and her ideal job would be in a ladies clothes shop, but she knew that as soon as any new employer saw her address, she wouldn't have a chance in hell of getting the job. She was feeling a bit down with Gerard leaving for England, as she liked him and thought that maybe someday they would get it together. But she wanted to stand on her own two feet.

She walked along the quiet street that was lit by the old street lamps. A car approached from the other side of the road and the driver slowed down and wound down the window. A man whom Imelda thought looked about forty or forty-one was driving, and he had a slightly balding head that reflected the yellow light from the lamps.

"Probably looking for directions." thought Imelda, as she stopped to see what he wanted. He said something to her, but it was a kind of loud whisper which she found hard to understand. She decided to cross the road to see what he was saying. She smiled at the driver, who as she got closer to the car looked very nervous.

"Hello, I couldn't hear what you were saying. Are you looking for directions?" she smiled at him.

He went quite red in the face, and swallowed hard.

"Are … hhemm … are you doing business? How much?" he whispered.

She was taken aback for a second, but then she remembered that the docks area, where she was walking had a reputation for working girls from years before. But in the last few years, the police patrolled every night so it was difficult for women to work as prostitutes.

She laughed, and said, "Fuck off! I'm not on the game!" The driver went a bright red and started to wind up the window,

"Sssorry miss … I …" he stuttered, then his foot slipped from the clutch, and the car shot forward and cut out. He hit his head on the steering wheel as the car shuddered to a sudden stop..

"Oh feck," he shouted as he rubbed the bump.

Imelda laughed at the way he had been flustered, and how he looked so nervous.

"Ya gobshite," she laughed as she went around to the passenger side of the car.

She opened the door.

"Is your head alright?" she asked genuinely as she felt kind of sorry for him.

He rubbed his head, and a weak smile came across his face.

"Err sorry, yes, I'm OK. Sorry for thinking you were a prost … a working girl …" he tried to explain.

She looked at him, as he mumbled his words and she felt sorry for him.

"I have me best frock on, and make up. God, do I look like a prossie? Thanks a lot," she laughed as she pulled the rear view mirror around to look at her face. She pulled her lipstick out of her bag and applied it looking in the mirror.

"Oh, I'm sorry, I didn't mean to insult you, it's just I heard that I could! Well, you know," he said shyly.

She looked at him and thought, "Jesus, he's not that bad looking, and not as old as he looked from a distance." She ran her fingers through her black hair and stood straight to straighten her skirt. Then she leaned back into the car to talk to him.

She pointed her finger at him and lectured, "If your wife saw you here with me, she would probably have your guts for garters".

"Oh, I'm not married, I live with me mother. I don't even have a girlfriend," he stuttered.

A few drops of water started to drop onto the windscreen. Imelda looked at the rain starting.

"Oh feck, me hair, it'll go all frizzy," she said out loud.

"Right, the least you can do is give me lift to Chapelgate, and I'll forgive ye for mistaking me as a prostitute," she quipped, as she sat into the seat and closed the car door.

"Yes, yes, no bother. Again, I'm sorry – where will I drop you?" he said as his car pulled away from the footpath.

"The Bell. Do you know it?" she asked.

He nodded. As they drove away, Dermot and Patrick were driving by and Dermot noticed Imelda in the front seat of the car. Patrick was reading some notes for his sergeant's exam and hadn't seen the car, or Imelda.

"She can't be on the game, can she?" Dermot asked himself.

Imelda sat and looked across the seat at the driver and thought to herself, "He's not bad looking at all. Fuck I've had sex with uglier looking blokes for free. He's willing to pay, God, he must be an awful fucking eejit."

He looked over at her and smiled. She smiled back.

"How much?" she asked.

"What?" he replied, not understanding the question.

She studied him and then she asked again.

"How much do you pay, or is this the first time?" she asked.

"Well, I actually never went off with a pros ... a girl, but a lad I work with pays a fiver," he replied.

"A fucking fiver, well bollix to that, and there's me givin it away free," she laughed.

He nearly crashed the car as she blurted it out. He let out a nervous laugh. Within minutes they were approaching The Bell, and as he started to indicate to pull in she turned to him.

"Go straight on," she said.

"But this is where you wanted to go. I can't drive you too far – I've got to ... " he protested.

"Straight on, I'll tell you where to go. Now just drive," she said, and she put her hand on his crotch.

The car swerved a little and then he settled. They drove for a minute or so.

Imelda broke the silence.

"Right I'll do it with you for a fiver," she said.

He shot a glance towards her.

"Are you sure? I don't mind if you want to go home," he said.

"Do you want a fucking ride or not?" she snapped.

"Err, yes ... Yes! Where will we go?" he asked.

At the back of the factory where Imelda and Angela and the girls worked, there was a gate that led into a yard. The gate was never locked, and Imelda knew that they would be away from the road and prying eyes.

*****

Dermot turned and followed the car that he had seen Imelda in. As it slowed down at The Bell and indicated, he thought to himself that she had maybe gotten a lift from a friend, and his first suspicions were unfounded. The car then pulled away again, and the indicator went off. He saw it swerve a little. He decided to follow it, but the radio crackled to life. Patrick looked up from his paperwork and picked up the handset. He answered the radio and they turned the car and sped off to where the radio operator had directed them.

"Fuck it I would like to know where they were going," thought Dermot.

"Who were we following?" asked Patrick.

Dermot shook his head. "No-one – just a hunch, but it was no-one. We'd better get on this call," he replied.

Patrick proceeded to write in the journal on his lap. "I'll keep an eye on that one" thought Dermot.

*****

"Do you want to do it in the back seat or the front seat?" asked Imelda.

"Is the front seat OK with you?" he said, as he leaned across and pulled a lever beside her seat.

The back of her seat shot back. Imelda wasn't expecting the seat to fall away from her back and got a shock.

"For fuck's sake, will you let me know what you're going to do before you do it," she laughed, as she was suddenly looking at the ceiling of the car.

"Sorry about that. I thought you knew that the seats recline," replied the driver, going red in the face with embarrassment.

"Recline, what does that mean when it's at home?" replied Imelda.

He started to take his coat off and was having trouble getting his hand through the sleeve.

She lay back in the seat waiting and looked at him as he tried to take his trousers down.

"What the fuck are you doing?" she snapped at him.

"I'm trying to get me man out," he replied sheepishly.

"Look, just relax and let it happen. I'll let you know what to do," she said.

He looked at her and nodded like a little boy being told what to do.

141

"Right, put your seat down as well, and just take it easy," she said as she leaned into him.

As he lay there he closed his eyes, and she thought to herself, "Jesus apart from his bald patch he's not that much older than me. I quite fancy him". She started to kiss him on the mouth. He just lay there and didn't respond to her kiss. She pulled her mouth away from his and said, "Will you kiss me back, and try and get into the mood?"

"Oh, is it alright to kiss you? I thought that prostitutes didn't allow kissing," he replied.

She slapped him in face playfully.

"If you're paying me for a ride, you're going to get a fucking kiss as well. Now kiss me," she laughed as she threw herself on top of him and kissed him while reaching into his trousers.

He kissed her and put his arms around her shoulders, pulling her towards him. She had stockings and suspenders on, as she didn't like tights.

Then he put one hand down to touch her thigh and when he felt her warm flesh at the top of her stocking he started to tremble. Imelda couldn't stop giggling to herself at his antics. He was making funny sounds and gasping for breath.

"Are you alright? she asked him.

"Uh … Uh … Yes… I..." he stuttered. She felt him going hard and decided to take the situation in hand, literally.

She started to put him inside her and he was getting really worked up now. After a few minutes she was really enjoying it, and as he was thrusting in and out – he groaned as he came. The sweat was trickling down her temple as she also came.

"God he was good, not like some of the wankers I've been with before. Fuck me and I'm getting a fiver. I'll never give it away again," she thought to herself.

"Well did you?" she asked him.

He was sweating and trembling and Imelda thought he was going to have a heart attack.

"Yes I have finished," he said.

She climbed back into the passenger seat and took a headscarf from her bag and wiped herself.

"I never thought I would be wiping myself with this scarf when I put it into me bag tonight," she said to the driver, as he tried to zip himself up.

"Oh Jesus Christ," he screamed as he had caught his penis in his zip. He pulled the zip back down and sorted it. Imelda felt a little sorry for him.

"Thanks Miss, that was lovely. You were very good. I don't have very much experience – I find it hard to talk to girls," he replied.

"Miss who the fuck! Oh, I never told you me name. It's Imelda. And what's your name? Jesus that's the first time I've done it with anybody without knowing his name," she laughed.

"Oh, Liam – me name is Liam. I work in a hotel, well bar manager. What do you do, Imelda?" he asked.

"Well, me day job is in this factory here, but after tonight I'm thinking of changing careers," she laughed.

They both laughed at her joke.

"Well, if you need a reference!" quipped Liam.

She threw him a scorned look.

"Oh! Oh, I wasn't being smart," he replied sheepishly, as he saw the look on her face.

"Jesus, he's afraid of his own fucking shadow, the feckin' gobshite," she thought to herself.

"I was only feckin' jokin', Liam – relax," she laughed.

They both laughed.

"Right! Money, and drop me to The Bell … please, Liam," she requested.

He reached into his jacket pocket and took out a wallet.

"Listen, can I see you next week?" he asked, as he took out five pounds.

Imelda took the money and saw he had more fivers in his wallet. She reached across and pulled another five pound note from the wallet. Liam just sat there and didn't stop her.

"Well, now I'll have to meet you, because you've paid me already," she said as she pushed the two notes into her bra. "Now drive," she ordered.

He drove towards The Bell.

"So you're not married – do you live on your own?" she asked.

"I live with my mother," he confirmed.

"What age are you Liam? I mean you don't look that old up close, it's just your bald patch that gives you an older look," said Imelda.

Liam didn't know whether to be vexed or pleased as he knew there was a compliment in there somewhere.

They drove towards Chapelgate, and as she felt the two notes against her chest, she thought to herself as the car pulled in beside the bar, "Men are so fucking stupid. The small head, ruling the big head!"

"Ten o'clock here, Liam, and don't be fucking late, or I'll keep the money and you can get someone else! Right?" she said to him.

He nodded.

"Yes, I'll be here. Er … thanks, you were very good, I mean I never had …"

She interrupted him.

"No need for that Liam, just be here," she said, as she jumped out of the car and walked straight into The Bell without looking back.

Chapter Fifteen

"Well, what do you think? Will we be millionaires when we return?" said Jem to Gerard.

Gerard looked at Jem.

"We're coming back in three months for the fucking wedding. Millionaires? I don't think so," he laughed.

Jem thought for a split second. "No, ye know what I mean Ger, for fuck's sake – but in a couple of years?" he replied.

They were standing at the front of the ship, and to the left far in the distance they could see the silhouette of the coast of Dublin, and lights flickering on and off. The wind caught Gerard's breath, and the feeling was quite exhilarating.

"Jesus, Ger. Pity bout poor Lar's da. What?" said Jem, as he looked into blackness ahead of him and tried to catch his breath.

Gerard looked ahead and agreed with Jem.

"Mr Burke, poor bastard, he was a hard worker, and he only started to make a few bob since Larry took over. Did you know that, Jem? The poor fucker worked his socks off and never got a break."

They stood there in silence for ten minutes while they sucked on their cigarettes.

"We have to go to London to meet Larry's uncle, Jimmy. Larry said he would put us up for a day or two, but fuck me, Jem, we are bringing over some great fucking news. His brother-in-law's death," said Gerard.

"Yeh, Ger the bearer of bad news, that's a great start," replied Jem.

"So the craic is, we meet him at Hueston station and he puts us up for few days, then we earn our keep," said Gerard.

Jem was silent for a few seconds and looking confused. Gerard noticed this.

"What's wrong Jem?" asked Gerard.

"Hueston station, that's back in Dublin beside Phoenix Park isn't it?" replied Jem.

Gerard looked at him and shook his head.

"There is a Hueston station in fucking London as well. Millionaires me bollox. If you're the best that Ireland has to offer we are going to come back paupers, and will ye hold that fucking cigarette properly. You are holding it like a girl" joked Gerard.

Jem smiled.

"I heard he has a few bob and he's into some dodgy stuff, but if we keep in with him we should do OK! Millionaires!"

"Who knows, Jem? Who knows?" replied Gerard, as he turned and went into the bar to get drunk.

Jem stood on the front deck of the ship. This was is first time out of Dublin, let alone the country. He was nervous about the future. He wished he had Gerard's confidence. Even when he worked with Joxer on the cart, Joxer took all the decisions. He decided he would try and be more positive in front of Gerard. He didn't want to let him down. He looked into the blackness of the Irish Sea. The spray hitting his face made him think of all the men and women who had taken this trip before him not knowing what the future held for them.

*****

Imelda could hear the song as she entered the bar.

"The Dillon's, fuck me do they ever go home," she thought to herself as she entered The Bell.

"There will never be, a portrait of my love" sang Mr Dillon.

Imelda saw Angela in the corner with Mick, and she headed for them.

"Do them pair ever go bloody home?" she said to Angela, as she sat in beside them.

Imelda opened her small bag and took a five pound note from it and gave it to Mick.

"Be a love, Mick, and get us a glass of beer."

Mick took the note and his eyes lit up.

"Five pounds, – Jesus, rich bitch," he quipped.

She stuck her tongue out at Mick.

"And one for you and Angela," she snapped back.

"You didn't get wet. How come?" asked Angela.

"I got a lift off an old fecker. He was lost so I gave him directions. He was looking for the five lamps. I tried to tell him the directions, but in the end I took him there and he brought me back," lied Imelda to her friend.

Mick came back with her drink.

"Jesus, Mick, poor Larry. God help him," said Imelda, getting away from the subject of the lift.

"He was trying to reach the gutters. The woman who owns the house was saying that she asked Larry and his father if they could clean out the gutters. He tried to reach the gutter and he slipped from the ladder," said Mick.

"God help Larry, he'll take this hard," replied Angela.

They sat there in silence not knowing what to say. Their thoughts were with Larry and his mother and sisters. Imelda looked around at the people who were sat in their usual places in the lounge of "The Bell". She saw Mrs Pluck as usual sitting with Ossiler. Mr O'Brien, the owner standing behind the counter with his red puffed face, cleaning glasses and chatting to a customer at the bar. Mr and Mrs Dillon, in their usual seats, and of course, Mr Dillon still singing his heart out.

"I've got to get out of Chapelgate. I need to change my life, and soon" thought Imelda to herself.

She turned to Angela.

"I hope Gerard and Jem do well in England," she said.

"I'm sure Gerard will be ok, but poor Jem, He's never been out of Chapelgate in his life," replied Mick.

"Well he has Gerard to watch out for him at least, but if he was on his own I think he would be back on the next boat," said Imelda.

Mick got up to go to the toilet and Imelda turned to Angela.

"You're starting to show your bump, do you think you will keep working much longer? asked Imelda.

"God, Imelda I haven't even thought about it. I feel great and well able to work but you know what the girls are like in the factory, they will have their snide remarks, so I suppose I'll have to pack in soon," replied Angela.

"Don't mind them bitches, If they pass any remarks at you, I'll feckin' deal with them," snapped Imelda.

Angela put her hand on Imelda's.

"Thanks Imelda, I know I can count on you," she replied and smiled at her friend.

Imelda smiled back.

"I'm thinking of looking for another job myself Angela. I'm fed up with that place," she said.

"You're too good for that place, you deserve better," said Angela. Mick came back from the toilet and sat down beside the girls. They sat there in silence listening to the last notes of Mr Dillon's song wafting across the smoke filled bar.

"A portrait of my love!" sang Mr Dillon, finishing the Matt Monroe song, and the few people in the bar clapped.

*****

Larry sat at the fire as the flames flickered in the darkness of the front room of his mother's flat. He had a glass with brandy and some lemonade in one hand and a cigarette in the other. The neighbours had long gone, and his two sisters Paula and Noleen had consoled their mother and taken her to bed. His oldest sister Paula, who was married, was sitting beside him now on her father's chair. His younger sister Noleen had gone to bed. Larry stared into the fire at the flickering flames. There was a silence in the room. Paula sat beside Larry, stroking him on his arm.

"I told him to wait for me, Paula," said Larry, as he took a sip from the glass.

"Lawrence, don't blame yourself," replied Paula.

They sat in the dark till the early hours talking about their father, and the way he would go cleaning windows every day even when it rained, and he would be cursing the weather. They recalled the week he had earned no money at all, and that weekend their mother had not got enough money to get Larry's father's good "Sunday suit" from the pawn shop.

Like most people in the inner city of the sixties, clothes, suits, shoes would be hauled each Monday morning to the pawn shop, and the money would be used to keep food on the table until Friday's payday.

That Sunday morning, Mr Burke had watched from his top floor flat, the other men all dressed in their Sunday best, head into The Bell. They recalled how he said nothing to their mother about it.

She scraped together money from the girls, and said to him, "Larry, go on over to The Bell. I have ten shillings – here, Larry," she offered her husband.

He nodded his head and said, "Ah, thanks, Chrissie, but I wouldn't go for a pint in me work clothes. Mr Foley and the lads are all in their Sunday best. I'd feel out of place without me good suit to wear."

In her naivety she turned to him and said, "But, Larry, they know you have a suit! Go on over now and have a pint."

He looked at her and smiled.

"I have a better idea. How about I get Noleen to buy a couple of bottles of Guinness and we will share them over the Sunday dinner," he had replied.

"He was a real gentleman, Paula. A real gentleman," said Larry, as his sister gripped him on the arm.

*****

Imelda said goodnight to Angela and Mick, and walked towards her flat. She was thinking to herself about what had happened with Liam, and how she had nearly ten pounds in her purse, and with the money she had from her uncle, she had a chance now to get a flat on her own and try and get a new job. She thought if she bought some new clothes and had a new address she might be able to get a shop assistant's job in a clothes shop. She loved her clothes and loved fashion and had a flair for it. She only earned five pounds ten shillings a week in the sewing factory, after forty hours' work.

"He thought I was on the feckin' game. Jesus, I must look like a prostitute," she thought to herself, as she walked by Mattie's sweet shop and stopped to look at her reflection in the shop window.

Her black hair swept back over her shoulders, and her red lipstick enhancing her pretty face, she had often been likened to Liz Taylor, or Sophia Loren.

A car pulled into the reflection and she spun around. Dermot Kelly wound down the window.

"Miss Bradshaw, how are we this evening? Modelling a new range of fashions are we? Or are we looking for business?" laughed Dermot sarcastically.

Imelda knew the two detectives from their constant presence around Chapelgate, and once when she was with a lad having sex at the back of the church, she saw the two detectives watch her from their car. At the time, she was a little tipsy, and she got a kick out of knowing they were watching.

She had no fear of authority, whether it was the church or the police. She smiled and walked towards the car.

"Now Detective Kelly, if I was on the game, I don't think you could afford me, but on the other hand you get your thrills from watching, am I right?" she quipped back.

Patrick let out a little giggle and turned to Dermot.

"Come on Dermot, she'll tie you in knots that one!"

Dermot liked her attitude and the way she used her sexuality as a weapon.

He laughed back and said, "Now don't let us be catching you with strange men."

She kneeled at the door of the car, and as she did, her skirt went up her thigh, revealing the top of her stockings.

"Would you protect me if I needed protecting, Detective Kelly?" she purred in a low sexy voice.

Dermot smiled back at her.

"Go straight home girlie, and don't let me see you getting into any strange cars," he replied, and he tipped the side of his nose with his finger.

She stood up in surprise and smiled.

"Good night, lads. It's way after my bedtime, and me ma told me not to talk to strangers," she said.

She turned and walked towards her flat, and as the car pulled away she smiled at Dermot Kelly. He smiled back as he passed her and turned to Pat.

"She's a feckin' sexy little minx, that one," he said.

Pat hadn't seen her smile at Dermot as he was tuning into the radio.

"She's trouble Dermot, mind her. Come on, let's get back to the depot – I'm knackered. Are we still on for dinner next week at my house?" he replied.

"Yes, yes, Mary's looking forward to it. She could do with some adult company. She has been stuck in the house, since she had the baby," he replied.

They drove towards the depot, and Dermot Kelly thought to himself, "Jesus, she's a sexy minx".

Imelda watched the car speed away.

"Fuck, there is no way he saw me getting into that car tonight," she thought. She put her hand into her bag and felt the notes. "Fuck me, a fiver for a ride. The fucking gobshite, I'd have rode him for nothing if he had bought me a drink. And that detective, he's a crafty one! I like him, though, but I'll have to be careful around him," she thought to herself as she opened the front door of her flat.

"It's only me," she called out.

Her mother was sitting watching the television. "Where's Da?" asked Imelda.

"He's gone to bed. When he heard about Mr Burke, Lord have mercy on his soul, he took it bad. He was good friends with him," replied her mother.

Imelda nodded. "Poor Chrissie, she'll be lost without him," replied Imelda. She went into the small scullery and put the kettle on. "Tea Ma," she called out.

"Please love, two sugars and a drop of milk," replied her mother.

Imelda mouthed the words in parallel to her mother's voice. For all the years she had been making tea for her mother, she would always add on the two sugars and drop of milk line, as if she was going to forget how her mother liked her tea. She smiled to herself at this.

She brought the two cups of tea and sat on her father's chair facing her mother.

"I'm thinking of moving out and getting my own flat Ma," said Imelda.

Her mother looked over at her daughter and couldn't help admiring how attractive she looked.

"I think that would be a good thing to do," replied Mrs Bradshaw, much to the surprise of Imelda. "You're a good looking girl and smart with it. Yes, I think that would the right thing to do," repeated her mother.

"You don't mind?" asked Imelda

"Imelda I've known for a long time you are frustrated with your life here and to be honest I actually thought you would gone off to England with Gerard Foley, but I'm really glad you didn't," replied her mother.

They talked for a while and Imelda stood up and told her mother she was heading to bed. As she got to the door leading into the hallway her mother spoke.

"Imelda, your uncle Paddy. He went back to England before he was due back. Did you say anything to him? Did something happen between you two?" asked her mother.

Imelda feigned surprise.

"No I don't think so. I didn't say anything to him, and for anything happening between us, sure he gave me fifty pounds for meself. No, I'm as surprised as you why he cut his holiday short. Anyway goodnight Ma, see you in the morning," replied Imelda as she left the room.

Lying in her bed listening to the Beatles '*Love love me do*' on her radio she thought to herself. Her mother was more aware of things than she gave her credit for.

Chapter Sixteen

Gerard sat in the Red Lion bar waiting for Larry's uncle Jimmy to arrive. He had been told to meet a lad in a car park in central London who would give him a bag, and he was to take it back to Jimmy in the Red Lion bar. He had done a couple of these transactions for Jimmy, and was getting fifteen pounds for every pick up and drop from Jimmy. Gerard wasn't told what was in the bag, and once he got the money he didn't really care. He sat and waited.

From the day Gerard and Jem had met Jimmy in London, he had looked after them like a real uncle. He had found them a small bedsit, and told them he would look after the rent, as long as they did some 'pick ups and drops' for him – they were not to ask any questions, and just to do what they were told. He told them if they stuck with him they would be OK for money.

"Gerard, that's great, you have the bag," said Jimmy, as he sat into the seat beside Gerard.

There was a jukebox blaring out a popular song by the group the Mamas and the Papas, 'San Francisco' and the bar was full with people. A lot of them were dressed in hippy dress, with beads and long hair. Gerard noticed that it was far removed from The Bell. Jem came back from the bar with a pint for Gerard and one for himself.

"Ah, Jaysus, Jimmy, here you have this. I'll get another one for meself," said Jem, as he put the two pints down on the table. He returned to the bar. Jimmy turned to Gerard.

"Make sure you keep young Jem in the dark, Gerard. He's a nice lad, but not up to speed with how things work here. Do you understand?" said Jimmy, as he patted Gerard on the shoulder and slipped an envelope into his hand.

Gerard understood where Jimmy was coming from. Since they had arrived in London, Jem was like a child in a sweetshop. He was very naïve. He had managed to get himself involved in a fight one evening in the Red Lion, and Jimmy wasn't very pleased when he found out.

Jimmy had told Gerard to keep a low profile in and around the areas where he had sent them for the pick ups, and told Gerard that if Jem got into any more fights or brought any attention to himself, he would be out of the bedsit and out of favour with Jimmy. So it was down to Gerard to look after Jem and keep him in the dark regarding any business they were doing for Jimmy.

Jem came back from the bar with another pint.

"Where's Jimmy? I have a pint for him," he asked Gerard, as he noticed that Jimmy had left the bar.

"He had to go, Jem. Listen, Jem, he wasn't too pleased about you getting into that row the other night, so try keep a low profile. We're on good fucking poke here, and we don't have to fucking work on building sites like the rest of the paddys that come over here. Do you hear me, Jem?" said Gerard.

Jem looked at Gerard a bit confused, and a little hurt.

"But I just stuck up for meself, Ger. Fuck me but that bollox pushed me in the back and called me a queer. I ..." Gerard didn't let him finish his sentence.

"Jem, just keep a low profile. I would have sorted that fucker for you outside. We are working for Jimmy and he needs loyalty, and we should just shut the fuck up and listen to Jimmy. He won't steer us wrong – do you hear me, Jem?" pleaded Gerard to Jem.

Gerard liked Jem, after all they had been pals since the first day at school together but the last thing he needed right now was to wet nurse him.

They sat there, and Gerard saw that he had hurt Jem's feelings.

"Are you looking forward to going to the wedding, Jem? We'll be like bleedin' millionaires with the new suits we bought," said Gerard to Jem, trying to cheer him up. Jem brightened up and smiled.

"One more week for the wedding, Ger and then celebrate Christmas and New Year in Dublin with all the lads. Jaysus, it will be great," said Jem.

The wedding was set for two weeks before Christmas, and Gerard, as best man, had to be back in Dublin for it.

When he had told Jimmy about having to go back to Dublin Jimmy was excited.

They were sitting in Jimmy's car, a black Rover with cream leather seats. Jimmy wasn't flash like the London crime bosses he'd done a lot of business with. Most of them drove big black Jaguar cars, and they dressed in smart tailored suits. They drew attention to themselves. They demanded respect and got it. Jimmy was more inconspicuous. He dressed in brown suede shoes tweed jacket and beige trousers. He didn't stand out in the crowd. He dressed more like a businessman or a bank manager than the gangster he was. He gave Gerard good advice on how to handle himself with the London gangs. He told Gerard to remember that they were strangers in a foreign country and never trust any of the fuckers no matter how well he knew them.

Jimmy would pass for a typical English country gentleman.

He told him he would give him one hundred pounds to take a bag to a pub in Dublin city centre. He was to meet someone who would give him a package and he was to bring it back to London with him. But he told Gerard that he would have to return a few days after the wedding, and therefore he would be spending Christmas and New Year in London.

Jimmy didn't go back to Dublin for Larry's father's funeral, as he said he was too busy. He confided in Gerard one night that he had liked Larry senior a lot, and he often offered him money when he would go to Dublin on holidays, but that he would never take it.

"He was one of life's true honest men, Gerard. But where did it get him? Not a fucking pot to piss in, and old before his time, God bless him," he told Gerard.

"Look Gerard you're a quick learner, but when I say jump you say how high. Don't ever try to take over my operation. A few have tried and failed. So keep that in mind and we can make money. Do we understand me, Gerard?" said Jimmy.

"I'm here to "learn and earn" Jimmy so just tell me what you need doing, and I'll do it," replied Gerard.

Gerard and Jem sat in the Red Lion for the evening, and later on two girls had come in and sat beside them. When the girls heard their accents they sat closer to them, and struck up a conversation. The girls loved the Irish accent and that's what attracted them to the lads.

Later the four of them ended up going to a house party together. Later at the party someone put a saucer containing tiny purple tablets on the table in front of the lads. Jem knew they were some sort of drug, and he had never taken one before – Gerard told him not to.

But when Gerard got drunk, he had left the room and gone off with one of the girls they had met in the bar.

The other girl had her arm around Jem, and she picked up two tablets and popped them in her mouth. She leaned across and kissed Jem. As she opened her mouth and Jem opened his, she slipped one of the pills into his mouth. At first he pulled back a little, but then he just swallowed it. After a couple of minutes he felt himself drift and he saw amazing colours revolve around the room. The girl beside him was saying things to him, but her words sounded muffled and her mouth was moving slower than normal. The sounds of Joe Cocker's 'With a Little Help From My Friends' blared through the large speakers and filled his head. Everybody seemed to be just floating as they danced. He spun around and around as he danced, and then he blacked out.

*****

Gerard's eyes opened, and he could hear the muffled sounds of music coming from somewhere in the distance. He looked beside him, and in the darkness could just about make out the shape and the long hair of the person beside him. He couldn't remember going to bed, and he looked around for his bearings, but it was hard to see in the darkness. He remembered having a lot to drink.

The smell of sweat and stale smoke in the room filled his nostrils. He got out of the bed and he was still fully dressed. He reached into his pockets and found his cigarettes. He struck a match, and from the light he could see bodies lying around the bedroom. He put his hands in his pockets again to check that he still had his money.

He didn't like it when he had had too much to drink. He liked control.

The walls were painted with peace signs and squiggles of shapes – he recognised as hippy signs and the flower power movement that was popular in London of the sixties.

He sucked hard on his cigarette and he heard a noise from where he had been lying on the bed. The long hair of the body he was lying beside covered the person's face. The voice that came from it startled Gerard.

"Hey man, where are we, man?" the man's voice called out.

Gerard was very confused.

"Fuck me! That was a bloke I was in bed with. Jesus did I do anything? Did he do anything?" he thought to himself in a panic, as he checked that his zip on his trousers was still pulled up.

Gerard had heard that blokes slept with blokes – 'queers', they called them – and that there were a lot of them in London. He remembered Jimmy telling him and Jem that people were a bit different in England, and life was even more different here in London.

As he left the room he saw a mass of bodies lying around the floor and on top of each other. He didn't recognise the place, but by the drawings on the walls and the state and dress of the people lying around, he reckoned he was in a hippy squat.

He looked for Jem and couldn't find him, so he opened the door and left the house. He didn't recognise the area, and decided to walk until he saw a landmark so he could determine where he was.

It was dawn, and the cloudy November sky wouldn't let the weak sun shine through to the grey buildings of London.

He walked through the empty streets. His life had changed so much since he had arrived in London. From his bearings, he knew he was in the Islington area of London. He passed the Angel bar, a place he had done business in for Jimmy a few weeks before. He pulled his jacket around himself and walked through the grey cold streets heading for the tube to take him to where he lived.

*****

Jem smelled the urine even before he opened his eyes. His throat was dry and he needed something to drink. He couldn't remember where he was, or had been. His eyes wouldn't open. All he could remember was drinking a pint with Gerard and two girls in the Red Lion. He could here clanging and shouting in the background. Then he heard the key turning, and as he opened his eyes he looked towards the direction of the sound of the door opening, he could see the white shirt and black tie of the policeman as he stood in the door.

"Oi, Superman, wakey wakey!" the policeman called to Jem.

Jem blinked and he could see that the policeman held a mug of steaming tea out to him.

"Jesus Mary and Joseph, where the fuck am I? Oh, thanks, guard," said Jem, as he took the mug from the policeman.

"Well, you're a very lucky boy, you would be in the morgue right now, paddy, if my colleagues hadn't taken you off the building last night. Actually the building you thought you were going to fly off, sunshine!" laughed the burly policeman.

Jem sipped the hot sweet tea.

"Building – what building?" asked Jem.

The policeman shook his head.

"Look, me little Paddy friend, you must have taken a lot of drugs, because you were going to jump from a building in Notting Hill that had scaffolding around it. You don't remember that? You had your coat draped over your shoulders like blaady superman, Gohrd, we 'ad a right larf at yer!" replied the policeman, in his cockney accent.

The policeman turned and left the cell laughing as he did.

"Get your head together and we'll let you out later," the policeman called back to Jem.

Jem was sitting on the smelly mattress.

"Oh fuck, what sort of drugs did that girl give me last night? He thought to himself as reality kicked in. "I can't remember a fucking thing," he thought to himself. He looked around the cell and realised that he missed Chapelgate. He didn't like London. He sipped the scalding tea. "This is the only thing I like about fucking London. The tea is lovely," he thought to himself.

Jem was released after giving his details to the desk sergeant in the police station, and he was told he would have to attend court in a week's time. He gave a false address – he knew if Jimmy found out he would flip.

He was being charged with being drunk and disorderly. As he walked down the road he recognised some buildings and he knew that he wasn't very far from the flat he shared with Gerard.

"Fuck! What will I say to Gerard? Jimmy told us never to come to the attention of the police. He told us to … What were the words he used … slither through the long grass. Fuck! Ger will go mad when he finds out." thought Jem.

He hoped Gerard wouldn't give him a bollicking. The fight he had gotten himself into a few weeks before upset Gerard no end. They hadn't got what you'd call a steady job and the last thing they needed was to draw police attention to themselves.

*****

Gerard sat in the room waiting for the kettle to boil. He had expected Jem to be there when he got back to the bedsit, but he wasn't, and that was nearly two hours ago. He was to go and book the train and boat tickets for their return to Dublin in a week's time. He looked out of the first floor window, up and down the road. The bedsit was small but clean, and as Jimmy paid the rent on it, they didn't have to worry about a landlord.

"Where's the little bollocks gone?" thought Gerard to himself.

He took the money from his pocket and opened the tea canister which held his savings. He took out a roll of notes and took off the elastic band holding them.

"I'd have to do an awful lot of robbing in Dublin to get this amount of wedge," he thought as he counted out the notes. He put the canister back on the shelf.

He looked out the window again.

"Where's that little bollocks gone?" he thought to himself again.

Gerard saw the familiar figure walking up the street and thought to himself, thank God Jem is safe. In some ways Gerard felt responsible for Jem.

"Hi Ger, what time did you get home last night?" said Jem, as he entered the small room.

"Jaysus, Jem, I was worried about you. Them girls we went off with last night, they were hippies, and them fuckers do drugs. Remember what Jimmy said to us – don't take fucking drugs or we will be out of this place pronto," replied Gerard.

"I didn't take drugs. I … I … went back to her place and stayed the night, Ger, honest." lied Jem.

Gerard looked at Jem. He looked rough and smelled bad.

"You'd better get yourself cleaned up. Have you any bread left from last night. I gave you a fiver – do you remember?" said Gerard.

Jem pulled his pockets inside out.

"Jaysus, Ger. I must have been pissed. I haven't a bean. I'm sorry pal," said Jem, as he flashed Gerard a sheepish smile.

"Yeh fucking gobshite! It's a good job I look after the readies," said Gerard, slapping his friend across the head in a playful way.

*****

A week later they were getting out of Jimmy's car at the train station. They were getting the train to Liverpool, and then the overnight boat to Dublin.

Jimmy turned to Jem, and said, "Jem, son, you go on ahead. I just need a word with Gerard here. Now take care, son, and don't go getting into trouble." He shook Jem's hand.

"Right Jimmy, have a good Christmas, and we will see you in the New Year. Thanks Jimmy," said Jem, as he smiled and shook Jimmy's hand.

Jimmy turned to Gerard.

"Take care of that parcel with your life Gerard, and don't let it out of your sight. Your contact is Christy. You meet him in The Bog Road bar on Capel Street tomorrow evening. Don't fuck this up. He gives you a closed envelope and you bring it back here. You don't open it or interfere with it, Ger. Do you understand?" said Jimmy in a tone of voice that Gerard had never heard before.

Gerard nodded and patted the suitcase that the parcel was in. Jimmy looked around and leaned forward to whisper in Gerard's ear.

"This is big time stuff, Ger. Do this right, and I can move you up in the organisation. Do you understand?"

Gerard nodded again, and promised Jimmy he would guard the parcel, do the delivery, and return with the envelope after the wedding. Gerard was just about to turn and walk away when Jimmy called him back.

"One more thing, Gerard. Jem! He's out. Don't bring him back. Don't ask why – just don't bring him back. Good luck now, and here, take this as promised, but don't open it till you're near Dublin port, and tell them all I was asking for them," said Jimmy, and with that he started the car and pulled away from the train station.

Gerard turned and followed after Jem, who was on a 'Speak Your Weight' machine with his suitcase lying beside it.

Gerard looked at Jem and then he saw where he had left the suitcase and thought, "Anybody could just walk up and take it, and Jem would be none the wiser. No wonder Jimmy wants to get rid of him".

Gerard had already decided not to bring Jem back to London even before Jimmy had told him. He looked at Jem standing on the machine and thought to himself that Jem hadn't learned anything from his trip away. He was still the innocent Jem that he always was.

*****

It was seven o'clock in the morning, and Gerard stood on the front of the boat as it steamed into Dublin port. Seagulls were following the ship and swooping onto the deck to pick scraps of food from the viewing area.

To his right he could make out the Bailey lighthouse of Howth, and further on the Bull Wall to his right came into view.

As a child during the summer months he used to come to the beach at Dollymount to play and swim. Those days seemed a far cry, from where he was now. He looked around to see who was beside him. A man and a woman were standing a couple of feet away, pointing and talking to each other, but not minding Gerard. Gerard took the envelope from his pocket that contained the money Jimmy had promised him, and there was also a small envelope inside with 'Chrissie' written on it.

He counted out one hundred and fifty pounds, and a little note addressed to Gerard. It read:

'Give Jem twenty five quid, and he is not to return.

'Give young Larry twenty quid from me, and get your brother a wedding present for the other fiver. The hundred is for you, as promised, and the other envelope is for me sister, Chrissie. Keep your nose clean in Ireland, and when you get back I'll fill you in on our business. As I told you not to open this until you were in sight of the port, I know that you are now looking at Howth, or maybe the Bull Wall. Gerard, throw this note into the water, and I'll see you in the New Year.'

He laughed a little laugh to himself, as he squashed the note into a ball and threw it into the sea.

"Fuck me, but Larry's uncle Jimmy is one very clever man. I am going to learn a lot from him," he thought to himself, and he took a long deep breath through his nose and smelt the air that was Dublin of nineteen sixty-seven.

Chapter Seventeen

Dermot and his wife Mary pulled up outside Patrick and Helen's house. Helen opened the door and greeted them as they walked up the drive.

"Mary, you look great! How's the baby?" said Helen, as she embraced Mary.

Dermot greeted her and walked into the house, leaving the girls to catch up.

"Pat, where are you?" he shouted.

Patrick came from the kitchen with two glasses containing whiskey.

"Me oul mucker, here – take this!" replied Patrick.

The two men walked into the front room and sat in front of the television.

"By God, we done well getting them televisions, Dermot. What do you think," said Patrick, as he pushed the buttons on the new television.

Dermot had the same television in his house. They had investigated a theft from a stolen lorry a couple of days earlier, and when they came across the abandoned truck, it contained televisions and radios. As there was no- one around, they decided to put two televisions in the back of their car.

They didn't see this as stealing – they were just taking advantage of the situation. The report they filled out indicated that there were five boxes containing radios and two boxes containing televisions taken from the truck. The two men clinked their glasses together.

"God bless the job!" they laughed.

Mary and Helen walked into the room.

"Pat, can you get Mary a drink," said Helen to her husband.

Patrick nodded and went to the kitchen. Dermot looked at Helen and couldn't help noticing how good looking and well turned out she was. His wife Mary had let herself go over the past few months.

Mary was quiet, and Helen noticed she had put on a lot of weight.

"Mary, you look great. I'm glad we are having dinner together. It's been such a long time," said Helen.

"I'm piling on the weight, Helen, and since the birth I just can't lose it," replied Mary.

Patrick came into the room and gave the women a glass of white wine each.

"Cheers girls," he said as he raised his glass. They sat and chatted for a few minutes.

They had dinner in the dining room of the modern semi-detached house which was a far cry from the dwellings in Chapelgate Gardens.

"Mary, we are going to Pat's parents for the Christmas. We're looking forward to the break, to be honest," said Helen to Mary.

"We are staying home this year," replied Mary, and she drank a large glass of wine in one gulp. Mary had been very quiet during the meal, and Helen noticed this. Helen tried to bring her around and lift her spirits.

They sat chatting but Mary was finding it hard to engage in the conversation.

Mary drank more glasses of white wine, and towards the end of the meal she had started to feel a bit tipsy. Helen couldn't engage Mary in any meaningful conversation.

She noticed that the more she drank, the more she was talking about silly things.

It had been months since Mary had had a drink of wine because of the amount of time the new baby had taken up, and her depression had worsened, and just to go out shopping was a chore for her. She started to relax the more wine she drank, and Dermot was glad that she was loosening up and enjoying the company.

"Did you hear that young Foley, and that O'Donnell fellah, are back from England? I'd say they're up to no good over there. I saw them the other day, and they were like a couple of spivs," said Patrick to his partner.

"What's a … hic … a spiv?" asked Mary, who was getting a bit loud now.

"A cockney spiv? It's … er … be the hokey … it's … er, a slippery fecker, Mary. Someone who looks and acts sharp. That's right, Dermot, isn't it?" replied Pat.

"Yes, Pat, I think so. Jesus, we say spiv, but we don't know where we get it from, but it even sounds like it is! Am I right?" said Dermot.

They laughed at this analogy from Dermot.

"Dermot, are you boys OK for a top up while I'm in the kitchen," said Helen, who was starting to clear the table.

"Here, I'll give you a hand clearing in," offered Mary, as she tried to stand, but fell back into the chair. They all laughed at her attempt, and she just stayed where she was.

"Er, I think … hic … I'll stay here," she replied.

Dermot got up and went around the table to her.

"Come on into the sitting room, Mary. We'll be more comfortable there. Come on, Pat," said Dermot. They helped Mary into the sitting room. She was very unsteady on her feet.

Helen heard the voices from the front room, and was glad to see that Patrick had settled lately. He was sleeping better, and since they decided to go to the country for the Christmas, she noticed a big change in him. Dermot came into the kitchen for a refill.

"Thanks, Dermot. Whatever you said to him, it's worked. He's sleeping much better, and treating me better also. Thanks again, Dermot," she said to Dermot as he filled the glasses with whiskey.

"Oh, I don't think I done or said anything Helen. I think time is a great healer, and this feckin' oul job we do doesn't help. The stuff we see Helen, you wouldn't believe, but I'm glad he's coming round. The exams are keeping him focused and he will do well," replied Dermot.

"Mary looks well," lied Helen.

Dermot cocked his eyebrow.

"Helen, I know you mean well, but come on. She was a mess when we arrived. She's starting to relax now, but to be honest, she has that terrible oul depression," replied Dermot.

Helen smiled and nodded. "Sorry, Dermot, I should know not to lie to a guard. But really I'm glad to see her. Having a baby takes it out of you. I should know," she added.

Dermot walked up beside her and said, "Thanks Helen. Yes, the baby is taking it out of her, but the way things are going it will be our last baby. She hasn't let me near her since."

Helen touched him on his arm.

"It takes time Dermot. She'll come round," she said.

Dermot picked up the drinks and went towards the sitting room. He turned and said, "I know she'll be OK. Thanks Helen – you're a good friend."

The four of them sat in the sitting room until the early hours, and when Dermot got up to leave he indicated to Helen that Patrick had long since fallen asleep on the couch. Helen threw her eyes up to the air.

"It's the studying, he's hitting them books every night," replied Helen.

Mary was very drunk, and it took Dermot and Helen to get her onto the back seat of Dermot's big Ford Zephyr.

Mary was talking but her words were incoherent. Helen walked with Dermot and he sat in the driver's seat and rolled down the window.

"Do you need a hand getting himself to bed?" he asked just before he sat in the car.

"No, he's staying where he is on the couch. He'll only waken the little fellah," replied Helen, and then added,

"She'll be ok Dermot. It takes time to get over that old depression. Just give her the time." Dermot smiled and agreed with her. He waved to Helen.

"Thanks for a good night Mrs O'Reilly," he said as he pulled away from the house.

He decided to go through the city, passing by Chapelgate Gardens on his way to his home. It was one thirty in the morning as he went under the railway bridge.

Ahead of him at the side of the road he noticed a car pulled in with the rear lights on.

As he passed he saw Imelda Bradshaw getting out of a car, and as he drove by the car, he noticed it wasn't the same car as he had seen her in before. He slowed down.

Imelda never noticed his car as it passed her. She had just put five pounds in her bra and the man was begging her to meet him the next week. She was telling him she would meet him the next week, but only if he paid her in advance. The man was getting a bit agitated, and was trying to grab at her arm as she leaned into the car.

Dermot saw in the rear view mirror the man's hand grab at Imelda, and saw that she was trying to pull away. He pulled in to the side of the road and looked into the back seat at Mary, who was snoring loudly and out to the world. Dermot got out of the car and walked back towards where Imelda was clearly remonstrating with the driver of the other car.

Neither Imelda nor the driver noticed him as he came right up to the driver's door. He opened the door and the red frightened face of the driver looked back at him. His hand released his hold on Imelda, who looked shocked at the way Dermot Kelly was standing over her assailant.

"Right, what's going on here?" said Dermot in a low clear voice, to the driver.

"Who the fuck are you? Fuck off, or I'll call the police!" shouted the driver to Dermot.

He flashed his ID in one hand and his other hand held the man by the collar.

"Now I'll ask you again, or will we do this at the station," replied Dermot in a stern official voice. The blood drained from the driver's face.

"Er, guard, she tried to rip me off. I paid her for sex and she's trying to rob me," he lied.

Dermot looked at the startled face of Imelda. This man was old enough to be her father, he thought.

"So you admit to being with a prostitute, which is an offence and is contrary to section six, paragraph nine of the

…" He didn't get the chance to finish his sentence as the man then pleaded with him.

"Oh, guard, sorry I was mistaken, sir, I … I …" he pleaded.

Dermot leaned into the car and whispered into his ear:

"Get the fuck out of here or I'll run your details and call to your house and let your wife know what you get up to, you fucking maggot. Now I'm turning my back for two seconds. If you're not gone from here, you will be in a fucking cell in five minutes and your wife will have to come down and bail you out for procuring prostitutes!" And with that, Dermot leaned out of the car.

The man's face went white with fear. Dermot closed the door of the car.

The car pulled away from the kerb with the driver's door not fully shut. As he sped away, Imelda looked over at the Dermot.

She hadn't heard what he had said to the driver but she had to jump clear from the car as it sped away.

"Thanks, guard. He was … I … I …" she tried to explain to Dermot.

"Come on, I'll drop you to your flat," he said as he casually turned and walked back towards the car, with Imelda walking behind.

He opened the passenger door and she reluctantly sat in. A movement caught her eye in the back seat and she turned to see what it was.

She was taken aback at the woman lying in the back seat with her dress nearly up around her waist and her hair all tossed, out for the count and snoring.

Dermot eased himself into the driver's seat and put his finger to her lips indicating for her to not say anything. He grabbed the gear lever on the steering column put the car in gear and pulled away, and within a couple of minutes he stopped at the entrance of Imelda's block of flats. No words passed between them.

He turned and looked at Mary in the back seat and then looked at Imelda.

"Miss Bradshaw, I believe this is your place of residence," he joked with her.

She was a little taken aback, and she knew that he knew she was on the game, but she couldn't figure out his take on it. He had actually stuck up for her.

"I, er ... I ..." she tried to talk.

Dermot smiled, put his finger to her lips again, and leaned across and pulled the silver door handle.

As he lay across her, she quickly planted a kiss on his cheek, and whispered into his ear.

"Thank you, kind sir, you have saved a maiden in distress!" and with that she jumped out of the car and ran towards the flats.

"The little minx," he laughed, as he pulled away from the kerb and pointed the big grey Ford Zephyr towards his home. He heard a groan from the back seat, and then heard Mary throw up all over his car. He took out a cigarette, pushed the in car lighter to on, and rolled down the window.

Chapter Eighteen

Gerard walked into the flats and looked around at the scene. He was only gone a few months, but he felt like he had been absent for a lifetime. It was eight o' clock in the morning and it was cold, very cold and he could see the fog from his warm breath as it hit the ice cold air. He had his little duffle bag with his few things in. Jimmy's parcel was tucked into the arse of his trousers. He had put it there in case the customs men pulled him. He didn't know what was in the parcel and he felt very uncomfortable about not being in control of the situation, but he was carrying out Jimmy's instructions to the letter. He stood and looked around at the red bricked flats with their neat little doors and the laundry, hanging from makeshift lines outside the scullery windows. He felt strange. Like a warrior coming home from battle. He had seen another life, if only briefly, but he had seen another life. He headed for his old flat.

He opened the door of his mother's flat, and he heard her humming as she cleaned and worked in the small scullery.

"Where's the love of me life?" she heard Gerard call out to her. As he entered the scullery. She turned and the tears came to her eyes.

"Gerard, Oh God, Gerard," she cried out.

"I'm back. Ma. How's me Ma?" he called to her as he embraced her.

He hugged her and the familiar smells from his old home flooded his nostrils. His mother made a big fuss of him and sat him down. She gave him a sandwich filled with Irish back bacon and dripping with real butter, a taste he missed from his time in England.

His mother told him about the wedding plans and all the fuss, and that he was to meet Mick later for a fitting of the dress suits they would be wearing on the big day.

Gerard put a wad of notes in her hand and she gave him a look.

"Gerard my God this … This is a lot of money. Where did you get this amount of money, it's too much?" she pleaded as she looked in awe at the notes.

"Ma, I'm working all the hours God gives, and I'm doing well, now don't go worrying yourself. Tell me where's Mick?" he asked.

His mother tucked the notes into her apron and wiped her tears with the bottom of her apron.

"Oh Mick and Angela are great. They have all the plans for the wedding: and her Mother. Don't talk to me about that one. Fur coat, no knickers her. She wa …" Gerard stopped her in her rant.

"Ma, forget about that ould wan. Where's Mick?" he replied.

"Work! He's gone to work, he's after getting a regular shift at the train station. When you left he had a few casual shifts but they brought him into the office and Mr Swan, a lovely man, his bos …." Gerard interrupted his mother again as she was inclined to ramble on and on.

"Ok Ma, I'll just have this bit of grub and take a few hours in me old bed. I'll meet Mick later," he replied. He tucked into the food and his mother looked in admiration.

"My lovely boy," she thought to herself.

*****

Jem O'Donnell sat in the cold flat on his own. His father was at work and his mother, who was a cleaner in offices down at the docks, was also out. He had to get into the flat through a side window, as he hadn't taken any keys to the flat with him.. He had left them in the bedsit in London. Even though he was alone in the flat, he was glad to be back. He really missed the familiar things strewn around the small flat. He was having second thoughts about going back to London with Gerard, and hadn't told him.

"I'll wait till after the wedding to tell him. No need to spoil his time with the family," he thought to himself.

Later on in the morning Gerard woke up with the winter sun streaming into the bedroom. He could feel the warmth on his face. He was disorientated for a couple of seconds. Then he looked at the familiar posters on the wall.

"George Best, Bobby Charlton." The two best footballer's Man United ever had," he thought.

He rose and sat on the end of the bed. Mick had changed the room since he was last here. There was a CIE uniform pressed and hanging from a hanger on the back of the door.

He lit a cigarette and inhaled it into his lungs. The kick was good.

"'Players Navy Cut'. Best cigarette ever," he mused. Gerard was home!

Larry was walking through the flats when he heard Gerard's voice.

"Hey, ye dirty little bollocks, are you still robbing?"

He turned to see Gerard dressed in new Wrangler denim jeans, and a denim jacket and his hair was a lot longer than he remembered, even though he had only left Dublin a couple of months before.

"Look at you, ye long haired fucking hippy!" called back Larry.

They patted each other on the back and Larry stood back to have a look at Gerard.

"Jesus, you look fucking ... What's the word? You look different, Ger," said Larry.

Gerard put his arms around his friend and hugged him. It was the first time he had ever hugged his friend in affection. It just seemed natural to do this.

They pulled away from each other and Larry pushed his friend in the shoulder.

"OK hippy, tell me, what's the fucking story? Are you home for good or just a flying visit to get the wedding in?" asked Larry

"I'm going back over as soon as the wedding is over Lar."

They traded stories from the last few months and Gerard could see that Larry had something on his mind that he wasn't divulging to him but he decided to leave it for now.

"I have some stuff for you and your mother from Jimmy. Do you want to head to your place, Lar?" asked Gerard.

They walked towards Larry's flat, arms around each other's shoulder, talking non-stop.

Larry kissed the twenty pound note, and put the envelope behind the clock on the fireplace for his mother. He made Gerard a cup of tea, and they both sat in front of the fire, which was blazing in the grate.

Larry had not worked for a couple of days, as the weather was very bad, and he was broke. The twenty pounds came at the right time, he thought to himself.

"Well, how's me Uncle Jimmy?" asked Larry, as he took the cigarette offered by Gerard but he tucked it behind his ear. "I'll keep it for later," he lied. He had given up smoking.

Gerard struck a match on the sole of his boot, which were made of leather.

They were the new 'Beatle boots', made popular by the group, 'The Beatles'. Larry looked at how Gerard was so grown up looking, even if it was only a couple of months since they had left for England.

"He's a fucking good bloke, Larry. He's been looking after me and Jem since we got to London," replied Gerard.

"Well, you must be looking after him. He doesn't do charity! Are you both working for him?" asked Larry.

Gerard took a long drag from the cigarette, and Larry looked on and envied him, but he had decided a few weeks before that he was going to stop smoking. Well, it was Marie who suggested it, as her husband smelt the smoke in the bedroom one day, and Marie had to make up a story to cover the fact that Larry and her had made love in the bedroom most of that day.

"Work? Well, I wouldn't call it work, Lar. We just pick up packages and drop them. Once I had to go to a pub with him as a bit of muscle, just in case things got out of hand. We didn't bring Jem, he's a bit of a gobshite, Lar. I could do with you over there mate. As a matter of fact Jimmy told me not to bring Jem back. I don't know how to tell him," said Gerard.

"Well, things have changed here for me, Ger. I … I … can't really go anywhere because I …" he stalled.

Gerard looked at how Larry was stalling his words.

"Come on, spit it out. Have you got someone up the spout?" he joked.

Larry said nothing. Gerard took another drag from the cigarette and noticed the change in Larry's demeanour.

He shot up out of the chair.

"You did, you fucker! Who is it? Not Imelda?" said Gerard, hoping that it wasn't Imelda.

Larry looked down into the fire and then turned to Gerard.

"Remember the woman I told you about – Marie from Clontarf. Well, I …" He tried to finish his sentence, but Gerard interrupted.

"For fuck's sake, Larry, the copper's wife. Fuck! I don't believe it, you and and … Jesus Christ, Lar … what the …" he trailed off.

Larry shrugged his shoulders.

"It just happened, Ger. She's a lovely woman. I actually think I love her. No Gerard I do love her. Don't fucking slag me, but I love her Gerard" he replied.

Gerard couldn't believe the news that Larry had dropped on him.

"Jesus Lar, you have it bad mate. You really do love her, don't you?" said Gerard.

"She's just so sweet, she's gentle, she's …" He didn't finish as Gerard was imitating throwing up with his fingers in his throat.

"For fuck's sake mate, get a fucking grip. She's years older than you. She's probably using you to get pregnant, did you ever think of that?" replied Gerard.

"No Ger. It's the real deal mate. She said she loves me too," replied Larry.

"So she loves you too. So you told her you love her, yes?" asked Gerard.

"Well yes, kinda," said Larry.

"And she's going to leave her big fucking house in Clontarf and move in with you your ma and your sister. Tell me that's what's going to happen," said Gerard sarcastically .

"Well not really, we haven't talked about that far ahead," pleaded Larry.

"No, and do you know why Lar? She's fucking miles ahead of you mate. Cop on for fuck's sake," said Gerard in a mocking tone.

Larry got agitated and defensive. He knew Gerard had a good point because anytime he tried to talk to Marie about the future she would change the subject.

"I don't know Ger, I've had me doubts," replied Larry.

"Forget about her for the moment. Let's go and have a few pints before we go for the fittings for the suits. We'd better wet the baby's head as well. Come on, you can forget the fucking tea, let's go have a pint," said Gerard.

Larry smiled a weak smile, but he was in a quandary, as Marie had made it known to him that she was staying in Clontarf, and Larry would not, and could not be part of her baby's life. They had talked a lot since she had broken the news of the baby, and her husband hadn't even suspected that he was not the father.

Larry hadn't told anybody about the baby, and he was glad that he told Gerard. It was like a load off his mind, and he wanted to hear what advice if any, Gerard had to give him.

They decided to go to The Bog Road pub, and Gerard told him that he was doing business in there for Jimmy. Gerard had the parcel tucked down the back of his trousers, and though it was uncomfortable, it was safer than carrying it out in the open.

As they walked towards the city centre, Larry told Gerard that Marie was staying with her husband, and that they could still see each other, but she needed security for the baby. Larry told Gerard that Marie was a very loving person, and for once Gerard thought that Larry was acting in a more mature and grown up way than he had ever acted before. But Gerard could read between the lines. Larry out, baby in.

They walked and talked as they told each other more and more details about how their lives were changing as the months rolled by.

"We have to meet Mick later. He wants us to get measured for the monkey suits. He wants me to be groomsman," said Larry.

"Jesus, that's brill, mate, and I have to get them a wedding present, so we can get the whole lot sorted today," said Gerard.

They entered the bar of The Old Bog Road and Gerard looked around for his contact. The description of the contact was a guy with a beard about forty years old, and he would be wearing thick black rimmed glasses. His name was Christy. He would be at the far end of the bar near the toilets. So as they entered the bar straightaway Gerard spotted a guy at the bar that fitted the description.

The lads went straight to the bar and ordered two pints. The guy was eyeing them up, but didn't make a move.

"I'm Gerard. Are you Christy?" asked Gerard as he stood at the bar.

The guy said nothing, but he looked across to the long seat where there were two other men sitting having a drink. One of them nodded to him, and it was Larry who copped it.

"Larry Burke, Jimmy's nephew," said Larry, crossing in front of Gerard and putting his hand out to shake the man's hand. The man smiled and took Larry's hand.

"Sorry to hear about your father – you're the image of him," replied the man as he shook his hand.

"You must be Gerard?" replied Christy.

"Yes, I'm Gerard. I have that package for you – have you got the envelope?" replied Gerard.

The man indicated to go out to the toilets and Gerard followed. One of the men sitting on the long seat got up to go to the toilet. Larry put his foot across his passage.

"I think they can handle that alone. Larry Burke, Jimmy's nephew … and you are?" said Larry in as tough as a voice he could muster.

The man smiled at Larry.

"Paul, good friend of your uncle. No problem there," replied the man as he turned and sat back down.

In the toilet Christy was about to take the package from Gerard, but Gerard put his hand out.

"You have something for Jimmy?" he asked, raising his eyebrows.

Christy leaned back against the wall.

"Let me check the package and if everything is in order I'll come back later with the envelope for Jimmy," said Christy putting his hand out to take the package.

Gerard pulled back and held on to it. Christy patted Gerard on the shoulder.

"Me and Jimmy go way back, he can trust me. Just give me that now and later I'll pop back with the envelope," said Christy.

"I will call back later with it. Don't worry, just give me that now," he repeated.

Gerard remembered what Jimmy had said to him before – 'Trust fucking no-one' and he said to Christy, "Listen, I will hold on to this, and when you bring back the envelope I will give the package to you. Nothing personal, Christy, but Jimmy's the boss, and I just do what he tells me," said Gerard, who was feeling a little uneasy, as this man was very cool, and he made Gerard nervous. But he had to stick to what Jimmy had said.

"No envelope, no package," he relayed Jimmy's words to Christy.

Christy stood back and looked at Gerard.

"What if I take it off you? What would you do?" he teased.

Gerard was getting scared now. He looked at Christy, and even though he was older, he just looked hard.

"Jimmy gave me a job to do, Christy, and he's the boss, so if you try to take it, I will just have to put you down. As for them fuckers outside, Larry can deal with them – no fucking problem. Your fucking choice, mate." gulped Gerard, who was really scared, but he knew if he went back to Jimmy, he would have to face the consequences.

There was a prolonged silence.

"What makes you think you can take me down son?" said Christy in a low threatening voice.

Gerard had never felt as nervous in his life but he wasn't going to let Jimmy down. Jimmy had paid him up front and he always finished a job he was paid for.

He thought for a few seconds and decided to brazen it out. He was in the big league now. So in for a penny in for a pound he thought to himself.

He took a deep breath.

"Christy, this is the way this is going to play out. First of all. I'm not your fucking son. The name is Gerard, Gerard Foley, and don't forget that name. Second I'm walking out that door with this package and whatever happens between you and Jimmy after that is your business. So Christy, that's the way it plays out. Your choice. Bear this in mind, Jimmy will not be happy if you try and fuck him over," said Gerard.

Christy stood back and laughed a little laugh. He reached out at Gerard and tapped him in a friendly manner on the shoulder.

"Jimmy said you had attitude – he was right. By the way I'm the boss, not Jimmy, and you said and done the right thing there, Gerard. I like you. Here, take this, and tell Jimmy I agree with his choice. He'll know what I mean," replied Christy. With that he handed Gerard the envelope and put his hand out for the package.

Gerard was relieved at this change of circumstances.

Christy put his hand in his pocket and took out twenty pounds.

"Here, get a few pints for you and young Larry out there." He handed Gerard the money and turned to leave the toilets. He stopped and looked back. "You done good kid, but what if I hadn't have given you the envelope?" he asked in a joking way.

"Then you would be up twenty quid and unable to walk as well," joked Gerard.

Christy laughed.

"He said you had attitude. He was right. Take care Gerard Foley we will be doing a lot more business again." And with that he was gone.

Gerard took a couple of moments to get himself together. He had felt threatened and nervous after this encounter with Christy. He knew by Christy's demeanour that he was 'the boss'.

"Take care, Larry. Tell your uncle I will be in touch," said Christy, as he passed Larry at the bar.

"Slán leat, Dairmid," shouted Christy to the barman, as the three of them left the bar.

Gerard stood looking at his reflection in the stained mirror in the toilet. He had never felt that threatened before, and the encounter left him a bit drained.

"Are you OK, Ger?" asked Larry, as he entered the toilet.

Gerard threw some water on his face, and ran his fingers through his long hair.

"Yes, I'm OK now. Fuck me, that bloke was scary, Larry. Anyway, let's get a pint and catch up," replied Gerard.

They sat in the snug at the end of the bar when they noticed a man sitting a couple of seats away who was slightly drunk. He took out some sandwiches and he offered the lads one each. They shared his sandwiches, and struck up a conversation with him. He told them he was on the way to Kildare with a delivery of electrical goods, but he was gagging for a pint. He was telling them that he had won money on a horse the day before and went on the drink after he left the bookie shop so today he was very hung over.

He told them that when he picked up the truck that morning he was still drunk.

"Hair of the dog," he said as he picked up the creamy pint of Guinness and lowered nearly half the pint in one gulp.

Larry looked at Gerard and whispered, "No wonder he has a bleeding hangover drinking like that".

They started chatting and he bought them a drink, and then Larry returned the favour. He was telling the lads that he worked delivering electrical goods around Ireland for a distribution company.

When he went to the toilet he had left his keys and his cigarettes on the table.

Larry took the keys and went outside to look for the truck. He went around to the back of the pub and saw a small lorry parked against the wall of the pub. Larry opened up the back door and saw that there were boxes with various pictures of the contents they contained. Some showed radios, and the larger boxes showed televisions. He shut the truck and went back to the bar.

The man had returned from the toilet and was deep in conversation with Gerard. Larry winked at Gerard, and slipped the keys of the truck from the key ring and put them in his pocket. He put the rest of the keys attached to the key ring on the table whilst the man was distracted by Gerard.

"Here have a small one," said Gerard as he brought three glasses with what looked like whiskey back to the table. Two contained red lemonade and the other one which he gave to the man contained whiskey. A double whiskey! After a few of these the man was slumped into the seat sleeping.

Gerard and Larry left the bar and went around to the side of the building where the lorry was parked.

They looked around the street where it was parked and it was deserted.

They opened the lorry and as confirmed by Larry it was filled with boxes.

"Right Larry, if we drive it to Chapelgate we can strip it and sell off the stuff. Pay day," said Gerard. "Jesus this day just gets better and better," he thought to himself.

Larry jumped into the driver's seat and started up the engine. Gerard jumped in beside him and Larry pulled away from the kerb. The side of the truck scraped off the wall as Larry tried to come to terms with the controls. He had never driven a lorry this size before. They rounded the corner and hit a bike parked at the corner. Larry was sweating as he tried to steer it around another corner, and then a few streets away he turned into a dead end. As they approached the end of the street, Larry couldn't stop the truck, so he just turned the engine off and took the keys from the ignition. It shuddered to a halt and ended up so close to the wall that the passenger door couldn't open.

"Fuck, what will we do now," said Larry as he opened the door and got out onto the street. They had driven down a lane that was a dead end.

Gerard jumped out the driver's door. He walked to the back of the lorry and opened the door.

"Right, let's just take what we can carry," he said to Larry.

"Fuck me, the size of them boxes. Here, Larry, take this and this," said Gerard as he threw a couple of small boxes containing radios towards Larry.

Larry looked around to see where they had come to a halt. They were in a side street and it was very quiet and deserted.

Larry had a brainwave.

"Hold on for a minute Gerard, I'll be back," he shouted, and he turned and ran to end of the lane and turned onto the street and went into a shop they had passed two minutes before.

He came back a couple of minutes later with two rucksacks he had bought from the camping supplies shop around the corner.

"You're a fucking genius, Lar. Here, take this and this," said Gerard, and they pushed six boxes containing radios into the rucksacks. Three in each rucksack.

They stood and looked into the lorry before they closed the doors.

"Gerard, look at them televisions. It's a pity we have to leave them, said Larry

"Ah fuck it Ger, let's just take these. They are too heavy to carry," he replied.

Larry threw the keys of the truck into a bin, and they laughed as they walked away from the truck.

"Guess what Mick and Angela are getting from me for a wedding present?" asked Larry.

"I'm guessing it's going to be the same present I'm getting them!" laughed Gerard.

"Radios!" they both roared in unison, and they laughed as they ran from the crime scene, just like they had done hundreds of times before, when they were younger.

*****

Mick finished work and walked towards the city centre to meet Gerard and Larry. He had gone home for lunch, and his mother had told him about Gerard, and how well he looked, and of the money he had given her. She told Mick that, as arranged, they would meet him at the dress suit hire shop in Mary Street.

Mick sat down to a large bowl of stew that was his mother's specialty.

"Are you all set for your big day son?" asked his mother. Mick was tucking into the stew, but in between mouthfuls he was telling his mother that Angela's mother had taken over the whole wedding.

"That's what mothers do Michael. It's her job," his mother laughed.

The wedding plans had been completely taken over by Angela's mother and sisters. Mick would just nod and agree to any new details of the wedding day. All he had to do was to get measured for the suits with Gerard and Larry, and turn up on the day of the wedding.

They had everything covered for the big day. Dresses, suits, hotel, photographs.

Angela and Mick had put a small deposit on a private landlord's flat, a few minutes from Chapelgate. They had being saving hard for the small wedding, and also for pieces of second-hand furniture from Cluxton's for the flat.

Pancho and Joxer delivered the furniture free of charge to the flat as a wedding present.

Angela had asked Imelda to be a bridesmaid for her, along with one of her sisters, Linda. Mick wasn't very happy about this. Imelda had given up the sewing factory job, and had told her friends she had got another job as a shop assistant the far side of the city. But the word going around was that she had been seen getting in to and out of cars, and that she was prostituting herself.

Angela dismissed this as gossip, saying, "Just because she has gotten a nice job and wears nice clothes, the people of Chapelgate Gardens are jealous."

Mick was also doing well in work. His boss knew he was getting married, and he gave Mick a position in the lost and found department of the train station, and this brought extra money in his wages – also, a few little perks. Items that weren't claimed within a year, the staff had an option to buy them. It was amazing the items that were handed in as lost property. Mick was able to buy a complete set of plates, cups and saucers that were brand new and still in the box. He bought other items for the kitchen so all in all they were putting a nice little home together for a small amount of money.

Mick walked up the three flights of stairs to the top floor of the building, where the dress hire shop was. Angela had picked out the suits for the wedding. As he walked through the half open doors at the top of the building, he had to adjust his eyes to the dim light of the hire shop. He could make out a mannequin in the corner of the shop dressed in a morning suit complete with top hat.

He looked around and whispered, "Ehm, hello."

There was no response.

"Hello, is there anybody here?" he called out again.

A movement caught the corner of his eye. The arm of the mannequin moved upward towards its top hat, and a voice came from behind it.

"Good afternoon, sir. I shall be with you shortly."

Mick jumped back in surprise and called out, "Jesus Christ!"

Gerard came out from behind the mannequin.

"Gerard, you fucker," laughed Mick.

"Frightened the shite out of ye there, brud," he said to Mick, and approached his brother with a big smile. They put their arms around each other.

"How's it going Mick?" asked Gerard.

"Fine Ger, and you?" asked Mick.

"Good. I'm good," he replied.

Larry came out behind the mannequin also, and watched Gerard and Mick hug each other, laughing at the joke they had played on Mick.

"You look fucking great, Ger – and your hair, what's going on there?" laughed Mick.

"He's like a hippy, isn't he, Mick. Them Brits are turning him into a hippy!" replied Larry, as he tried to involve himself in the conversation.

"Hi Larry, Yes, you're right, a bloody hippy!" laughed Mick, as he patted Larry on the shoulder.

"The bloke is gone downstairs to get something. He should be back shortly," said Larry, as he refused the cigarette offered to him by Mick.

"That's grand, Larry. Sorry, I forgot you were off the fags. Ger, here, take one, God, you look great. How's things going over there? Are you doing OK?" said Mick, as he struck a match and lit the cigarette.

Gerard and Mick talked for a few minutes about the past few months, and about how Mick and Angela were looking forward to the wedding.

"The Foley wedding!" announced the man as he walked in on the trio.

They all looked to where the sound came from, and saw the small man in the waistcoat and the glasses stuck on his forehead walking towards them.

"Right, I have to measure each one of you, and then you can pick the suits up next week – on the Friday. The wedding is on the Saturday, yes?" snapped the man in a squeaky voice.

"That's right. I'm the groom," said Mick.

Mick stepped forward and offered himself to be measured first.

"My fiancée has already given you a deposit. Is that right?" said Mick, as he held his arms up as the small man measured him.

Gerard and Larry looked at each other and Larry mouthed the word 'fiancée' to Gerard and they both laughed together. Mick looked over his shoulder and he knew that Larry had been slagging him about the word 'fiancée'. He smiled at them, saying, "Piss off, ye pair of bastards!"

The man measured Mick with the tape, and was writing all the details in a small notebook.

"OK, that's you done, Mr Foley. Next!" the little man said.

Larry stepped forward, and the man dropped to his knees and began to measure Larry's inside leg. Larry looked down at the bald patch on the man's head and he looked across at Mick and Gerard. Larry rolled his eyes, and put his head back, indicating that he was receiving oral sex from the kneeling man. At this the two of them burst into uncontrollable laughter.

The man squinted through his glasses at the two lads. He somehow knew that they were slagging him.

"Right, you're next," he called to Gerard.

He was used to the way some lads would take the piss out of him, but he didn't mind, as he knew that most of the lads would have had a few drinks on them and would be in high spirits. In fact, he didn't need to measure any of them, because he was so long tailoring that he could measure and get the correct size of most men to within an inch of their correct size just by looking at them.

"Right that's it. Pick the suits up on Friday," said the little man.

They left the shop and decided to go back to Chapelgate and to have a pint in The Bell. As they walked towards Chapelgate, Mick noticed Larry and Gerard carrying the rucksacks.

"Is me wedding present in that rucksack?" he asked Larry.

Gerard and Larry looked at each other.

"Well, a couple of them." laughed Larry, and he told Mick about the truck and the radios.

Gerard had already decided to give Mick and Angela some money for a present, and Larry had told Gerard that he would give them two of the six radios, and they could sell the other four, and he would just take a third of the money. But Gerard insisted that the four radios would be sold, and they would split the money fifty-fifty.

As they walked and laughed, they recalled the days when they had left school, and when they used to steal from the docks, and all the times they would cling to the back of trucks as they made their way to and from the docks with goods imported for the shops in the city.

Mick was telling the lads about how Angela's mother was organising everything.

Chapter Nineteen

Angela left the factory after work, and she was to meet Imelda outside, at the back gate. Imelda had arrived early and was waiting for Angela. She had left her job a few months before.

As Imelda waited for her friend she recalled the night that she brought Liam here to have sex with him. She had used this place on regular occasions as it was always deserted at night.

Imelda's life had changed since that night.

On Monday, Wednesday and Friday nights, she would take herself on her own, to the area where she had her first encounter with Liam. She was a bit nervous at first, as she would wait for cars to pull in and she would approach the driver. If she didn't like the look of the driver, she would just turn and walk away, and then the driver would just drive off. She decided to pick two customers each night – that earned her ten pounds each night, three nights a week. She would often question herself about what she was doing.

The men she went with were nearly always married, and she actually took pity on most of them. Some nights, when she would sit in the car with a man, he would only talk, and not have sex at all. She couldn't understand this, but the more she went with men, she realised in her mind that they were the weaker sex. Some of the men she met were not much older than herself, and most of the times she liked the sex with them. If she didn't like a man after she had been with him, she would not arrange to meet them, and made some excuse or other.

One night a man pulled into the kerb and she jumped into the car with him after they agreed on the price and what he wanted her to do. He seemed like a nice man about forty years old and judging by the ring on his finger he was also married. As they drove to where she normally went to have sex with men he started to ask her personal questions. Imelda started to get suspicious.

When he stopped the car at the back gate of the factory he turned to Imelda.

"Who looks after you?" he asked her. She noticed now that his demeanour had changed from when he had picked her up. There was a change in his tone of voice. Imelda was nervous.

He indicated that he would give her security.

"Terrible things can happen to a working girl on the streets," he said in an intimidating tone.

She didn't like the man, and she had already decided not to have sex with him. She thought to herself, "He wants to be my pimp. If I give in to this, I would be giving him most of me money, and he sounds like a nasty piece of work". She had to think quickly.

"I'm OK. I have a man – a detective – he's local. He looks after me, but give me your name, and I'll give it to him and maybe you can work something out with him. Actually you don't have to give me that, when I got into this car he had already taken the registration number. He was sitting in the car that was parked across the road. Do you remember seeing the car?" she lied.

The man pulled back in surprise and started to look around the deserted lane way to see if the car had followed. He didn't remember seeing any car parked across the road.

"But it could have been there," he thought to himself. Now he was nervous.

"Er … mm ... I was just enquiring. Look I forgot I have to pick up the missus. Here take this, and lets just forget about everything," he said as he took out a ten pound note and gave it to Imelda. "Look I have to go now, keep that and get a taxi back. I'm sorry I can't drive you," he mumbled. Imelda got out of the car and as the door closed he sped off with smoke coming from the wheels of the Cortina.

She never came across him again. She didn't know where she had got the idea, but she decided to use this story in future.

As she stood looking at the girls leaving the factory, she recalled the night she had sex with Liam in the yard, and how she realised how easy it was to make money. She stood in a doorway and kept out of sight from some of her old work mates. She didn't want any of them to see her, as she had heard that some girls had put it around that, 'Imelda was on the game'.

The girls poured from the back door of the factory, and most of them wore their work overall.

Imelda looked at her own clothes. She had started to buy more modern and expensive clothes than she was used to. She had the money and the time to shop. She had told her friends that she had a job on the south side of the city, in a ladies' clothes shop, and that was how she explained to Angela and her friends where she got her clothes. She told them she could get great discounts.

Angela walked with her sister Linda through the gates, and they heard Imelda call out. The three of them met up and Angela looked at Imelda's new clothes and praised her style.

"God, Imelda, that's a lovely dress – and your hair ..." Angela remarked, as she stroked the fabric of the dress.

"A woman bought it and brought it back to the shop because it was too small for her, and Mrs Fitzgerald, that's the owner, well she told me to take it, as she wouldn't put it back on the racks for sale. She's a lovely woman, and a great boss." lied Imelda.

The three of them turned and walked towards Chapelgate.

Angela told Imelda that Gerard had come back from England that morning for the wedding, and he was staying until a few days after the event. Her mother had met Mrs Foley at the shops, and told her about Gerard's return. Angela and her sister had gone home on their lunch hour and their mother told them all the news.

As they walked, Imelda heard her name being called behind her.

"Bradshaw, are you still on the game?" called out a girl from a group of workers who had just left the factory.

The girl who called out was Jean Reid, who worked with Angela. She was a bully. When Imelda worked at the factory, she kept well out of Jean's way. She wasn't afraid of her, but she just never wanted any trouble with her.

Jean had managed to get a couple of girls sacked through her bullying and manipulation of her workmates.

Imelda stopped and turned to face where she heard Jean call from.

"Don't mind her, Imelda, she's just bleedin' jealous, the bitch," said Angela as she tried to link Imelda and walk on.

Imelda pulled away from Angela and turned towards Jean and the few girls that stood with her.

"Ask your fucking da. He can't keep his hands off me, ye bitch!" shouted back Imelda.

Jean's friends held on to her as she tried to walk towards Imelda, furious at her answer. Imelda turned and linked Angela and Linda.

"Come on girls, let's go and meet the lads – we have to sort out your hen night, Angela," she said.

Imelda turned and stuck her two fingers up at Jean, then turned and walked on.

The three of them walked towards Chapelgate, singing, *"I want to be Bobby's girl, I want to be Bobby's girl. That's the most important thing to me."*

*****

Jem was standing at the corner of his flats complex when Pancho and Joxer came along, with their box car piled high with turf. Pancho was sitting astride the turf as Jem used to do, and Joxer pushed from behind.

"Jem, Jem, over here mate!" called Pancho, as he saw his old buddy leaning against the wall of Chapelgate Gardens.

Joxer heard him call out, and lifted his head to see where Jem was. The box car came to a halt, as Joxer came around to the front and walked towards his old workmate.

Pancho jumped from the top of the pile of turf.

"Jesus, you look great Jem. How's things in jolly old London?" mimicked Pancho in a cockney accent.

Joxer had a big smile on his face as he came up to his friend and patted him on the shoulder.

"Great to see ye, Jemser," he remarked.

Pancho walked over, and he too patted Jem on the shoulder.

"Well, are yis millionaires yet?" asked Pancho.

Jem laughed and shook his head.

"Jesus, Pancho. It's a bit of a mad place, that London. Me and Ger are working for Larry's uncle. We just drop stuff of from one place to another place. He gives Ger the money, and we have a flat that he looks after the rent," replied Jem.

"So you're doing the same job over there as you were with me!" suggested Joxer.

"Picking stuff up in one place and dropping it to another," said Joxer.

Jem squinted his eyes up.

"Er, yes, I suppose so … well kind of. But the pay is much better," replied Jem.

Pancho told Jem that he and Joxer were thinking of buying a little van. He told Jem that when they had dropped some more furniture into the second hand shop a couple of weeks earlier, the owner asked them to do some drops and pick ups of furniture, but they would need a van or a small truck. So they had decided to look out for a van and buy it between them.

When Jem heard this, and when he saw how Joxer and Pancho were getting on so well, he was happy for them, but he was also a little jealous. He was homesick and he missed his life in Chapelgate Gardens. On the way over from England, he had come out onto the deck of the ship for a cigarette on his own, and it was then that he had decided not to return to London. He knew Gerard would do better on his own in England, because Gerard was more confident, and sure of himself than he was.

When he saw Pancho and Joxer so close, and how they were starting to get some sort of little business together. Jem knew that he was out of the loop. He thought to himself that he would just end up on the dole now, or bite the bullet and go back with Gerard to London. But he really didn't want to go back. So he was facing a life on the dole. Pancho told him about how they had been putting money by every week to get the van.

"JAP Transport," said Joxer out of the blue.

"What the fuck is JAP transport" asked Jem.

"Joxer and Pancho's transport. Our initials," replied Joxer.

Pancho was smiling at Jem.

"What do you think, sounds great doesn't it?" said Pancho with a big smile on his face pleased at the prospect of having the name plastered all over their new van.

"Sounds great. Yes I think that's great," replied Jem. He felt really left out now.

They decided they would all meet in The Bell that evening, and catch up on everything that was happening.

Joxer pushed the cart and Pancho ran alongside, then climbed aboard the loose sacks of turf. As he sat astride the top of the load, Jem remembered how he used to sit up there, and he was the driver in *Stagecoach* with John Wayne, and Charlton Heston in *Ben Hur*. As he watched Joxer bent over pushing the cart, he thought to himself, "I miss all this!"

*****

Gerard was standing at the bar when Imelda, Angela, and Linda walked in. He noticed how grown up and mature Imelda looked, and her clothes looked more expensive than the normal Chapelgate local girl.

Imelda didn't notice Gerard at the bar as she entered.

She sat in beside Larry and Mick, and Angela sat down on the other side of Mick. Gerard couldn't help noticing that Angela was starting to get a bump – he realised he had been away a few months now.

He looked over and waved to Imelda, as she looked over to where Mick pointed when she asked Mick where Gerard was.

When he had left for England, he had put any sort of relationship with Imelda on the back burner. He remembered the night of Rory's funeral – how he satisfied her not far from where she was now sitting. He remembered the way she just dropped him on their return to her flat.

The night walking back from the hospital where Larry's father was laid out, and the conversation they had. He knew that Imelda's path and his path were not parallel. As he watched her smile and laugh with the others, he realised that she was right about the two of them.

"Would you get a load of him. Jesus, Ger, you need a haircut!" remarked Imelda, as Gerard put the drinks on the table.

"And you look fucking great, too. How're ye doin' Melda? You look good," he smiled back at her.

Imelda fluttered her eyelashes at him mockingly.

"You say all the right things to me. What are you after?" she replied.

"Angela, you're blooming. How are you kid? Linda, hello – haven't seen you in ages, kid. Can I get you a drink? Linda! One day me and you kid," said Gerard, as he greeted the girls.

Linda was very shy and her face went bright red at Gerard's joke.

Whenever Gerard talked to Linda, she would always go as red as a beetroot. She was only seventeen, but had a big crush on Gerard since she was about fourteen. Gerard went back to the bar and ordered the drinks for the girls. Imelda watched as he walked to the bar, and was distracted when Angela asked her a question.

"Am I right, Imelda?" was all Imelda heard.

"Sorry Angela, what did you say?"

"I was just saying to Mick and Larry that Gerard looks great," repeated Angela.

Imelda looked at Gerard and couldn't help notice the change in his appearance. He looked more mature and his long hair and the expensive denim jeans that were the fashion in London made him stand out. He seemed to have an aura of confidence about him.

"Suppose so! But don't fucking tell him that or he'll get a bigger head than he already has," said Imelda sarcastically.

Gerard returned to the table with the drinks.

"Here you are Angela, er, sorry future sister-in-law. Here Imelda that's for you, but ye wanna see what I have for your sister," joked Gerard. And he put the other drink in front of the red faced Linda. "Here Linda, now don't be lookin at me, get your own fella," he laughed. Linda was thrilled at the attention she was receiving from Gerard.

"Leave her alone Gerard, she can do better than you," joked Imelda.

The girls talked about the wedding and the bridesmaid dresses, and as they talked across Mick, he got up and sat in beside Larry Burke.

"You're fucked now. Mick. It will be 'weddin', weddin', now 'till you walk up the aisle, and then it will be 'baby, baby, baby' after that," laughed Larry.

Mick let out a little laugh.

"I know the wedding is one thing, but I'm really looking forward to the baby. I can't wait until she has it, Larry. I know we will be OK," replied Mick.

Larry thought about Marie and his own baby. He wouldn't be able to have the same relationship with his child as Mick would have with his own.

Gerard turned to Larry.

"Give me two of them there radios. I just sold one to O'Brien and one to Mr Fitzpatrick at the bar there," said Gerard. Larry reached out and took two radios from the bag.

He came back and put some money into Larry's hand and pocketed the rest.

"Thanks, Ger," said Larry, as he put his into his pocket. "He's only here a day, and I've just been getting money from him since he got here." thought Larry to himself.

Gerard turned to Imelda and offered her a cigarette.

"Thanks, Ger. Well, have you a girlfriend over there in London?" she asked.

Gerard pulled hard on the cigarette and sat back, then blew the smoke into the air.

"You know me, Imelda. I have no loyalties to anyone. No time for girlfriends. Just work and make money," replied Gerard.

"What do we say about loyalty Larry?" asked Gerard to his friend.

Larry laughed and together Gerard and Larry said, "If you want loyalty. Buy a dog" and they both fell around laughing at their old sayings.

"What is it you do over there anyway?" asked Imelda.

"A bit of this, and a bit of that. Just stuff for Larry's uncle," replied Gerard, non-committal.

Imelda smiled at him in a way that acknowledged that was all the information he was going to give her about the work he was doing in London.

"Jem and me have a nice little flat, though. Well, it was a nice little flat when we got it, but it's a bit of a tip now. We are not very domesticated!" laughed Gerard.

"You need a woman to look after yous!" laughed Imelda.

"So how are you? I heard you got a new job," said Gerard, as he changed the topic of conversation. Imelda took a sip from her glass and shrugged her shoulders.

"Yeh – a clothes shop in Grafton Street. I wasn't going to spend me life in that sweatshop of a factory," replied Imelda.

"So how did you land a job like that? Do they know you're from Chapelgate?" asked Gerard.

"Where the fuck is Chapelgate? I live in Clontarf," replied Imelda.

Gerard laughed at her reply.

"You're sharp one Imelda," he replied.

The door of the bar opened and Pancho came in, followed by Jem and Joxer, who were laughing and joking. They headed straight for the lads and sat down.

Pancho and Joxer shook Gerard's hand and told him he needed a haircut.

"You're like one of them bleedin' hippies. Flower power and all that," stuttered Joxer.

"Here Joxer put on one of them hippy songs on the jukebox," said Larry and he handed Joxer sixpence.

"Jukebox, what bleedin jukebox" exclaimed Gerard.

"Ahh Mr O'Brien got one in a few weeks ago. The Dillon's are going mad since he got it in," replied Larry.

"Jesus you turn your back for five fucking minutes and the world changes in Chapelgate Gardens" joked Gerard. They all had a good laugh at Gerard's sarcasm.

Pancho turned to Angela and said, "Your mother was looking for you, Angela. I told her we were all meeting here, and she told me to tell you that the photographer wanted to talk to you and Mick."

Angela turned to Mick.

"I think we should go back to the flat and talk with him. He needs to know a few things about the church and stuff," she said.

Mick nodded and said, "OK, I'll just finish this pint and we will head up."

Linda got up and said, "Don't worry, I'll tell him to pop over here." and she was out the door in a flash.

They decided to stay and wait for the photographer to come to them.

"We're buying a van, Ger, and setting up a transport company," said Pancho, as he returned from the bar and sat beside the lads.

"That's great, Pancho! Jesus, you guy's must be doing well," replied Gerard.

"We're making a few bob – isn't that right, Joxer?" replied Pancho.

Joxer nodded as he sipped his lemonade from a bottle through a straw.

"We have our logo and all Ger. JAP. Transport. Joxer and Pancho's transport," said Joxer.

"Well, me and Jem were talking to a bloke in London and he had a transport company but it went bust. Isn't that right Jem said Gerard. Jem laughed and nodded.

"Larry O' Sullivan Ger, that was him. He put his initials on his van too but couldn't get any work. LOST Transport," replied Jem.

They all had a good laugh at this joke. Joxer didn't laugh. He just didn't get it.

Jem felt a bit left out as the lads discussed the van with each other. He tried to change the topic of conversation.

"Me and Ger are flying over there in London – that right, Ger?" he said.

Gerard nodded and said, "Yes, we are doing OK, only thanks to your uncle, though, Lar."

"Would you think of going over, Larry?" asked Imelda.

Larry shook his head.

"No fucking way. I'm doin' alright here. Why would I want to deprive all them ould wans I'm keeping happy out there in Clontarf?" he laughed.

Imelda looked over at Larry.

"You're a dark horse, Lar. No girlfriend in Chapelgate, and all the girls after ye. You're a good catch. So who's the lucky lady?" quizzed Imelda.

Larry got a little flustered. Gerard noticed and turned to the rest of them.

He wanted to take the conversation away from Larry.

"Listen, a few weeks ago I was in this pub in London, and this girl came over to me and tried to start a conversation with me, but I was doing business for Jimmy. So I couldn't really get talking to her until I had finished the business I was doing for Jimmy, so Jem, tell them what I said to her – tell them," he said.

Jem started laughing.

"I couldn't believe me ears, lads. He turned to her and said, 'Listen, love, you look like shit, but come back to me when I have a few more pints in me, and you might look a lot better.'"

They all laughed at this, and Jem put up his hand to get their attention.

"Listen, that's not the best part. About an hour later, she came back over and said to Gerard, 'Are you drunk enough now?'" and they all laughed even louder.

"Hussy," said Angela.

"Slut'" laughed Imelda.

"But that's the way they are in London, Angela. The women are very forward, and not at all like the girls in Dublin," replied Gerard.

"Sluts!" replied Angela.

They all laughed at Angela's outburst. The door opened and Linda walked into the bar, followed by a man of about fifty, wearing a hat and a camera slung around his neck. He introduced himself to Angela and Mick and asked them a couple of things he needed to know about the plans for the wedding day. Mick bought him a drink and he sat with them for about ten minutes. He got up to go, and Gerard looked at the camera around his neck.

"Have you any film in that yoke?" he asked.

The man looked at the camera.

"Yes, this is always on the ready. It's one of them new ones that gives you the picture in two minutes. Polaroid, that's what it's called," he replied.

"Right, come on, you guys. Let's get all of us in this picture. I don't think we have a photo of us all together," he said as he put his arms around Imelda to his left and Larry to his right.

Pancho got in beside Larry, and Jem and Joxer got in beside Linda, Mick and Angela. The man stood back from the group and put the camera to his eye.

"Cheese!" they all chorused.

The flash caught Gerard by surprise. The man pressed a button on the camera and a piece of paper spat out of the front of the camera. He pulled it out and blew on the glossy side of the paper.

"Here you are, boys and girls," he said, as he handed the photo to Angela.

Larry nodded over to Gerard.

"Give him that other radio, Ger, will you," he said.

Gerard gave the man the box and thanked him for the picture. They all poured over the black and white photo and it started to come clearer as it dried. Imelda looked at the photo and it captured them all against the stained wallpaper of The Bell. She noticed that they were all looking at the camera except for Gerard. He was looking to his left at Imelda. She was the only one that noticed this.

"Here, give me that," said Larry, as he took a pen from the inside pocket of his jacket.

He turned the picture around and wrote on the back of it. *Pancho, Larry, Gerard, Imelda, Angela, Mick, Linda, Jem, Joxer. The Bell, November '67.*

"Now, that's the first time we've all been together in a picture," he remarked.

The music in the background playing on the jukebox was the Mama Cass song 'San Francisco, with flowers in your hair'" Over the years that followed every time Gerard heard that song it would remind him of that night.

They stayed in the bar for the rest of the night, and later the picture which had been passed around all night, lay on the table. During the night someone had rested a pint glass on the photo and it had a brown ring on it. Gerard picked it up and put into his inside pocket. Nobody noticed him taking it, or so he thought. Imelda noticed Gerard putting it into his pocket.

They all left the bar at different times, and it was Gerard and Larry who ended up together, worse for the wear from all the drink they had consumed that day. As they made their way back towards Larry's flat, Larry told Gerard about the previous few months with Marie.

Chapter Twenty

Larry looked up and down the road outside Marie's house. He wheeled his bike around to the back of the house and knocked on the door. Marie opened the door and smiled. He kissed her as he entered the house.

"Mr Window man, stop, we will be seen," she laughed as she walked backwards into the kitchen. Larry and Marie had become close over the past few months, despite her being married and the age difference between them. Larry touched her stomach, which was slightly swelled.

"How's our baby?" he asked.

Marie stroked Larry's head and he looked at her.

"I love you, Marie, and I know we discussed it about you're staying with your husband, but really he doesn't deserve you," he said.

"We talked about this, Larry. I like you a lot Larry, but I'm married. I know you want me to leave him, but it wouldn't work. You're a great guy and you deserve to live a little before settling down," she said to Larry.

In fact, Marie loved Larry, and she was thrilled she was carrying his baby. But she needed stability, and she knew that Larry couldn't give her the lifestyle she wanted. She also didn't want to tie Larry down. He was still only twenty years of age. Things were also changing in her husband's life. He had been promoted a few weeks earlier, and when he told her of the new plans for their life, she had to sit and think of her future. She had decided on a plan, and she would just keep things to herself for the moment.

"The lads came back the other day from England – you know, the lads I was telling you about. Gerard, and Jem. They came back for the wedding next week," he said to Marie

Marie knew that Larry's life was so different from the life she lived. She attended functions with her husband, and talked about politics, current affairs, and the state of the economy.

Larry was a kid to her. But she loved his stories about his life, and the fact that he satisfied her sexually and that he was there most days was a bonus for her.

Her husband treated her as a housekeeper, and at functions he made sure she talked to the right people who could help his career. He played golf and went to GAA matches with his superiors, and everything was geared towards him and his career. She didn't dislike her husband – she found him to be self-absorbed and not very attentive to her. Even when she told him of the baby he took the news calmly and raised a little smile.

"That's great news, Marie. What, with my promotion and the baby, things are going quite well, would you agree?" he replied when she told him.

Larry and Marie made love that afternoon, and there was more passion from Marie as she held onto Larry, and as she climaxed she cried into his shoulder.

Larry just felt the tears fall onto his skin. He didn't ask her why she was crying.

"Probably the hormones," he thought to himself. He had seen his sister go through her pregnancy and the times she would just burst out crying for no apparent reason. 'Hormones', his mother would say.

They lay there, and Larry talked non-stop about his friends and his life. Marie stroked his chest and thought of all the days they had lay beside each other, and the sweat falling from their bodies as they made love in the sunny afternoons during that summer.

Later, when he was leaving the house, she stood at the back door. As he walked towards the back gate, she called out to him.

"Larry, come back for a second," she called to him.

He put his bike against the gate and walked back to her.

"What?" he asked, looking puzzled.

She took his face in her hands and pulled him towards her. She kissed him full on the lips and held his face tightly.

"I feckin love you Lawrence Burke." she said to him as she let his face go.

Larry looked at her puzzled.

"It's your hormones," he laughed at her.

She watched him walk with his bike out of the gate. She stood there until he turned at the top of the lane and he was out of sight. She came back into the house and went into the back bedroom where the suitcases were arranged on the floor. The cardboard boxes packed flat on the floor were waiting to be filled with the contents of the house. She knelt down and started to put clothes into the case. The tears rolled from her face again, and onto the sweaters that she was folding.

*****

It was three days before the wedding, and Imelda had just emerged from a blue Ford Anglia car and walked along the road towards Chapelgate. It was only ten fifteen, and she already had fifteen pounds in her purse. Liam, her very first client, had picked her up at nine thirty, and he paid her extra for oral sex. Then he dropped her at a bar in the city, where she had arranged to meet another man. She had been with this man before, and even though he paid her the five pounds, all he ever did was talk while she played with his penis. Sometimes she would have to stifle the giggles as he would just ramble on talking rubbish – sometimes repeating the same word over and over. But she knew when he was about to come, because he would lift himself up slightly and then would repeat the words, "Marilyn Monroe, Marilyn Monroe … M … M … M … MARILYN!" as he climaxed.

The grey Zephyr pulled slowly alongside her. It was so quiet that she got a fright when she heard Dermot Kelly's voice.

"Imelda, can I have a word?"

She turned and saw that Dermot was all alone in his car. The car he had dropped her off in, on the night she had the trouble with man who was giving her hassle.

"Oh God, you gave me a fright there, Detective," she said, as she approached the car.

The door opened and she sat in the front seat. He pulled away and drove to a bar the far side of the Liffey. On the way to the bar Imelda looked at Dermot and realised that he seemed more afraid of her than she of him.

She tried to strike up a conversation, but he just said, "Wait, we'll talk in the pub."

It was a quiet bar, very smoky and dark. They entered the snug area, a place normally used by ladies, as the main bar was nearly male dominated. He tapped on a glass panel, and when it opened a bald man peered through the hatch.

"Good evening, Dermot" the man said to Dermot as he wiped a glass with a cloth.

"A pint and a glass of Guinness, Sean, thanks," replied Dermot, and he turned and sat in beside her.

"Imelda, what are ye playing at, girl?" he said in a friendly tone of voice.

She looked at him but she didn't feel threatened or intimidated.

"Detective, I'm ..."

"Dermot, call me Dermot," he interrupted her.

"Dermot, I'm doing no harm on anyone, and I make a few pounds. I don't want to end up working in that sweat shop of a sewing factory for the rest of me life, or till some fucker knocks me up and I end up in Chapelgate with a couple of fucking screaming brats and a waster of a husband," she snapped back.

"So we're not the maternal type, then?" he quipped back.

They both laughed at his frankness. The hatch opened and the drinks were put through, and then it closed as fast.

"Here, I'll pay for these," said Imelda, as she reached into her purse for money.

"No need. Free to all coppers here. A little perk of the job," replied Dermot as he picked the drinks up and put them down on the table in front of himself and Imelda.

"You've got to be careful out there on the streets. There is a nasty bunch going around. Tell me, have you not been approached already about protection?" he asked her, as he picked up his pint and buried his mouth into the creamy head.

"A few weeks ago, a little runt tried it on with me, but I told him that I had a detective as a minder. He hasn't bothered me since," she replied as she also picked up her glass.

"Cheers," she said.

Dermot nearly choked on his pint as he tried to laugh at her brashness.

"Jesus Christ, well you've some neck Imelda, I'll give you that," he replied.

She told him about the way she operated, but she was hoping to move from Chapelgate and get a flat, maybe in Rathmine's, but somewhere no-one knew her. She told him things that she had never discussed with anybody before, and even about her uncle and the way he had abused her before. She liked this man, and felt so comfortable with him, even though they were from different backgrounds, and he was about fifteen years older than her. Dermot felt the same way with her, and he told her things about his life that he would never in a million years tell to anyone, especially to someone from Chapelgate Gardens.

They sat there for over an hour and talked and talked.

Dermot looked at his watch and it showed eleven thirty.

"Listen, Imelda, I've no problem with you working, but keep off the streets. Leave it with me for a few days. I know a sergeant who has a house in Phibsboro. There are a few girls working from the house, and ... well ... the sergeant looks after them. He also gets them clients, and they are safe. I will sort something out for you kid, so don't do any more punters till I get in touch with you. Is that alright, chicken?" he replied.

Imelda looked at him.

"Why? Why would you do that for me?" she asked.

He looked at her, and she could see by his face that he was sincere.

"To tell you the truth, I don't know, but I like you, kid. I always liked you from the first ever time I saw you a few years ago, skipping along from school with your friends.

"I just wouldn't like to see you get hurt on the streets, even though I think you are well able to take care of yourself. But to be on the safe side, let me do this for you," he pleaded with her.

"Thanks Dermot, I will. But only on one condition," she replied.

"Er, what's the condition?" he asked.

"You look after me full time. I mean, if I get any trouble, I only want you to take care of it. Please," she pleaded back to him.

"OK. I'll be your guardian angel," he laughed back at her.

They left the bar, and as he drove towards Chapelgate she looked at his features. He was about thirty-five or six, and he was quite handsome in a quirky way. She reached across and touched him.

"You don't need to do that for me Imelda, really I am not looking for that from you. I worry about you that's all," he said to her. His tone of voice told Imelda that he was sincere.

"I know. I want to do this for you," she replied in a soft voice.

He started to get hard. She rubbed him and then she opened up his trousers and leaned across with her head in his lap. When he pulled in at the back of the factory where Imelda normally went with her clients, he turned the car lights out and took her by the shoulders and kissed her face. The seat went back, and she put her leg across him and pulled her pants to the side. As he entered her she moaned in pleasure.

*****

"The stag night is tomorrow, so where will we go?" asked Gerard.

The lads were sitting on the canal bank. It was freezing, and they were all huddled around a small fire. Mick was at work, and the lads were trying to sort a good time for Mick's last night of freedom. Jem, Gerard, Larry and Pancho sat at the fire. Joxer wasn't there, as he had the 'flu, so that counted him out.

"That hotel, Flanagan's, that's a great place to go," said Larry.

"Yep, I heard that was a great place for pulling the birds," replied Jem.

They all looked at Jem and then they laughed.

"You pulling birds, Jem? For fuck's sake, give us a break," said Gerard.

Jem blushed.

"Piss off, you's feckers," he laughed.

It was decided that they would meet in The Bell and go off to the hotel later in the night.

"The Bell will be packed tomorrow. "Buckets of Blood" is getting buried tomorrow, and he fucking knew everyone. So we would need to get there early," said Larry.

"Buckets of Blood" was a local character everybody knew. He was about four foot ten, and when he got drunk he would try to start fights. He would brag and boast about when he was younger, when he robbed banks and ran with a crew called 'The Canal Gang' – they would cut up anybody that got in their way, and then throw them into the canal. He would walk into The Bell and strut around pulling himself up to his full four foot ten inches saying hello to everybody he knew.

He always sat at the bar on the high stools but it would be an ordeal for him to climb onto the stool as he was so small.

People would humour him when he told stories, and pretend to be in awe. If he got the hump with anyone and started a fight, he would stand his full four foot ten inches and call out to his mates, "Hold me back, or I'll cut him to ribbons! There'll be buckets of blood, I swear … there'll be buckets of blood," he would shout.

It would be comical looking at him sizing up to a man six foot or more and shouting for his mates to hold him back. In all his days he had never been hit, nor had he hit anybody.

Gerard offered his cigarettes around to the lads, and Larry would have loved to have taken one, but he had promised Marie he wouldn't.

"Fair play to you, Lar, I couldn't give up the fags," said Pancho, as he sucked the smoke into his lungs.

"I just got fed up with the fags, and anyway they give you cancer," replied Larry as he looked and envied the lads.

"I don't give a bollocks, cancer or not, I love me fags," said Pancho.

Gerard threw a stone into the fire and turned to Jem.

"Jem, would you mind hanging back here for a few weeks. Jimmy asked me to ask you, I think he needs you to bring over a package for him," lied Gerard.

Larry and Pancho knew he was lying, and they looked at Jem to see his reaction. Jem was secretly delighted at this outcome.

"Er, yes, no probs, Ger. If that's what Jimmy wants, yeh, no probs," he replied.

Gerard was relieved at Jem's reaction.

There was an awkward silence.

Pancho broke the silence.

"Let's paint his bollocks," said Pancho out of the blue.

They all looked around at Pancho.

"Jesus, what's going on in that head of yours?" replied Gerard.

Jem secretly thought it was a good idea.

"Mick! Let's paint his bollocks! Why not?" replied Pancho.

Jem then piped in.

"Yeh, let's paint his bollocks!"

They all laughed at the prospect of Mick getting his bollocks painted.

"We can't do that, lads. Jesus, he's me brother." laughed Gerard.

They sat around the fire, throwing bits of wood on it and telling jokes.

"So what do you do for Jimmy?" asked Pancho, innocently.

Gerard looked at Larry in a knowing way.

Pancho, like Jem, was a little bit naïve, and Gerard didn't want to elaborate on the dealings he had been engaged in for Jimmy. Even Jem didn't know the gravitas of the business that was going on under his nose.

Jimmy had realised this the first day he had met Jem at the train station, and he had told Gerard not to give Jem any information regarding the drops and the pick ups. More often than not, Gerard went on his own to do the business for Jimmy.

"We just do pick ups and drops! Don't we, Ger," said Jem out of the blue.

Gerard threw another piece of wood on the fire.

"Yeh, just dropping packages off here and there. It sounds fucking dodgy, but I asked Jimmy and he told me that the packages contain money, backhanders for blokes that work in the council, who tell Jimmy where the next big building projects are being started. Then Jimmy sells the info on to big Irish building firms, and they go after the work from there. He's very clever," replied Gerard.

Larry looked at Gerard and a wry smile came across his face.

"Fuck me, Gerard Foley is the smartest bloke I've ever known. Where the fuck! How did he come up with that story?" he thought to himself.

"Now, that's being ahead of the posse," said Pancho, looking around the group.

Jem nodded in agreement. Larry looked at Gerard and nodded.

"Yes, that's thinking ahead of the posse alright." remarked Larry.

"Here, Jem, take this and get us a few cakes and a couple of bottles of milk, will ye? Fuck, I miss the Irish milk lads – isn't that right, Jem? The milk's poxy over there," said Gerard, handing Jem a pound note.

Jem nodded in agreement about the milk, and he took five pounds from his pocket and waved it around.

"It's all 1 right I have money. What cakes do you want?" he replied.

"Get me two apple rolls Jem. Thanks mate," said Gerard.

"Cream doughnut for me," said Larry.

"Come on Panch, let's get a few bottles of milk, and a couple of "Gur" cakes," replied Jem as he stood up and walked towards the gates.

Pancho threw a piece of wood onto the fire, and got up and walked off with Jem.

Jem was glad to have Pancho on his own, because he wanted to see if Joxer and Pancho would take him back on.

"After all, it was my job before Pancho's," he thought to himself.

They climbed over a small fence and headed for the creamery stores on Chapelgate road.

"Jesus, Jem, will you be OK for money waiting on Jimmy to call you back? You could go back anyway. Jimmy doesn't own you," said Pancho, as they strolled towards the shop.

"To tell you the truth Pancho I have a good few bob stashed away. Anytime me and Gerard are out Gerard pays for everything," said Jem.

"Do you get wages from Jimmy or what?" asked Pancho.

Jem thought for a moment. He realised that no, he didn't get any wages from Jimmy. Gerard would just give him a few quid every week. Some weeks he would give him twenty five quid, and other weeks fifteen. But he had nothing to pay from this. The food Gerard paid for. The rent for the flat, and the electric, Jimmy paid. So over the months he had saved quite a few pounds.

When he really thought about it he was just a passenger, for Gerard.

Jem kicked a stone in front of him and then he stopped and looked at Pancho.

"I didn't really want to go back, Pancho, and anyway, I think the police are looking for me. I got arrested a few weeks ago, and I never appeared in court, so I wasn't going to go back. I was glad that Ger told me Jimmy didn't need me, yet," replied Jem.

Pancho didn't want to bring it up, but he knew he had to say something about the situation with Joxer.

He was getting on so well with Joxer, and they were earning money.

But Jem had been with Joxer a lot longer than he had, and he knew that if Jem stayed in Dublin he might be pushed out of the partnership.

So he decided to bring it up with Jem.

"Pancho, Joxer and me are doing ok with the turf and even the furniture stuff for Cluxton is going to take off if we get the van. But if you're staying on here I will step back and you can go back with the Joxer fella," said Pancho.

Jem shook his head.

"No fucking way Pancho.. I wouldn't step in between you blokes. No way pal. I walked away and went to England. You two are getting on so I ain't going to fuck that up for you, no way," replied Jem.

Pancho was delighted at this news but he felt sorry for Jem. He was coming back to Dublin and he had no job.

Jem could see that Pancho was worried, and he had been a little jealous about how Pancho and Joxer were getting on so well.

"No Pancho, I will sort something for meself," said Jem.

"Thanks mate," said Pancho patting his mate on the back.

Pancho changed the subject

"Arrested, for what"" asked Pancho.

"I woke up in the cell Pancho, and the last thing I remembered, was taking these fucking pills that this bird gave me. I had a few flashbacks since then. I remembered standing on a scaffold with me jacket around me like a cape, like, like fucking Superman," said Jem.

"What sort of pills?" asked Pancho.

"Blue job's, don't know what was in them but they fucked up me head that night," said Jem.

Jem told Pancho about the girl passing the pills into his mouth from her mouth and how he remembered being in the flat with all the music and the lights.

"Pancho London's not for me mate. Too fucking mad for me pal," said Jem.

"What's the birds like?" asked Pancho.

"Rides. Their rides, Pancho mate. They're forward though. Fuck me, they just do it with ye. Ye don't even have to be going out with them. If they want you they just fucking tell you mate. Not like the chick's in Chapelgate," replied Jem.

Pancho laughed.

"Fucking chick's. Jesus, where the fuck did you pick that up," laughed Pancho.

Jem laughed with him.

"I know. Chicks, groovy, right on man. That's the way they talk Pancho," said Jem.

"Gobshites," laughed Pancho.

"I have an interview for a job already, Pancho, but don't say anything to Ger. I wasn't going back anyway, but I didn't know how to tell Ger," lied Jem.

Pancho was relieved at this news.

"Great, pal. Jesus, I was kind of worried that you would want to go back with Joxer," said Pancho.

"No, I'm moving on to bigger and better things. No offence, Pancho, but after London, I'm open to more exciting things. You know, Dublin is me lobster," said Jem.

Pancho looked at Jem.

"Dublin is a lobster? What the fuck does that mean?" he asked.

"Ah, a saying I heard in London, The world's me lobster, oyster or something like that. It means … well … it means that I can do and go anywhere, I think. Ah, fuck, whatever! Dublin's me lobster! That's me new saying, Pancho," said Jem.

"Come on, Panch, let's get something to eat for the lads," he replied, and they walked towards the shop.

*****

"Larry, come over with me. Jimmy asked me to ask you. He said your ma would be OK with the girls here. You and me, we could do well with Jimmy." pleaded Gerard to Larry.

Larry kicked a piece of wood and walked around the fire.

"It's not that easy, Gerard, I have to stand by her," replied Larry.

Gerard sighed out loud.

"Me bollix! You don't have to stand by her. For fuck's sake, she's a married woman, and she's fucking years older than you, Larry. What the fuck are you thinking of? For fuck's sake, snap out of it!" shouted Gerard, as he saw his mate sulking, and he spotted a change in him he didn't like.

Larry shrugged his shoulders.

"I know, Ger, but it will be my kid, mate. I can't just fucking head off to London. I owe it to the baby." pleaded Larry.

Gerard looked at his friend and saw him in a different light. He was a lot quieter now and he had even given up smoking.

"I can see he's changed, and that's because I've been away. Fuck me, that one will tie him in knots. He's lost his fucking balls, the gobshite." thought Gerard to himself.

"Larry, she's married to a fucking copper – and not just an ordinary copper by your stories about him. You're not even in the fucking running. If he gets the wind of the word about you, you're fucked, mate. You're out of your depth, pal. For fuck's sake, Larry! Cop on, it's them and us mate," pleaded Gerard to his best friend.

Larry looked at Gerard and could see his friend was upset over his decisions. But he had to stick around. Marie was a breath of fresh air to him.

"He was going to get out of Chapelgate, but he would do it with Marie. He had to save money, but he would do it," he thought to himself.

"Gerard, you don't know her. She's lovely. She makes me feel like a man. Gerard I love her" pleaded Larry.

Gerard took another cigarette from his packet and offered one to his mate. Larry refused it and shook his head.

"Lar, you're not thinking straight. She has you by the bollix, and you can't fucking see it mate. You won't even take a fag, for Christ's sake. She probably has you sitting down to take a piss," said Gerard.

Larry turned on his friend.

"Who the fuck do you think you are?" A fucking wet day in London, and you're "Ronnie fucking Kray!" Do me a favour, Ger, and fuck off back to London, and mind yer own business!" shouted Larry at his friend, and he turned and stormed off.

Gerard stood up.

"Lar! Larry. Come back ... ahh, for fuck's sake Larry," pleaded Gerard.

Larry was disappearing out of sight, and Gerard sat back on the grass.

"Fuck you, Larry Burke, fuck you," he screamed in his head. He sat there for a while, and the two lads came back with the cakes and milk.

"Here, Ger – where's Larry?" asked Jem innocently as he looked around for Larry.

Gerard stood up and took a cake from the bag and took a bite aggressively.

"I'll tell you where he is, mate – up his own fucking arse!" shouted Gerard.

Jem and Pancho looked at each other, confused.

Pancho whispered into Jem's ear.

"Fuck me, you turn your back for a minute and world war three breaks out," he laughed.

They both giggled. Gerard turned around and caught them giggling.

"And yous pair can go fuck yourselves," he laughed as he threw the cake through the air and it bounced off Jem's head.

Chapter Twenty-One

Mick left for work, and walked through the early morning drizzle. He had been promoted to a new department, and he liked his new position. When his boss had heard that he was getting married, he started to take an interest in Mick. He liked Mick, and he knew he would do well in the company. Mick wasn't looking forward to that evening, as the lads had organised a stag party, and he knew they would try and strip him, or do something stupid to him. But it was a tradition that the bride and groom would have to have a party a couple of nights before the wedding. He was to finish work at six, and he was to meet the lads at seven in The Bell. Gerard told him not to bring any money, as he was paying for the drinks, and they were going to a dance hall in the city, and he would pay for that too.

He had seen a big change in Gerard since he had returned to Ireland. He noticed how mature in his attitude he was.

He also noticed the money. Gerard had a lot of money to spend. He also noticed he never talked about his job. He was worried that Gerard would get himself into some real trouble. Not the "mickey mouse" robbing and stealing that he had been doing in Chapelgate, but real stuff with real consequences.

When Gerard had told his Mother he was returning to England after the wedding she was very disappointed.

"Just stay for the Christmas son," she pleaded with him one night.

But Gerard was adamant. He wanted to go back to London. He had big plans now that he knew that Chapelgate was not for him.

Mick and Angela were saving every penny that they could get, to put towards the wedding, but the hotel they had booked for the reception was looking for all the money up front. Because they were from Chapelgate Gardens, the hotel wanted to be paid before the reception went ahead. The hotel had been stung before, when a wedding party from another inner city complex had just paid a deposit, and after the reception, the manager couldn't find the bride or the groom to pay the balance.

As he walked, Mick thought to himself that all the fuss and the bother that comes with the wedding was well worth it as he only had to look at Angela and he knew she was the one for him.

Angela had arranged to meet Imelda that evening, and then they would meet the girls, and go on a night out as a hen party. Angela wanted just her sister, Imelda, and two of her workmates to be at the hen party. They were to go to a cabaret club, and then dancing. Angela was to start her holidays that day, so she had a couple days before the wedding to prepare.

Imelda lay in bed and looked around her room. She could hear her mother getting the tea and toast ready for her father before he went to work on the docks. Her father went to the docks every day to try and get casual work, and more often than not if he didn't secure work that day, he would just go to an early opening pub and try and get in with the ganger foreman, so as he might get picked for work the following day. The docks were regulated by a system that wasn't fair, as the casual workers were picked on a day to day basis, and if you were a good worker, or knew the foreman, or bought your way in by way of a bribe to the foreman, you would get work. But the unemployment situation meant that there were always too many men for too few jobs.

She lay there in the dark with just a small shaft of light coming through at the top of the door, where there was a glass panel. She sat up and reached out, and picked up a little box hidden under her bed. She opened it up, and took the twelve pounds from her bra and put it with the rest of the money in the box. She looked at the money and couldn't believe how quickly she had accumulated such an amount. She was earning on average fifteen to twenty ponds three nights a week and the money she had from her uncle Paddy was still in the box. She had been looking for jobs, and also for a flat as her mother had been asking her too many questions. She was buying new clothes and she would explain it away to her mother that the shop she worked in was changing the window display and the owner gave her a big discount on them. But she had no job and her mother was asking if she could come to the shop to see where she worked. Time was ticking for Imelda.

She heard her mother coming towards the bedroom door, and she quickly pulled the bed covers over the tin box.

"Melda! Melda! I have your tea, love," called her mother, as the door opened and the room filled with more light.

She sat up and fixed her pillows behind her and pushed her long hair back off her face.

"Thanks, Ma. Pass me my bag will you, and give us that ashtray off the press, please," she said to her mother.

Her mother did as she asked and left the room, and Imelda heard the muffled voices of her father and mother. She lit a cigarette and took a long drag, then took a long sip from her cup.

"Mmmm…this is a lovely cuppa," she thought to herself.

She pulled her knees up to her chest and stared at the half open door. She tried to make out what her mother and father were talking about.

"I hope I get something today, chicken. I bought that bastard a heap of drink yesterday, and he swore to me that the ship that arrived last night had my name on it," she heard her father saying.

"Well, after plying him with drink, and the money you'll spend on the fecker after today, that's if he does pick you, it's hardly worth the bother, and that's the truth," replied her mother.

Angela was used to this conversation, as she'd heard it hundreds of times before. She knew her father. Given the chance, he was a good worker, but the system that operated on the docks was archaic and very flawed. But that was the system that operated at that moment in time. Imelda had been earning a lot of money lately, and she had come to terms with the morals of it – not that she had really thought much about the morals of having sex with men for money. As she saw it, she was giving herself to boys and not being respected, but now she controlled things with her sex. She had developed a kind of sixth sense whereby she could read situations before they happened. She could think fast on her feet, and sometimes she even surprised herself with her replies to a smart punter, or when she would talk to anyone in authority.

When she left her job at the factory, she had told them she was starting a new job, and even went to the trouble of asking for a reference. She had to create a new life for herself outside Chapelgate, and she would make stories up about things that would have supposed to have happened in the clothes shop that day.

She would describe to the girls how women with rich husbands would pay large amounts of money for dresses, jackets, and lately because she was starting to buy nice shoes, she told them the shop also sold shoes. She told her mother that she was off every Tuesday and Thursday, and that her starting time for Saturdays was eleven thirty. This meant that Mondays, Wednesdays and Fridays she would leave the house at ten in the morning and head into the city for the day. She knew that she would have to get her own flat eventually, because she didn't want to be hanging around the city all day. There was only so much shopping a person could do. But her love of fashion and clothes, meant her days were filled with learning. What new designers were in. What type of shoes and handbags went with what clothes.

*****

At eleven thirty that morning she was in a shop in Grafton Street, a shop she would go to at least once a week to buy a dress or a top. But a couple of weeks, before she had gone into this shop, before she had spruced herself up and gotten her hair done. That particular morning, as she browsed through the rails, she noticed the shop owner keeping an eye on her.

She thought to herself, "God, I've loads of money and that "Wan" is watching me! She must think I am a shoplifter or something." That day she bought a lot of dresses and tops in the shop, and went straight to the hairdressers and had her hair done. She made sure that from that day she would look the part with her hair, and clothes, and since then, when she went into any shop, the assistants never gave her a second glance.

Imelda realised that if you looked the part, you could get away with anything. She decided then that, no matter what, if she hadn't much money, she would always look as if she had.

She wandered through the rows of clothes looking at the colourful fabrics. She heard the woman behind her call her, and she turned to see what the woman wanted.

"I hope you don't mind if I ask you a favour, but my assistant is after phoning in sick, and I'm on my own. Could you look after the shop for about two minutes? I need to go to the toilet." asked the owner of the shop, a woman of about fifty, who was dressed impeccably.

Imelda had built up a relationship with the lady over the last three weeks. As she would wait for the lady to ring up her purchases and bag them, they would make small talk. The lady didn't realise that a few months before, she had been observing Imelda in case she stole something.

Imelda looked so different now. Her make up, hair, clothes. She had transformed herself.

"Of course. You go ahead, I've plenty of time," replied Imelda, as quick as a flash.

The lady smiled and touched Imelda on the side of the arm, and hurried off to the back room. Imelda walked around the shop and caught her reflection in the mirror. She was dressed in a grey suit and white blouse. Her flaming dark hair was tied up in a high pony on her head, and it shone, as she had it conditioned every time she had it done. The new red lipstick, and expensive make she wore, made her look very attractive. She could have passed for any one of the models, she saw on the pages of the fashion magazines she read.

She had been having her hair done every week now, because she could afford it, and it showed. She stood at the back of the shop and looked down at the racks of expensive clothes. Grafton Street was not the cheapest street to shop in Dublin.

She thought to herself, "If I had come in here a few months ago in my work overall from the sewing factory, I wonder would she have asked me to look after the shop while she went for a piss."

"Excuse me, miss? Do have this in a larger size?" asked a woman from the dressing room, who appeared from behind the dressing room curtain.

Imelda had been putting dresses that had fallen to the floor back on to the racks, and the lady thought she was an assistant. She recognised the dress the lady had, as Imelda had bought one the week before.

"Yes, I have that dress myself, and I have that in a black. What size, and colour do you want?" asked Imelda, in a voice that she only used when she shopped in the posh shops she frequented.

The lady stood out from the cubicle.

"What do you think? A ten?" she asked.

Imelda looked at her and realised the woman was more a twelve in size, but she didn't want to embarrass her.

"They are a very small fit. I had to get a twelve, and I normally take a ten," replied Imelda, and she walked down the aisle and returned with the dress in black.

A few seconds later the lady came out of the cubicle and asked Imelda her opinion. As Imelda talked to the lady, the owner came back from the toilet, but stood at the door and observed Imelda.

"What do you think?" asked the woman.

Imelda looked at her. She was about forty, and her nails were manicured and her hair was well looked after. She looked as if she wasn't short of money.

"Here, take a look at this bolero jacket with the dress. It makes you look slimmer," said Imelda, as she took a jacket from the rail.

The lady walked up and down towards the mirror, and she agreed with Imelda.

"It does, and you're right, the ten is a small fit in this style. I really need a twelve. I'll take the dress and the jacket. Can you wrap them for me?" asked the woman.

The owner was just about to butt in, but Imelda took her by surprise.

"What shoes are you going to wear with them? Because I have a pair of black sling backs, and with the dress, it sets off the whole look" lied Imelda.

Imelda knew where the shoes where, as she had been in the shop so many times. She brought the shoes, which were very expensive to the woman and showed them to her.

"Shoes are my weakness," squealed the woman as Imelda helped her put them on. The woman walked up and down the aisle in the shoes, and Imelda told her that they would be lovely with the dress and it would be a shame if she didn't have them to finish the look.

The woman looked at the price of the shoes and frowned.

"God they are a bit more expensive than I thought. The hubby will go mad if I overspend," she replied.

Imelda could see that this woman wasn't short of money so she pushed her a little more on the sale.

"But sure aren't you worth it. I bet if it was a set of golf shoes for himself he wouldn't think twice about asking you if he could buy them," joked Imelda.

The woman thought for about two seconds and replied.

"You're right, he wouldn't give me a second thought if he wanted something for himself. Can you wrap them for me?"

"Oh, I don't wor …" she couldn't finish her sentence, as the owner came from behind the door as soon as she heard Imelda try to explain to the lady that she did not work at this shop.

"That's fine, we will wrap that for you," said the owner, as she came up to Imelda and smiled at her.

The lady went into the cubicle to change.

"Thanks for looking after the shop for me. Do you have a few minutes miss? Sorry, I don't know your name." whispered the owner.

"Imelda – it's Imelda," she replied.

Five minutes later, the owner, June Clooney, sat talking with Imelda, and they were sipping coffee from two china cups. Imelda had never tasted coffee before. She liked the bitter taste from it.

"I hope you didn't mind me asking you to look after things, but the girl I have is always letting me down, and when she is here she just stands around. She never helps the customer. But she's a daughter of a friend of mine, and I promised her mother I'd give her a job," said June to Imelda.

"I didn't mind. I'm not busy today, so it was no problem. But why keep her on if she can't do the job? Some girls would kill for a job here," replied Imelda innocently.

June thought for a moment.

"I don't know why, but her mother and myself go back a long way, so I suppose I think I am being loyal. But I know the girl doesn't want to be here also – she only comes in because her mother makes her. I wouldn't mind, but she doesn't need the money – her father is a millionaire!" laughed June.

"I wouldn't mind meeting a millionaire myself!" laughed Imelda.

"I hope you don't mind me prying, but do you work?" asked June.

Imelda was on the spot but she held herself together.

"I'm in between jobs at the moment. I was manufacturing supervisor in a sewing factory, but I like the retail end more. I have been applying to some of the large department stores for a position as a buyer," lied Imelda.

June poured out another coffee and offered one to Imelda.

"Would you like a job here, as an assistant? I saw you with that customer, and you know and I know that the last time she fitted into a size ten was when she was walking up the aisle. Then you pushed that jacket on her. The shoes! How did you know they would go with the dress?" asked the woman.

"Well I like fashion and let's face it she would be better buying the shoes here rather than anywhere else would you agree?" replied Imelda.

June nodded in agreement.

"You have a knack for sales Imelda. I think you would like it here, so what do you think" asked June.

Imelda was surprised at the offer and couldn't believe her luck. She hesitated for a couple of seconds.

"Don't jump at this job just yet girl. Deep breaths," she thought to herself as her legs went to jelly.

"Well, I am after applying to other stores," she bluffed.

"Look, Imelda, sometimes in large stores it takes years to climb the ladder to be a buyer. I go to London twice a year on buying trips, and if you show any initiative, maybe, just maybe, I can bring you with me on my next trip. I can teach you a lot in the rag trade," replied June, who secretly hoped Imelda would take her up on her offer.

"Imelda" reminded June of herself when she was younger. There was something about Imelda that she liked.

Imelda's legs were shaking now.

"Jesus, this woman is begging me to take a job. Take it – take it," she was screaming to herself.

"I think I would like to work here, June. Yes, I will take the offer. When do I start?" replied Imelda who couldn't believe her luck.

"Are you able to start now?" asked June.

Imelda got off her chair and put her bag down on the counter.

"I'm all yours," she said, and offered her hand to June.

"Imelda Bradshaw," she said, as she formerly introduced herself to June.

"June Clooney, welcome to the firm," replied June.

*****

Angela met Mick in Talbot Street at one o'clock. They were both on their lunch hour, and they sat in a small café sipping tea and eating chips.

"Is everything sorted for the hotel? The rest of the money, I mean." asked Mick.

Since they had decided to get married, the whole proceedings and arrangements were taken out of Mick's hands. Angela's mother was in charge of the whole thing. Mick's mother was glad to take a back seat, because since Rory's death, she was having bad bouts of depression.

"Are you looking forward to your hen night?" asked Mick, as he smiled at Angela.

She raised her eyes up to the sky.

"Mick, I hate them sort of nights as it is ... but my hen night? I hope the girls don't go too heavy on the celebrations. The last hen night we had, they all went mad. I never drank as much in me life, so I'm going to take it easy tonight, Mick. What about the lads. Have they anything planned?" asked Angela.

"I hope not, Angie. The wedding is in two days, and you know me with the drink. If I get drunk it takes me a week to get over it! By the way, Gerard gave me this towards the wedding," said Mick, as he took the twenty pound note that Gerard had given him that morning from his pocket. Angela took the money and put it into her little clutch bag she had beside her. "My God Michael, Gerard seems to have a lot of cash on him since he came home. I just hope he's not into anything illegal" replied Angela. Michael shook his head. "He'll be fine. Gerard Foley looks after number one. Don't you go worrying about him" replied Michael reassuring her.

She held his hand and looked into his face. Mick was embarrassed and looked around the café. There were a few people sitting in the café, but no-one was taking any notice of them.

"Angela, stop staring at me," he whispered, and giggled as he squeezed her hand tight.

"Mrs Michael Foley," she said.

He looked at her face and then to the little bump in front of her.

"The Foley family," he said as he touched her belly.

She took his hand.

"Mick Foley, I will make you a good wife," she said to him.

"And I will make you a good husband, Angela Hopkins," he replied.

They stayed holding hands in the café for the rest of the lunch break.

Chapter Twenty-Two

The Bell was packed with people from the funeral of "Buckets of Blood". Mr Dillon was in top form with his singing.

The jukebox was out of order and the Dillon's were delighted.

As Gerard, Mick, and Jem entered the bar, they could hear him singing a Matt Monroe song, 'From Russia with love'. The pub, which was full of people, was hushed to hear Mr Dillon sing.

"Good on ye, Bertie!" shouted a man from the back of the house, as Bertie Dillon paused and took a breath.

"Shuuuurrup!" shouted a drunk from the other side of the bar.

"Any sign of Larry?" asked Gerard to Pancho, who was sitting in a corner of the pub trying to hold on to seats in the packed pub, for the lads.

"Shuuuurrup!" shouted the drunk again.

"Shuuuurup your fucking self!" shouted back Gerard.

"Ssshhhhhh …" hissed the crowd at both of them.

When Bertie Dillon finished, he shouted out, "God bless Buckets of Blood!" and he picked up his pint and drank a mouthful.

Gerard repeated himself.

"Any sign of Larry," he asked. He hadn't seen Larry since they had had a row the day before.

None of the lads had seen Larry since he walked off after the row with Gerard.

Gerard was worried about his friend.

"Maybe I was too harsh with him," he thought to himself.

*****

After the row with Gerard, Larry went to Clontarf to see if Marie was at home. As he cycled towards Fairview a car passed on the other side of the road going towards the city. He recognised Marie in the passenger seat and her husband was driving. Larry stopped and watched as they drove by. He noticed Marie was laughing at something her husband had said to her in the car. She never noticed Larry as she passed by.

He decided to keep on going towards Dollymount and walk along the strand to clear his head.

He went right to the end of the Bull Wall at the entrance to Dublin port. A very large cargo ship was leaving for somewhere in the world. He thought of what Gerard had said to him about going to London. He mulled it over in his head and after an hour he headed back towards Chapelgate Gardens. He had decided to stay put and try and be part of Marie's life, and his baby's life.

"Fuck Gerard Foley. Who does he think he is? Giving me advice! He doesn't even know Marie," he thought to himself.

The next afternoon, Larry was in good spirits as he rambled around Clontarf. The weather was after improving, and the rain had stopped. He had a lot of work to catch up on, and this meant more money. He had decided to forget about the row he had with Gerard, and he vowed to meet the lads that evening and have a great night on the town with them. He was going to let Gerard know that he was staying put in Dublin, and when he had enough money he would get Marie to move in with him. And when the baby was born, they would be a proper family. "Marie loves me" he thought to himself.

He was cleaning windows about ten houses down from Marie's house. The truck parked outside Marie's house didn't grab his attention straight away, but after cleaning the back windows on the house, he came around to the front, and knocked on the door to get paid. He looked towards Marie's house, and saw a man in a brown overall walking out with a large cardboard box in his arms, which he put in the back of the truck.

The door of the house opened and he was distracted from looking down towards Marie's house and the truck parked outside.

"Hello, Mrs Kavanagh. How's the back today?" asked Larry to the woman who had opened the door.

He always made small talk with the customers when waiting for his money.

"Agony! I'm a martyr to me back." cried the woman.

She counted out his money.

"There you are now Larry. You're losing a customer, I see," she said, and indicated towards the truck outside Marie's house.

Larry was confused, and he looked up towards the house.

"How do you mean, losing a customer, Mrs Kavanagh?" asked Larry.

That lovely lady – the policeman and his wife – they moved out yesterday," she said.

Larry was taken aback.

"Mov ... moving! Where? Jesus, where?" said Larry in a startled voice that took the lady by surprise. He turned back to the woman and asked again.

"Moving? When? Where?" he pleaded.

"I ... er ... I don't really know. Does she owe you money?" asked Mrs Kavanagh innocently.

Larry didn't wait for her to hand him the money, but he ran towards the truck. The man was just getting into the back of the truck, and was positioning the box he had just put on it. He was surprised when Larry called out.

"Hey mister. Where's the people from the house?" Larry called to the startled man.

The man looked at Larry and could see he was upset.

"Why should I tell you? Who are you?" asked the man.

Larry realised that it must look strange, the way he was carrying on, in front of this man and Mrs Kavanagh. He settled down and lowered his voice.

"I'm ... I'm the ...er, window cleaner. Where have they moved to?" asked Larry, and he smiled shyly at the man.

The man looked at Larry cautiously.

"They owe me money for cleaning the windows," said Larry.

The man saw Larry back down, and thought to himself.

"Jesus, they must owe him a lot of money". He came over to Larry and knelt down in front of him.

"Galway, actually Oranmore," replied the man.

Larry was devastated. He stared at the man.

"Galway! When?" he pleaded.

"Yesterday. I know the other driver, Pat, he took a load yesterday, and he couldn't manage to fit everything on one load. That's why I am picking up the last few bits and bobs. I can give them a message if you want. I'll be heading down first thing in the morning. They probably forgot to pay you. I can pick up the money from them and meet you here tomorrow night with it, that's if they give it to me," said the man, as he looked at Larry, who had just turned and walked away, saying,

"No, it's alright. It's OK ... er, thanks."

The man stood on the back of the truck scratching his head.

"Feck me, he must have been owed a right few shillings, the way he's reacting," he thought to himself.

Larry went back to Mrs Kavanagh, who was still standing at the door with the money in her hand.

"Does she owe you anything? She might have forgot about it," she said.

Larry looked at her blankly.

"No, it's fine ... I ... no, it's fine, but thanks. No, she owes me nothing," said Larry.

"I think he got a promotion or something but when I was talking to "herself" at the shops the other day she was telling me that they were moving to the country and her husband was starting in a new district. Lovely people and what with the new baby on the way," said Mrs Kavanagh.

Larry tried to hide the hurt he felt. He just smiled sheepishly and nodded to Mrs Kavanagh. He couldn't even bring himself to speak.

He took the money, turned, and walked off, wheeling his bike. He walked towards the seafront and sat on one of the many benches that were dotted along the seafront.

"I must be the biggest fucking eejit in Dublin."

Larry felt betrayed. "They must have been heading to Galway yesterday when they passed me," he thought. He felt sick in the stomach.

Gerard was right – she doesn't give a fuck about me. How could I not see this coming?

Larry sat on the bench thinking about how only the other day, Marie had been so nice to him. They had made love. How could I have not picked up the signals. She had it all planned out," he thought to himself.

"So where to from here? If I follow her, she'll tell me to fuck off. The baby – I'll never see it. Maybe just as well – who'd want me as a father? The fucking bitch," he talked to himself on the bench for over an hour. He then decided on what to do for the future. "Why? Why?" was all he could repeat to himself.

He cycled back towards Chapelgate with the ladder chaffing the side of his leg.

"I'm a fucking nobody that's why! A fucking nobody that's what I am," he thought to himself.

*****

Imelda was shown the ropes by June, and they got on very well together that first day. June had seen something in Imelda that reminded her of herself when she had first come to Dublin in the late fifties. June was impressed with how quickly Imelda picked things up, and the enthusiasm she had in the work.

Just before five o'clock, June said to Imelda that she could finish for the day. Imelda had told her about her friend, Angela, and the hen party they had organised for that evening.

"Imelda, come in at two o'clock tomorrow, because you might have a little hangover in the morning, and with the wedding on Friday, just come in on Saturday at eleven. Is that ok?" said June to Imelda, as she was putting on her jacket to leave for the day.

"Thanks, June, but I don't do hangovers! I'll be in here at ten in the morning and the same on Saturday," she said.

June was impressed. Earlier that morning, when she received the phone call from her friend's daughter, she thought she would never get a good shop assistant. She thought to herself that not only had she a good shop assistant in Imelda, but maybe a good right hand woman. Imelda walked towards the door, and then June called her back.

"Imelda, you never asked what the wages are, and you never gave me your address." asked June.

Imelda realised that, yes, she hadn't asked about wages, or given her address. That was something she didn't want June to know.

"Phibsboro. I live in Phibsboro, and I'm sure the wages will be better than my last job, June. Good evening, and I will see you in the morning," said Imelda, and she turned on her heel.

*****

Larry looked around the packed bar for the lads.

"Larry!" shouted Gerard when he saw his friend.

"Shuuuurrup!" shouted the drunk again.

Gerard, Mick, Jem, and Pancho looked over at the drunk and shouted back.

"Shuuuuurup yourself, ye bollix!"

They laughed at the way they had all shouted in unison.

Larry sat down beside Gerard, and he slapped Mick across his cheek in a friendly manner.

Gerard was glad to see his mate Larry. He was afraid that Larry wouldn't have come to the stag night because of the row they had.

"Can I get you a pint mate?" said Gerard to Larry as he put his hand out to his friend. "Sorry, Larry. I was out of order mate. I was trying to look out for you so don't mind me," said Gerard.

Larry shook Gerard's hand and smiled back at him.

"No need for apologies mate. You were right," replied Larry.

"No I wasn't Larry. You do what you think is right mate. Don't mind me I just see the bad in people. I can't help it," replied Gerard.

"Gerard just get me a fucking pint and give me one of them Woodbines, I'm gasping for a smoke," laughed Larry and he patted his mate on the shoulder. "I'll fill you in on the story later mate, but will you just get me the pint," laughed Larry.

Gerard offered him a cigarette and smiled.

"It's good to have you back," said Gerard.

"Last night of freedom, mate." Larry said to Mick as he popped the Woodbine into his mouth and struck a match.

"So much for giving up the fags, I knew you wouldn't last," laughed Jem.

"Go and ask me bollix," replied Larry and he sat own and laughed with the boys.

"Here, mate, are you OK?" said Gerard as he sat in beside his friend and put a creamy pint of Guinness beside him.

Larry stood up and lifted his pint towards Mick.

"Lads, may I give a toast to my good friend and former partner in crime, who has fallen to the enemy. He fought a brave battle to stay single but as we all know. There comes a time when the small head rules the big head. I give you Mick Foley. Cheers and good luck mate," said Larry and he lifted his Guinness to Mick.

The lads laughed at Larry's little speech and then Mick rose to his feet as the lads all called for "Speech! Speech!

Mick picked up his glass.

"Fuck you very much for that lovely speech Larry, and to all you losers, I thank you also," laughed Mick.

As he sat back into his seat the lads all raised their glasses to him.

They chatted and joked for the next hour and planned out the evening.

Larry turned to Gerard when he got an opportunity to talk to him in private and confided in him. Larry told Gerard what had transpired since they last talked. Gerard put his arm around his friend. "Fuck her!" was all he said.

"Bleeding women! They are all split with the one axe, aren't they mate," said Larry, and he took a long drag from the cigarette he had been longing for, for weeks.

Gerard smiled back at him.

"Are you alright, mate?" he asked.

Larry took another drag from the cigarette, and squinted his eyes as he blew out the smoke.

"She's gone Ger. Galway! You must think I'm a right mug?" replied Larry.

"No way Lar. But women can wreck your head can't they?" said Gerard.

"I suppose so. I've learned a good lesson Ger," replied Larry.

Gerard put his pint up to Larry.

"You're not the first and won't be the last to be fucked over by the enemy mate, so put it behind you. Get off the cross we need the wood," replied Gerard with a laugh.

"When are we leaving for London?" he replied as he clinked his glass with Gerard.

Mick, Jem, and Pancho heard Larry and looked at Larry and Gerard.

"We leave on the next stagecoach, pardner!" mimicked Gerard, and he grabbed his friend around his neck with the palm of his hand, and pulled both their heads together.

"Queers! I seen it in London – it's fucking full of queers," said Jem, as the other two looked on.

Gerard and Larry grabbed Jem and wrestled him to the ground, laughing.

"I'll give you fucking queers!" shouted Gerard and he and Larry grappled with Jem jokingly.

Pancho looked at Mick.

"Larry going to London as well. For fuck's sake, Mick, there will be none of us left in Chapelgate," he remarked.

Mick looked at the three lads rolling on the carpet of the bar.

"I know, Pancho! Would ye look at them, they are like kids. Gerrup outta that," laughed Mick.

"Shhhuuuuurrup!" shouted the drunk.

Mr Dillon turned to the drunk.

"You fucking sssssshhhuuuuurup!" he shouted.

The whole pub went into hysterics.

"Here's to Buckets of Blood, the only man in Chapelgate with the balls to fight anyone" shouted a man from the bar.

A shout of "To Buckets of Blood" went up all around the bar.

*****

Imelda looked at her watch. It was five fifteen and she was rushing to meet Dermot Kelly at the High Tide Bar. She was to be there at five, but the walk from Grafton Street took longer than she thought.

She entered the snug area, and Dermot was reading the Herald as she came in. There were two women in the far corner. They were fruit and vegetable stall holders from the markets, and when Imelda came in, they looked at each other. Imelda stared back at them. They turned to each other and resumed their conversation.

"Imelda, I thought you weren't coming," said Dermot, as he tapped the window to the hatch.

She sat in beside him with her back to the women. He ordered her a glass of Harp lager and sat back down.

"Well, how are you?" he asked her.

She looked at him and she had realised from the last few times they had met, that he was nicer than the man she thought he would be. When she used to hear the people in Chapelgate give out about the police, and the way they hassled the youths from Chapelgate, she didn't think that they had feelings. She thought that all coppers were nasty.

But her few intimate encounters with Dermot had changed her attitude of Dermot Kelly.

"I'm better today than yesterday. I got a job," she replied, and she opened her bag for her cigarettes.

The hatch opened, her drink was put through, and the hatch closed as quick.

"A job? That's great, Imelda. So you don't want me to sort that thing out for you with the flat, and ... well, you know," replied Dermot.

She took a sip from the glass, and shook her head as she swallowed the cool liquid.

"No. I want you to sort that out for me, Dermot. Please don't let me down," she pleaded.

"But you are working now, so you won't have to do that ... well, the other thing, any more," replied Dermot.

She looked at him and let out a little laugh.

"Have to? What do you mean by have to? I want to, Dermot. Want! This is my life, and my body, and if I want to do something I do it," she laughed.

Dermot was a little confused.

"But you have a job now. I just thought ... well ..." said Dermot.

"Just because I like sex, it doesn't mean I have to give it away, Dermot. Anyway, when can I move in?" she asked.

Dermot just looked at her and knew she was determined to go ahead with the plan. He told her about his friend 'the Sergeant', and about how he used to work the beat years ago. He told her about how he had seen the beatings the street girls got from their pimps and the punters.

So one day he set one girl up in a house he owned which he had set out in bedsits. As the other tenants moved out, he moved a couple of more street girls into the bedsits.

"But he runs a very strict house, and the girls like working from their bedsits" said Dermot

Imelda nodded.

"I've talked to him about you and he has a place coming vacant very soon. He's willing to rent it to you," said Dermot.

"He looks after the girls. The rent on the flat is a lot more than the normal, but you will be safe," said Dermot.

"So no more punters from the street?" asked Imelda.

Dermot took a drink from the glass.

"No. You see, the thing is, he won't allow that. He has a woman who looks after the house. She holds a client list, and you just tell her the hours you want to work and she sends the man to your flat. Usually after a few weeks or months you have your regulars and you just make your own arrangements with them. You just make sure you pay your "Rent!" On time, every week," replied Dermot, emphasising the word rent.

"The only thing I will tell you Imelda is that you will meet a better class of punter. In fact you will meet people you wouldn't expect to meet, I mean politicians, policemen businessmen and the like," said Dermot.

Imelda nodded and then a wry smile crossed her face.

Dermot noticed this.

"What? Tell me Imelda Bradshaw what's going on in that little head of yours?" he laughed.

"Better class," she exclaimed. "So even though these pillars of society cheat on their wives with prostitutes, just like the painter or the bricklayer, who pay over the same money, then they are, in your words. Better class! Do me favour Dermot! A fucking punter is a punter," replied Imelda with a tone of sarcasm in her voice.

Dermot took in what Imelda had said and couldn't help agreeing with her.

"What sort of a creature am I dealing with here?" He thought to himself. Imelda I'm sorry for insulting your intelligence," he said to Imelda.

"I call a spade a spade," Dermot. "Don't get me wrong Dermot, I sell me body for money. But If I ever get married and, if I ever meet the right man. I will be faithful because if I love a person then I give that person my body and soul," she replied.

Dermot nodded in agreement and couldn't help agreeing with Imelda's simple logic.

Imelda was pleased with the way things were working out between her and Dermot. She liked him, and when they had sex, he was very gentle and loving. She never took money from him, and she knew that she had one over on him.

But she would never betray him.

The two women were watching Dermot and Imelda with interest. They knew Dermot was a policeman as he often had dealings with them when investigating crimes in and around where they sold fruit.

Imelda was aware the two women were taking in the scene and she just threw them a look.

They looked away quickly.

Imelda finished her drink and Dermot asked her if she needed a lift, but she said she would walk to meet Angela and the girls outside the factory for Angela's hen night.

"Do your friends know what you work at?" asked Dermot innocently.

"Yes they know I work in a boutique! But selling my body for a living! That's not work Dermot," she replied with a little laugh.

She put her fingers to her lips and kissed them, and then she planted them on his cheek.

"Be good," she said, as she rose to leave. And as she passed the two women she stuck her tongue out at them.

The two women stopped talking as she left, and resumed as the door closed behind her.

Dermot looked down at the women. One of them smiled back in a sarcastic way.

"Good evening, Sir ," she said through her broken teeth.

Dermot stood up and polished off his pint. The hatch opened and he threw a pound note on the counter.

"Look after the ladies for a drink there," he said to the barman, and he headed for the door.

"Thank you, detective. May God bless you and yours." called back the two women.

"That's the Bradshaw young wan," said one of the women, as the barman put the two glasses of Guinness in front of them.

"Slut," said one woman.

"Brazzer," said the other, and they cackled as they clinked their glasses to each other.

After they took long sips from the free drink, one turned to the other and said, "A Gentleman always stands the traders a free drink. God bless him."

The other agreed.

"A real Gentleman!"

Chapter Twenty-Three

The lads left The Bell and headed towards the city centre. Mick had had three pints of Guinness and he was feeling tipsy, because he hadn't been drinking regularly at the weekends, as he and Angela were saving every penny.

Gerard had his arm around his brother, and they were talking about the wedding day.

Mick talked about Angela and the baby, and Gerard could see that he was very happy. He envied Mick because he had met someone he loved. Gerard would have liked to have what Mick had, but the only woman he had any sort of relationship with was Imelda. Even that relationship was difficult. Imelda had outlined her situation to Gerard the night before he left for London. She was more advanced in her years than any other girl he had ever met, even the girls he had met in London.

They walked on towards the city centre and had decided to do a pub crawl of all the bars.

Larry talked to Jem about the window cleaning round.

While he was sitting on the seafront contemplating his future, he had decided to give Jem the window cleaning round. He could trust Jem to drop money in to his mother every week, as a payment for giving Jem the window round. The business was quite lucrative since Larry had taken over. He had built up a lot more customers, and with the relationship with Marie, he had been in a nice place. That was before his world fell apart.

"You pay the mother every Friday, Jem, right? And you know the consequences if the money stops," said Larry, half joking, but whole in earnest.

Jem crossed his heart with his finger.

"Jesus, Lar, mate. You know I'll drop the few bob in to your ma. I wouldn't let you down, and if I get a good week, I'll put extra in. You know me – I'll do that." promised Jem.

Larry knew that Jem was sincere and he also knew that Jem would give his mother extra money if he had a good week of window cleaning.

"No, Jem. Just drop the same amount every week, and that's all. When I get back, I'll take it over again. That's if things don't work out for me over there," said Larry.

"Thanks Larry. I won't let you down," said Jem.

"I know Jem. I know!" replied Larry.

Pancho was relieved when he heard that Jem was taking over Larry's round, as it meant that him and Joxer could go ahead with the plans for the van. They had a drink in one pub then moved on to another during the evening.

Larry was worse for the wear with all the drink as he couldn't hold his drink and got very drunk very quick.

But by half eleven that night they were all very drunk.

*****

Imelda met the girls in a bar beside the factory. They would often have a drink there on Friday, after a long week working in the factory. Angela was sitting chatting with the girls when she saw Imelda standing near the door.

Larry was in the toilet of the Old Bog Road at the end of the night. He heard his name being called, and when he turned around it was " Christy" the man Gerard had given the package to for his uncle Jimmy.

"Hello there. Larry, isn't it?" asked Christy.

Larry looked at him and remembered him from that day.

"Oh yeh. Hello, Christy, Yeh, I'm Larry, Jimmy's nephew," replied Larry, as he tried to hold himself steady at the urinal.

"I thought I'd recognised you. Listen, if you come in here tomorrow afternoon, I'd like to run something by you." suggested Christy.

Larry looked at him suspiciously.

"Er … you can ask me now. I've a few drinks on me, but I ain't drunk" slurred Larry.

Christy laughed a little to himself.

"OK. Listen – do you want to come and do some business for me?" he asked.

"Thanks Christy but it turns out I've decided to go to London with Gerard," replied Larry.

Christy patted him on the back.

"That's fine son. Welcome to the firm, and tell Jimmy I'll be over in a few weeks," replied Christy, and with that he just left the toilets.

Larry finished and came out to the bar, where Mick was slumped over the arm of the seat, asleep.

Gerard was at the bar chatting to two girls. Jem and Pancho were deep in conversation beside Mick. Gerard caught Larry's eye.

"Lar, over here," he called out to his pal.

Larry walked over to Gerard, and was introduced to the two girls.

"Larry, this is Collette … and Grainne," said Gerard.

Larry tried to stand still, but his legs were giving him a hard time, and he swayed back and forth. Gerard wasn't as bad – he could hold his drink, unlike Larry. One of Larry's faults was that he couldn't drink much alcohol, as he got drunk after just a couple of pints.

*****

The girls were having a great time in one of the larger hotels, where there was a band playing. During the night the lead singer sang a song for Angela, and he came down from the stage and sat beside her, flirting and holding her hand.

Imelda paid for a few rounds of drinks, and the group noticed. She told them about her new job, but she said that she had been working there for weeks. She also told them how she was thinking of getting her own flat. Angela was proud of her friend, as she had heard that she had been seen getting into strange cars. She always defended her friend.

241

Imelda was talking to one of her old friends from work, Teresa. A shy pretty girl who had gotten married a couple of months before.

She noticed that Theresa had been looking at her watch all through the night.

Theresa was married to a local lad who had a fierce reputation as a boxer and nearly every weekend he would always be in some sort of trouble. Teresa had a bruise over her eye, and even with all the makeup she had applied on her face the bruise was still visible.

Imelda noticed the bruise.

She confided in Imelda that her husband was beating her up regularly and, any time she went anywhere, he would question her on her return.

"So he hit you because you were late coming home from work. The dirty little bollocks I'd fucking stab him in his sleep if he done that to me Teresa. Why don't you just leave him?" said Imelda to her friend holding her hand and comforting her.

Teresa was crying.

"I love him Imelda and he can't help it. He just loses his temper and lashes out," replied Theresa.

Imelda could see that no matter what she would have said to Teresa, it would fall on deaf ears. Teresa would not leave her husband and her life would be one long series of beatings and abuse. Imelda couldn't understand why women stayed married to men who beat them or abused them.

Imelda listened to Teresa and comforted her but, she knew that Teresa wouldn't take any advice, so Imelda didn't offer it.

The girls were having a great time and danced all night.

Later the girls went to the chipper for chips, and Imelda paid. Imelda decided not to overdo the drink that night. She wanted to make a good impression in her new job. Angela was glad that they didn't do anything crazy to her, as she was starting to get big in the belly, and also she tired easily since she had become pregnant.

They walked towards Chapelgate after they had left the chipper. Angela told Imelda of her fears and her hopes for the future.

"Mick is a nice guy, Angela, and you are lucky to have met a nice guy, because believe me there are some nasty men out there," said Imelda.

Angela was linking her friends arm and she hugged her.

"I know, Imelda, He is very considerate and generous," replied Angela.

"Jesus, who would have thought that "you" would be the first to get married out of the gang?" Imelda questioned.

Angela patted her belly. "Well we hadn't much choice Imelda," she laughed.

"Is he good in the sack, Angela?" asked Imelda.

Angela giggled and pushed her friend away.

"Imelda Bradshaw, you're feckin' mad!" laughed Angela.

They walked on, and the other girls were walking ahead.

Angela looked at her friend and said to her, "Imelda, do you know what they are saying about you since you left the job?"

Imelda didn't want to tell Angela about her double life.

"It's just jealousy Angela. I don't give tuppence for what they say about me. But Angela, I love me job so fuck them," replied Imelda.

Angela looked at her friend and was proud that she had gotten a good job and seemed to be doing well.

"You're right Imelda, fuck them. Jealous that's what they are, just fucking jealous," said Angela.

"Listen, Angela, you're getting married on Saturday, but tomorrow meet me for lunch at my shop. That will sort out the gossips, and you can look anybody in the eye when they try and run me down," replied Imelda.

"Imelda, you don't have to prove anything to me. You're my mate, so the rest can just piss off. You don't need to prove anything to me. Whatever you tell me, well that's good enough for me 'Melda," replied Angela.

Imelda looked at her friend.

"No, I want you to come and meet my boss, and I have a surprise for you." laughed Imelda.

"What's she like?" asked Angela.

"Well I can tell you this Angela. She treats me well and the pay is very good. I want to do well in the shop and who knows in a few years I'll have my own shop," replied Imelda.

Angela squeezed her friend's hand. "Imelda you'll go far. You were always the bravest in the group. I really believe you will have your own shop one day," said Angela.

They walked on, and Imelda took out her cigarettes and offered her friend one.

"I'm trying to give them up, Imelda. They're supposed to be bad for the baby," said Angela.

"That baby will be fine! Now fuck off and take yourself out of your misery and have a fag! Did you ever hear the saying, 'All smokers are happy people'?" laughed Imelda. .

"Is that true? I never heard that saying before." remarked Angela innocently.

Imelda took a drag from her smoke, and blew the smoke out in a long drawn out blow.

"I don't know – I just made it up!" laughed Imelda.

Angela looked at her friend.

"Imelda Bradshaw, you're a mad bitch," she said, and they walked towards Chapelgate arm in arm.

*****

"Is your friend alright?" Collette asked Gerard. Larry and Gerard had been chatting to the two girls at the bar.

Collette and Grainne had gone into Dublin city that night after finishing work.

Collette worked in the department of agriculture as secretary, a job her father, who was a prominent politician, had gotten for her.

Grainne worked in a different department.

The girls had struck up a conversation with Gerard early on in the night. Collette asked Gerard where worked and his answer impressed her.

"I'm a sound engineer for a band, "The Hustlers" from Liverpool" lied Gerard.

With his long hair and his clothes that were bought In London, he looked different from the rest, so his story was believable.

They chatted for a while and later Collette asked Gerard if he wanted to go to a party. When he saw how Larry was behaving, he decided to leave with the girls and go to the party.

Mick was trying to look after Larry and Gerard decided that maybe it was time the lads headed home.

Jem and Pancho were still deep in conversation.

"Just give me five minutes to sort out a taxi for the lads," said Gerard.

Gerard talked to Mick and then to Jem and Pancho and they helped Larry outside.

A taxi was just dropping a person off at the bar and Gerard grabbed the door and pushed Larry into the car. Mick jumped into the front and Jem and Pancho piled into the back beside Larry.

The taxi man wouldn't normally have taken a drunk but he had no choice as Gerard had literally hijacked the taxi.

"Will yer man be allright? I hope he doesn't throw up in the back."

"Yeh, he'll be OK once he gets a bit of fresh air," said Gerard.

"Chapelgate Gardens mate and here take this," said Gerard putting two pound notes into the drivers top pocket. This was double the fare and the driver relaxed as he was paid up front and twice the price.

Mick looked at his brother.

"Thanks Ger," he said and then the taxi pulled away.

Gerard went back to the bar and joined the girls.

"Right where's this party?" asked Gerard.

*****

The taxi pulled into the far end of Chapelgate flats complex.

"Right, Larry here we go," said Mick helping his friend from the taxi. Can you manage, Mick?" asked Pancho.

Pancho and Jem stood either side of Larry and they walked towards Chapelgate.

"Larry's bollixed, Mick," said Jem.

They swayed and stumbled towards Chapelgate. Mick was feeling a bit sick now after the drink and car ride. He stopped and turned towards the wall and threw up on the pavement.

"Oh God, the world is spinning. Stop the world, I want to get off," he shouted.

"The poor bastard! It'll be a long time before he gets out with the lads after the wedding." laughed Jem.

Larry looked up at Pancho and Jem and they could see that indeed Larry was very drunk now, and his jaw was slack and his eyes slightly glazed.

"Where are we, Mick?" asked Larry.

"We are in fucking bits with the drink, that's where we are mate!" laughed Mick as he wiped his face.

It would be a long time before the lads would be able to have a drink together. From that night until the next time they would be together, a lot of unpredictable things would happen to each individual.

*****

Dermot watched the lads sway from side to side as they entered the flats complex. Patrick and Dermot were on the late shift, and had just pulled into a side street to have a cuppa from the thermos flask supplied by Helen.

"Somebody's going to have a sore head in the morning," stated Dermot, nodding his head towards the lads.

Patrick sipped on his steaming tea and tapped his cigarette into the ashtray in the unmarked police car. Even though it was unmarked, everybody in Chapelgate Gardens knew it was a police car.

"That's the Foley lad, Mick. He's getting married this week," said Dermot.

"He's the eldest, yes?" said Patrick.

"Yes, he's a good sort, but that Gerard – he's the other brother – he's just back from London."

"Wouldn't trust him as far as I'd feckin throw him, Dermot. I'd keep an eye on that one," said Patrick.

They watched as Jem and Pancho struggled with Larry.

The lads disappeared into the flats complex.

Dermot took a drag from his cigarette.

"I wonder where the other Foley lad has gotten himself, Gerard, I wonder, has he gone back to England?" said Patrick.

"He's a sharp one. Never lets the guard down, him. I'd keep an eye on that fellah. The sooner he gets back on the boat to London the better." Said Dermot

"I'd say he'd be keeping us on our toes, my friend, if he was running around Chapelgate," replied Patrick.

Dermot nodded in agreement with his partner.

"No, he'll be here till after the brother's wedding I'd say," replied Dermot.

"How's things with that Bradshaw girl? Are you putting her with the Sarge?" asked Patrick.

Dermot had been telling Patrick about the meetings with Imelda, and how he had caught her in the car that night with the irate punter.

"Be careful around that one," said Patrick.

Patrick was over his brief bout of depression, and had decided to try and sit the detective sergeant's exam the following year. This took a lot of time to prepare for, and he hadn't been drinking much after work, the way they used to. Dermot would keep him updated about his relationship with Mary, his wife, with Imelda, and with his informers, who were few.

Dermot had only one informer in Chapelgate, and he was Fatser Larkin. He would give Dermot snippets of information, and Dermot would turn a blind eye to what Fatser got up to. Once, Fatser tried to get money from Dermot for information, and Dermot knew that he would have to let Fatser know who was boss. So that particular day, when Fatser asked him for cash and said he would give him information, Dermot pulled him into the police station and locked him up for five hours.

After his shift finished, he took him out of the cell and told him if he ever tried to look for money, he'd have his arse in a cell so fast, his head would spin.

Dermot had heard that Gerard and Jem had been in London, and since they had come back they were spending cash like it was going out of fashion. Fatser had informed Dermot that he had heard they had sold a couple of radios a few weeks earlier. Dermot told Patrick about the radios.

"They must have been from the truck we got those televisions from. The robbing fucking bastards," said Patrick, as he realised that they had acquired televisions from the truck also.

They both laughed at the irony of it. There wasn't much going on in the inner city that Dermot and Patrick didn't know about.

"So she's going to be in Phibsboro?" said Patrick.

"I talked to the Sarge, and he said she would be OK to move in soon. She's not a bad sort, Patrick, and Jesus, she's trying to get herself out of Chapelgate. You can't blame her trying to better herself," said Dermot.

"Do you remember we saw her a few years ago with that lad at the back of the church?" laughed Patrick.

"Yes, she was just a kid then, but she's grown up now," said Dermot.

"Fair play to the Sarge, He looks after the girls," said Dermot.

"Jesus boy, he's well paid for it. The rent! I mean, OK, it's protection money, no matter what way you look at it, but don't be under the illusion he's running a charity house for wayward fucking girls – it's a fucking brothel! Well policed, but still a brothel, Dermot," said Patrick.

"I know, Patrick, but you have to admire the way he runs that little operation. I also know he has no other places. He keeps it sweet and tidy," said Dermot.

"It's his pension, Patrick. You couldn't blame him. I mean, stuck behind a desk, no perks, like the odd TV or the suits we got there last year from that shop break in. He has to look after number one," said Dermot.

"Well I suppose you're right Dermot. Let's face it after thirty years in this job the pension is not much, is it Dermot?" said Patrick.

Dermot agreed.

"How are things with Mary?" enquired Patrick.

Dermot shook his head and replied.

"She's not good, Pat. Her sister came over a week ago and stayed for a few days. Only she was there. The kids wouldn't have been looked after. I have to work, and she stepped in for us, thank God."

"Helen was worried about her since the night in our place. Helen picks up on things, and she noticed Mary was getting that … what's this they call it … post-natal depression?" replied Patrick.

"We're getting there, Patrick," replied Dermot, who was interrupted by the radio breaking in about an incident in Fairview Park.

They threw the cigarettes out the window and drove away from Chapelgate.

*****

Gerard sat with the girls at the bar and he was making up stories about working for the band. Collette and Grainne were twenty years old and by their accents and their dress Gerard knew that they were middle class.

"So where's this party" asked Gerard.

Collette got off her seat and said, "Right let's go. It's at my house," she replied. The three of them left the bar and when they got outside Gerard stood in the road to hail a taxi.

"What are you doing Gerard?" asked Collette.

"We need a taxi, Howth, that's where you said we are going, am I right? Well it's a long bloody walk," replied Gerard.

Collette pulled a set of keys from her handbag.

"I'm driving. Come on Grainne," she said as she turned to walk towards a little Mini car parked outside the pub.

"Jesus," Gerard thought to himself, her own fucking car, this one's loaded,"

Whilst he was talking to the girls he didn't use swear words and he put on a slight London accent just enough to impress the girls. He had told them he had been in London for a few years and the band was doing really well. The girls had heard of the band also, and apparently they were going to be the next big thing on the music scene. The girls were impressed.

As they drove by the "Five" lamps Grainne made a comment about Chapelgate Gardens.

"Is this part of your dad's constituency" asked Grainne.

Collette looked around at the road leading to Chapelgate.

"Yes it is. He bloody hates coming here when the elections are on," replied Collette.

Gerard remembered Collette had told him her full name and the penny dropped with him, and he knew her father as "Brennan" the TD who represented Chapelgate. He would only see him at election times doing the rounds in the pubs buying drink and everybody patting him on the back saying what a "Great man" he was.

"He always says that it's a good job he only has to go down there every couple of years for to get the votes," said Collette.

"Where do you come from, like where did you grow up Gerard?" asked Grainne, out of the blue to Gerard. He was caught on the hop.

"Well in London for the last few years but I'm from Killester. Well the parents live there" lied Gerard. He had to think fast. He wasn't going to let the girls know he was from Chapelgate. "What about you Grainne. Where are you from?" he asked, turning the question back on Grainne.

"Sutton, my parents have a business there," replied Grainne.

They drove to Howth and as the Mini pulled up outside the big house at the top of the hill Gerard was impressed.

The lights were on in the house and Collette had told him that her brother was having a few friends around as their parents were away.

As they were walking up the long gravel drive Grainne walked ahead and Collette pulled on Gerard's arm. She pulled him towards her and kissed him on the lips.

"Fuck me I'm in here," thought Gerard.

Chapter Twenty-Four

Imelda awoke at seven, hearing her mother come into her room with a cup of tea.

"Imelda, do you want anything to eat love – toast, an egg, anything?" she asked Imelda.

Imelda sat up in the bed. She hadn't had much to drink the night before, because she knew she would have to be sharp for her first real day in her new job.

"No Ma, tea will do. I'm putting on weight anyway. I hope I'll fit the bridesmaid dress tomorrow – I'm huge," she replied.

"Would you go way out of that! Since you started that job in the clothes shop you look great. Better than that oul sweat shop you worked," replied her mother.

She sat in her warm bed, and the lamp on her dresser barley illuminated the room. It was sill dark outside.

She looked around and realised she would be moving out soon. Her mother would be a little upset, but she'd get over it.

"Anyway, she will be delighted that I will still be able to give her money every week, even though I won't be living here," she thought to herself.

She sipped her tea, and the steam rose from the cup in the cold room. She looked around at the pictures on the wall – her pin-ups. The Beach Boys, Adam Faith, John and Paul ... the real Beatles. She remembered the morning after her uncle had left for England. She remembered that the night before she had idolised him, and when he had left her bed after doing what he had done, and the hatred for him and the strange way she felt. She knew he had taken her virginity, her trust in him – how could he? The days and weeks after, should she tell, who do I trust? Is this a part of growing up? She had changed from that day. She lit a cigarette, and leaned back into her pillows, mug of tea in her hand.

At nine o'clock she walked through the flats complex. She was wearing the new dress she had bought the day before in the shop that she was about to start work in.

When she was working in the sewing factory she only wore an old nylon overall.

Today as she walked through O'Connell Street dressed up for work she felt alive. She was really looking forward to her first day in the job.

She was excited, and knew that her life was changing rapidly. Her clothes were much more expensive than the clothes her friends, which were few, wore. Her need to be independent was paramount in her mind. The relationship with Dermot. She felt grown up and mature.

The way she handled the woman in the shop the day before – the same woman who a few months before followed her around the shop, thinking she was a shoplifter, because of the clothes she wore. This woman now talked to her with a respect. She realised she had to look the part at all times.

"This is a good day for Imelda Bradshaw," she thought to herself, as she walked with her head in the air through Dublin city that day in nineteen sixty-seven, daring anybody to take that feeling away from her.

*****

"Jesus! Me fucking head!" thought Larry, as his eyes tried to focus on the yellow smoke-stained wallpaper in the front room of his flat. He was still dressed, and there was a blanket thrown over him. He tried to remember the night before. Flashbacks came flooding into his brain.

"The two girls, getting sick … oh God, me head," he thought to himself.

He looked at the basin beside him, and couldn't remember who had put it there. He rubbed his eyes and sat up in the armchair.

His back was hurting, and there was a pain in his neck. His mouth tasted strange.

"Fuck me – the cigarettes! Me mouth feels like I've chewed cardboard. I'm never smoking again," he thought. He held his head between his hands and looked down at the cracked and tea-stained oil cloth that covered the floor. He heard a noise in the scullery. It sounded like someone was humming, the song his father hummed while he worked.

"Is that you, Ma?" he called out.

There was no reply. He got up and walked into the scullery. The humming had stopped. He looked into the small scullery and there was no-one there. He scratched his head.

"Jesus, am I hearing things?" he thought to himself.

He was to meet Jem later, to show him the window cleaning round.

He made a cup of tea and walked to the window. He lived at the top of the block of the three story flats complex. He could see The Bell and he remembered the time his father sat at the window looking at the men going for a pint and how he couldn't go because his suit was still in the pawn shop. He had little giggle at what his mother had said. 'Sure they know you have a suit,' she had said.

He wondered what was ahead for him in London. He thought of Marie and how she had left for Galway. His life had turned upside down that day. "Fuck her," he said to himself and he reached into his pocket for his battered pack of cigarettes.

As he stood looking out on the surrounds of Chapelgate his thoughts were disturbed by his mother calling out to him.

"Larry are you up? I'll make you a cuppa in a minute love," she called out.

"How am I going to tell her I'm going away," he thought to himself.

"It's OK Ma, stay in bed I have a cup of tea for you," he called out.

*****

Gerard and Mick sat at the table. Gerard was tucking into bacon, eggs, sausages, and fried bread. He was leaning across the table for the sugar for his tea. Mick looked on at Gerard and couldn't believe that his brother was eating the greasy mess that was in front of him on the plate.

His mother came to the table with another plate.

"Here, Michael, eat this, you'll feel better," she said, as she put the plate in front of him. He loved his bacon and eggs normally, but this morning the look of the runny eggs, swimming in the lard they were fried in, put him right off his appetite.

"Ma, that's the one thing I've missed. The fried breakfast – the real butter, not that oul margarine they serve up to you in England. They don't do it like you do over there in London," said Gerard to his mother.

She was happy to have her two boys sat together at the table. She remembered the times when the three of them would be sat around the table, and Rory would be stealing from their plates, and the banter that went on between them. She missed that. She missed Gerard after he had left for England. She missed the noise in the flat as her boys would taunt each other.

"She missed the noise!". When she came in from the shops, she would hear the lads talking and shouting, and sometimes fighting with each other. "She missed the noise!"

"What time did you get in this morning son? You're bed wasn't slept in?" asked his mother, as she put two more sausages onto Gerard's plate.

"Thanks Ma," said Gerard as he patted his mother on the bum..

She laughed and went back into the kitchen.

"Where did you end up last night Ger?" asked Mick.

Gerard let out a little laugh.

"If I told ye that, I'd have to kill ye" joked Gerard.

Gerard told him what had happened the night before.

*****

The house was packed with people. They were all in their twenties and Collette introduced Gerard to her brother. As he sat and listened to the music blaring from the record player Collette brought over a bottle of beer and sat beside him.

"Nice house," said Gerard and he took a swig from his bottle.

"Dad bought it from a builder a few years ago. He was looking for planning permission and Dad was on the council at the time, so he pushed it through for him. So he sold this house to Dad for a song," replied Collette.

"It's not what you know it's who you know," said Gerard under his breath.

"What?" asked Collette.

"Oh nothing, I was just admiring the place. You're lucky to have a rich father," laughed Gerard.

She smiled at Gerard.

"I suppose so. But what's the point of being a TD if you don't get any perks. He was able to get me job in the civil service without even having to do an exam. It's not what you know it's who you know Gerard," she replied.

"Funny that. I was thinking the same myself," said Gerard.

The party went on until about two and everybody had left the house and Gerard found himself alone in the sitting room with Collette asleep on his shoulder.

He got up to go to the toilet and Collette just rolled over and curled up on the couch.

The house was silent as he made his way to the toilet which was on the first floor.

He heard a sound from the bedroom to the left of the toilet and as the door was slightly opened he looked in. Lying on the bed snoring heavily was Collette's brother and beside him was Grainne. They were both naked. Gerard couldn't help notice Grainne's body lying with her leg draped across the bed. "She's a fucking ride" thought Gerard.

He went into the toilet and as he descended the stairs he looked at the photographs that adorned the wall.

All of them were of Collette's father, photographed with various famous people.

"So this is where our 'Man of the People'," lives thought Gerard.

He looked at Collette asleep on the couch. She's a nice girl though. He looked around the sitting room. There was expensive crystal glasses, and silver ware on the expensive antique furniture.

A couple of months ago he would have stolen some of this stuff and sold it, but he was past that now. He knew he was on a different path. He was making money.

He opened another room on the ground floor, that looked like a study. The large desk, had photographs of Collett's dad Mr Brennan with various prominent people, who Gerard recognised from the television. The large bay window overlooked Dublin Bay, and Gerard could just make out in the early morning sunrise, the spire of the Church in Chapelgate.

"Someday I will own a house like this," he thought to himself. He went back into the room to where Collette was sleeping.

He woke Collette and asked her to phone for a taxi. She rubbed her eyes.

"What time is it Gerard? she asked.

"Four thirty. Do you want something to drink?" he asked her.

She asked for a coke and when he returned from the kitchen with it, she had stripped off and, was lying on the carpet in front of the gas fire in her bra and pants. She patted the ground beside her.

"Come on," she said to Gerard in a low sultry voice. He handed her the bottle, then took off his T-Shirt. He lay down beside her and, he put his hand inside the cup of her bra. Collette smiled and grabbed at his jeans……

An hour later as he left the house and went into the cold dawn morning he looked back at the house. Collette was standing at the door in a flimsy silk wrap.

. The taxi had just pulled in to pick Gerard up.

She waved to him and he waved back.

"Kilester?" asked the man.

"I fucking wish! No Chapelgate Gardens," replied Gerard.

Gerard told Mick about his encounter with politician's daughter.

"Jesus Gerard your life is full of surprises," said Mick

"Tomorrow is the big day, pal. Are you nervous?" asked Gerard.

Michael looked a sorry sight. His eyes were red and bloodshot. His stomach ached, and the smell made him nauseous.

He looked at Gerard and said, "Ger, how much drink did I have last night?"

Gerard laughed at his brother.

"Not much. Jesus, Mick, you're a real girl. You used to be able to put them away no problem. Your fucking eyes are like piss holes in the snow!" laughed Gerard.

Mick felt his stomach rumble. He put his hand to his mouth and ran for the toilet. Gerard cut the thick sausage and dipped it in the yellow egg.

"Poor bastard – he's fucked. Jesus, I miss me ma's cooking," he thought to himself.

*****

Angela and Linda were getting ready to meet Imelda that afternoon. She stood in the bedroom and looked at the wedding dress hanging on the back of the door.

Linda helped Angela with her shoes. Angela found it hard to get her shoes on, as her feet were starting to swell.

"Angela, Imelda has lovely clothes," said Linda to her sister, as she kneeled in front of her.

"That's because she works in a clothes shop, and she told me she gets loads of discount off them," replied Angela.

"What's the name of the shop again? She told me, but I forgot," said Linda.

Angela turned and looked at her bump in the mirror. Linda was looking up at her.

"Feck! I'm huge. The shop, I think it's called Lady B, or something like that, but it's somewhere we can't afford to shop on our few pittance," replied Angela.

Linda stood up and straightened her skirt.

"Right, let's go and meet Lady B. I can't wait to see the face on that fucking Jean Reid, when I see her and tell her about Imelda's shop. She's a fucking bitch that wan. I can't wait to put her in her place. Did you know she's saying that Imelda's on the game?" said Linda.

"Imelda Bradshaw is getting herself a better life. That Reid one has a cheek, sure everybody's been up on her," said Angela.

"I heard she was trying to chat up Gerard Foley the other night in The Bell," said Linda. Angela raised her eyebrow at this news.

"He wouldn't be bothered with her. He has taste, and she wouldn't even be in the running," said Angela.

"Yes in her dreams," replied Linda.

"Don't mind that bitch. She's just jealous. Imelda is the salt of the earth – she'd give you her last penny. Don't mind that bleedin' bitch, Linda," said Angela.

*****

Imelda was standing outside the shop when June arrived.

"Someone is keen!" remarked June as she greeted Imelda.

"Well, first day, and well … you know … I just want to learn the ropes," said Imelda.

"Well, we need a cuppa first, so let's get that sorted," replied June.

They sat in the back of the shop among the rails of clothes, covered in plastic wrapping.

June asked Imelda about her life, and what she had been doing since she had left her last job. Imelda created an illusion of a life for June. She told her she had worked as a supervisor in a sewing factory, but had fallen out with the owners as she wanted to progress as a buyer of fabrics. And also she wanted to get to know more about the rag trade.

The lies tripped off her tongue, but she knew if she had told June her real life story, warts and all, she would be out the front door of that shop as quick as her legs would carry her.

June was also telling Imelda about where she came from and her path in life, and Imelda liked June more for her honesty with her.

They talked for half an hour before they opened the shop, and Imelda told June about her friend Angela, who was getting married the next day.

"I want to buy her something nice from the shop. That's why I was here yesterday, June, so if she picks something out, can you take the money from my wages?" asked Imelda.

"With a twenty five percent discount, of course," replied June.

Imelda decided to go out on a limb as they discussed her friend.

"June, I hope you don't mind, but could I ask a favour from you?" she said.

June looked at Imelda wondering what the favour was to be.

"Fire away," she replied.

"Well, when I left my job, I told the girls I had another job to go to. I didn't want to let myself down in front of them. So I told them I had started work in a clothes shop since I left the other job," said Imelda.

"Don't worry, Imelda, your secret's safe with me, and if they ask, you've been here months. I know you want your friends to be proud of you, and I can see you are determined to get on in life. Something tells me you will," replied June.

"Thanks June," replied Imelda.

Chapter Twenty-Five

Larry had to meet Jem later that day and bring him to Clontarf. He had to show Jem how he worked the system, with the gutters, and how to clean the windows properly, because he didn't want to lose the window cleaning round, as he had made it into a nice little earner.

If things didn't work out in London, he needed to have something to come back to. His father had built the round up over the years, and he wasn't going to just let anybody take over. Also, his mother needed money coming into the house, as the widows' pension wasn't enough, and she needed to bridge the gap with the extra money.

Jem walked along the path towards Larry. He was wheeling a bike, because Larry had told him he needed to borrow a bike for a few days, until Larry gave him his own.

Larry had written out in a diary all the customers, and the prices, and the dates. He had also written little tips in the back page, about some of his customers. "Mrs Reid" is a good tipper, "Mrs O'Leary" tries to get out of paying, "Mr O'Neill" stands watching as you clean, but he's a nice man; since he retired he likes the company and the chat. The "Old Lady" in sixty-eight is just fucking mad. Larry jotted down these little snippets for Jem, so it would help him get to know the customers. Larry Burke loved lists. He loved writing things down. He loved seeing the columns of numbers in between the blue lines of the jotter. When he had started work with his father. His father would have everything in his head. No dates or names. This was why he lost so much of his earnings to memory lapse. When Larry wrote all the customers in the book, his father couldn't believe the amount of customers he had.

"How's the head, Larry? Jeez, you were in a right state last night," said Jem, as he stood the bike against the wall and took his packet of player wills cigarettes from his pocket, offering one to Larry.

Larry shook his head.

"No, Jem. I'm going to give up again. Me throat was in bits this morning," replied Larry.

They discussed the diary and the entries relating to his customers, and the prices for each house, as some were bigger than others.

Jem pored over the entries.

"Which oul wans are you ridin?" asked Jem, and he looked into Larry's face like a little boy waiting on sweets from his father. Larry pushed him in the shoulder.

"I made that all up, Jem, for fuck's sake. Now don't go trying to get into any of me customers' knickers!" laughed Larry.

Jem was a little disappointed.

"They were all just stories?" he enquired.

"You are so fucking naïve, mate! Now listen, this book is the bible, so don't lose it or let it out of your sight," replied Larry.

They went through each page, and Larry noticed that Jem was taking him seriously, and absorbing everything he was saying. He was surprised, because Jem acted like kid most of the time, and the lads thought it was because he spent too much time with Joxer, who was slightly retarded.

"Thanks for the chance," said Jem to Larry.

"Look Jem, if things don't go according to plan over in London for me I'll be back. So look after the work and don't let me down," said Larry.

Jem shook his head and said, "No way Larry I won't let you down, I promise," said Jem.

Larry looked at his friend.

"I know you won't Jem. I know," replied Larry.

"Right, let's go and relieve some people of their cash," said Larry, as he took his bike and skipped off, throwing his leg over the crossbar and the ladder that was tied to the bike. This was a new ladder, because Larry couldn't bring himself to use the ladder his father had fallen from. Larry cycled and started to tell Jem about how to stuff the gutters when he realised that he was cycling alone. He stopped the bike and looked behind and saw Jem running towards him, wheeling his bike.

"You'd want to get on that thing – we have a good distance to cycle," said Larry, and he was about to take off again, when Jem called out.

"Lar, I don't know how to go on a bike."

Larry stopped and looked behind again at Jem.

"You can't be fucking serious, Jem! You never learned to go on a bike?" asked Larry.

Jem looked a bit sheepish at Larry.

"I never had a bike before, Lar. It's not my bleedin' fault!" replied Jem in a hurtful tone.

Larry looked up towards the sky. Then he looked at Jem, who just stood there beside the bike, he couldn't ride.

"Right, for fuck's sake, we'd better get you sorted," said Larry, and he parked his bike against the wall. His head was still a bit sore, and he thought to himself, "Jesus, I could have done without this today". He spent the next half hour holding the seat for Jem, as he tried to balance himself on the bike. Jem was like a child, and had run into the wall twice, as he couldn't get it through his mind the aspect of turning the handlebars.

Eventually Jem got a grasp of riding the bike and Larry decided it better they cycle on the foot path, just in case Jem fell in front of a car.

Larry thought to himself, "God, for all the years I've known Jem I never knew he couldn't cycle. And you think you know people," he thought.

They cycled towards Clontarf, with Larry helping Jem as they cycled side by side. Jem fell, a couple of times, but by the time they got to the first house, Jem was cycling on his own. For the rest of the day, Jem was introduced to Larry's customers, and they cleaned some windows and removed a slate from a gutter that Larry had planted a few weeks before. Larry was surprised at how easy Jem fell into the work. Most of his customers were women, and they loved Jem. He had a way of talking to women which made them feel sorry for him.

He had a type of effeminate side to him. Even the way he held his cigarette was like a girl. As he had been working with Joxer, and most of the customers were women, he felt at ease talking with them.

They sat on the wall overlooking the seafront near the wooden bridge linking Dollymount with main Clontarf road.

They were taking a short break and eating Tayto crisps and drinking two bottles of red lemonade.

"These will be two things I'm going to miss in England Jem. Gerard said he can't get any Tayto or red lemonade anywhere over there," said Larry.

"You can't fucking beat a package of Tayto," said Jem as he munched on the crisps.

"I heard Imelda Bradshaw is on the game," said Jem out of the blue.

Larry had heard it also but he knew Imelda. He knew she was easy when it came to sex, but he couldn't imagine her on the game.

"That's bollock's Jem. Don't let Gerard Foley hear you saying that. He likes Imelda. A lot," replied Larry.

"I don't believe it either Larry. Cunt's down there in Chapelgate just want to take a fucking pop at anybody who gets on in life, the fuckers," replied Jem. Then he added, "Larry don't tell Gerard I said that, will you," pleaded Jem sheepishly.

"Don't worry Jem I wouldn't say that to Gerard. Now come on we have people to swindle. I've two more pieces of slate left, now who will be the lucky ones'" laughed Larry.

They jumped on their bikes and cycled towards Clontarf. Jem lost his balance again and rode straight into a lamppost.

*****

Gerard sat in "The Bell" on his own, in the corner. He drank the pint of Guinness and thought to himself, "That's another thing I miss about Ireland – the Guinness. The Guinness in England is piss!"

Mrs Pluck was sitting with the owner, Mr O'Brien, and he was pointing out parts of the bar that she had to clean. He watched them walk through the bar and into the toilets. There were two men at the bar sitting on the stools sipping pints of Guinness. He felt good in himself. He looked around the smoke-stained walls, and remembered the nights he had spent in the pub with his mates. With his father, and his brother. He remembered the year before last, when his mother and father had an anniversary party in the bar.

It was the first time Rory was allowed to come into the bar. His two married sisters had been there also. They lived out in the new Coolock housing estate, where they had managed to get social housing from the local authority.

The afternoon sun streamed into the bar, and the smoke could be seen rising from his cigarette. The wedding was the next day, and he was meeting Mick in an hour, and the rest of the gang were to join them later. The reception was to be in the The Star Hotel, just ten minutes from Chapelgate Gardens.

Gerard had given his father an envelope with fifty pounds in it towards the wedding. He knew that his father wouldn't have much money on the day, so he had given it to him to buy the drink for the main toast at the wedding. He wanted his father o feel like a millionaire. Even it was only for a day.

As he sat there, he pondered the last few months, and how his life had changed. Last year, he was picking up odd jobs, and robbing lead and scrap metal, or robbing the odd truck.

Mick had managed to get Angela pregnant, and they were getting married. Poor Rory had been killed. And Larry's "Da", poor bastard, he thought to himself.

Then there was Larry's uncle Jimmy! He was glad Larry was returning to England with him. As he sat there, he felt the money in his pocket. Since he started working with Jimmy, he had never been without money. He went over to the phone when it rang. He was waiting on this phone call.

"The Bell," he said into the mouthpiece.

There was a moment of silence.

"Gerard, is that you?" replied Jimmy from the other end.

Gerard was about to tell Jimmy about the drop off, and how things went, but he was interrupted by Jimmy, who said "I know Gerard, I know, and Larry is coming over, I hear."

Gerard was taken aback.

"Fuck, how does he know that?" he thought to himself.

"Yes, he's fed up here. I was telling him that Jem would not be going back, and he decided to come back with me, but listen Jimmy, how did you know he was ..."

He didn't get to finish his sentence, as Jimmy interrupted him.

"Gerard, it's my job to know things, son. Now the package you got, you have it safe?" asked Jimmy.

They discussed what Gerard was to do with package, and then Jimmy said that it was important that he had to have the package before Christmas.

Gerard hadn't realised that Christmas was only three weeks away – with all the hustle and bustle over the wedding, Christmas was an after-thought. Gerard and Larry would be returning to London a few days after the wedding. They would be spending Christmas and New Year in London.

"Gerard I liked the way you handled the "Christy" fella. I am moving you up in the organisation. Keep your nose clean over there, and I'll see you in a couple of days. Tell Larry welcome to do the same" replied Jimmy Burke and with that the line went dead, as Jimmy hung up. "Typical Jimmy" thought Gerard.

He sat down and took another sip from his pint.

"Fuck me! That Jimmy is hundreds of miles away, and he knows what's going on here. He's a clever guy." thought Gerard.

As he sat there at the bar a picture behind the bar caught his eye. It was a picture of Mr O'Brien standing beside Collette's father. Life is fucking strange he thought. He raised his glass to the picture.

"You have a lovely daughter sir," said Gerard as he toasted the picture of Collette's dad.

As he did this, Mr O'Brien and Mrs Pluck walked into the bar from the toilets.

They saw Gerard talking to himself and lifting his glass towards the picture and take a gulp from it.

They looked at each other.

"England! That's what it is. England it makes them all mad," said Mr O'Brien. Mrs Pluck nodded her head in agreement.

*****

Angela and Linda walked back from the Lady B laden down with bags.

"Now, I can't wait to see that feckin' Reid wan, and tell her about Imelda's job. Do you believe me now about Imelda? She's not on the game – she is after getting herself a very good job and we're the proof. That wan is just jealous," said Angela to her sister.

"I'd love a job like that. Imelda is so lucky to work with all them lovely clothes, and her boss, she's a lovely woman," remarked Linda.

Imelda had given Angela a lovely suit. It was for her to wear after she had had the baby. It was grey, and the fabric was expensive. Imelda also put two blouses into the bag, even though Angela protested that she already had enough. June watched Imelda with her friend, and saw a side to her and a quality that was rare. There was also a silk scarf in the bag that June had given Angela as a wedding present. The girls walked towards Chapelgate with the bags, laughing and singing.

Later, back in the shop, June watched Imelda as she talked to a customer.

June had talked to Angela and her sister Linda, and she knew they were from an inner city flats complex. Because of the cost of the clothes that she sold in the shop, she would not come across people from that social background. She knew that Imelda would have come from that social background but was trying to better herself. June knew only too well what that was like, as she had done the same many years before.

June had come from a very run down area in Limerick city. She emigrated along with her sister to America and worked hard for ten years until she returned with enough money to start a business. At forty-six years of age she was a very wealthy woman. She never married as she liked her independence. She had a lot in common with Imelda.

*****

Larry came into The Bell, followed by Jem. Gerard saw the lads and he waved to them.

"Larry, Jem," he called out.

The lads sat down and Larry turned to Gerard.

"Twenty fucking years of age, and he can't ride a poxy bike! Did you ever see the like, Gerard?" said Larry.

Gerard looked at his friend in disbelief.

"Me bollix, he can't ride a bike?" asked Gerard.

"Fuck off, yis pair of cunts!" replied Jem, as the lads took the piss out of him.

Jem went to the bar to get the pints and Larry sat in beside Gerard.

"Jimmy knows you're going over to London with me. I know! Don't ask me how he knew, but he was able to tell me. Jesus, Larry, nothing gets by him," said Gerard.

Larry shrugged his shoulders.

"Me ma's brother, Jimmy – but you're right, he's as sharp as a blade," said Larry.

Gerard explained to Larry how he was to open the package and split the contents between them, and how he was to get off the ship separately at the other end.

Gerard had hidden the package that Christy had given him in his flat, and didn't know exactly what was in it, but by its bulk, it was more than likely cash.

"Well how're you feeling today?" asked Gerard.

Larry shook his head.

"I was bollixed this morning. But I'm a lot better now. Just showing Jem the ropes today. He has taken to it like a duck to water, well except for the bike. Nearly sawed the bollix off himself cycling with the ladder and bucket on the bike," laughed Larry.

Jem came back from the bar and put the glasses on the table in front of the lads.

"What's the joke," he asked as he sat into the seats putting three pints on the table.

Larry and Gerard were sniggering.

"Ahh fuck off you pair of fuckers," he said as he picked up his pint and smiled thinking how he nearly killed himself that day on the bike.

"Well, here's to Mick and Angela," said Larry, raising his glass.

"Mick ... and Angela!" chorused the three lads.

"Is he joining us later? It's his last night of freedom," asked Larry.

"I think he's meeting the "Minister for war" and Angela and then popping in for quick pint before having an early night.

Jem looked puzzled. "Minister for War?" he asked.

"The future mother in law" replied Gerard and Larry in unison. They both laughed at how they were thinking on the same lines. A thing that they did often.

"Well where did you get to last night, you dirty devil?" said Larry to Gerard.

Gerard told him about Collette and how she drove him to her house. When he told him who her father was, Larry raised his eyebrows.

"Fuck me you landed a right little bird there. Her own car and daddy a TD," said Larry.

"Did you ride her?" asked Jem.

They both looked at Jem and he had a moustache of cream from the Guinness along his top lip. He looked comical.

"Of course," they both chorused together.

"I have her phone number. I told her I was with a band and we were touring Ireland for the next few days but when I go back to London I'd give her a call," said Gerard.

"Jesus Ger, you're an awful fucking liar," laughed Larry.

Gerard laughed.

"I know. I know," he laughed.

Mick was walking along the street with Angela's mother. They had been in the hotel to finalise the seating plans. He had to make sure that everybody was seated in the right seats, and to keep certain factions of Angela's extended family apart from each other, as there was bad blood between them.

Angela's mother took over, and as the manager was off that day the young receptionist had to put up with Mrs Hopkins.

Mick sorted his family seating in minutes and left them to it.

The Foley clan got on well together, so the seating arrangements were simple to organise for them.

He walked towards Chapelgate when they left the hotel.

Mick recognised the familiar gait on one, of the two women walking in front of him. He ran towards Angela and caught up with her.

"Have you any money left?" he laughed out loud.

The girls turned, and Angela thrust the bags towards him.

"Here take these, Mick, the mother of your child is a bit knackered," she laughed.

He took the bags from her.

Mrs Hopkins caught up with them.

"How're you girls, did you see Imelda?"

"Yes she's great Ma. She works in a lovely boutique in Grafton Street," gushed Linda. Mrs Hopkins made a face. "So she's not on the game?" she snapped. "Maaa!" replied Angela scolding her mother.

Angela took the bags from Mick.

"Here Ma, take these home will you?" asked Angela.

Mrs Hopkins took the bags and said goodbye to them.

"Well, how's Imelda? Does she really work in a shop?" said Mick.

Angela threw him a look.

"Mick, she gave me a lovely suit to wear, for after the baby is born," said Angela.

"Mick, you would want to see the shop she works in, and her boss is great. Imelda speaks real posh when she's in work." added Linda.

"Did you sort the seating and the bill for the meal with the manager of the hotel?" asked Angela.

"Yes, your two aunts that hate each other are at either end of the room, so hopefully things will be OK tomorrow. There is a new manager. He wasn't there but the receptionist sorted out the bill and the seating," replied Mick.

"Did me ma give the receptionist a hard time?" asked Angela.

"Is the pope catholic?" replied Mick.

They walked towards The Bell, and Angela told Mick she was only having one drink, and that it was unlucky for the bride to see the groom the night before the wedding.

As they entered the pub, Gerard shouted, "Well, here's the happy couple!"

Mick smiled and pretended to search around the bar. "Mr and Mrs Dillon! Where?" he joked. Angela thumped him. "Stop that" she replied laughing.

The six of them sat together, and Linda was delighted to be part of the group. Larry noticed her watching him, so he tried to ignore her. She was just a kid to him.

"I swear, Gerard, she has a great job," replied Angela.

"So she's not on the game?" said Jem, and they all looked at him.

"Do you know what? You're a feckin' dickhead! That's my friend you're passing comments on. She gets a good feckin' job and tries to better herself, and then people like you try and take her down. I expected better from you, Jem." Angela snapped.

Larry shook his head and looked at Jem.

"She's right, you are a fucking dickhead," said Larry.

There was a silence at the table. They had all heard that Imelda had been seen with a couple of different men, but nobody wanted to believe it. Angela looked at the lads.

"She has a great job, and she's trying to better herself. There is no way she's on the game, and if I hear anybody saying any different, I'll feckin' go through them," snapped Angela again.

"Sorry about that Angela," said Jem sheepishly.

Linda felt sorry for Jem.

Linda stood up, saying, "I think we should go, Angie, we've loads to do,"

Mick nodded to Angela.

"Yeh, love. I think you should get home and prepare for our big day," he said.

He stood up and gave Angela a kiss on the cheek. Larry and Gerard made a face at each other, and Mick caught them.

"She's going to be me wife, now piss off slagging me," laughed Mick.

Jem stood up and went over to Angela.

"I'm sorry, Angela, I was out of order. You're right, I am a dickhead," he said.

Angela saw that Jem was genuine.

"I'm sorry for snapping at you, Jem," she said, rubbing him on the shoulder in an affectionate way.

As Linda and Angela left the bar, the boys sat down, and all eyes were on Jem. He picked up his pint and took a sip from it. Gerard, Larry, and Mick looked at him. He looked back.

"What!?" he said.

The three lads looked at him.

"Dickhead," they chorused.

They stayed in the bar until eight that evening, when Larry and Gerard decided to head into the city and try and pick up a couple of girls. Jem and Mick headed for the flats. Gerard and Larry bought some chips in the local chipper, and they ate them from the bag as they walked towards the city.

Chapter Twenty-Six

Imelda woke up early on the morning of the wedding. Her mother came into the bedroom with her tea.

"Here – do you want toast, love?" asked her mother.

Imelda rubbed her eyes and sat up.

"No, ma, just a fag, and pass me that bag over there will you?" asked Imelda.

Her mother bent down and picked up the bag that had 'Lady B' on the side.

"How's the new job? That's the first time I've seen you bringing anything back from it," replied her mother.

Imelda pulled a scarf from the bag and gave it to her mother.

"Here. That will go with your outfit for the afters of the wedding. You're coming to the afters, aren't you?" asked Imelda.

"I wouldn't miss it for the world. Angela Hopkins is a lovely girl, and Mick Foley! They'll make a lovely couple," she replied.

"I hope the day goes well. That bitch of an aunt is going to the wedding. You know, the one that causes all the trouble," replied Imelda.

Her mother stopped and thought for a couple of seconds.

"Oh, that little fucker – the one that's married to her mother's brother. Yes, I know her, she's always causing fucking trouble. I knew her before she married Angela's uncle – she was a fucking slut. If she had sticking out of her what she had sticking in her, she'd be like a fucking hedgehog!" laughed her mother.

Imelda burst out laughing.

"Ma Bradshaw, you're terrible," she exclaimed, and they both burst into hysterics, imagining the prospect.

"Angela and Linda were in the shop yesterday. I told her to come in and meet my boss. June is lovely Ma. Anyway I gave her a suit and a couple of blouses," said Imelda.

Imelda liked her little chats with her mother in the morning. She was going to miss these little moments with her. She took the opportunity to bring it up about moving out.

"Ma, June has a bedsit in Phibsboro and she has tenants moving out soon. I'm thinking of taking it. How would you feel about that," asked Imelda.

Her mother wasn't surprised.

"To be honest Imelda I had an idea. I saw a few little things in your wardrobe the other day I was cleaning your room. I wasn't spying on you love but they just fell out of the bag," replied her mother.

Imelda had been buying things in preparation for her move to the bedsit, a kettle, cups and saucers, and other kitchen things.

"I should have told you earlier but what with the new job. Sorry Ma," said Imelda and she reached out and held her mother's hand.

"Imelda you're going places and don't let Chapelgate hold you back. I think you're doing the right thing. I'll miss you but go for it my baby," said her mother and a little tear came to her eye.

They hugged for a few minutes and then Imelda said, "Right, I have a wedding to get ready for".

*****

The young priest looked out at the altar and saw the flowers that were being prepared by Angela's mother and her sister Linda. He was taking the wedding, as the canon of the church refused to perform the ceremony because the bride to be was pregnant. It was a contentious issue in the church, and things were changing, but changing slowly.

He looked around the church and could see the how different it looked with the fresh flowers.

Mrs Hopkins nodded to the priest.

"Good morning, Father. Lovely day for it," she called to the priest.

He nodded back and smiled.

"The flowers are so lovely Mrs Hopkins. I'm sure it will be a great day," he replied.

He went back into the sacristy to prepare his homily for newlyweds. He looked at the text of the speech he wrote, and scribbled a couple of lines out and replaced the wording with more acceptable wording.

"If the heads in Rome let the people use bloody condoms, there would be a lot less shotgun weddings," he thought to himself.

The parish priest came into the sacristy and picked up the text, and he perused the words.

"You can't say that, or that, and you certainly can't say that," said the parish priest.

He continued reading the text.

"You can take that bit out there, and that. God Almighty, you've a lot to learn about being a priest! Did you get the donation envelopes from the family yet?" asked the parish priest.

The young curate shook his head.

"The mother is out doing the flowers, so I am assuming she will drop it in here before she leaves," replied the young priest.

"Right, but make sure you get it before they leave," snapped back the parish priest, as he left the room mumbling to himself.

The young curate went back to the text and tried to keep focused, but couldn't help thinking back to the night before, as he sat in the club in the city, where the clientele were mainly young men. It was a club another young priest had told him about before he had left the college for his new post in Chapelgate Gardens. He wasn't in his priest's outfit, just a sweater and slacks. Since he had left the company of the other lads in the training college, and had been ordained, he found it lonely in his new surroundings of Chapelgate Gardens.

Larry's eyes blinked as he awoke to unfamiliar surroundings. He could smell a sweet perfume fragrance. He was lying on a couch, and the noise coming from the other room had awakened him. He sat up and as the room came into focus he remembered the night before. The noise coming from the room got slightly louder.

"Gerard! the randy fucker," he thought as he smiled to himself.

He looked around the room and saw the large television, and the large speakers on each side of the record player. He got up from the couch and walked into the open plan kitchen of the house that he had found himself in.

He lit the gas cooker and put the kettle on it. He looked out at the panoramic view that was Howth. He saw the early morning boat from England heading into Dublin Port, steaming by in the far distance. The same boat he would be on in a couple of days' time.

He lit a cigarette and turned to look at the modern kitchen with its brand new Formica counter tops and built in presses.

The kitchen looked out on to a lawn that fell away from the house, with the entrance to Dublin Port in the distance. From his memories of Howth and the surrounding areas, he knew he was in a house near the top of Howth Head. He made a cup of tea and walked back into the sitting room. He saw the expensive furniture with the crystal glasses and silver wear, and he noticed the photos on the wall. "So this is where Gerard ended up the other night" he thought to himself.

He looked on the coffee table at the three empty glasses and the half empty bottle of Jameson whiskey. The night before came flooding back to him.

He remembered now where he was and what had happened the night before.

He sat in the leather armchair and tried to recall the night before. They had been drinking in a bar in the city, and he had decided to go on soft drinks, as he was still feeling a bit sick from the night before. They decided to go to one of the top class hotels in the city, and were surprised they had been admitted.

Larry walked back from the bar with two drinks, a glass of orange and a pint for Gerard. A very drunk man bumped into him and the drink spilled everywhere. The man just walked away without apologising, and Larry was going to give him a slap, but decided not to. It wasn't every day that someone from Chapelgate Gardens was admitted to "The Gresham Hotel", one of the top hotels in Dublin.

Gerard saw what had happened.

Larry put the drinks on the table and sat in beside Gerard.

"Forget it mate – he's drunk."

Gerard thought the guy looked familiar.

"Look, we are in a nice hotel here, so let's just see how the other half lives," said Gerard.

They sat in a corner and talked about what they were going to do when they got to London. As they were talking, a girl came up to the table.

"I'm sorry about my brother knocking into you. He's very drunk," she said to the lads. Larry was quite surprised by her interjection.

"How did you know I would be here tonight?" said Gerard to the girl.

Larry was puzzled at this encounter.

"Collette, I think you met my friend Larry," laughed Gerard and he stood up to let Collette into the seat beside him.

"You wouldn't remember me but I remember you Larry," she said as she put her hand out to shake Larry's hand, then she sat in beside Gerard kissing him on the cheek.

"The Hustlers," she said.

Larry thought for a moment "What's the fucking Hustlers?" Then the penny dropped and he remembered Gerard's yarn he had spun to Collette.

"Are you staying here with the band?" she enquired.

"No, Larry is staying with me at my parents in Killester. Larry's the rigger," lied Gerard. We came by boat with the gear, and the rest of the band came by plane," he replied.

Unknown to Larry, there was a famous group staying at the hotel, and they had just come over from England for an Irish tour. It had been in the papers. Gerard assumed the band were staying in the hotel, that's why he brought Larry, and he was hoping Collette would turn up. He wouldn't phone her. She would have to chase him up.

Gerard liked Collette but he was thinking of the future.

"Politician's daughter! It's not what you know it's who you know," he thought.

Larry didn't know what to make of Gerard's banter, so he just nodded his head. One of the reasons they were allowed entry to the hotel was because the doorman thought they were with the band as well. The long hair on Gerard made him stand out slightly.

Collette, asked Larry and Gerard to join them at their table.

Her brother Sean turned out to be a nice guy. He hadn't realised that he had bumped into Larry, and he hadn't remembered Gerard from the night before. He was very drunk.

Collette asked Larry and Gerard to come back to the house in Howth.

"Where's Grainne?" asked Gerard.

"Who the fuck is Grainne?" thought Larry.

"They have split up, that's why he's drunk," replied Collette.

"Is he coming with us?" asked Gerard, nodding towards her brother.

Collette laughed.

"No, he's hooked up with some of Dad's political cronies. I think he's staying here tonight, they all have rooms booked," she replied.

So they left the hotel and Collette drove them to her house in Howth. Larry didn't speak much as he didn't want to drop Gerard in it as he didn't know the extent of the stories he had spun Collette. Larry sat in the back and Gerard sat in the front of the Mini.

"Well, did you miss me?" asked Gerard.

Collette looked across at him as she drove along.

"Don't flatter yourself Foley," she laughed.

When they got to the house all three sat and talked and Collette opened a bottle of Jameson.

She told them about all the dignitaries who had come to the house over the years to meet with her father.

"Where's your dad tonight "asked Larry.

"Him and Mam are away. Some government business in Europe I think," replied Collette.

They sat and talked for a while then Collette and Gerard went to the bedroom leaving Larry with the Jameson bottle.

The last thing he remembered from the previous night was the large whiskey he had before he blacked out.

He looked around at the large spacious room.

"If Rory were let loose on this house, he'd clean the fuckers out!"

So this is where Gerard ended up in the other night.

He heard Gerard and Collette in the bedroom.

"The lucky bastard," he thought to himself.

He looked at the photos on the walls.

"I've seen this fucker before," he thought to himself, as the familiar face of the man in each photo looked back at him. He recognised most of the faces, as they were famous people.

Collette came into the sitting room and said good morning to Larry. He looked at her and thought to himself, "Gerard is a lucky bastard, this bird is beautiful looking."

"Tea, coffee?" she called to Larry.

"No thanks Chloee, I'm OK. I have a tea," he replied. "Chloee, where the fuck did that come from?" he thought to himself.

She stopped and turned to Larry.

"Ooohh, that's so sweet! My dad is the only one who calls me Chloee … aaahh," she said and she walked to Larry and hugged him.

Larry was a bit taken aback, and thought to himself, "People with money really are a different breed – they act different."

He hugged her back, but wasn't used to this sort of affection.

"Er … where are your oul… wan … parents?" he said, nearly saying "oul wan", which was the normal term he would use if he was talking to someone from Chapelgate.

"Paris. Daddy's on business, something to do with the Common Market, or something," she replied.

"Oh right, the Common Market. Does he have a couple of stalls, like … at the Common Market?" asked Larry innocently.

Collette looked at him. Then she laughed.

"You showbiz people, you're always making fun of serious people," she laughed.

"The EEC. Daddy is a politician. You know him – look at the photos. Now do you know who he is?" she laughed, and she turned to make two cups of coffee.

She returned to the bedroom with the coffee. It was then that Larry realised that the man in the picture was always on RTE television, as he was high up in the government. He looked at the famous people in the photos again and thought to himself, "Fuck me! Who'd have guessed me and Gerard would be in a famous person's house." Then he thought, "Jesus, Gerard is shagging his daughter! Fuck me, the lads would never believe us."

He walked around the sitting room and he decided to himself that one day he would love to have a house like this.

Gerard walked from the bedroom and saw Larry.

"Can you believe this bird, Larry? She thinks I'm the "Dog's Bollox" laughed Gerard.

"Well dog's bollix or not ye cheeky fucker. Here, we'd better get out of here. It's half seven – the wedding is today." whispered Larry.

"Jesus yes your right Lar, we'd better get a move on," replied Gerard.

"We have to go, we have a meeting at ten." Lied Gerard.

He hadn't told her the real reasons he was in Dublin.

Collette came over to Gerard and planted a big kiss on his lips.

"Give me a keepsake," she begged.

Gerard thought about something, and as quick as a flash he took the boat ticket he still had on him from his pocket, and gave it to her.

"Here, this is my phone number in England," replied Gerard and he scribbled a couple of numbers on the ticket, adding a 'with love xxxx Gerard Foley'.

"I'll keep this forever," she gushed.

She had ordered a taxi for them earlier, and they heard the wheels crunching on the gravel outside.

As it pulled away from the house, Gerard looked back at Collette and waved.

"Fuck's sake Ger you've landed a right one there pal," said Larry.

"Think future, think big time Larry. She could be useful to us in the future," he whispered to Larry.

"What the fuck is going through Gerard's head," thought Larry.

The taxi driver turned to the lads.

"The Gresham, is that right?"

Gerard had heard Collette order the taxi, and the destination she gave was the Gresham, where she assumed they were going for the meeting.

"No mate, Chapelgate Gardens," said Larry.

The taxi driver looked in the mirror at the two lads.

"Oh, I was told The Gresham," he said, and was confused by the change of destination. Most taxi drivers were reluctant to drive into Chapelgate.

Gerard took out a couple of notes and threw them into the seat beside the driver.

"Don't worry, mate, we've got the money," said Gerard, and he leaned back into the seat.

"Fuck me, mate! Who'd have believed we were in your man's house," laughed Larry.

The driver drove towards Chapelgate. As they drove by Clontarf Larry pointed out the road where Marie lived.

"So our old saying is true isn't it Lar?" said Gerard.

Larry remembered another saying they had.

"Stick it to them before they stick it to you," he said.

Larry looked out the window at the familiar houses some of which he had spent many hours cleaning the windows on. He passed by "Marie Whites" house and the hurt hit him. "Fuck her. Fuck me me for falling in love with her. Fuck her" he thought to himself.

He was glad he had decided to go to London with Gerard.

*****

Mick looked across at his brother's bed. He realised that it hadn't been slept in.

"I hope the fucker hasn't gotten himself into trouble," he thought to himself. He put a pair of jeans on and went to the scullery, where his mother was cooking the breakfast in the large iron pan.

"Sit down there, son, and I'll feed you for your big day. Did Gerard not come home again last night?" she asked.

Mick scratched his head.

"Him and Larry went into town last night, but he'll be OK, Ma. Sure, he's a big boy now, living in London," replied Mick to his mother, and he kissed her on the forehead.

His father came out of the bedroom.

"Well, son, the big day – what," he remarked to Mick.

Mick acknowledged his father. "Yes, Da – this time tomorrow I'll be a married man," he replied.

The two plates of rashers, sausages, eggs and black pudding were put in front of the two men, and Mrs Foley returned with two steaming mugs of tea. They sat at the table and she looked at her son.

"She's a good girl. Treat her well, Mick," she said to her son.

"I will, Ma, you can be sure of that," replied Mick.

They ate, and then Mr Foley, who never spoke much, turned to his son.

"Rory would have loved to be here. He looked up to you Mick – you know that, son," he said.

His mother smiled.

"He'll be here in spirit, love," she said.

The front door opened, and Gerard and Larry came into the room.

"Where the hell were you two bowsies?" smiled Mrs Foley, and she got up to put on more breakfast for Gerard and Larry.

"Morning Mrs Foley," said Larry.

"Good morning Larry, how's your mother? replied Mrs Foley.

"She's grand, but she's not happy about me going with Gerard.

"Don't worry about her, I'll pop over the odd time and keep an eye on her. Now the pair of yis sit down there and I'll feed ye," replied Mrs Foley.

Gerard grabbed Mick around the neck in a playful way and ruffled his hair.

"The big day today, brother," he laughed.

Mick grabbed his brother and called out, "Get away you mad bastard!"

Larry sat at the table.

"How are ye, Mr Foley?" he asked.

"Grand, Larry. So you are heading over to London with the Gerard fellah there. Fair play to ye, your father would be proud of ye. He was a good man, Larry," replied Mr Foley.

Larry nodded his head.

"I know, Mr Foley, I miss him," replied Larry.

The lads sat at the table, and Gerard told Mick about the night before.

Mr Foley had no interest in the conversation, and he read his paper as he ate. Mick laughed when he heard the story.

"It could only happen to you guys. London better watch out," he laughed.

Larry thanked Mrs Foley as she put the fried breakfast in front of him. The lads discussed the wedding and what they were to do at the church and the reception.

Mrs Foley stood in the kitchen listening to the laughter coming from the room. She put her fingers to the little necklace on her neck, the one that Rory had given her. As the tears fell from her eyes, she didn't know if they were tears of sadness at Rory not being here, or happiness because of the laughter coming from her lovely sons. She lifted the corner of her apron and wiped her eyes.

Chapter Twenty-Seven

Dermot Kelly had just left the police station. He had received a phone call from the Sarge to tell him that there was a flat available in the house in Phibsboro for his friend. Dermot had no prior arrangements with Imelda to meet her. He knew she was to be bridesmaid at the Foley wedding, so he decided he would go to the hotel to see her when he had finished his shift later that day.

"You're a happy camper today, Dermot. So who was the phone call from?" asked Patrick, as Dermot sat into the car. Dermot smiled back at Patrick.

"The Sarge. He has a flat for the Bradshaw girl, so I can move her in soon," replied Dermot.

Patrick smiled and shook his head.

"Be careful there, mate, don't let the small head rule the big head. You've a lot to lose, if she messes with your life." remarked Patrick.

Dermot looked out of the window of the car as it pulled away, thinking to himself.

"I'll be OK. Imelda is a good sort, she won't mess with my head."

He turned to Patrick and said, "I'm on top of things, Pat, don't worry about me. Just you make sure you pass them exams for your promotion."

Patrick was going for his sergeant's exam soon. If he passed it, he knew that it would certainly mean a move of station and possibly a new city. He knew his time with his close partner was coming to an end.

*****

Angela was standing looking at herself in the mirror. The bump was bigger, and the dress wasn't sitting right, she thought. She started to cry. Imelda saw the tears start to flow.

"Here, we'll have none of that," she said to Angela.

"It's too small on me. I've grown bigger since the fitting," she pleaded to Imelda.

Imelda fixed the dress and the veil, and pulled the bodice down over the front. She took the flower bouquet and handed it to Angela.

"You look a million dollars, pet," said Imelda.

Linda agreed with her.

"Oh, Angela, you look stunning. Wait till Mick sees you," she replied.

Angela's mother, Linda, and Imelda stood back to look at the bride to be. Her mother started to cry, which started Angela, which in turn started Linda. Imelda looked at the trio.

"Right, you can stop that blubbering. "You three are a right pair!" laughed Imelda.

They went into the sitting room where a few of the neighbour's had called in to see the bride. It was mostly women, as the men usually went to the pub.

Angela's mother sat and talked to Imelda's mother as she sipped on a lemonade.

"She look's beautiful," said Imelda's mother nodding towards Angela.

"I know I'm going to miss her," replied Mrs Hopkins.

"Imelda is moving out soon. We're losing our babies," said Imelda's mother.

"They're growing up too quick. I heard Imelda has a new job. The girls were with her yesterday and told me that she has a lovely boss and she treats her so well," said Mrs Hopkins.

Imelda's mother nodded as she looked over at her daughter. She looked so confident and in her bridesmaid dress she looked like a film star.

"She'll go far in life," she thought to herself.

*****

The lads were dressed now and on their way to The Bell. Mr Foley felt proud as he walked through Chapelgate with his two sons, and the wad of money in his pocket gave him confidence. They all looked well in the dress suits.

Mr O'Brien put four pints in front of the lads when they got to the bar. It was tradition for the groom to have a couple of pints before going to the church.

Gerard turned to Larry.

"I'm going to take it easy on the beer today Lar. I don't want to let Mick down by getting drunk. I'll get drunk later in here when we come back," said Gerard.

Larry nodded.

"Yes good idea Ger, but I think I need a few beers. I need the "Hair of the Dog" to settle meself," he replied.

Mick turned to the lads.

"Thank Ger, I know you gave the ould fella a few quid," said Mick.

"The least I could do Mick he's the Da," replied Gerard.

"Will you two miss Chapelgate?" asked Mick.

Gerard shrugged his shoulders.

"No job, no girlfriend, no prospects. Don't think so Mick. You're fucking lucky mate. You've found a diamond, and that doesn't happen too often" replied Gerard.

Larry agreed with Gerard.

"She a fucking "Keeper" Mick," said Larry. They chatted and laughed for a few minutes and then they heard the familiar voices of Pancho, Jem, and Joxer enter the bar.

"Would you look at the fucking suit that Joxer's wearing," whispered Larry as he looked to see Joxer walk towards them with an old fashioned pin stripe suit, and a bright blue and silver grey, tie, which looked like something straight from the nineteen forties.

"He looks like Humphry fucking Bogart," laughed Gerard.

The lads all greeted Mick with slaps on the back.

"Where did you get the suit from" asked Larry trying not to laugh.

"It's me da's," replied Joxer innocently.

Gerard kicked Larry in the leg.

"Fuck off, don't make fun of him," he whispered. Then they both laughed into their pints.

The lads talked for a few minutes and over the noise of the bar they heard a familiar voice. It was Fatser Larkin and he was talking to his only mate in Chapelgate, Micks'er Boyle.

Pancho put his pint on the counter, turned and walked over to where Fatser was sitting. He stood and stared at Fatser. There was an uncomfortable silence in the bar. Fatser went white in the face. He said something to Micks'er Boyle and they both stood up and hurried out of the bar without finishing their drinks. Pancho stared them all the way to the door.

He walked back to the lads.

"Fucking maggot," he said. Joxer was proud of his mate.

After a few more pints Gerard looked at his watch.

"Right you shower, come on or we'll be late for the future Mrs Foley and she won't be too pleased," he shouted. The lads lowered back the pints and headed for the church.

As they walked towards the church Pancho and Jem couldn't help noticing the way Joxer's trousers were flapping in the wind. They were giggling like children behind Joxer's back. Larry walked up behind them.

"Grow up yis pair of fuckers," he said and he flicked his finger hitting Jem on the ear.

"Fuck off Larry that hurt," cried Jem rubbing his ear.

*****

The young priest stood on the altar facing the groom and the congregation. He was feeling a bit nervous as this was his first wedding to officiate.

He knew Mick and Larry, but couldn't remember seeing Gerard before. The organ whirred into action, and the soft notes from the large pipes wafted over the people. Mick shuffled from one foot to the other, and he wanted to turn around and look at Angela, but she had told him to wait until she was standing beside him. Gerard was a little nervous, and he looked at Larry, who was also nervous.

Angela looked stunning, and as she came down the aisle she drew gasps from the women in the church of "oohs and ahhs". Imelda and Linda walked behind her.

As Imelda passed by the girl that she had had a run in with outside the factory, Imelda threw her a look.

Angela walked up and stood beside Mick. He looked at her and smiled.

"I love you," he whispered into her ear.

The church was full, as everybody in Chapelgate knew the Foleys and the Hopkins. Both families were respected in the community.

The priest went through the wedding vows with Mick and Angela, and everybody had a little giggle when Angela found it hard to get her ring on her finger.

During the readings, Imelda looked at Gerard. She let her mind drift and imagined herself getting married, and the only face she could imagine standing beside her was Gerard. She was staring at Gerard, and suddenly he turned and caught her stare.

For a couple of seconds she hadn't noticed him looking back, but then she realised he was looking back. He winked at her, and she stuck her tongue out at him. They smiled at each other.

The ceremony was over in half an hour, and as the couple came through the doors, people threw handfuls of confetti at them. The photographer, who had been popping up in all areas of the church during the ceremony, was now hanging from the church railings taking snaps.

"Would you look at the photographer – he's like a monkey!" remarked Larry, as he watched him run about taking photos.

Gerard, Imelda, Linda and Larry were standing outside the church, and cigarettes were offered around. Larry refused the cigarette.

"You're really taking the no smoking seriously, aren't you, Larry." remarked Imelda.

Larry nodded his head in agreement.

"I didn't think I would want to give up, but to be honest Imelda, I feel better in the morning since I gave them up," he said.

They stood looking at Mick and Angela as they posed for the photos.

"Right, drink! Are we ready for the hotel?" asked Gerard.

The arrangements were that two cars were booked to take the bride and groom and bridesmaids and groomsmen to the hotel. There was a bus hired to take the guests to the hotel. The lads agreed to get the bus to the hotel, and the girls went in the car. Gerard got on the bus and made sure all the guests were ready to go. He looked out the window and saw the young children milling around the bus.

The driver was ready to go, so Gerard turned to him and said, "Listen, hang on here for a minute, and I will get some change for the "Grushee."

The Grushee was an old tradition and a way of sending children away from the bus as it pulled away from the church. Gerard took an empty confetti box and went through the bus collecting loose change from the passengers. When he got to the end of the bus he opened the emergency door and called out "Grushee", then threw the loose change as far from the bus as he could. The children all ran after the change and descended onto the rolling coins and away from the bus. The bus driver looked in the mirror and saw his opportunity to pull away. Ten minutes later they were disembarking the bus.

"Handy little journey, thank God!" thought the driver, as Gerard handed him the envelope with the cash.

When Larry, Jem and Gerard entered the hotel, they headed for the bar. Imelda was sitting with Angela's family, and the aunt who caused trouble at family get togethers, sat in the far corner with her husband. She was under strict orders not to cause trouble.

Gerard had to see the manager about the meal and the timing for the speeches. The manager had never met Gerard, as he had been dealing with Mick, but he had only taken over as manager a few months before, and he wasn't happy having the residents from Chapelgate Gardens in the hotel. He had heard that after most weddings from Chapelgate, there was always a situation where a row would start up. He wanted everything to go smoothly, so he had decided that as soon as the meal was finished, he would try and clear the bar as quickly as possible.

His predecessor had taken the booking and he thought to himself, if he had been manager at the time he wouldn't have booked it in.

The wedding party hadn't booked the room for a band and a dance after the meal, so he was glad that they would all be gone by eight or eight thirty. In fact, the plan was, that Mr O'Brien had invited them all back to The Bell, and he would provide music, and provide sandwiches later in the night.

Mick and Angela were glad for Mr O'Brien's offer, as they were running out of money for the wedding, and booking a band wasn't cheap. Also, the drink prices in the hotel were far more expensive than in The Bell.

Mr O'Brien was glad to cater for the afters, of the wedding as he needed the business.

During the meal, the manager came into the room to see how things were going, and as he left the room, Imelda noticed him walking from the room.

"Where do I know that bald patch from," she thought to herself.

Gerard gave a good speech, and at one stage he mentioned Rory, which brought a tear to his mother's eye.

He recalled the story about the night Mick had worn his mother's cardigan back to front and Mick blushed with embarrassment. Mick thumped him in the leg playfully.

"Fucker," he whispered at his brother.

Angela laughed but put her arm around Mick.

"He's just jealous Mick. You looked great that night, don't mind him," she whispered to her husband.

After Gerard had finished his speech he raised his glass.

"Let's all stand and toast Mr and Mrs Foley," he shouted.

Everybody stood and toasted the couple.

Imelda looked at Angela and wondered if she would ever be sitting where she was.

"Someday, you'll be doing the same," she heard Gerard whisper into her ear.

Imelda smiled and fluttered her eyebrows at Gerard.

"Are you asking?" she replied.

"Too much living to do before that, but if you're still around! You never know," laughed Gerard.

Imelda leaned over and kissed Gerard on the cheek.

"In your dreams," she replied.

They had a little laugh together at this banter.

The young priest also pitched in with a few words and told some stupid jokes, at which the people laughed out of politeness.

During the young priest's speech, Jem couldn't help notice, the priest was nervous. As Jem had been away in London and also as he never went to mass, he hadn't noticed the priest around Chapelgate before. He didn't know why but he felt something strange in himself, when he watched this young man.

The young curate, was a bit nervous as this was his first wedding and his first reception representing the church.

Mr Foley made a speech and told everybody to have a drink on him. With the money that Gerard had given he felt like a millionaire.

Gerard had decided to keep off the drink, for Mick's sake – as he was best man he wanted everything to go smoothly. After the speeches and the meal had finished the guests returned to the main bar of the hotel.

Larry, Gerard, Pancho, Jem, Joxer, Linda and Imelda sat in the corner of the bar. As Gerard had done his best man's job he decided to have a pint.

Mick and Angela sat with the Foley's and the Hopkin's relatives, and were thanking them for the wedding presents they had received.

They had received a lot of presents and it was a great start to their married life having the basics to start a home of their own.

Angela went to the toilet's to fix her make up and loosen her dress which she barely fitted into as she was getting bigger by the day.

Imelda followed her and they talked as Angela applied more make up. Imelda helped Angela with her dress.

"Well Mrs Foley, how do you feel?" asked Imelda.

"I can't believe it Imelda. It won't be long before I have the baby. Time goes by so quick Imelda," replied Angela.

"You're telling me! Jesus it doesn't seem like a year since you started going out with Mick. Now married and the baby. Jesus, Angela where does the time go," replied Imelda.

They hugged each other and Imelda knew that her friend would have a different life and Mick and the baby would come first.

As the day wore on, everybody drifted from the room to go back to The Bell

Gerard, Larry, Pancho, Imelda, Linda, Joxer and Jem were the only ones from the wedding party left in the hotel, as most of the guests had retired to The Bell.

Jem was in deep conversation with Linda and Gerard tipped Larry on the arm and nodded towards them.

"Another lamb to the slaughter by the looks of things," he said.

Larry nodded in agreement and Imelda turned to the lads.

"What about you fuckers? Who's going to nail you two down," she said.

"No chance Imelda, I'm staying single. Why marry and make one woman miserable when you can stay single and play the field and keep them all happy?" he replied.

"And you Gerard?" queried Imelda.

"Collette has her sights on him," replied Larry.

"Collette!" exclaimed Imelda.

Gerard was annoyed at Larry's outburst.

The rest of the group looked at Gerard.

"Dark horse Ger," said Pancho.

Larry told them about the night before, and how Gerard and himself had ended up going back to the house of the prominent politician.

"That bollix," said Jem, when he heard who the politician was.

"Well, his daughter loves our Gerard" remarked Larry, smiling.

Gerard laughed.

"Well, who would blame her? I mean, look at the body," he replied, as he stood up and flexed his arm muscle.

The girls squealed and laughed.

The manager heard the noise and looked across at the last few from the wedding party. He could see the five lads and the two women, who were sitting with their backs to the bar, laughing and joking.

He called the young barman over.

"Do you see that shower from the wedding? Well, don't serve them any more drink. I've heard about that crowd from Chapelgate," he said to the barman.

"Oh, they are OK. I know one of the lads – he cleans windows for my aunt in Clontarf. His father died a few months ago.

"My aunt said he was a nice chap. I don't think they would start trouble. Anyway, they are the last of the wedding party. After the bride and groom left, the rest of the wedding party left not long behind them," replied the young barman.

The manager turned to the barman.

"Just don't serve them any more drink. Who's the manager? Yes! Me, so just do what I instruct you to do. OK?" he snapped.

Even over the noise of laughter, Imelda heard the manager snap at the barman. She looked over at the commotion at the bar, and realised who the manager was.

"Well, fuck me sideways. Who would have thought? Mmmmm ..." she thought to herself. The manager walked away and the young barman stuck his two fingers up behind the manager's back as he went through to the kitchen.

"Wanker," the young barman thought to himself.

"She's a very nice girl, Collette, but I'm going back to London. No settling down for me," said Gerard.

"No, she "Was" a nice girl, wasn't she Gerard," said Larry to his friend.

"Well, she slept with you, mate! Nice? Eh, no, I think desperate would be the fucking word I'd use, Gerard." laughed Larry.

The rest of them laughed at Larry's retort.

"So who is this mysterious girl you're hiding" asked Imelda, who was a bit jealous after finding out Gerard had slept with Collette.

"I heard about that "Bloke" Her father, the politician man. He's supposed to have swindled money from the government, or something like that," said Joxer.

They all looked at Joxer, because he never spoke unless he was asked a specific question.

Most people thought he was slightly retarded, but in fact he was very clever, and read the papers every day, cover to cover. But Joxer was painfully shy.

"Er, he, the politician, I heard he put the wrong information in his expenses for last year, and he is being questioned about it, or something," said Joxer to the gang, clearly embarrassed at the attention he was receiving.

"I read about that. He asked for travel expenses from his holiday home in Kerry, even though he lives up there in Howth. It was in the papers," said Linda, agreeing with Joxer.

She smiled at him.

Linda was delighted to be with the gang, as she was a lot younger than most of them, and it was only since the wedding plans that she had been involved with Angela's friends.

"Robbin' bastard," said Jem, and he emptied his pint.

"That's not robbin'," said Larry.

Jem looked at Larry in surprise.

"Of course it's robbin'. If he lived in Kerry, it wouldn't be robbin', but he lives in fucking Howth, Lar, for fuck's sake!" replied Jem.

"He's making money from a situation. It's not robbin', because he is an upstanding politician, and think of the knock on effect. If the people suspect that this '"Upstanding Politician' is on the take. Where would the world be. We would have anarchy in the streets of Dublin. It's not his fault he has two houses, and can't remember where he slept the year before, when he was putting in expenses. " replied Larry sarcastically.

Gerard smiled and nodded in agreement.

"If he can afford two houses, why does he need to rob? I mean that's just stupid," said Linda. Gerard turned to Linda and said. "Linda Larry is being sarcastic.

"That's not being stupid, Linda, that's being fucking greedy.

"He has two houses because he can get away with things you or I would be locked for. Linda, life's not that simple. They take it because they know the rules don't apply to them," laughed Gerard sarcastically.

"Now get me another drink someone, before my throat dries up," laughed Gerard.

Larry jumped up.

"My round," he said.

"Stay where you are this round is on me. I am the best man after all," replied Gerard

"I'll get them in, and we'll head down to The Bell after this one, yeh?" said Gerard.

As he got to the bar he noticed for the first time that one of the policemen who had told him about Rory's accident was sitting at the end of the bar reading his paper.

*****

Dermot Kelly had slipped into the hotel bar hoping to see Imelda, and maybe catch her on her own, and tell her about the bedsit. As he sat and watched from a distance, he could see her with her childhood pals, laughing and joking, and he thought to himself that when she was with him she was so mature and grown up.

The keys of the bedsit were in his pocket. He had given the 'Sarge' a deposit from his own pocket. He would get it from Imelda later.

Earlier the manager nodded to the detective in recognition as he had been in before and the manager knew he was a policeman.

*****

Gerard noticed that the detective didn't even look up to acknowledge him, even though he knew who Gerard was.

"Prick!" thought Gerard to himself.

"Er, three Guinness, one Fanta orange, one pint of lager, and two half pints of lager," asked Gerard of the young barman as he approached him.

"I … em … I'm sorry, but the manager told me that you can't have more drink. I'm sorry, it's not me – it's the manager," said the young lad behind the bar who was embarrassed.

Gerard was taken aback.

"We are with the wedding party. You've seen us here all day. What's the problem?" asked Gerard, as he raised his voice slightly.

The barman went red in the face and said, "It's not me. I've no problem serving you, but the manager, he's …"

"Where's the manager?" replied Gerard, who was beginning to get agitated.

Dermot heard Gerard raise his voice, and he looked up from his paper.

The manager, who was in the back, heard Gerard, and he came through to the bar to confront him.

As he entered the bar, he saw the familiar face of Dermot Kelly at the bar, and his spirits went up.

"That's great, that detective is still here. Now I can sort these feckers from Chapelgate out," he thought to himself, as he brazenly faced up to Gerard.

"Do you have a problem, sir?" asked the manager in a sarcastic tone, as he stood square to Gerard.

Gerard looked at the manager, and his receding hairline showed his shiny forehead.

"Well, the barman is refusing us a drink, and he says that you told him not to serve us any more. Is that right?" asked Gerard.

Imelda noticed that Larry was watching Gerard at the bar, and she turned around to see what was happening.

Larry got up and walked towards Gerard. Imelda followed.

Dermot Kelly put his paper on the bar and listened to the conversation between Gerard and the manager.

"Bloody hell, Imelda is coming over towards the bar. This could get messy," thought Dermot as he saw Larry walk towards the bar followed by Imelda.

"What's the problem, Ger?" asked Larry.

The manager looked at the two lads and folded his arms. If there was going to be trouble, he had the law on his side, and he was just at the end of the bar.

"He's refusing us a drink, Larry. Can you believe that? And the amount of money Mick and Angela's wedding brought to this fucking place today," said Gerard, who was raising his voice now.

"Look, we are leaving after this drink sir. Our wedding party has put a lot of money into this hotel today," pleaded Larry in a lower tone of voice that Gerard had used.

The manager shook his head.

"I'm the manager here, the boss, and I can refuse whoever I like. Now if you would finish up over there and leave the premises I won't have to get the police," replied the manager in a cocky patronising voice.

Larry looked at the manager and was about to remonstrate with him when, out of the blue, Imelda stood between Gerard and Larry at the bar, and put her hand on Larry's arm.

"I'll take care of this, Larry. You and Gerard go back and sit down," said Imelda.

The blood drained from the manager's face as Imelda confronted him.

"Right, that will be three pints of Guinness, one Fanta, one pint of lager and two half lagers … and I think detective Kelly at the end of the bar could do with a refill, and of course, "Those drinks are on the house", isn't that right , Liam?" she ordered.

Liam looked at Imelda, and even though she had been in the hotel all day, he hadn't recognised her as the girl he met once a week and with whom he had sex.

He had told her the most intimate things about himself. Things that he would never reveal to anybody.

Imelda stood smiling at Liam. He was flustered and his hands started trembling.

Gerard looked at Imelda, then the manager. Dermot Kelly looked up from his paper when he saw Imelda confronting the manager.

The young lad behind the bar couldn't believe what was happening in front of his eyes. He had seen the manager tear strips off the waitresses if they got any orders wrong and he knew he had a very bad temper.

"Fuck me I pity that girl, he'll go fucking mad at her," thought the lad.

There was a silence, and you could have heard a pin drop. Imelda broke the silence.

"Could you drop those drinks to the table, please we are waiting?" she said, and with that she linked Gerard and Larry by the arm and walked them away from the bar back to their seats.

Liam the manager snapped out of his trance.

"Er … Er … Get that order ready and drop it over to the table," said Liam, who was sick in the stomach now.

"But I thought you said I wasn't …" The barman didn't finish his sentence.

"Just bring them to the table, and a pint for the detective as well," replied Liam, as he smiled weakly at Dermot Kelly and walked in a daze towards the kitchen.

"Are they on the house like the lady said?" asked the lad.

"Yes," he heard Liam call out as he walked towards the kitchen where he stayed for the remainder of the night.

Dermot Kelly had seen everything that had happened in front of his own eyes, and still couldn't understand it.

"That girl has a power over a man, and by God I don't know what it is, but I'd better watch myself," he thought to himself as he watched Imelda Bradshaw swagger back towards the table with Gerard Foley and Larry Burke.

The lad looked at the detective and shrugged his shoulders. He couldn't believe what had happened right before his eyes.

He got the drinks ready for the table.

"Imelda, what the fuck?" pleaded Gerard, as he sat down in his seat.

Larry and Gerard looked at Imelda, waiting for an explanation. The others hadn't copped what had just happened.

"He comes to the shop with his elderly mother every week, and she just loves me.

"I think she secretly wants me to go out with her son, but as you can see, he's a prick. But she's a lovely woman. If I tell her what went on here today, she would fucking kill him. He's a fucking mammy's boy," lied Imelda.

The young lad put the tray in front of Gerard.

"I wanted to serve you, lads, but that prick told me not to," said the lad, who didn't know how the lads would take him.

"Forget it, pal. Don't beat yourself up," said Gerard.

The young lad smiled and was relieved, and he went back to the bar.

"Nice one, Imelda," said Larry, and they all cheered with their full glasses, and raised them to Imelda.

She took a sip from her drink and turned to see Dermot raise his glass to her. She smiled back at him. Only one person at the table caught this encounter.

"Now what the fuck is going on there!" thought Gerard Foley.

Chapter Twenty-Eight

A couple of days later, Jem wobbled on his bike, and ladder, making it difficult for him to reach the pedals. Larry saw him come towards him and thought to himself, "Fuck me, he'll cut the bollocks off himself the way he's cycling that bike!" Jem nearly fell over as he stopped beside Larry, who had to catch him by the shoulders.

He straightened himself and turned to Larry, saying, "Thanks, Lar. I'll get the hang of it."

Larry let out a little laugh.

"Yeh, no probs, Jem, you will. Now have you got the book with the customers' names and the prices in it?" he asked.

Jem waved it in front of Larry.

"Here, I have it here, Lar," replied Jem.

Larry saw how casual Jem was with the work diary, and he shook his head at Jem.

"For fuck's sake, Jem, that book is very important. Don't wave it around like that. Look after it, it's the brains of the business. It "IS" the business, so take care of it," said Larry.

Jem could see that Larry was passionate about the business, and was finding it hard to hand it over to him.

"I'll take care of it, Lar, don't worry. In fact, I'll write all the names and addresses in duplicate in another book, for safety!" replied Jem.

"OK, Jem, I know you will. Now let's get out to Clontarf, and I'll show you the rest of the round," said Larry. He was glad to see that Jem was going to copy the book, even though he already had a copy of all his customers' details hidden in his mother's flat.

They rode out to Clontarf, and Larry went to great lengths to make sure Jem was introduced to his customers, and that they knew who Jem was. The last thing Larry wanted was another cleaner moving into the area, and the customers thinking Larry had put him in.

Jem pulled up outside Marie's house.

"You're forgetting this house, Larry. It's in the book," said Jem, as he started to take the ladder from the bike.

Larry looked at the house.

He looked up towards the bedroom and remembered the first time he had made love with Marie in that bedroom, and the afternoons in the summer when they would lie there, with the afternoon sun shining through the lace curtains.

"Larry! Larry, snap out of it, and give us a hand," chided Jem as he struggled with the ladder.

Larry turned and said to Jem, "No, they moved, so we can give this house a miss."

"This is the house Rory Foley turned over Jem, remember, just before he was killed," said Larry.

"Poor Rory. Gas little fucker wasn't he Lar?" said Jem.

Larry agreed with Jem.

Jem put the ladder back and took out the book.

"Better cross her out, then," he said as he opened the book at Marie's entry.

"She must have been a good customer, Lar – you have a star beside her name," said Jem.

Larry took the book from Jem, took the pen, and put a line right through her name.

"There now – that's the end of that," he said, as he handed the book back.

For the remainder of the day, Larry gave Jem tips on the little scams he had developed, and told him that once he gave Larry's mother a set amount of cash every week, he could earn as much as he wanted, or the weather would allow.

"If the ma doesn't get the money on Friday, I'll be over by the Monday, Jem, so don't mess me around, right?" said Larry to Jem, but he knew he didn't have to say this, as he knew Jem wouldn't cross him.

"Lar, I'd never let you down," said Jem, who was actually hurt that Larry would have the thought that he would try and cross him.

Larry looked at Jem, and he knew his words had hurt him.

"I know, Jem. Sorry, but you know what I'm like. I know you won't let me down," said Larry, and he gripped his friend on the shoulder and gave him a squeeze. "Sorry Jem" he replied.

"What time are we meeting this evening? You and Gerard's last night in The Bell." asked Jem.

Larry and Gerard were catching the late boat to England at ten that evening, and they were all meeting in The Bell at seven.

"Seven, Jem, and you're fucking buying, you tight fisted fucker!" laughed Larry, as he tousled the hair on Jem's head.

"Fuck off, Lar, I'm trying to grow me hair like Gerard's!" laughed Jem as he tried to comb back his long hair.

They continued on the round for the remainder of the day.

A little Mini car passed by Larry as he descended the ladder. Collette looked at the familiar face.

"No it couldn't be him. Must have a double," she thought as she drove on towards the city to meet her parents on their return from Europe.

Larry never noticed the car passing.

*****

"Well what do you think?" asked Dermot, as he showed Imelda around the large comfortable bedsit in Phibsboro.

She was impressed as she looked around the well-furnished large room. There was a small kitchen tucked away in the corner, separated by a partition wall. There was a door which opened into quite a large bathroom. The bathroom hadn't a bath, but had a large glass-walled shower.

"I think it's perfect!" exclaimed Imelda, as she stood looking at her first flat.

Dermot sat in the comfortable sofa that fitted in between the large bay window.

"Right, the deal is this, Imelda," he said, as he sat back and took two cigarettes from a pack.

He put both in his mouth and lit them together. As she looked on, it reminded her of the night Gerard had done the same, as they walked back from the pub after Rory's funeral. She sat in beside Dermot and took the cigarette.

"The Sarge runs a tight ship here. He organises the clients. They are all well to do – solicitors, businessmen, you know, no wasters or dirty old raincoat brigade. Only his clients allowed, Imelda, so no freelancing. Is that OK by you, now?" said Dermot.

"OK, yes, that seems like a good system. So he knows I work in the day, and only night time suits me?" Imelda asked.

"All the girls have day jobs, Imelda, and the operation is very low key. There are four flats, and you only do as many clients as you want. The Sarge has a system he operates. You get the money and keep it all. But, and here's the But! You pay your rent! Every week … and it is not cheap. Now, here, look at this – that's the price of the room every week, and it's paid on Monday morning. Every, Monday morning on time, and no excuses. Is that OK for you?" said Dermot, as he handed her a slip of paper with the rent amount on it. The slip of paper had Paid scribbled across it.

"Did you pay this for me?" asked Imelda.

"Yes but don't worry about it, it's to give you a start," replied Dermot.

Imelda reached into her bag and took out the neatly rolled notes.

"Here take this," she said as she handed him the notes.

Dermot pushed her hand away.

"No, forget it," replied Dermot.

Imelda pushed her hand back towards Dermot.

He knew by her demeanour that she was paying no matter what. He knew he couldn't argue with her.

Imelda had been earning much more money lately, than she had been earning in the sewing factory. She carried out a quick calculation in her head, and with the wages from the shop, which was a lot more than she would have expected, and the money from her other activities, the rent would not be a problem to meet every week.

"This is fine, Dermot," she said, as she handed back the slip of paper.

"OK, that's it, Imelda. Now, you understand your rent is Monday morning, and no freelancing. Are you OK with that?" repeated Dermot.

Imelda looked around the large room, and was pleased that she was about to embark on a new chapter in her life.

"Thanks, Dermot. When can I move in?" asked Imelda.

"Yesterday!" laughed Dermot, and he stood up to leave.

Imelda looked around again, and stubbed her cigarette out in the ashtray.

"Can you drop me to work? Please?" asked Imelda.

Dermot looked at her and smiled.

"Cheeky little minx. OK – come on," he replied.

As they drove towards Grafton Street, Imelda looked at the world passing her by. Her life had changed a lot in one year.

She loved her job, and June treated her like an adult. Her wages were almost three times the wages she got at the sewing factory, and she received large discounts on the clothes she bought. They stopped at the corner of Trinity College and she opened the door to get out. She turned and looked back at Dermot.

"Why? Why are you looking after me?" said Imelda.

Dermot was taken aback at her directness.

"I don't know, Imelda, really, I don't know, but I like you, and I wouldn't like to see anything happen to you. Does that answer your question?" he replied.

She got out, closed the door, and reached back into the open window.

"Thanks, you've been very good to me," she replied, and with that she turned and walked towards Grafton Street.

He watched her walk away and thought to himself.

"Why am I helping her?" He put the car in gear, and pulled away from the kerb towards the station.

There was something about her. He wasn't in love with her or anything like that. It wasn't the sex either, but he had to admit to himself he liked the sex.

It was something he just couldn't put his finger on.

*****

Mick and Angela were walking along the harbour in Howth. They watched the seagulls swooping on the trawler, as it unloaded the boxes of fish onto the pier.

It was a cold day, but dry. Angela was eight and half months pregnant, and with her heavy winter coat on, she didn't look pregnant. She was very neat.

They had booked into a bed and breakfast in the harbour town after the wedding, and were enjoying the few days away from Chapelgate Gardens.

"It was a great day, Mick, I think everybody had a good time," said Angela.

Mick had his arm around her shoulder, and he squeezed her tightly.

"You looked lovely, Angela. I'd say the photos will be perfect," replied Mick.

They walked towards the end of the pier, and just before they got to the end, Angela stopped and put her hand to her stomach. Mick stopped and looked at her, concerned.

"Are you OK?" he enquired.

She walked to a bench and sat down.

"Yes, just a little pain shot up me, I'll be ok," said Angela. "Yes, of course I'm OK- just a bit of heartburn. That black pudding we had for breakfast was gorgeous, but it gives me terrible heartburn," replied Angela, and she smiled at Mick.

But she knew it wasn't heartburn, the pain was much lower in her stomach.

They sat there for a few minutes, and Angela got another stabbing pain. Her face winced as the pain shot through her. Mick looked at her, even more concerned.

"Angela, is it the baby? Are you OK?" he questioned.

"I'm grand, Mick, and the baby is not due for another few weeks, so don't panic," she replied as the pain died away.

They sat and watched the birds swooping and fighting over the scraps of fish that were being pulled apart by the excited creatures.

*****

Pancho and Joxer looked at each other and smiled when they saw the red van drive into the flats complex. The driver, Noel, a gypsy traveller, looked at the two lads as they approached the van.

He jumped out of the Ford Transit and put his hand out to shake hands with them.

"Noel. Hello," he said, as he shook Pancho's hand and then Joxer's.

The lads introduced themselves, and proceeded to walk around the red Transit van. One of the back doors was white, and Joxer pointed this out to Noel.

"A lick of paint will sort that, sir, and the inside is spotless. For the money, it's a bargain," replied Noel.

Pancho looked at Joxer.

"Well, what do you think?" he asked.

Joxer nodded his head.

Pancho turned to Noel and asked, "Can we have a test drive?"

Noel jumped into the passenger seat and Pancho jumped in beside him. Joxer sat in the driver's seat. He had only driven a car twice before. He paid for two driving lessons with a driving school, and he had also read up a manual about how to learn to drive.

He would practice in his bedroom with a plunger for a gear stick, and the lid of a pot as the steering wheel. He sat in the van and realised it was bigger than the little car he had the two lessons in, but he was determined to drive the van.

The gears crunched, and the van shot forward. They drove around the square in the middle of the flats complex, and as he picked up more speed, the jolting stopped, and it rolled along smoothly.

Pancho was impressed with Joxer's driving skills.

"The engine runs like a kitten, and the inside is spotless. The previous owner delivered flowers, so the springs and shocks are in great nick," said Noel, and he winced when Joxer missed a car parked on the corner.

They drove out of the complex and headed for the docks. The van rolled along the cobbles, and Noel was right, the van sailed over the bumpy road, as the springs absorbed the bumps.

Twenty minutes later, Pancho counted out the pound notes in front of Noel.

He put the last fiver into Noel's hand, and said, "Right, there you go – One hundred."

Noel rolled the money up, but took a five pound note and gave it back to Pancho.

"Here – this is the "luck money," he said, and then he spat on his hand and shook Pancho's hand, which was an old traveller tradition.

"Ah Jesus, thanks, Noel," said Pancho, and he waved the fiver at Joxer, who was still inspecting the van by kicking the wheels.

A large Ford Zephyr pulled in behind the van, and Dermot Kelly got out and walked towards the lads.

"Well, what have we got here?" he remarked sarcastically.

"Hello, sir, how are we today? I've all the paperwork for the van, sir," said Noel, and he reached into the glove compartment of the van and took out the log book.

Pancho and Joxer just stood looking at Dermot, as he walked around the van, inspecting the paperwork. He went back to the car and gave Patrick the details of the number plate to radio into the station, to see if the van was stolen. They waited for a reply.

"Well, what do you think? Could it be stolen?" asked Patrick.

"No, I don't think so. I've come across that fellah Noel before. He has a caravan out there in Coolock – nice young fellah, but you know travellers. You have to check everything out with them."

"Two ten, negative on that vehicle." the voice crackled from the radio.

"That's fine," replied Patrick into the handset.

Dermot walked back towards the three lads.

"There you go, lads, and don't forget to tax and insure the thing before you go ripping up the roads of Chapelgate

Gardens," said Dermot, as he handed the logbook back to Noel.

"Thanks, guard," replied Noel.

As the Zephyr pulled away, Pancho whispered, "Wankers" under his breath as it passed him, and he smiled at the two men in the car.

"Well, at least you know it's not stolen!" laughed Noel, as he patted Joxer on the back.

"Right, do you need a lift?" asked Joxer, as he took the keys from Noel.

"Coolock will be fine. Don't forget to get the insurance sorted," replied Noel.

Pancho looked at Joxer and they both laughed.

"Bollox to that!" they both chorused.

As they drove through the flats complex some kids ran after the van, and two of them hung on to the back as it jumped and jolted through the streets.

Chapter Twenty-Nine

"She will be fine," said the ambulance man, as he helped Angela into the back of the ambulance. Mick was panicking, and he held her hand as she cried out with pain.

"Relax, Angela. We'll soon be in the hospital," whispered Mick into her ear.

"Relax? That's easy for you to say – the pains are crucifying me," she screamed.

The ambulance screamed through the small village towards the city.

"When are you due the baby?" asked the ambulance orderly, as he hooked Angela up to an oxygen mask.

"I'm not due for another, three or four weeks, according to the doctor," she replied, as she gulped in the oxygen.

"How often are the pains coming – like how many minutes in between pains, I mean?" he asked Mick.

Mick shrugged his shoulders.

"I don't know, but they are frequent," he replied.

Angela gripped Mick's hand and her nails dug into his skin. He smiled weakly at Angela, even though her nails were hurting his hand.

"Right, there we are, and counting," said the ambulance man.

As the pain receded, Angela released Mick's hand. When the next pain came and the ambulance man timed how long between the contractions, he opened the little hatch to the cab.

"Put your foot down, and radio ahead. We'll be lucky to make it to Fairview never mind the Rotunda," he told the driver.

"Right, let's see how far you have dilated," he said, as he kneeled at Angela's feet and told her what he was going to do.

*****

"June, I have locked up out the back, and the stocktake you asked me to do is done," said Imelda.

June was amazed at the way Imelda had picked up the details of the job. Earlier in the day, June had gone to lunch to meet her friend, and while she was out, she had asked another friend to go to the shop and be a difficult customer. She wanted to see if Imelda could handle a situation when June wasn't there.

That afternoon, June's friend went to the shop and asked Imelda for various items, and was short with her, and in general tried to get Imelda to lose patience with her. But Imelda was able to handle the woman.

As she rooted through some stock at the back room for an item the woman had asked for, she thought to herself that this woman was going out of her way to try and get her to lose her patience.

So in a flash she came to the conclusion that June was setting her up to test her. In fact, getting to know how June worked, she wouldn't have expected anything less. So she came into the shop with a big smile on her face and fawned over the woman.

Imelda brought a scarf that had just come into the shop and wasn't even on display yet.

The woman had been in the shop so often that she thought she had seen all the stock but when Imelda brought the scarf to her to show her the woman ended up buying it.

June sat with Monica, eating her sandwich in the small café around the corner from her shop. Catherine walked in and joined them.

"Well, you're right, that girl is a one off! She was so helpful, and I was a bitch to her. Even I would have lost my temper with me if I behaved like that," she gushed, as she sat in beside her friends.

"I'm glad. I like her, and it's so bloody hard to get a good assistant. She has something, hasn't she, Catherine." stated June.

"Yes, there's a quality to her, you know. It's like she's in charge, but you have a good one there, June, so hold on to her," said Catherine.

"Look, I wasn't supposed to be buying anything but your little test has cost me," laughed Catherine.

June noticed that the scarf was from the new stock.

"She's good," she thought.

June sipped her tea.

"I sure will hold on to her. I'm taking her on a buying trip next month to London. I'm going to see if she has an eye for fashion. I'm not getting any younger, and I need someone to keep the shop going when I'm in hospital in a couple of months. So I think she can handle things," she replied.

*****

"Can I start work at ten thirty tomorrow, June? I'm moving to a new flat in the morning." asked Imelda.

"Sure you can, Imelda. Take your time, we don't get busy until about half twelve. That's OK, Imelda, take your time. You're moving from Phibsboro then?" replied June.

"No, a bigger flat came up, and I got in touch with the landlord. It has more room than the one I'm in," she lied.

"By the way, Imelda, do you have a passport?" asked June.

Imelda was taken aback.

"A passport? No, I was never out of the country. Why?" asked Imelda, confused by the question.

"Well, I think you should apply for one. We are going to London on a buying trip at the end of next month, to have a look at the summer collection," replied June.

Imelda nearly fainted.

"London, God ... London!" squealed Imelda, and she ran to June and hugged her.

"That's great, June! Thanks, I won't let you down, I swear," Imelda squealed again.

June hugged her back.

"I know you won't, Imelda. I have great plans for you," replied June.

"I'll put the kettle on. Ooohh, thanks, June!" Imelda exclaimed, as she went to the kitchen to make the tea.

June looked at her protégé walking towards the kitchen, and thought to herself, "She reminds me of me when I came to Dublin in the early fifties, but I doubt if she has had to do what I did to get where I am today!"

*****

Gerard came to Larry's flat and knocked on the door. Mrs Burke answered, and was delighted to see Gerard.

"He's just packing his few bits. Go on in to him," replied Mrs Burke.

"Here, we have to split this package up between us, Larry," said Gerard, as he took the bulky package that he had picked up in the Bog Road pub.

Gerard opened the package, and wasn't surprised that it contained bundles of cash, but he was surprised it was sterling and US Dollars.

"Fuck me, Ger! How much is in that bundle?" asked Larry.

Gerard carried out a quick calculation, and reckoned it amounted to about fourteen to fifteen thousand. What the lads didn't know was that the cash was the proceeds of a bank robbery, and it was easier to get rid of sterling and dollars in London as opposed to trying to pass it off in Dublin.

The package Gerard had brought over from Jimmy contained drugs. LSD, purple hearts and various other types of uppers and downers. Larry split the money into two bundles, and they decided to leave it in their bags in the flat, and to pick the bags up on the way to the ship. The plan was to meet Mick and Angela, Joxer, Jem, Pancho, Imelda and Linda in The Bell later that evening.

*****

"Jesus that ambulance is certainly ripping it up," said Pancho, as he sat in the front of the van waiting for the traffic lights to change colour.

Joxer was staring straight ahead, and he was more confident in the driving seat now. He had driven to Coolock and back, and as they sat at the traffic lights in Fairview, the ambulance sped by. They had no idea that Angela was about to give birth in the back of that same ambulance.

*****

Mick was out of his depth in the back of the ambulance, as the orderly checked and rechecked Angela's progress. She screamed again, and the orderly told Mick to tell the driver to pull in and help with the birth.

"This baby is coming, and it's not waiting for the hospital!" the medic told Mick.

Five minutes later, as Mick wiped Angela's forehead, the two medics helped Angela with the birth, and the baby slipped from between her legs. Mick could make out the small head covered in blood, and then the umbilical cord. He heard the first cries of his little baby, and he saw the baby's face, all puffed up.

Angela cried when she saw her little baby.

The medic wrapped the baby in a blanket and handed it to her.

"It's a girl!" exclaimed the medic, smiling at the happy parents.

Mick looked at his little baby girl. The tears just flowed from his eyes, and he looked at his new bride. The woman he vowed to spend the rest of his life with, holding their little baby. The two medics smiled at each other and congratulated one another.

"Is this your first delivery, John?" he asked his partner.

"Yes, the first," replied John.

"Thanks, lads," said Mick to the two medics.

"All in a day's work. Don't mention it, and congratulations!" replied John, and he joined his partner outside the ambulance for a much needed cigarette.

Angela looked at her little bundle.

"That's your daddy, and I'm your mammy," said Angela to her baby.

Mick looked at them both.

"Jesus, I have to look after them both now. That's a lot of responsibility – I hope I can do it," he thought to himself, as he held the baby's little hand between his thumb and forefinger.

*****

Dermot drove into the car park of the police station and Patrick turned to him.

"If I get the promotion, I'm likely to be moved to another police station. Are you OK with that Dermot?" asked Patrick.

Dermot could see by his friend's expression that was upset that he would most likely be transferred.

"Listen, Patrick, onwards and upwards. It's a hard job, this, so take the promotion and don't worry about me. We can still get together for a few pints now and again," replied Dermot, as he punched his partner in the arm.

"Thanks, mate, you've been there for me. You know, when the young fellah … the train accident … thanks mate," said Patrick.

"Just look after yourself, and don't go catching too many villains. Leave some for us!" laughed Dermot.

They walked towards the door of the station.

"Has that Bradshaw girl moved in, yet?" asked Patrick.

Dermot looked at his friend.

"Er, no, she's backed out. I think she bagged a good job, so I think she's got out of that line of work," lied Dermot.

"Maybe it's just as well. She's far too clever for us, Dermot. I've seen her cast her magic over you – just be careful there, Dermot! Be careful," said Patrick, as he opened the door into the station.

"Thanks, Pat … thanks," replied Dermot Kelly.

Chapter Thirty

Gerard looked at his watch as he sat with Larry in The Bell, and said, "Mick was supposed to be back from the few days away. Angela and him said they would come and have a pint with us before we leave."

The bar was quite full for that time of the evening.

"It's early yet. Sure the lads are not here yet," said Larry.

Just then, the door opened and Pancho and Joxer walked in. Pancho saw Larry and Gerard and called out.

"Do you want a drink, lads?"

Gerard got up and told Pancho and Joxer to sit, as he was buying. As he stood at the bar, Linda walked in and looked around the pub.

"Is Angela and Mick here yet?" she asked Gerard.

"No, they'll be here later. Sit down and have a drink, and if you're a good girl, I'll set you up with Pancho!" laughed Gerard.

The five of them were sitting laughing and talking, and Imelda came over to the table.

"Right – where are the two explorers?" asked Imelda sarcastically.

Gerard looked at Imelda, and couldn't help notice that she looked so mature. Her clothes and her hair made her stand out from the other girls in Chapelgate.

"Oh, Imelda, that jacket is so gorgeous," said Linda, as she saw how well Imelda looked.

"Perks of the job, Linda!" replied Imelda. "Where's Mick and Angela?"

Gerard stood up to get a drink for Imelda.

"You look good today, kid," he said, as he passed her to go to the bar. She fluttered her eyelashes at him mockingly. He smiled back.

She sat beside Linda, and showed her the new nail polish she was using.

Jem walked up to Gerard.

"Mine's a pint, mate," he whispered in Gerard's ear.

Gerard hadn't seen Jem sneak up behind him.

"You bollix – you frightened the shite out of me," he laughed, as he got Jem in a headlock.

Jem straightened his hair, which was starting to get really long now.

"Ger, I ... I er hope you didn't mind me not going back to London with you," said Jem to his friend.

Gerard looked at Jem and put his arm around him.

"No, you're fine, mate. Now fuck off before you have me in tears," he laughed, as he gave Jem his pint.

As Jem walked towards the table where they were sitting, Gerard looked at him and thought to himself.

"Jem would never have made it in London. He would stay in Chapelgate and most likely marry Linda, or someone like Linda. He would have children and be a good father and husband. He would get drunk on Saturday night, and Linda would give out about him to her friends. But really, she would love him and look after him. By the age of thirty he would be set in his ways."

Gerard wasn't going to go that road. Not for him, the smell of urine on the steps leading up to the flats in Chapelgate. Not for him, the pawn shop odour from his suit as he sat with the men in The Bell on Sunday mornings. Not for him the daily struggle to keep body and soul together. He was shaking this life from his back and moving into a real life. The world was out there – what was it Jem had said? – 'The world's your lobster'... or something like that," thought Gerard to himself as he watched the group together.

"It's a girl," he heard Mick say in his ear. Gerard spun around and saw Mick standing beside him.

"It's a girl, Angela – she had a girl ... today ... this afternoon, Gerard!" laughed Mick.

Gerard hugged his brother.

"For fuck's sake, Mick! Congratulations, brother."

They told the gang and a cheer went up.

Mr O'Brien came out from the bar when he heard the noise.

"Take it easy there, now. Hello, Mick. By the way, congratulations on the wedding," he said to Mick.

"We've just had a baby today, Mr O'Brien," replied Mick.

Mr O'Brien scratched his head.

"By God, you don't waste any time, do yous," said Mr O'Brien as he walked away from the table.

Half an hour later Mick got up from the table and told Gerard he had to go and tell his mother and father, and Linda said she would tell her mother. Gerard walked to the door of the bar with Mick. As they stood outside saying their goodbyes, Mick caught his reflection in the window of the pub and remembered the night he and Gerard stood toe to toe to fight, when he had realised he had his mother's cardigan on. That was nearly a year ago.

Mick looked at his younger brother.

"You fucking take care of yourself, and don't go getting caught robbing. Well, just don't get caught, right?" said Mick.

"Don't you worry about me, Mick. You'll never take me alive, copper! That will be my last words, brud!" replied Gerard.

As Gerard returned to the bar, Mick looked at his reflection again.

"Is that really me? Mick Foley?" he laughed, and walked towards Chapelgate flats.

*****

"So I will meet you both at eight in the morning," said Imelda to Pancho and Joxer.

"At your place, Imelda. Right, eight it is. This is our first job with the van," replied Pancho.

Pancho, Joxer and Jem said their goodbyes to the lads. Larry looked at Jem.

"Good luck, Jem, and don't let them oul wans in Clontarf get the better of you. Remember, do it to them before they do it to you," he said.

Twenty minutes later, Larry slipped back to the flat to get the bags. He checked to make sure the money was still in the bags. He kissed his mother, and both his sisters.

"Tell Jimmy we were asking for him," said his mother.

Gerard moved in beside Imelda. They were to wait until Larry got back, and the three of them were to walk to the boat.

"Do you remember what you did to me here the night of Rory's funeral?" asked Imelda.

"Did you like it?" replied Gerard.

Imelda turned and looked at Gerard.

"Do you have to ask?" she replied.

Gerard took two cigarettes from the box, put them in his mouth, and lit them together.

"Here," he said as he offered her the cigarette.

She took the cigarette and drew hard on it.

"Is it true? The rumour." asked Gerard.

She smiled at Gerard.

"Are you not doing anything illegal over there in London?" replied Imelda, with a smile.

"Imelda Bradshaw, you're far too clever for Chapelgate. Why not try London?" he asked.

"Funny you should say that. I'm going on a buying trip to London next month," she laughed.

Gerard laughed mockingly and then he caught the look on her face.

"Fuck me! You really are, aren't you? Jesus, Imelda, you will go far," he replied.

Just then, the door opened, and Larry stood there with the two travelling bags in each hand.

"Right, let's get the fuck out of town," he mimicked, in cowboy style.

*****

Imelda, Larry, and Gerard walked towards the departure area where the boat was pulled in. The glass-fronted building where the people entered was crowded. Imelda hugged Larry.

"Look out for him," she said to Larry.

She turned to Gerard and said, "You look out for him."

She turned and walked back towards Chapelgate, and as she did she looked over her shoulder at the lads. They walked towards the boat, jostling each other.

She walked and thought about how her life was changing so fast. But she was in charge of changing it. She loved her job. She loved the thoughts of her new flat. She liked the fact she would only have to work from her flat. No more strange cars. No more hiding …

"Are you doing business, love?" she heard someone say from behind.

She stopped and looked at the big car that had stopped beside her. She walked over to the passenger window.

"If you're not careful, I'll get the police for you," she said.

The driver leaned across and pulled the silver handle of the door of the Ford Zephyr, and it opened.

"Well, it's just as well that I am a policeman," said Dermot.

Imelda got into the front seat and planted a kiss on his lips.

*****

Larry and Gerard stood at the front of the ship as it sailed out of Dublin. .

"Listen, Larry, we have to look after each other's back over there. We are going to be moving up a notch … like big stuff," said Gerard.

"I know, Ger. I've nothing to lose, mate. That bitch is going to have my baby. A baby I'll never see. She fucked with me head, Ger," said Larry.

Gerard patted his friend on the shoulder.

"Snap out of it, Larry. You were never going to be together, and in your heart of hearts you know it's true. Listen

– go to the bar and order me a pint. I just want to finish this smoke," said Gerard.

Larry nodded his head in agreement.

"I know you're right, pal. Right – see you in the bar," he replied.

*****

The wind blew into Gerard's face, and the taste of salt from the spray was on his lips. He reached into his coat pocket and took out the photo. He looked at the black and white picture with the brown ringed stain on it. He turned it over and read the writing.

Pancho Larry Gerard Imelda Angela Mick Linda Jem and Joxer The Bell November 1967

He noticed he was the only one looking at Imelda. He put the picture away, and little did he know that he would take it out and look at it from time to time as the years would roll by, and his life would take him on an adventure. He took a drag on his cigarette, and flicked the butt into the wind. He turned and walked back to meet Larry in the ship's bar.

The End